THAT WEDDING

THAT WEDDING

JILLIAN DODD

Jillian Dodd Inc.
Madeira Beach, FL
Jillian Dodd and The Keatyn Chronicles are registered trademarks of Jillian Dodd, Inc.

ISBN: 978-1-946793-72-0

Books by Jillian Dodd

The Keatyn Chronicles®

USA TODAY bestselling young adult contemporary romance set in an East Coast boarding school.

Stalk Me
Kiss Me
Date Me
Love Me
Adore Me
Hate Me
Get Me
Fame
Power
Money
Sex
Love
Keatyn Unscripted
Aiden

That Boy Series

Small-town contemporary romance series about falling in love with the boy next door.

That Boy
That Wedding
That Baby
That Divorce
That Ring

The Love Series

Contemporary, standalone romances following the very sexy Crawford family.

Vegas Love
Broken Love

Spy Girl™ Series

Young adult romance series about a young spy who just might save the world.

The Prince
The Eagle
The Society
The Valiant
The Dauntless
The Phoenix
The Echelon

For my husband,
Thank you for making me believe true love, the fairytale kind,
actually exists.

My favorite part of the whole night.

SATURDAY, SEPTEMBER 9TH

PHILLIP'S HOLDING MY hand, leading me toward the hotel elevator. We just left our engagement party. I still can't believe I'm engaged to Phillip Mackenzie, the boy I've known forever.

As we step into an empty elevator, Phillip inserts a key and presses the number for the top floor. I'm about to say something, but before I can, he has me pinned into the corner.

He sings about love in an elevator.

I start to laugh, but my laugh is smothered when he kisses me deeply.

I forget what I was about to say. It's hard to concentrate when his hands are running up my dress. The elevator dings, and the doors open, but Phillip doesn't stop kissing me.

"Um, Phillip, where are we going?"

"Maybe I have a few more surprises," he says slyly.

"I think I've had enough surprises for one day," I tease.

He scoops me up and carries me out of the elevator.

"Phillip, put me down. You're not supposed to carry me over the threshold until our wedding night. You'll jinx us!"

He doesn't put me down, but he stops and looks at me seriously. "Are you really gonna marry me?"

"Yeah, I think so. I said yes. Twice." I wrap my arms around his neck. I really don't want him to put me down.

He wrinkles his nose at me. "You also said no at least four times."

I stick out my tongue at him. "What did you expect? You asked me to marry you on our first date. I'm sorry, but that was a bit of a shock. Are you going to put me down?"

"Nope."

"Phillip …"

He leans his face in close to mine. "I'm carrying you into the bedroom, not over the threshold."

The simple mention of Phillip and me in a bedroom sends flames blazing through my body.

"The bedroom is good," I whisper.

He slides in the key card, opens the door to the suite, kicks the door shut with his foot, and carries me past the gorgeous living room and straight into the bedroom.

I eye the king-size bed. The fluffy comforter is turned down. There are chocolates on the pillows. I can't wait to dive in.

Phillip carries me past the bed.

"Hey, you skipped the bed."

"I told you, I might have another surprise."

"And I told you, I can't take any more surprises. If there's a pastor and a wedding party in there, I swear, I'm running the other direction. I'm not marrying you tonight."

He chuckles. "I should've thought of that. We could be on our honeymoon right now."

"No way I would've agreed to that. It's bad enough we got engaged on our first date."

He sets me down in front of another set of double doors and tilts his head at me. "It's bad?"

"You know what I mean—not bad, just really weird."

He loops his arm around my shoulders. "Open the doors. Trust me."

Of course I trust Phillip. He's been my best friend my whole entire life. Plus, based on the room's layout, this has got to be the door to the bathroom. I sling open the double doors and step into a marble room ablaze with varying sizes of flickering candles. There's a huge roman tub in the corner, full of water with rose petals floating across the surface.

I turn around and grin at him. "This might be my favorite part of the whole night."

"I thought it might be. I figured, if you said yes, we'd need a little time to relax after the party."

"And if I had said no?"

"I could've just come up here and drowned myself," he says with a laugh.

He grabs me and has me dangling above the tub before I can scream, "Don't you dare!"

Phillip's been picking me up and throwing me into pools and lakes ever since he got strong enough to do it.

"Wouldn't be the first time," he says as he pretends to drop me.

I'm pretending to be horrified, but really, all I keep thinking about is how strong Phillip is. How I love the way he makes me feel.

But I have to tease him. "We know what would happen if you dropped me in. I'd get out and take you down. Show you that you're not as tough as you think you are."

"Why do you think I always threw you in? You'd get out of the pool, chase me down, and jump on top of me. It was kinda hot."

I laugh at him. "You're being bad, Phillip, but I kinda like it."

Phillip is so damn cute. He was always a cute boy, but the older he's gotten, the sexier he's gotten. His short brown hair, that smile, the deep brown eyes with their golden flecks, and that sexy voice. I don't think there's anything I don't love about Phillip.

I wrap my arm around his neck and pull him into a long, delicious kiss. "Plus, you'd ruin the dress."

"That'd be a shame. You look amazing in this dress, but I bet it'd look even better off." He sets me down and slowly unzips the back of my dress. "I really thought you were gonna say no at the party even though you said yes earlier."

"I was gonna say no."

Phillip's hands glide up my back. He slides the dress off my shoulders, which makes it hard for me to remember why I said no. I'm pretty sure whatever question he asked me right now, the answer would be yes.

"I'm really glad you said yes," he says as his lips graze my shoulder.

God, he's adorable.

"I'm glad I said yes, too. Can you believe we're gonna get married? Can you believe Pastor John told me we need couples counseling?"

He turns me around to face him, kisses my neck, and unhooks my strapless bra. It drops to the floor. He cups my face in his hands. "He's probably right. You do need counseling, and the first thing we're going to counsel you on is, how you should always say yes to me. Do you have any idea how crushed I was when you slammed the ring into my hand and marched away?"

I instantly feel bad. Bad that I could make Phillip even a teeny bit sad. "You know, even if I had said no, it wouldn't have been because I didn't wanna marry you. I just thought maybe it was too soon to get engaged." I grab both of his hands, hold them tight, and look into his eyes. "Phillip, I'm sorry."

"For what?"

"For Cancun. For tonight. I love you. I'd never do anything to hurt you on purpose. I just …"

"It's okay. I got so excited and caught up in planning it that I didn't stop to think about how crazy it sounded."

"Are you changing your mind? Do you wish you hadn't?"

"No, this is exactly where I wanna be."

"In a bathroom with me practically naked?" I ask with a laugh.

He leans down and strips off my thong.

"Make that completely naked."

He wraps his strong arms around me. "With you. Naked is just a bonus. Get in." He holds my hand to help me into the warm, fragrant water.

I lean my back against the tub to relax, but then I notice Phillip's taking off his shirt. I watch raptly. I've seen Phillip's chest a million times—he and Danny were always running around with no shirts on—but it still takes my breath away. Especially now that I know exactly what it feels like. Now that I've run my hands across his abs, felt his weight on top of me, and massaged every square inch of it. I used to rub his back when we were just friends. Even then, I loved feeling every muscle, every curve, but now, all I can think is how hot he looks and how lucky I am. All of a sudden, the bath feels ten times warmer, my face feels flushed, and other parts of me seem to heat up as well.

"I thought you were gonna say no. What changed your mind?"

"I was gonna say no. I was really mad at you. I couldn't believe you sprang that on me. We'd just agreed to kinda keep it a secret. Then, boom! You tell me we're at our surprise engagement party, and everyone knows!"

He chuckles. "You were really pissed. You even cut my hand with the ring."

My eyes get big. "I did?"

He walks over and holds his hand up. Shows me a teeny little scratch. "My war wound," he says in a very fake pathetic voice.

I grab his hand and kiss the scratch.

"So, what made you change your mind?" he asks.

I am about to answer, but then he unbuckles his belt. I watch his slacks fall to the ground and then his boxers. All I can do is stare at his beautiful body.

"You're totally checking me out, aren't you?" he says, busting me.

"Maybe."

He does a few silly bodybuilder poses. His muscles ripple across his broad chest. He's being goofy, but he's naked.

Which makes me feel very serious.

He slides into the tub with me. I lean back against him as he absentmindedly cups water in his hand and pours it down my chest.

I sigh. Close my eyes. *This must be what heaven feels like.*

"You're avoiding the question."

"What question?"

Did he ask me a question?

"I asked what made you change your mind. You haven't told me yet."

"You distracted me with nakedness."

"I'll have to remember that. Seriously, tell me."

"When I was looking out into the crowd, telling them I said no, I saw you standing there. You looked sad. You weren't even looking at me. You were staring down at my ring."

"Go on," he says.

He runs his hands down both my arms. I close my eyes again.

"Then, I wondered what you would do after I said no. Like, would you still date me? Would you give up on us forever? And, just as I was about to say no again, I spotted Danny and Lori. My mind flashed back to when we were walking home after their big engagement. Do you remember how you asked me if I'd ever want to be surprised like that in front of a bunch of people?"

"I do remember. Why do you think I did it? You said you thought it would be amazing to know a guy had planned all of that just for you."

"I realized that. That's when I knew I had to say yes. I realized you had done it all for me. The three-dozen roses, sending me to the spa with your sister, the gorgeous dress, all the charms, the limo, the scavenger hunt, the ring, the party—all of it. I still can't believe you did all that. Planned it all out."

"I was trying to impress you. Did it work? Do you like the ring?"

I pull my hand out of the warm water and hold it in front of us. The diamonds sparkle. It looks the way I feel—sparkly, glittery, full of promise. "The ring was a slam dunk."

"You seemed shocked that I'd kept the drawing of your dream ring."

"I was shocked. What made you keep it?"

"When you looked at the other jewelry, Danny ripped the drawing off the pad, threw it at me, and said, 'You'd better save this; you'll need it someday.'"

"Did you laugh at him?"

"Not really. I hoped he was right. We'd had a conversation about you a couple of months before that. You asked me to your winter formal."

"I remember wishing you were my real date, not just my friend."

"I felt the same way. Then, you came to my spring formal with me, remember?"

"Yeah, but we went as friends. Again."

"Danny chewed me out about that. Said I was a chicken for not asking you for real. Got me to admit I was in love with you."

"So, you kept the drawing and had the ring made. It is my dream ring, but it was just that, Phillip. A dream. You spent way too much on this. On the ring, the party, all of it."

He lowers his voice and whispers into my neck as he's kissing it, "I'd spend everything I had on you." Then, he laughs and runs his hand across his eyebrow. "Actually, I pretty much did. I might have to live with you now."

"You have been living with me."

"I've been spending the night with you."

"Are you trying to guilt me into letting you live with me? I know you live at your parents' for free."

"Yeah, but it's not as much fun there as it is at your place. Speaking of that, I think we should go see if that bed's as comfortable as it looks."

We get out of the tub and quickly dry off. When he picks me up and carries me into the bedroom, I'm pretty sure I know exactly what kind of fun he's referring to.

Sparkly, gooey, and magical.

SUNDAY, SEPTEMBER 10TH

WE EVENTUALLY HAVE to leave the cozy cocoon of our hotel suite and get back to reality. Reality starts with our usual Sunday night dinner at the Mackenzie house. I've been to many Sunday night dinners there. I grew up next door to them, and Mr. Mac and my dad were fraternity brothers and best friends. I've always been close to them, but when my parents were killed in a car accident my senior year of high school, they pretty much made me one of their own. I don't know what I would've done without them or the Diamonds.

Still, I'm nervous for dinner.

I'm officially going to marry their son, and I know it sounds odd, but I feel like I need to make a good impression. So, I put on a pair of dark jeans, a new flouncy pale peach top with rosettes at the neck, and a pair of silver heels.

I look romantic and happy.

Now, I see why Lori started trying to set me up with Phillip as soon as she got engaged to Danny. She felt all sparkly, gooey, and magical, and she wanted her friends to feel that way, too.

I get it now.

I feel pretty sparkly, and I *cannot* stop looking at the sparkle on my finger during the drive over.

JILLIAN DODD

But, when we get there, Mrs. Mac doesn't seem to notice my sparkle, how I'm dressed, or how Phillip keeps being quite naughty and running his hand dangerously high up my thigh under the kitchen table.

No.

Mrs. Mac is focused on one thing.

Which is good because I can't seem to focus on anything other than the fact that, if Phillip doesn't stop it, I'm going to drag him up to his bedroom and show him *exactly* how I feel about him.

Oh, sorry, where was I?

Oh, yes, I was saying, Mrs. Mac is focused on one thing.

And that thing is wedding planning.

Seriously? We've been engaged for, what? Twenty-two hours! And she's ready to start planning?

I mean, I'm still in shock that I'm even dating Phillip, let alone engaged to the boy.

Isn't there some kind of engagement buffer? Where you get a few days, weeks, months to get used to the idea before people start bombarding you with questions about an event you're totally not mentally prepared to deal with?

The answer to that question is *apparently not* because she's already prepared a wedding spreadsheet of some kind. Not surprising really since she probably has to make a spreadsheet before she can do laundry to make sure she does it in the proper order. To say this woman is organized is a supreme understatement.

She hands it to me, and I scan it.

Looks pretty typical. Once we figure out when we want to get married, then we'll be happy to use her list and start planning.

But I'm not in any hurry to get married.

We need to date for a while first.

Ashley, Phillip's sister, says, "So, JJ, I would recommend you start by picking a theme and your colors."

"A theme?" *What is this, a frat party?* "What kind of wedding theme?"

"Oh, wow," she says. "There are so many things you could do. You could have it black tie, casual, country, or beachy. Fairy-tale weddings are big right now. You could do, like, a fall wedding or even a Halloween wedding!"

"A Halloween wedding! Like a black-and-orange wedding? How fun would that be? We could have people dress up and hand out candy!" I laugh. *Ha!* "Phillip, did you hear that? We could get married on Halloween! We could just have people ring the doorbell and stand outside, and we could get married in the entryway. We could be all dressed up and then go out and get candy for our reception! Our favors could be dozens of eggs, forks, Fruity Pebbles, and toilet paper!"

"PHILLIP DAVID Mackenzie!" Mrs. Mac yells. She squints her eyes and gives him the mom glare. "You told me you had *nothing* to do with the Robertsons' house that Halloween."

"What Halloween?" he asks innocently.

"The year their whole sidewalk was covered in Fruity Pebbles. Then, it rained, and the color stained their sidewalk. We thought it was never going to come off! You swore to me that you had nothing to do with it!"

Phillip scrunches up his nose and laughs. "What are you gonna do, Mom? Ground me? Besides, I was in charge of the forks, not the Fruity Pebbles." He gives me a pointed grin, so his mom will think it was my idea.

"Jadyn!" Mrs. Mac scolds.

"Uh, so maybe a Halloween-themed wedding is a bad idea," I say, quickly switching the conversation back to something that won't get us in trouble.

Besides, the Fruity Pebbles was all Danny's idea, but we won't mention that. Knowing Mrs. Mac, she'd be calling his mom.

Ashley continues, "Well, you could do winter wonderland or,

like, a down-home country-style wedding. Some people even have Nebraska-themed weddings. You both love football; maybe you should do something like that."

"I do love football, but I don't think I'd want that for my wedding."

"So, what do you want?" Phillip's mom asks.

"I have no idea. I got surprise engaged on my first date less than twenty-four hours ago. I really haven't gotten that far yet." They both stare at me like I'm nuts, so I'm like, "Phillip, what kind of wedding do you want?"

"Um ..." he says eloquently. "I don't know. The kind that involves us getting married?"

Mrs. Mac and Ashley both roll their eyes at him in that *he's just a man; what could he possibly know* way.

"JJ, have you seriously never pictured your wedding? Every little girl dreams of her wedding day," Ashley admonishes.

Gee, apparently, I'm a failure as a girl.

All I ever dreamed about was marrying a prince, but that was really as far as I got. To me, it was all about finding the right boy. I guess I sorta thought, once you found the guy, the wedding would just fall into place.

I mean, think of *Cinderella*. The whole story was about her and Prince Charming's courtship. It's only at the very end that the wedding bells ring, birds fly, and they kiss. No one asked Cinderella what kind of themed wedding she wanted. The wedding just happened.

Didn't it?

I know most of my sorority sisters have planned out their ideal weddings. I listened, thought they sounded amazing, and encouraged them. But my wedding seemed so far off that I never really thought about what I'd want. Plus, you have to remember, my two best friends are Phillip and Danny.

Boys.

I can tell you with all certainty that they never once stood around the pool table, planning their dream weddings. The only real discussions we ever had about weddings involved Danny praying some girl wasn't pregnant, so he wouldn't have to marry her.

"Uh," I say, "honestly, not really. We used to have weddings for Barbie and Ken, but those mostly involved a wedding in front of Phillip's Lego castle. They'd drive off in her Barbie Jeep and then have a Barbie baby. And, sometimes, they would go on a honeymoon to the blow-up Barbie pool where they would kiss, swim, and get their hair wet. Oh!" I giggle. "And, sometimes, instead of Ken, she would marry G.I. Joe."

"Bigamy Barbie," Phillip quips as he sets a beer down in front of me.

"That's true, but you loved when she married Joe. You'd make him jump out of a plane or rappel down the wall, and then they'd get married. Joe always made a big entrance. It was all very exciting. Ken was sort of boring, but he was there for her when Joe went off to, I don't know, fight in wars and stuff."

Phillip laughs.

I can't help but laugh, too. We had so much fun when we were kids. "She also married Robin Hood. So, she was more like Trigamy Barbie," I tell Phillip.

"Trigamy?" Ash questions.

"Uh, maybe trigonometry?" I stupidly say.

"Oh my gosh." Phillip chuckles. "Are you both blonde or what?"

"Well then, what would it be called?"

"Polygamy."

"No, that's when you have many spouses. What's it called when you have just three, like Barbie did? It would have to be trigamy. Really, that's kind of a good idea. Like, I could marry Ken because he was pretty and would provide a good gene pool for kids. Then, there's G.I. Joe. He'd, like, show up whenever, you'd have wild sex with him, and then he'd be off again on some mission. And Robin Hood would take you on adventures. I think Barbie was on to something. She really did have the perfect life."

"Except when she got pregnant and didn't know if it was Ken or Joe's baby," Ash says sarcastically.

"Like Barbie would've had a big dilemma over that one. You know she would've just told Ken it was his baby. He wouldn't have known the difference. Ken looked good, but I don't think he was all that smart. But he'd be a good dad and stay home and take care of the kids while she was off with Joe or Robin." That's not a bad idea. "Hey, Phillip, can I have three husbands, too?"

"Hmm, I don't think so." He grins and shakes his head.

Ashley rolls her eyes. "So, are you saying you want a Barbie-themed wedding?"

Uh, no. I might not know much, but I do know a hot-pink Barbie wedding is not for me.

It seems the *theme* of tonight's dinner is for us to pick a theme. I swear, if they don't lay off, pretty soon, my theme is gonna be *I don't give a damn.*

Thank God the oven buzzer goes off, meaning we finally get to eat. And here's what I want to know: why aren't they asking Phillip these questions? He's the one who was so bound and determined to get engaged. I just want to have fun sleeping with him for a while.

MRS. MAC FALLS back a little during dinner, but apparently, it's not a full retreat because, after dinner, she sits us down in front of apple pie and questions us.

I told you before that she feeds you and gets you to spill your guts. That woman is sneaky.

Phillip's as clueless as I am on the whole theme thing, so he tells his mom, "I have no freaking idea." Then, he ditches me and takes his pie into the family room to watch football with his dad and Ash's husband, Cooper.

But Mrs. Mac will not be deterred. She gets up and grabs a large stack of the thickest magazines known to man.

Bridal magazines.

They practically break through the wooden table when she slams the stack down in front of me. Thankfully, I got my hands out of the way.

"I went through and marked everything I like in yellow," she tells me.

"And I marked everything I like in blue," Ashley adds.

When did these people find time to go through these monstrosities? If I tried to sit on the couch at home and flip through these, I'd make it all of about twelve pages before Phillip attacked me. Sex has been taking up a lot of our time lately.

Mrs. Mac continues in her sweet, *if you do this for me, I will bake you cookies* voice. "So, just flip through all the magazines and mark stuff you like. Then, we'll help you figure out a theme. So, what are you thinking for a date?"

"We haven't discussed dates yet, but I'm pretty sure we're going to have a very long engagement. Like, maybe a couple of years. We really don't need to start planning yet."

She gives me a little sigh. I see my opportunity to get away, so I grab the magazines and go sit in the family room. She's still staring at me, so I pretend to look interested and flip through a few pages. But, really, I'm looking at Phillip, who's sitting in his favorite chair, finishing his second piece of pie. He looks so adorable that I almost wish I had two of him.

That reminds me …

I grab my phone and look up the word *trigamy*. And I'm right! There is a word that means married to three people.

I glance over to Phillip and say, "It's trigamous."

"Cool," he says, not really listening because he's very into the game and his pie. He practically licks the plate and then turns to me with a grin. "So, you were wrong?"

"I was closer to right than you were. That's all I care about." I give him a sassy little smile.

He grabs me off the couch, pulls me onto his lap, and starts kissing me.

Why is it kinda funny that this boy, who managed to keep his hands off me for years, cannot seem to control those hands anymore? I'm a little embarrassed by this. We're in the middle of his family room, and everyone can see us! I cut the kiss short, but he won't let me get off his lap, so I get cozy, watch the game, and forget all about wedding planning.

MY CELL BUZZES on the side table.

Phillip grabs it, says, "Danny," and hands me it.

"Hey, what's up?"

"How about, tomorrow will be my first start as a freaking pro quarterback? Can you believe it?"

One of the first things Danny told me when he moved next door in fifth grade was that he was a great quarterback. I remember telling him he was a bragger. He told me that he wasn't bragging; he was just confident in his skills. Turns out, he was right about that since he went on to be a state champion in high school, got recruited to play for Nebraska, won the national championship his senior year, came in second in the Heisman race, and won every quarterback award there was. He went on to be the second pick in the draft.

Last week, the starting quarterback got a concussion, so Danny finished the game. With his blond hair, dreamy blue eyes, killer body, and good-old-boy attitude, he's also quickly becoming the poster boy for hot quarterbacks everywhere. His pro jersey, with Diamond across the back, became their hottest-selling jersey before he ever stepped foot on their field. He's making his first professional start tomorrow in a *Monday Night Football* game.

"Yeah, I can believe it. I've always believed in you, and I'm so excited I get to be there!"

"Jay, you *have* always believed in me. I should probably thank you for that."

"Yeah, you should!"

"Remember my freshman year in college?"

I laugh. "I do. You thought it sucked."

"Well, it did! I was the big man in high school. State champion winner. MVP. First team, all-state. Five-star recruit. Then, I went to college and *nothing*. I got freaking redshirted. I guess I just figured it would stay easy, be like high school."

"Danny, you know as well as I do that it didn't come easy in high school. Yeah, you were better than most kids, so it looked easy, but those of us who knew you knew how much time you devoted to working out, how many freaking passes Phillip and I caught for you, all the times you stayed after practice, the camps, all of it. You've always worked for it. Are you nervous? Are you comparing this to your freshman year?"

"I might be a little nervous. I've moved up a level. What if I can't compete?"

"You already competed on that level when you finished the game last week. You did awesome. You'll do awesome."

"You know, I still visualize us playing in the empty lot between our houses before every game, and that pic of you two is hanging in my locker."

"That's so cool."

"My priorities are different now. I have an amazing wife, and pretty soon, we'll have a baby. But, when I'm out there in a game, I play because it's fun. Because I love it."

"I know, Danny."

"The guys have been giving me all kinds of crap about the picture though. They want to meet this flag-bikini girl. They've also been making up funny stories about you two. Like, Phillip's my gay lover. You're my mistress. You're the one who got away. You're a Vegas hooker. Some think I don't even know you. Like, I found the pic of you both going up for a pass on the internet or something. One of these days, I might tell them the truth, but for now, their wild guesses are kinda fun."

"So ... Daaaannyyy Diamoooond! Are you ready for some football—a Monday night partyyyyy?" I exaggeratedly sing the *Monday Night Football* anthem.

"We'll see," he tells me. "We'll see."

In a blaze of glory.

MONDAY, SEPTEMBER 11TH

WE'RE DRIVING TO Kansas City for the game and listening to sports radio. There's a lot of speculation that Mark Conway's football career is over due to concussions and that he's going to retire soon.

If it's true, I'll be happy for Danny, but I feel bad, too. I wouldn't want Danny to go out that way, having a concussion end his career. I want him to go out in a blaze of glory. He needs confetti raining down on him, fans cheering him, raising the Super Bowl trophy over his head for the third time when he announces his retirement.

Danny calls me. He must really be nervous.

"Hey, what's up?"

"Do you remember that day after prom, how we talked in the hammock?" he asks.

"Of course. That was the day you told me, if we dated, it would ruin our friendship."

"Do you remember what you told me?"

"Not really." I don't remember exactly what all I said that day.

"You told me that I had greatness in me. That I was doing what I always wanted and what I was meant to do."

"Oh, yeah, the football talk. I remember that. I thought you

19

were talking about what I said about us. You know, when you broke my heart."

Danny laughs. "We both know I did not break your heart."

"I still say you did. Ahhh, the one who got away."

I giggle and wink at Phillip. He rolls his eyes at me.

"Jay, back to football."

"Oh, sorry."

"Do you remember after we lost the Texas game? I'd had those two interceptions, and the press—who the week before had thought I was the second coming of Christ himself—threw me under the bus and decided I was overrated?"

"Yeah, I remember. It sucked."

"You told me that it didn't look like I was having fun out there. That, when I stopped having fun, the whole team did, too. I remember yelling at you. Because how could I have had fun when I was either getting sacked or running for my life? But, when I watched the game film, I realized you were right. When I'd started falling apart, the team had come with me. You told me I was like the captain of a sinking ship. That, if I let the water get to me, it would get to my crew, too. That I needed to be the leader. Tell them it didn't matter, that the water was good for the boat, and we were gonna make it to land. You told me I had to lead my offense, be the calm in the storm. That, if I wasn't confident, they wouldn't be either."

"Wow! I was really supportive, and apparently, I'm quite brilliant at motivational sports analogies. I should totally be on ESPN."

Phillip chuckles in the seat next to me.

Danny laughs, too. "Don't get too puffed up. You also used to say, 'Screw it. It's just a game.' Tell Phillip he gets points for making me go in the backyard and toss around the football."

"I'll tell him, but only if I get bonus points for taking you to the bar."

"I'm not sure that was the smartest thing."

"So, why are you calling? You need a little pregame pep talk?"

"Maybe."

"Hmm, okay. I still believe what I said back then. You were born for this, and you're exactly where you belong. You can perform under pressure like no one else can."

Phillip bursts out laughing, but that's because his mind's in the gutter.

Danny says, "I like it so far," but then he bursts out laughing, too, and is like, "although that last part sounded a bit sexual. Has Lori been telling you how amazing I am in bed?"

"Uh, no," I say, but then I laugh again. "Well, maybe I've heard a little, but you know what I mean. I'm talking defensive pressure, which I don't think you'll have much of tonight because you have an offensive line most quarterbacks would give their left nuts for."

"True."

"So, Daniel-son," I tease.

"Oh boy, movie references. You aren't gonna start telling me to wax on, wax off, are you?"

"No, I have a better one. Remember the old movie *Iron Eagle*? Where that kid flies a fighter plane to go rescue his dad?"

"Yeah."

"Your offensive line is like his plane. They're going to protect you. You're the iron eagle that can't be brought down, can't be stopped. You'll hold your ground. You'll scramble. You will not take a sack."

"That's pretty good. I like it."

"Good, 'cause, after you win tonight and the reporters are all like, *Oh, Danny, you're so ah-mazing*, I expect you to say, *I owe it all to Jay*."

Danny chuckles. "That's why I love you. See ya after the game."

WE'RE AT THE stadium. I was so excited that I packed a ton of tailgating food and lots to drink. The Diamonds came, too, but didn't bring the RV, and they're kicking themselves because Lori has to pee a lot. Mrs. Diamond says pregnant women always have to pee. She was gushing on about how Lori's glowing. And she is. Lori is beautiful, but her strawberry-blonde hair looks thicker, her cheeks look slightly flushed, and although she's still her normal, skinny self, she looks just a little fuller. Sexier. She looks amazing.

We drink beer in front of her, but I feel funny, doing shots. I don't want her to feel left out. So, not bringing the RV turned out to be a blessing in disguise because, while she's waiting in line to use the Porta Potties, I get out the Jägermeister, which is a good thing because I'm probably more nervous about Danny starting than Danny is.

WE GET TO our seats early, so we won't miss a thing. I'm expecting our conversation to be about the game. But the topic is not Danny's starting, the fun tailgating, the 9/11 memorial silence, the blimp, the roar of the crowd, the gorgeous weather, or the stealth bomber flyover. The topic Lori wants to discuss is my wedding.

She questions me, "So, how do you want your wedding to be?"

"I just want it to be nice. Pretty flowers, a pretty dress, a fun party. I love parties."

She rolls her eyes at me. "Yes, we all know you love partying, Jade. But this is your wedding. It's not supposed to be some drunkfest. Although how about a New Year's Eve wedding? Confetti, hats, noisemakers—and I won't be a moose yet."

"I like the idea, but that's way too soon! We're going to have a long engagement."

"So, have you set a date?"

"No. You were at our party. We've been engaged for two days.

Why does everyone keep asking me that? It makes my head hurt!"

Phillip leans over and whispers in my ear, "Or maybe it's the Jäger." He pats my back and says, "I think we're gonna need a few more beers here."

He runs to get beer while Lori continues talking, "I'm not trying to pressure you, but we're thinking about taking a babymoon. I was trying to figure out when would be a good time to go ..."

What the heck is a babymoon?

I am gonna interrupt her and ask, but she keeps talking, "And I know you haven't asked me yet, but I assume I'll be your maid of honor."

"Matron of honor," I remind her. "You're married."

"Oh gosh. Matron? Really? That makes me sound so old. There needs to be a different name for that. We need to come up with something. Like, you could really hurt people's feelings with those labels. I'm married, yes. But I'm not matronly, and I don't want to be a matron. And what about the poor woman who's thirty-five and never been married? Are you going to call her a maid of honor? You might as well call her an old maid because I'm sure that's how it'd make her feel. We seriously need to rethink this."

I wonder if I'm going to get a word in edgewise. Or get to watch the game.

"And here I was, stupidly thinking my wedding day was supposed to be about my and Phillip's undying love."

"Oh, hush," she says. "Don't be such a whiner."

I stand up and cheer loudly. Danny just made a great pass, and they've moved the ball down to the red zone.

"I promise to okay my date with you before we make it official. Now, what the heck is a babymoon?"

"It's a vacation that you and your husband go on before the baby's born. It's time to relax and connect while it's still just the two of you."

"That sounds like a vacation."

"Yes, Jade, it is a vacation," she says with a sigh. "They just call it a babymoon because of the timing. I mean, a honeymoon is just a vacation, too."

"Yeah, I suppose. Can we please watch the game now?"

THE GAME WAS so exciting. It was a purely offensive battle. Danny played really well and threw for over three hundred yards. It was back-and-forth scoring. You could tell it was going to come down to who had the ball last. Unfortunately, it was the other team. We lost by a field goal with only three seconds on the clock. Bummer.

WE WERE SUPPOSED to stay at Danny and Lori's, but they're remodeling their house, and it sounds like it's a disaster right now. Mr. and Mrs. Diamond are staying there since one of the guest rooms is done, but we didn't want to stress Lori any more or have to sleep on the couch, so we got a hotel.

Phillip pulls me down on the bed. "Do we need to start talking about wedding stuff? My mom seems to think we do, and I heard Lori asking you about it."

"Eventually, we do. I guess it depends on when we wanna get married."

"I'd marry you right now if I could," he says while running his hands through my hair.

"Awww, Phillip." I give him a big smooch. "I know everyone thinks we need to start, but I think we need to take our time. Enjoy this. Lori told me tonight that she's going to be my special bridesmaid and when I could and couldn't have the wedding."

Phillip laughs and says quietly, "Control freak."

I laugh, too, and then I say, "I'm still seriously in shock that we're even engaged! It sorta feels like a dream. If it wasn't for this ring on my finger, I don't know if I'd even believe it happened."

Phillip gets a naughty look on his face. "A dream, huh?" He quickly pins me down on the bed. "Oh, Princess, you're definitely awake. Maybe I need to remind you of that."

He reminds me by recklessly kissing me and pulling off my shirt.

LATER, WE'RE LYING here, exhausted and grinning at each other.

"Still feel like a dream?" he asks.

He's slowly running his fingertips up and down my leg, which makes me kinda feel like I'm in a dream.

"Yeah," I say, "a hot, sexy one."

"Okay, so I saw you were flipping through the bridal magazines Mom gave you. Did you see anything you liked?"

"Phillip, the game was on. Do you really think I was looking at them? I was just flipping to make her happy."

"I heard Ash say we need a wedding theme. What does she mean? Like the frat parties we used to have? Like a boats and hoes wedding?"

"Not funny, but, yeah, I guess. Really, I have no idea what she means. I'm pretty sure all the weddings we've been to have just had a color scheme, not a theme."

"Your favorite colors are turquoise, orange, and purple. Those going to be our colors?"

"They sound awful together. Turquoise might be pretty though. What color would you want?"

He kisses the top of my forehead. "Doesn't matter. This wedding is all about you."

"No, it's not! Hey, don't think you're gonna get out of helping me plan by saying that. This wedding—if we even have one," I tease, "is going to be all about us."

"I like us."

"You wanna talk about colors and wedding themes all night?"

"No, I think I can come up with something a little more fun than that," he says. He rolls on top of me, kisses me, and makes me forget about weddings again.

planning a wedding sounds like no fun.

WEDNESDAY, SEPTEMBER 13TH

I'M BACK AT work. Thankfully, my boss is a huge Danny Diamond fan and let me take off a few days to go see his first game. Okay, so I had to bribe him with an autographed football, but whatever works.

So far, the day has been a disaster. It's bad enough, trying to get caught up, but now, I'm frantic because the blueprints I sent with a courier first thing this morning have still not arrived at their destination. I've wasted so much time trying to track them down.

My phone rings, and I stupidly don't look at the caller ID before I say, "Jadyn Reynolds," because I assume it's the messenger service.

I hear Mrs. Mac's voice. "JJ, we really need to have a wedding-planning meeting. Do you realize all that has to be done? Even if you don't want to get married for a year or more, we've got to get started. I'm assuming, by now, you've had a chance to go through the bridal magazines and mark the things you like?"

"Uh, not really yet. We went to Danny's game, and I'm at the end of a project at work. It's, like, crunch time, and you know Phillip has been super busy at work, too. In fact, we're both working late tonight."

She doesn't get the answer she wants to hear, so she snarls,

"Fine. You have homework. I want you to go through the magazines I gave you and flag everything you like. And tell my son that he needs to go through them with you. Bring them to the house Saturday morning."

I say gently, "Um, that probably won't work because we're going to a game-day party."

She huffs at me and sounds a little pissed. "Fine. Be here early for dinner on Sunday. Let's say three o'clock. And tell Phillip to jot down ideas as well—never mind, I'll tell him. Oh, I'm also supposed to remind you that Pastor John wants you to call him right away. Something about couples counseling."

I get off the phone and am like, *Homework and couples counseling?*

Seriously?

Planning a wedding sounds like no fun.

All that's on that boy's mind lately.

THURSDAY, SEPTEMBER 14TH

I HAD TO work late again tonight, but when I get home, Phillip is waiting with Chinese takeout and a bottle of wine.

It even has a cork and everything.

He greets me with a kiss and opens the wine. "So, I talked to Lori about wedding-planning stuff the other day. She told me about a wedding show, where a celebrity wedding planner can take the worst themes ever and turn them into something beautiful. I recorded a few, so we can watch them tonight while we eat."

"Watching TV sounds perfect. I'm tired, stressed, and starved. I didn't even get time for lunch today!"

We spread our feast across the coffee table, sit on the floor, eat, and watch a couple of shows.

And, wow! Lori was right. He can take the tackiest theme and make it amazing.

Maybe I need a wedding planner.

Phillip flicks off the TV, and we talk about possible themes for our wedding. Most of the couples had a reason for their theme. We talk about the swings, football, princesses, and Barbie. None of them seem right.

But, pretty soon, the food is mostly gone, the wine is completely gone, and wedding themes seem to be the last thing on

Phillip's mind.

He leads me into the bedroom, throws me on the bed, and pounces on me. I have a fleeting thought that maybe our theme should be sex because that seems to be all that's on that boy's mind lately.

I'M HAPPILY SPRAWLED across Phillip's body when I joke, "I think our wedding theme might have to be sex."

"A XXX wedding?" Phillip asks.

We get silly, talking about ideas for our XXX-themed wedding.

The celebrity wedding planner would be hyperventilating!

"I know." I giggle. "We could use furry handcuffs for napkin rings."

"We could have personalized condoms as our favors!"

"Oh … listen to this! We could use those big dildos that stand up on their own, and we could, like, cut the tips." Phillip winces when I say that. "And we could use them to hold the table numbers at the reception!"

Phillip tickles me. I giggle and tickle him back.

"I'll use a vibrator as the base of my bouquet! It could vibrate through the whole ceremony. Can you just picture that? Everyone's all serious, and it's just sitting there, shaking."

"You're silly," he says. Then, he attacks my chest with kisses. "I have a better idea. We could do a *Phillip and Jadyn Make a Porno* video."

"We could show it at the reception!" I scream.

"Maybe we should practice a few moves right now," Phillip says sexily.

And, uh, yeah, we do.

Practice, I mean.

Sorry, no videos.

AFTER ROUND TWO, I give Phillip my pouty face.

"What's the face for?" he asks. "We just had amazing, mind-blowing sex. Again. I even impressed myself."

I roll my eyes at him. "I don't know about mind-blowing."

I laugh, but he totally knows I'm lying. It's really hard to lie to someone who can read your mind. And it was oh-my-gosh-scream-it-from-the-rooftops incredible. But I don't tell him that. I don't want him to think he's, like, all that. He needs to keep working toward a goal or something.

"Plus, I think you're just using me for sex." I try to look sad.

He laughs a huge, hearty laugh. "Yeah, I am."

I can't help but grin with him.

"But I'm just trying to catch up."

"Catch up?"

"Yeah, so the sex and the friendship are even."

"We've been best friends for a really long time."

"Yes, I know. I really do have my work cut out for me," he jokes. "I just feel balance is important in our relationship." Then, he says, "Speaking of that, Sunday night, when you were sitting on the kitchen island at my parents' house, I had this flashback. Do you remember the night you were all upset about your date with that Mark guy you had a crush on? He tried to attack you before dinner, so you got pissed and made him bring you home. You came over, all upset about both him and the fact that you'd dumped Dillon because of him. Do you remember that?"

"Yeah, you were just getting home from Danny's, and if I recall, you weren't much help because you were tipsy and thought the whole thing was hilarious and my own fault."

"Well, that, and all I could think about was how hot you looked, how I really didn't blame Mark for wanting you, and how I really just wanted to do you right there on the kitchen island. I even had dreams about it. Do you remember what you wore? Lisa must have dressed you. You had on a short plaid skirt, little white

31

blouse, a navy cardigan. You kinda looked like a naughty schoolgirl."

"Phillip! *Your mother's island! And* you used to have naughty dreams about me?"

"Oh, yeah. Lots of them. Good ones."

"Like what?"

"I don't know. They would start off with us doing stuff we'd normally do. I never really remembered those parts, but you'd end up attacking me. Like, one time, we were sitting on the hood of my car, looking at the stars. All of a sudden, you straddled me and attacked me. It was a good dream."

a little freak out in my mind.

FRIDAY, SEPTEMBER 15TH

LAST NIGHT, I laughed and smiled about Phillip's dreams, but now that I'm at work, trying to focus on pulling some figures together for a budget meeting I'm about to go into, my mind is still thinking about it.

Because it's sorta bugging me.

I mean, shouldn't *he* have attacked *me* in his dreams? Shouldn't that have been his dream?

I'm about to have a little freak-out in my mind when my cell vibrates.

Apparently, Phillip has shared our wedding theme with Danny because I receive a random text.

Danny: *Groom's cake = strippers jumping out!*

Oh, wow. That's funny!

Me: *Groomsmen dress like Chippendales. Meaning a tuxedo with no shirt for you!*

Danny: *Gonna have to work on the abs some more.*

Me: *Yeah, right. What are we up to now, an eight-pack?*

Danny: *Gotta keep the core strong, baby. ;)*

Me: *Got a meeting. Gotta go.*

I go to my project meeting. During the meeting, I keep getting texts from Danny. Nobody notices this, except the guy who is sitting next to me and is kind of a creeper. He always makes slightly sexual comments to me. He's never crossed the line really. He just kinda creeps me out. I can tell he's reading my texts because he just almost burst out with a laugh. He tried to hold it in, which caused him to snort coffee up his nose and have a mini choking fit.

10:08

Danny: *Bridesmaids = sexy schoolgirls.*

11:22

Danny: *Bridesmaids all dressed in different sexy outfits.*

11:23

Danny: *One a sexy schoolgirl, one a French maid.*

11:47

Danny: *Reception = all couples swinging. Provide masks for anonymity.*

11:49

Danny: *Whips and chains for party favors?*

It's very difficult for me to concentrate during the meeting, and every time I see my phone light up, I sneak a peek and want to die laughing. Finally, we break for lunch, and although Danny's texts have been entertaining, my mind is still on Phillip's dreams.

I go out to my car and call Lori.

I need to talk about this and probably shouldn't do it at my desk where everyone can hear about my sex life.

Especially the creeper.

As we were walking out of the meeting, he said, "Sounds like you have some fun when you're not at work," and, "Hmm, I thought your fiancé's name was Phillip. You're a naughty girl, aren't you?"

And I tried hard not to gag in front of him.

Lori answers, and I'm like, "Phillip told me he used to have naughty dreams about me." I don't even say hello.

But she goes with it. "And that surprises you?"

"Well, yeah, actually, it did, or I wouldn't be calling you about it."

"Oh, Jade. What am I going to do with you? You're so oblivious."

"Hey, don't judge! I need help and advice, and I called you, but never mind."

"Oh! You called *me* to ask for *advice*? You never do that! You always call Danny."

"I know, so help me!"

She makes a little noise that lets me know she's quite proud of this. "Oh, well, continue."

"Okay, so in Phillip's dreams, I attacked him. So, does that mean his subconscious thought was that I was hot for him and wanted to attack him, or does it mean his subconscious was hot for me and wished I would attack him, so, in the dreams, I did? Like, if he was hot for me, why didn't he attack me in the dreams?"

"Does it really matter? He wanted you. He's always wanted you, and now, you have him."

"It kinda matters to me."

Lori sighs. "Jade, for a girl who barely gives anything she says or does a second thought, oh my gosh, you way overprocess everything in your mind when it comes to Phillip. Why don't you put that brain to better use and start planning your wedding?"

"One, I like the boy. And, two, I *am* working on the wedding."

"Really?"

"Well, sorta. We watched that show you told us about, but we also drank a whole bottle of wine, and then Phillip kinda attacked me. Lori, he's so freaking sexy. And the sex? Oh my gosh, the sex is so ..."

"Jade, I thought you wanted my advice." She is not impressed.

"I do."

"But you're not gonna take it, right?"

"Well, I'm not going to forget about this, if that's what you mean. I can't!"

"Why does it matter?"

"I'm trying to determine why I attacked him in the dreams because I have a wild idea."

"Wow. Now, I'm really impressed you're asking *me* for advice. Aren't wild ideas, like, Danny's specialty?"

"Yes, they are, but I called you because I'm thinking about making those dreams come true."

This sinks in, and she says, "Oh my! As in act them out? Oh, Jade, he'll like that!"

"Well, I hope so, but if I don't understand the dream, it won't be right."

"Hmm, hang on. I'm gonna get Danny and put you on speaker. I actually might be in over my head on this one. We need a boy's opinion."

I knew I should've just called him in the first place, but I'm happy I called Lori first because she seems so happy about it.

I hear Danny's deep voice go, "What's up, girls?"

And I'm like, "So, last night, Phillip told me that he used to have naughty dreams about me."

Danny says, "So? Big deal. We both did."

"You did?" I say.

"Well, a couple, sure. I mean, we were together all the time."

"Danny! Did you dream about me or lots of girls?"

"Well, duh, lots of girls."

"Crap. Now, I'm depressed. Phillip probably did, too."

Lori chimes in and explains to Danny, "Phillip told her he used to have naughty dreams about her, and for some reason—that reason being, she's oblivious—she was surprised by this."

Danny says, "Jay baby, pretty much all of Phillip's dreams were about you."

"He told you about them?" Lori and I say at the same time.

"Well, yeah, some of them. We've always talked about everything. You know that."

"Dang, I thought you guys told me everything, too. Now, I'm sad."

"Don't be. In high school, our dreams were certainly more exciting than what we were actually doing."

"Danny, you did plenty of *doing* in high school."

"Not really. Think about high school sex. It was do it quick, don't get caught, pray her parents don't come home early, pray she doesn't get pregnant. Not exactly dreamworthy."

"I think Jade was considering trying to fulfill some of Phillip's dreams," Lori says.

"Like his fantasies? Wow, lucky guy. He'll definitely like that."

"Well, I was thinking about it, but now that I know he had them about other girls, I don't know if I want to."

Danny says, "Jay, come on, like, all his dreams were about you."

"He told you that?"

"Kinda, yeah."

"So, what you're saying is that you really don't know?"

"No, they were mostly about you. I know that because, when they weren't and they were about, like, a Victoria's Secret model, he would tell me. And, most of the time, he wouldn't tell me who the girl was. I would ask, and he would always say, 'It doesn't matter.' It all makes sense now. It had to be you. So, you wanna make his dreams come true, huh?"

"Yeah, but which one? If you talked about it, do you remember ... did he have, like, a favorite?"

"Yes, actually, he did. It involved you and me getting it on in that little tent we used to camp in."

"So, it was a threesome?" I ask.

Lori says, "I can't imagine Phillip dreaming that."

"Oh. My. Gosh!" I say. "Is Phillip bisexual?"

Danny chuckles. "Oh, wait. Maybe that was my dream."

Lori humphs.

I'm like, "Danny!"

And he goes, "Ha-ha. I'm just kidding. And, jeez, Lori, I was fourteen. Okay, so back on track here. I remember one he used to have a lot. We were at the ball field, and someone attacked him on the hood of his car. Of course, that was you. Remember how the three of us used to do that? Sit there, drinking my special Gatorade-vodka mixes and eating sunflower seeds? But there was also a Spin the Bottle one that I never really understood."

Lori is like, "I know that one! Jade, remember when I told you it was time to play Spin the Bottle again?"

"Yeah." I can't help but smile about that.

"Did that happen?" Danny asks.

"Kinda. Remember when Mary Beth had a crush on him, and he was in the closet with her for seven minutes of what was probably pure hell at Lisa's fourteenth birthday party?"

"I did hear about that part. He told me he wouldn't kiss her because she was gross and mean to you."

"Awww, really? That's so sweet. Phillip's so sweet."

"The story, Jay?"

"Oh, yeah. So, later that night, we played Spin the Bottle, and the bottle landed, like, right between Mary Beth and me. He pointed the bottle toward me, and then he kissed me. He was just trying to piss MB off. That was the last time I really kissed him until after your engagement."

"Makes sense now. So, Jay, did you have any dreams like that, and how many were about me?"

"I didn't have any dreams about you like that, but I do vividly remember one I had when I was dating Jake. We were all playing football. I was mad at Phillip because he was being a jerk about something, so I accidentally/on purpose tripped him, and we both fell down."

"The flag-bikini day?" Danny asks.

"Yeah, that's it. I was mad because he'd told me he didn't like my swimsuit. Remember how he was so pissed and was sitting on top of me?"

"Yeah."

"Well, that happened in my dream. He leaned down to yell at me, and instead, he started kissing me and, um, doing a lot of other stuff, too. You sorta disappeared."

"I think I did disappear that day. It looked like he was gonna do you right there in the grass. I think I told you to get a room."

"The dream really upset me back then."

"Why?" both Danny and Lori ask.

"'Cause Phillip was like my brother. It was like, I don't know, practically incestuous."

"Jay."

"Well, he was, and the problem was, I liked it and kept wishing I'd have the dream again. I felt very conflicted."

Lori says, "Oh my gosh, you two were so dumb."

Danny intercedes, "Okay, so here's what I think. You should take him to the ball field. Wear a ball cap and those cute little braids like you used to, but sexify it. Wear something hot, like a teeny little baseball shirt with major cleavage—well, as much as you have anyway—and some short shorts with tall socks and high heels. Get him on the hood and then, like, straddle him, tease him a little, and then—"

"Danny!" Lori interrupts. "I think we all get the idea."

"Oh, dang. Sorry."

"Danny, if I do this, will he think it's weird?"

"Dude, if he thinks it's weird, you have my permission to dump him."

AFTER WORK, I start planning. Phillip planned all that stuff for our engagement, and I think this will be my little engagement gift to him.

A series of naughty events.

A little trip down memory lane of my own.

I wish wedding planning were this fun.

We can't do it all in one night, so I think it'll be a weeklong event.

I'm going to have fun with this. Okay, let's brainstorm. We'll do the baseball field. Maybe the swings at the elementary school. Camping in a little tent. His mother's kitchen island. And maybe it would be fun to have a prom night redo. The same room, the hot tub. Hmm.

My phone chimes. There's an email offering me last-minute deals on airfare. I click through it and see Cancun is on the list.

OMG! That's it.

It's like fate!

I call Phillip and tell him he's mine every night next week and not to make any weekend plans.

He's like, "Why?"

And I'm like, "Maybe I have a few surprises of my own."

My phone vibrates with another text from Danny.

Danny: *Done with practice. Guys LOVE your idea and think a hot nurse bridesmaid is in order.*

I book flights to Cancun and make reservations at the resort where we stayed for Danny and Lori's wedding. The lowest point in my relationship with Phillip. Time to make some happy memories there. *Oh, I hope he likes this!*

Vibrate.

Danny: *And a dirty cop. They also think, if all women would plan XXX weddings, guys would be much more excited about the planning process. You might be on to something.*

I ignore Danny's text because I need to finish planning. I grab my purse and head out to my car. I'm gonna run to the sporting goods store and find a little baseball shirt, and then I'm gonna hit Victoria's Secret for one of those bombshell bras. I think that should give me the look Danny had in mind.

I'M RUNNING LATE to meet Phillip. We're going out for a nice dinner, and then we're meeting some friends at the bar.

Danny calls me. "What are you doing? Why aren't you replying to my brilliant texts?"

"Your XXX wedding ideas are brilliant, and I appreciate your help. And I didn't reply because I've been busy trying to plan Naughty Dream Week. Phillip's gonna love it. I mean, I think he will. I hope so anyway. I'm taking him to Cancun next weekend! We're gonna have a Cancun redo! And, right now, I'm rushing to meet Phillip for dinner."

"Let me guess; you're late as usual?"

"A bit. And I shouldn't be. It's our second date!"

"So, Jay baby, speaking of dates, have you set one yet?"

"Screw you, Danny."

I hang up on him, but my phone immediately vibrates. He's calling me back.

I answer with, "Eff off, baby!"

I'm totally making fun of Danny, and he knows it. Since he started playing professional ball, practically every other word out of his mouth is *baby*, which is hilarious because, even with all the girls Danny dated, he never called a girl that. He always remembered their names.

I hear a voice—a voice that is not Danny's—say, "Hello? Is this Jadyn Reynolds?"

"Uh, yes, this is she."

Oh my gosh, who in the world did I just tell to eff off?

"JJ, this is Pastor John. I was hoping to set up a time for us to get together and talk."

Oh. Shit.

I'm probably going to hell for this.

Can you get sent to hell for accidentally telling a pastor to eff off?

"Uh, I'm sorry about that. I thought you were someone else. Um, Mrs. Mac said something about couples counseling, but we aren't getting married for quite a while, so there's really no rush."

"I'd still like to talk to you. Could you come see me tomorrow morning before the game?"

I want to say no, but I feel like a little kid who's in trouble. It'd be like telling the principal, *Sorry, I'm not going to your office.*

"Uh, sure."

"Great. See you then."

Just for dramatic effect?

SATURDAY, SEPTEMBER 16TH

PASTOR JOHN IS sitting behind his desk when I walk in. He stands up to greet me.

Pastor John is about the same age as Mr. and Mrs. Mac. He's not that tall, but what he lacks for in height, he makes up for in attitude. He's really a great guy, and he makes going to church both fun and a learning experience. He baptized Phillip and me, taught our confirmation classes, took a group of us on a mission trip one summer, and was really nice when my parents died. I've known the man my whole life.

He hugs me and says, "So, you and Phillip are engaged."

"Yeah, you were at our engagement party," I say as I sit in one of the two blue-checkered chairs in front of his desk.

He slides into the chair behind his desk. "I'm curious, did you say no onstage just for dramatic effect?"

"Not really. I was thinking about saying no. I told him I was gonna say no."

"I wondered about that. His parents had told everyone he was asking you at dinner and that, when you came down, it meant you'd said yes. I noticed when he went up onstage with you that he put the ring on your finger. I thought he would've done that before."

"He did. I said yes at dinner, but I got mad at him when I figured out it was an engagement party."

"Why?"

"He had just agreed we wouldn't tell people yet."

"Why wouldn't you want to tell people such happy news?"

I roll my eyes at him. "Pastor, you know we got engaged on our first date. You've been marrying people for a long time. Ever seen that?"

"Actually, no. That's part of why I wanted to talk with you. But, first, tell me why you said yes."

"That's easy. I said yes because I love him."

Pastor John nods.

"And you don't have to worry. We're not rushing into things. We're gonna have a very long engagement."

"I see," he says.

He seems frustratingly noncommittal. I thought he'd agree that it was a good idea.

"Do you think that's bad or something?"

"I'm not here to judge you, JJ."

"Then, why am I here? Why did you wanna talk to me? I know getting engaged on your first date is a little unusual, but it'll be a great story to tell our kids someday."

"Would you want your children to do the same?"

"Well, no, but I've known Phillip my whole life. It's not like I just met him."

"Yes, but being friends with someone is different from being in a relationship with them."

I wanna say, *Damn right. Sex makes it a whole lot more fun*, but I don't. I'm in church. And hell doesn't sound like much fun. I'm just saying.

He says, "I'll be honest with you. Phillip's parents are a little concerned about this."

"Are you serious? Mrs. Mac keeps pushing me to plan the

wedding."

"It's not the planning part or the fact that you're marrying their son. They love you. They're just a little worried that you've never dealt with your parents' deaths, and they are afraid it might affect your future with Phillip."

That comment sorta gets my panties in a wad, so I have a hard time keeping the smart-ass out of my tone. "I dealt with it."

"If I recall, you refused counseling," he says with an equally snippy voice. "At least from me. Did you talk to someone that I don't know about?"

"I didn't need counseling. Obviously, I turned out fine. I graduated from college, and I have a good job."

"Yes, on the surface, it would appear you have, but I also heard, when you and Phillip tried to date before, you pushed him away."

Are you kidding me?

"I *didn't* push him away! We were having fun, drinking and dancing, and *he* ditched *me*! He's the one you should be talking to about this."

I'm mad, but I also know that he's sort of right. I kinda did push Phillip away. I was scared, but it had nothing to do with my parents.

I mean, except for the whole being-alone thing.

What's this all about?

Pastor John looks frustrated with me. He runs his hand down the sides of his small brown beard. "I will talk to Phillip. You'll have to go through couples counseling here if you want me to marry you."

"Well, like I said, there's plenty of time for that."

"JJ, what we find is that, sometimes, when a person's suffered a loss like yours, they tend to push people away without realizing it. Sometimes, they feel it's easier not to love than to love with their whole heart and risk experiencing another loss. Is that why all your past relationships have been so short? Have you pushed people away?"

What the hell?

What is he? Is he in some kind of pastoral CIA? Where does he hear this stuff?

"I don't push people away. I've had the same friends for years and made a lot more at college. And, as far as guys go, they usually stopped dating me because they couldn't handle that we were all so close. And I've dealt with my parents' deaths just fine. You were at the funeral. I stood up and spoke. I dealt with it. I'm fine."

So there.

He says quietly, "Some people feel abandoned."

Abandoned?

His quiet words knock the wind out of me.

Before I can even think, I'm standing up, leaning across his desk, and yelling, "My parents didn't abandon me! They never would've left me. They loved me!"

Then, I remember, he's a pastor, I'm in church, and I probably shouldn't be yelling. But there is no way in hell I'm gonna stay and listen to this bullshit.

Sorry, God, but I'm not.

"Look, this has been a great chat, but I'm afraid I have to go." I walk toward his door.

As I'm opening the door to get the hell out of there, he says, "Is this how you typically deal with conflict? Do you run away from it? Avoid it?"

It takes everything I have to calmly say, "We don't have a conflict, sir. If we did, I'd stay here and fight you. You've deeply offended me, and I have nothing more to say." I turn around and mutter under my breath, "And I'll be damned if you'll be counseling or marrying me."

Sorry for cussing in church, God, but I hate him. I really do.

As the door closes, I hear him mutter, "Wanna bet?"

I SIT IN my car, shaking slightly and feeling like I could throw up. *What the hell does he know anyway?* Just because he sees me occasionally at church doesn't mean he has a clue about me. I never run away from conflict. I've always stood up for myself. Even against Danny, who is the most stubborn person I know.

And what is that stuff about my parents abandoning me? I've never felt abandoned. Ever.

Alone, sure.

I mean, I am alone. Family-wise.

And, yes, I refused counseling. What good was counseling gonna do me? I wasn't going to sit around and talk about how they were gone. I was already painfully aware of that fact.

I GO MEET Phillip.

"So, how'd it go with Pastor John? What'd he want to talk about?"

"Um, nothing really," I lie. "I don't think I want him to marry us, Phillip."

Phillip is taken aback by my comment. "Why not?"

Fortunately, we have just pulled into the parking lot of the bar where we're meeting a bunch of friends to watch the college football game. I quickly hop out of the car without answering.

I don't usually say this, but I could seriously use a drink right now. I'm still feeling shaken. I'm not sure what to tell Phillip about why I don't want Pastor John to marry us. If I do agree to counseling, I'll have to tell him what he said.

And what he said is something I don't wanna talk about.

Phillip casually takes my hand as we walk across the parking lot.

I take a deep breath. I don't know what it is about Phillip, but when he holds my hand, I feel like I could take on the world.

I don't need a drink, just Phillip.

"So, why don't you want him to marry us?"

"He's just getting old. I want our wedding to be cool," I lie. Badly. We were just at a wedding he did that was very contemporary.

Phillip looks at me kinda funny, but when we walk in the bar, Joey immediately slaps Phillip on the back, hands us Fireball shots, and makes us cheer, "Go, Big Red."

While I try really hard not to cry.

You'll love me more after tonight.

MONDAY, SEPTEMBER 18TH

I'VE PUSHED MY run-in with Pastor John to the back of my mind. The man knows nothing. I'm also going to have to find a new church, which sucks because I know practically everyone there. I've also decided to push all the wedding planning nonsense to the back of my mind. Phillip and I are gonna have some fun first, and fun begins today with Naughty Dream Week.

I'm super excited about this, but I'm also feeling a little nervous. What if he thinks it's silly?

Danny told me that Phillip would love it, so I'm going to do it even if it means making a bit of a fool of myself. What do they say about fools in love?

I forget, but anyway.

I want to surprise Phillip, but I also think anticipation is half the fun. So, to clue him in a little, I snuck in the bathroom after he was asleep and wrote in lipstick on the mirror.

You + Me = Dreams

It must be bugging him because he just texted me.

Phillip: Dreams?

Me: Yeah. ;)

Phillip: Like sweet dreams???

Me: More like your dreams!!!

Phillip: I'm living my dream.

Me: Well then, maybe I shouldn't do it.

Phillip: Do what?

Me: My plan. ;)

Phillip: What plan? You're driving me nuts.

Me: That's sort of the point. It is Naughty Dream Week after all.

Phillip: Naughty Dream Week?

Me: Yep. Get ready to live your dreams. And be home by 7. We're going out for pizza and beer first.

Phillip: Yum. Where are we going?

Me: Johnny's.

Phillip: I haven't been there in forever.

Me: I know. :)

Phillip: Did I have a naughty dream about Johnny's Pizza?

Me: I don't know. Did you?

Phillip: I love you.

Me: You'll love me more after tonight.

I look a bit ridiculous at Johnny's. I'm wearing the bombshell bra under a tight little baseball shirt.

And I do magically have amazing cleavage.

Phillip knows that the extra cleavage is kinda fake, but he doesn't seem to mind.

He keeps staring at it.

Probably wishing it were real.

Anyway, I nixed Danny's idea of shorts because I thought ...

well, I thought they might prove to make things more difficult, if you catch my drift. So, instead, I'm wearing the teeniest denim miniskirt known to man.

It barely covers my ass, and we'll hope I don't have to bend over to pick anything up, or the world will see my blue-and-white-striped thong. Yes, it's even striped like a pair of baseball pants! I'm totally into this!

I completed the look with tall white athletic socks and these wedged heels that sorta look like tennis shoes. I even did the braids and the baseball hat as Danny suggested. He seemed to get into that part, so I hoped Phillip would have the same response.

I will admit, the overall look is pretty damn sexy.

Or, at least, Phillip thought so when I came out in it.

He whistled at me, and then he asked me very seriously if I was really going to Johnny's dressed that way.

He said, "You know, it is a family place."

I took that as a compliment. Figured maybe Danny does know what he's talking about occasionally. I just laughed and wouldn't tell him anything else.

Over a pitcher of beer and some yummy pizza, he says, "That outfit is smoking hot, and I'm not complaining, but I don't get how the whole dream thing fits in."

I tell him, "Oh, this is just the preparty. Dreams don't start until after dark."

He nods in understanding while his eyes happily float back down to my fake cleavage.

I MAKE HIM drive to the old ball field. We park in the back parking lot, and I spread a blanket over his hood. I pull two Gatorade bottles out of the little cooler I had stashed in the backseat and then hand him a bag of sunflower seeds.

He takes a drink and says, "I think I get this now. And I like."

We lie there for a while, holding hands, drinking Gatorade,

talking, and staring at the stars. When I figure it's time, I straddle that boy and start making out with him like crazy.

Although this whole dream thing is supposed to be for Phillip's benefit, I'm really enjoying myself. Phillip has my shirt unbuttoned and is kissing the fake cleavage while I'm trying to undo his pants.

All of a sudden, car headlights wash over us. I see a police car pulling into the lot. The cop parks and turns on his big spotlight. I quickly roll off Phillip and try to button up my shirt.

There goes my big plan.

All we really got to do was make out!

"Oh my gosh, Phillip. It's the cops!"

To myself, I say, *Nothing going on here, Officer. Nothing at all. Just innocently sitting here, looking at the stars.*

But then I whisper to Phillip, "Can we get in trouble for this?"

"I don't think so. We're not really doing anything wrong."

"There's *vodka* in the Gatorade!"

"We're legal now, Princess. Chill. I doubt he'll open the Gatorade. It's not like we're sitting here, swigging out of a vodka bottle, and most of the Westown cops are pretty cool."

An officer shines a flashlight in our eyes and says, "Well, I'll be damned. JJ Reynolds. How the hell are you?"

"Cookie!"

Cookie is obviously a nickname, but that's all I've ever known him by. He used to play Wiffle ball with my dad on Sundays, and he also helped Phillip get me to the hospital the night my parents died.

"Are we in trouble?" I ask him.

He changes his voice, deepens it, sounding like a tough cop. We can tell he is just teasing us, so we go along with it.

"You kids been drinking?"

I hold up the Gatorade bottle, shake my head, and pray I'm a good liar.

Cookie seems to accept the lie because he says, "Well, how about drugs?"

Phillip smiles and holds up the bag of sunflower seeds.

Cookie finally determines that we're not in any trouble. "Well, it doesn't look like it then." His flashlight trails down my outfit, and he says knowingly, "Some little getup you got on there. Trip down memory lane?"

I laugh nervously. "Sort of. Phillip and I used to come here and stargaze when we were in high school. When we were just friends," I make a point of saying, so he'll think that there's only been stargazing going on.

Like, in theory.

"Heard you two got engaged," he says with a grin. "Congrats, kids. Have a nice evening."

We can hear him snickering all the way back to his car.

As he pulls out of the parking lot, I say, "Phillip, I'm so sorry. That totally ruined the mood."

Phillip gives me a big grin. "Hell no, it didn't. Almost getting caught just adds to the excitement. Get back over here. I need to finish my dream."

He quickly undoes his pants and pulls me back on top of him.

Losing my virginity. Again.

WEDNESDAY, SEPTEMBER 20TH

LAST NIGHT WAS pretty amazing. I dug out the exact outfit I'd worn the night he wanted to do me on his mom's kitchen island. The little plaid Abercrombie skirt with the white blouse and navy cardigan. I added high heels and white thigh highs, and then I took him to the swings out behind our old elementary school. We talked and swung. He teased me and told me how he'd always had a thing for me and that he obviously was quite intelligent and a visionary to have known the girl he wanted to marry at the mere age of ten. I laughed and called bullshit.

I think he just got lucky.

We kissed on the swings just like we had the very first time he kissed me, when he pulled my swing over and planted a big, fat kiss on my lips. But, this time, he didn't run away. He kept kissing me. He was up for doing whatever at the playground, but, well, I just couldn't bring myself to do much more than kiss. I mean, kids play there!

So, we decided to go parking in a cornfield instead, which was way fun, too. It'd been a long time since I'd been parking.

TODAY IS THE day we're supposed to do it on his mother's kitchen island. After last night, I'm not sure if I can do that either, but I'm sure he could talk me into it. I think Phillip could sweet-talk me into just about anything.

I call Mrs. Diamond to try to enlist her help in getting the Macs out of their house, but I find out his mom is hosting Bunco tonight, which means there is no way I am gonna get them out of the house. So, I quickly have to switch things up and decide on a prom night redo.

Phillip had a date for the prom. I forget who she was, but I do remember he had big plans for her. He'd even gotten a hotel room with a hot tub. But she got drunk on champagne, threw up at the dance, and got taken home early.

I hadn't really wanted to go to prom. I was supposed to go with my boyfriend at the time, Jake, but then I found out he was cheating on me. That was the same night as my parents' accident. Prom was a week later, and it just didn't seem right for me to go. Danny offered to take me. At first, I refused, but everyone thought that my parents would've wanted me to go. Plus, at the time, I was kinda hot for Danny.

I thought that, after prom, I would be busy losing my virginity to him. I figured losing it to a friend instead of a jerk boyfriend would be a good idea. But, just as things were starting to get good, Danny passed out, and I ended up sitting in the hot tub with Phillip.

As usual, it was sweet and probably a little romantic, but also as usual, nothing happened between us.

But, tonight, things are going to happen.

I check into the hotel right after work. I take rose petals and sprinkle them all over, put some champagne on ice, and lay out a tray of chocolate-covered strawberries. Granted, we didn't have those things on prom night, but we should have. And Phillip was the guy I should've lost my virginity to.

I go home, put on a sexy dress, make Phillip wear a suit, and take him out to dinner.

As I LEAD Phillip down the hall to our hotel room, he's grinning. "So, are we reliving prom night?"

"Well, not reliving exactly. We're having a prom night redo."

"I'm not sure what that means, but I assume it means we're gonna do more in the hot tub than talk."

"Well, maybe. So, here's the storyline. We're both seniors. I've liked you, probably loved you, for a while. You finally got brave and asked me out, and you're hoping that I might be willing to part with my virginity tonight."

Phillip's eyes gleam. He's so adorable, especially when he totally gets into character. He pins me against the hotel room door. "So, you know, Billy is having that big party tonight."

I nod my head. "Uh-huh."

"I was thinking maybe we might wanna skip it."

I get into my nervous virgin role. "Oh, well, I don't know. I mean, what would we do, just sit in our room?"

He leans in and kisses me. "I was thinking of something a little more fun." He opens the door. "Look." He looks at what I've done to the room and mutters to me, "Damn, I'm good." Then, he shuts the door and has me on the bed before I have a chance to even think about what to do next.

He intensely kisses me and expertly moves his hands across my dress. I'm ready to lose my virginity right about now, but that wouldn't fit my character. I pretend to be nervous about where things might be heading. "Um, I saw champagne."

"Oh, yeah, there is champagne." He seems to have already forgotten the champagne chilling in front of us.

I made him forget the champagne! Yay for me and my sexiness!

He opens the bottle and pours champagne into real crystal flutes. No plastic cups for this prom night redo! He takes off his jacket, unbuttons his shirtsleeves, and takes off his tie. I only have on a dress, so I reciprocate by sliding off my shoes.

He saunters to the bed with both glasses crossed in one hand

and a strawberry in the other. He sits on the bed and holds the strawberry up to my mouth.

I open my mouth, thinking he's going to feed it to me. He puts just the tip of the strawberry against my lips. I try to suck a little of the chocolate off, but just as I do, he pulls the strawberry back out. He keeps sliding the strawberry across my lips and occasionally lets me suck some chocolate off. He's so teasing me with the strawberry.

I'm pretty sure no high school boy would ever think of this suggestive little game.

I leave my lips sexily parted and make a little girlie noise, and he pushes the strawberry deeper into my mouth.

I take a little bite.

He gives me a satisfied grin, hands me a flute, and pops what's left of the strawberry in his mouth.

"Here's to the perfect night," he says, clinking my glass with his.

We each take a drink. He takes the glass away from me, sets it on the nightstand, pulls me up off the bed, and unzips my dress.

I act nervous.

Really, it's not that much of an act. It's feeling kinda realistic.

He sweeps me back onto the bed and starts doing exactly what I imagined the guy I would lose my virginity to would do. I'm just saying, if you ever have the opportunity to have a lose-your-virginity redo, I'd highly suggest it because this is going to be good. Certainly much better than the drunken frat house romp that really happened.

He's going slow, kissing every inch of me, patiently, tenderly.

There's some song in the musical *Rent*. I forget how it goes, but it's something about sweet little kisses.

That's what this reminds me of.

He's covering me with thousands of sweet kisses, but when he starts to take off my bra, I realize that, if I want to play this out in character, I need to stall because I'd be nervous.

So, even though my body is majorly disagreeing with me, I say, "Do we get to use the hot tub?"

Phillip looks at me with those steamy dark eyes. It's funny how, when he looks at me and tells me he loves me, I see all the golden flecks in his brown eyes, but when he wants sex, those same eyes get all dark and fiery-looking. I know the hot tub is about the last thing he wants to get into right now, but he goes along with it.

"We shouldn't let it go to waste." He turns on a riot of bubbles, strips naked, and hops in.

Yum.

I pretend to be nervous about his nakedness. "I didn't know you were getting a room with a hot tub. I don't have a swimsuit."

"Oh, I don't think you need one of those. Just get naked and get in. Promise I won't look."

He says he won't look, but I can tell by his grin that he's totally lying. I can't help but laugh. He used to say the exact same thing to me in high school when I was changing out of my softball uniform in the backseat of his car. I always caught him looking in the rearview mirror.

I act like I'm shy, but I'm really trying to torture him with a little striptease. I slowly take my bra off. When I catch him peeking, I slowly slide my underwear off, too. I turn around, neatly lay them on the dresser, grab the champagne bottle, and slide in next to him.

He immediately pulls me on top of him and presses his lips to mine. We make out in the hot tub for a really long time. I'm actually shocked at how slow he's going. I've been ready for him to throw me on the bed and have his way with me since we walked in the door, but he continues his slow, sexy way.

When I seriously can't wait anymore, I try to spur him on by saying, "You know, I've never done this before."

Phillip runs his hand through my mostly wet hair. "I know,

Princess. That's why I'm going slow. I want you to be sure. I want it to be special."

And, yes, I melt at that because that's so what I wanted to hear.

I slam the rest of the champagne, get out of the tub, grab his hand, and make him join me.

Then, I engage in a little naughty slowness of my own.

I take a towel and dry off every single inch of Phillip's amazing body. Of course, I leave the best parts for last. When I start drying off *that*, he can't seem to wait any longer. He picks me up, lays me on the bed, and proceeds to take my virginity.

Like, again.

Slightly bigger than I expected.

THURSDAY, SEPTEMBER 21ST

I GET A text from Phillip while I'm at work.

Phillip: *Naughty Dream Week is fun.*

Me: *Glad you think so.*

Phillip: *It's also making me like one of Pavlov's dogs.*

Me: *How so?*

Phillip: *I'm horny, just thinking about what's coming up tonight.*

Me: *Coming up? LOL! Pun intended?*

Phillip: *You're bad. Yes, and no. I wanna know what we're doing tonight.*

Me: *I can't tell you!*

Phillip: *But I need a hint. :(*

Me: *Hmmm ... okay ... there will be lots of snacking involved.*

Phillip: *Snacking? Are you my snack? ;)*

Me: *Can't tell ...*

Later, he wants to know more.

Phillip: *Are we pretending it's Friday night, we just got home from a football game, and you're gonna make us nachos and popcorn?*

Me: *I don't know. Did any of your naughty dreams include Danny? 'Cause I don't think he'd be down for that.*

Phillip: *Is that a no?*

Me: *That's a no.*

Phillip: *I really need another hint.*

Me: *Fine. Think warm summer nights.*

Phillip: *Are we gonna drink from a keg in a cornfield and go parking again?*

Me: *Nope. :)*

Phillip: *One more hint, please!*

Me: *Think younger. Middle school, backyard kind of nights.*

Phillip: *Are we going CAMPING?*

Me: *Maybe ...*

Yesterday, Phillip's mother didn't cooperate with my plans. Today, the weather isn't cooperating. I was gonna set up Phillip's old tent, but it poured this morning. The ground is still a soggy, muddy mess. So, during my lunch break, I buy a shiny new tent. I take it home and set it up in my living room.

At the store, they don't actually have the tents set up. They just have these little dollhouse-sized versions. They're adorable. The tent I picked out is so cute. It's green with two rooms and a skylight—but it's maybe slightly bigger than I expected it to be.

Okay, it's *a lot* bigger than I envisioned.

Phillip used to tease me about my inability to calculate distances. About how there was no way I would ever be able to design anything.

I would always say back, "You know why women are bad at measurements, don't you?"

He'd turn red and say, "Shut up," because he knew what I was gonna say.

I'd always finish the joke anyway, holding my fingers about three inches apart and saying, "That's 'cause guys always tell us that this is six inches."

Danny was never embarrassed by that joke; in fact, he often fired back, "Only looks like about an inch to me." Of course, implying that he's huge. Let's just say, Danny has a big ego and leave it at that.

To get the tent to fit, I have to move the couch up against the kitchen table. It's also blocking the hallway, so you have to climb over the back of it to get to the bathroom, but that's a minor detail. I focus on making the tent a den of seduction. I climb over the couch, strip the comforter and blanket off my bed, and spread them across the tent floor. Then, I add every pillow and throw that I own.

AFTER WORK, I make up bowls of all Phillip's favorite middle school candy and a batch of popcorn, and I fill a small cooler with beer. I change into little pajama boxers and a tight tank top. I even go sans bra just for the heck of it, and before I know it, Phillip's home.

My plan is to pretend like we're in middle school. We'll eat popcorn, munch on candy, drink some beer, and I'll challenge him to a game of strip poker. We'll play cards and slowly get naked. Phillip will be so overwhelmed with desire for me; he won't be able to control himself. He'll attack me, and it'll be amazing.

MY PLAN GOES astray the second Phillip walks in the door and runs straight into the tent. He backs up and laughs at the huge tent in the middle of the living room. He looks so darn cute. I just can't help myself; I tell him, no clothing allowed, strip that boy naked, and lead him into the tent.

So it's my fault you're lying?

FRIDAY, SEPTEMBER 22ND

I CALLED PHILLIP'S parents and told them what I'd planned for this weekend. I even spilled my guts to Phillip's dad about what had happened at Danny and Lori's wedding. Seeing as he'd heard the rumors, I thought I'd set the record straight. He was all for me making it up to Phillip.

I'm up at five a.m., which is way earlier than even Phillip usually gets up. I hear the phone ring, and Phillip hits speaker.

His dad's voice booms into the room. "Son, I hear you're taking the day off."

Phillip says groggily, "Uh ... what? Who did you hear that from?"

"Your mom."

"Mom? Why would she ... oh no, is she making us do wedding planning? I don't think JJ is ready for that, and I'd really rather come to work."

I hear his dad say, "I think you'd better talk to your future bride about that. Have a great day."

Phillip looks confused when I come into the bedroom and say, "Hey."

"What's going on, and why the heck are you up so early?"

"Well, I have a little surprise for you, sweetie."

"You only call me sweetie when you want your way. We're doing wedding planning with my mom all day, aren't we?"

"Nope, but you'd better hurry up and get dressed. We have a flight to catch."

"A flight? Where are we going? I'm not packed."

"I packed for you, and we're going on a Naughty Dream road trip."

Phillip grins big and wipes the sleep out of his eyes. "Really? So, where are we going?"

"It's a surprise."

"Is it somewhere I dreamed about?"

"I don't know, honestly, but I think you hoped it'd go differently. And that's all I'm saying."

WE GET TO the airport, and of course, he sees where we're going.

"Cancun, huh?"

"Yeah. You good with that?"

"Oh, yeah. Are we staying somewhere we might have stayed before?"

"We definitely aren't staying at that dive we stayed at that one year for spring break, but, yeah, we might be."

"Lori and Danny's wedding?"

"Bingo. You're smart."

"And what are we gonna do there?"

"Probably the same things we did when we were there for the wedding."

"That wasn't fun."

"Well, there might be some new twists to the story this time, but I'll warn you; just like at the wedding, I got us separate rooms."

"You're such a liar."

"Stop asking me questions I don't want you to know the answers to, and I won't have to lie."

"So, it's my fault you're lying?"

"Absolutely."

He flicks the end of my nose. "Watch out. It's gonna start growing." Then, he laughs and tells me, "You know, Dillon and Neil told me yesterday, with this whole Naughty Dream Week, that I've been spending way too much time with you. That we've been *hiberdating*."

"Hiberdating? What is that supposed to mean?"

"It's like I'm hibernating. I'm not seeing my friends because I'm always with you."

"You have always, always been with me."

"Yeah, but we've been spending quite a bit of time alone."

"Are you saying, you don't like the time we spend alone?"

"No, I'm just saying, our friends miss us and are giving us crap. I'd hiberdate you forever if I could."

WE GET TO Cancun and immediately head to the beach. This time, I'm relaxed and happy. I'm not feeling the stress or pressure to be with Phillip. I'm with him because I want to be.

We drink fruity drinks, which I'm still convinced contain some kind of love potion, go jet-skiing, and lie on the beach. After that, we go back to our room to *take a nap*. We do sleep a bit. Like, after.

WHEN WE WERE here before, I had big plans. I was going to take Phillip dancing, get him a little tipsy, and then invite him back to my room. But, as we all know, last time, I drank a little too much, ended up dancing with other guys, and made Phillip really mad. He thought I wasn't trying, that I didn't want a relationship with him, and we were lucky to have stayed friends. The next day, at Danny and Lori's wedding, he pretty much ignored me.

But not this time. This time is the way it should've been. Romantic dinner, fruity drinks, and dancing only with him.

We dance together and have a blast. Last time, I danced with other boys. This time, I couldn't even tell you for sure if there were other people on the dance floor. I only have eyes for Phillip.

After dancing, we go for a walk on the beach, and I ask if he wants to come back to my room. He teases me and says that he doesn't want me to think he's that easy, but then he does, and we definitely make up for the last time we were here.

Let's sit down.

SATURDAY, SEPTEMBER 23RD

THE BEST PART of waking up this morning was having Phillip in bed with me. We lounged in bed, ordered room service, tanned on the beach, snorkeled, parasailed, and then came back to our room to get ready for dinner.

When I'm dressed and ready, Phillip takes my hand and says, "Let's sit down."

My mind immediately flashes to the hospital. I can see the waiting room. I can smell the popcorn. I can picture the doctor telling me to sit down. I can hear him say that my dad isn't going to make it.

What horrible thing is Phillip going to tell me?

I try to prepare myself. *He's breaking up with me. He has cancer. He's joining the Peace Corps. He's going to become a priest. He doesn't really want to marry me. He's in love with someone else. He's really gay. He found out he has a baby. He made a mistake.*

I suck in a deep breath and hold it in my chest. I don't say anything. I just squint my eyes at him and try to shut out whatever pain is coming.

"Breathe," he says. He tilts his head and studies my face. "It's good news."

I let out a sigh of relief. "Oh, I didn't know what you were gonna say. I just sorta flashed back to that night at the hospital when the doctor made me sit down and told me about Dad."

Pain flashes across Phillip's eyes. He reaches out and runs the back of his hand across my cheek. "I'm sorry I scared you."

I smile at him, grab his hand, and kiss it. "It's okay. So, tell me your good news."

His eyes brighten. "You know how we recently signed that big deal at work?"

"Yeah."

"Well, part of that deal is that we have to open an office in Kansas City. That means, both Dad and I are going to have to spend more time there."

"That's exciting! And cool, too, since Danny and Lori are there."

"Well, there's more." He has a huge smile plastered across his face, and I can tell he's really excited about all this. "So, because of this, I got a promotion. I'm going to run the Kansas City office."

I throw my arms around Phillip's neck. "I'm so proud of you!" I have to tease him a bit though, so I say, "Must be rough, having your dad be your boss. So, wait. Does that mean you'll be traveling a lot?"

"Um, well, no. We kinda need to move there."

"Seriously? That'd be so cool! I'd love to live close to Danny and Lori! But jobs aren't easy to find. Like, with the economy, a lot of people I graduated with still don't have jobs. I'd have to find a job first, I guess."

"You already have a job there, if you want it."

Phillip's grin has turned into a sneaky smirk.

I can't help but smile back at him. "Why don't you tell me everything?"

He's practically bouncing with energy and starts talking fast. "The first thing we have to do is find temporary offices. We've already bought some land, and we're going to build our corporate headquarters on it. You can design the whole thing from the ground floor up. Wouldn't that be awesome? We'd be working together!"

I stare at Phillip for a few beats. *Design my very own building? Is he serious? That's, like, my dream!*

"How long have you known about all this?"

"It all just fell together in the last week, Princess. How 'bout we discuss the details at dinner? We can negotiate your pay over some good wine."

WE GO TO dinner, eat some food, and drink some great wine. Phillip keeps talking excitedly about his new job, about the new building, about living close to Danny and Lori, and I can't help myself; I get really excited, too. It would be cool to design a building on my own. That's what I went to school for, but at the job I have now, it'd probably be years before I ever got something like this as my own project.

Phillip assures me that I'd have lots of freedom; that he wouldn't boss me around; and that, once the project is done, I could find a job there and start my own business or whatever I wanted to do.

Before I know it, I'm agreeing to it all.

AFTER DINNER, WE walk along the beach for a while. It's amazing how just being together, holding hands, and not saying a word can be so romantic. I feel like we're the only two people on Earth.

We find an empty hammock and lie together in the moon-light.

"Talk to me about our wedding," Phillip says. His body is always so warm, and with his arms wrapped around me, I barely feel the cool ocean breeze. "Do you want a big wedding or a small one?"

"I kinda think I'd like a big wedding. All our friends. A fun party."

"I agree. What about colors?"

"I'm not sure. Do you have any ideas?"

"Just please don't make me wear a white tuxedo. I think black looks best."

"I like black, too, but black makes it more formal."

"I think a wedding should be formal, don't you?"

"Yeah, I do." I sigh. There's something I need to tell Phillip, but it's gonna be hard to talk about. "Phillip, I have a confession. I kinda lied when I said I'd never planned my dream wedding. Well, I didn't really lie; I never planned it. It's just that there was this time when my mom and I talked about my wedding when I was little. I just always sorta assumed that's how it would be."

Phillip rolls in the hammock and faces me. "Tell me about it."

"We were at a wedding. I was young, maybe eight or nine. Mom pulled me on her lap and said, 'Someday, you're going to get married just like this.'

"And, since then, that's how I've always thought my wedding would be. The wedding and the reception were held in a big ballroom. I remember being impressed by the huge, sparkly chandeliers. I told her I wanted candles in my bedroom like the ones flickering on our table. She told me I couldn't have candles in my bedroom, but I could have them at my wedding. She told me candlelight was romantic, and my wedding would be romantic because the day would be all about love. I told her the bride looked like a princess, and she told me that, someday, when I married my prince, I would, too. I told her I wanted to marry Daddy. I remember the way she laughed. I loved her laugh. She told me I couldn't marry him because he was her prince. That I would find my own prince someday. I remember there were gorgeous flowers on the tables and a huge cake that had as many layers as my age. I think it was eight. We ate cake, and then my dad scooped me up and danced with me."

I'll never forget dancing with my dad at that wedding. The way he twirled me around, the smile on his handsome face, how he seemed so big and strong compared to me, how I always felt safe when I was with him.

"That sounds beautiful." Phillip closely studies my face and then runs his fingertip across my cheek and feels my tears. "Are you crying? You never cry. The last time I saw you cry was the night of the funeral."

I shrug my shoulders. "I try not to cry. I want my parents to be proud of me, so I have to be strong. And you've seen me cry. I cried on the beach in Cancun."

"You were drunk."

"I also cried onstage at our engagement party."

He runs his fingers through my hair. I lean closer to his neck and smell him. Phillip always smells so dreamy.

"Twice in four years." He kisses me softly and says, "You know, you don't have to be so strong. Especially with me."

He's so sweet. I feel so incredibly lucky. Really, that's what makes me feel like crying. I love him so much, and I'm still so afraid of losing him.

"You don't have to shut your emotions away. It's okay to feel sad. It doesn't make you a crybaby."

I nuzzle my face into his neck and kiss it. "I know, Phillip. I love you, and I don't care what anyone thinks about our fast engagement. I can't wait to marry you."

He leans back and smiles at me. "Do you really mean that?"

"Of course I mean it."

"Hmm, well then, maybe now would be a good time to tell you the rest of it."

"The rest of what?"

"When we move, I want us to buy a house together."

"Well, yeah, it wouldn't make much sense to get separate places."

"I also think we should be married when we buy the house."

"But that means …"

Phillip nods his head. "Yes, that means we'd need to get married soon."

"Really soon."

"Yes," he says tentatively.

I snuggle back into his shoulder and let out a content sigh. "Okay."

"Okay?" he asks with disbelief. "You're agreeing, just like that? No fight? No freak-out?"

I kiss his shoulder and then up the side of his neck. "I'm done freaking out, Phillip. Why would I freak out when I've never been happier in my life?"

BACK IN OUR room, I change into a sexy little nightie. While we're brushing our teeth, I say to him, "You know, we still haven't discussed what you're going to pay me. I'm very expensive."

He looks up and down the nightie, which is a very sheer lacy thing, as in no lady parts are being hidden, only slightly obscured. "Yeah, I figured."

"Maybe we should discuss my salary in bed?"

"Oh, no," he tells me seriously. "I never mix business with pleasure. And, if you're gonna work for me, there are gonna have to be a few rules."

"Work for you? No way. I think I need to be an independent contractor or something."

"No go. You work for me or no deal."

I put on my pouty face.

He smiles, smacks my butt, and winks at me. "Now, go get in bed, and we'll discuss your career."

I'm pretty sure I can work this to my advantage.

I expected you to throw a fit.

SUNDAY, SEPTEMBER 24TH

I WAKE UP early. Way early. My mind is reeling over all I agreed to last night. I think about how I didn't freak out. About how I know Phillip's the one. About how I'm gonna have to plan a wedding fast. About how his parents are going to be the ones to freak. How his mom is going to push me to plan the wedding the way she thinks is best. How I want to plan the most amazing, romantic wedding ever. I was serious when I said I couldn't wait to marry Phillip.

We're sitting in bed, eating breakfast, when I tell Phillip I have a few demands. "You know, I was pretty amazing about this whole change-jobs, move-to-a-new-city, quickly-plan-a-wedding thing."

"I was pretty shocked about that. I really expected you to throw a fit."

"Well, I do have a stipulation."

He rolls his eyes at me. "I should've known you'd have demands."

"Not demands. Just one demand. One I'm very serious about."

He tilts his head at me and looks concerned. "Okay, what is it?"

"We aren't telling anyone about this when we get back. I'm talking no one. Not Danny, not Lori, not your parents, *no one*. We need some time. I'm gonna go back and quit my job but not tell anyone. I think, since we just finished that design project, they won't ask me for two weeks' notice. If they don't, then I'm gonna spend the week doing some wedding planning. I need to gather ideas on my own. We need to talk about things, figure out what we want. The minute we tell your parents, they're going to ask a million questions. Your mom's gonna be the one to freak. I want to have some sort of a game plan first. I want this wedding to be about us. About our relationship. I'm not going to let your mom make me do stuff. You're gonna have to stick up for us. If this week goes well, we'll tell your parents next Sunday at dinner. Can you agree to that?"

Phillip nods his head and smiles at me. "Yeah, I'm good with that." His face gets that soft look, the look where I swear he can see straight into my soul. "You know, even though your parents are gone, they're still with you."

"Yeah, I know, and I think they're really glad I'm with you."

I BUY EVERY bridal magazine available at the airport and excitedly look through them on the flight home. I even mark a bunch of things I think are pretty. Phillip starts out strong, but pretty soon, his eyes glaze over—probably from having to endure page after page of white lace—and he goes to sleep.

I have no idea what I want for my wedding.

But I do know one thing. I know who I want to marry.

We may need cocktails for that.

MONDAY, SEPTEMBER 25TH

I CAN'T BELIEVE I did it, but this morning, I walked into my boss's office and told him about my new job offer. As expected, he didn't ask me to give two weeks' notice. He was excited for me, wished me the best, and offered the company's services for anything I needed outsourced. I cleaned out my desk, said good-bye to everyone, and was back home by noon.

I hope the rest of our plan goes this easily.

SINCE THE MAIN focus of most bridal magazines is the wedding gown, I figure that might be the best place to start. I call Katie and Lisa and ask them to join me. They've been advising me on what to wear since we were kids.

We meet at a bridal store, and Lisa immediately takes charge. She's running from dress to dress, screaming, giggling, and basically making a fool out of herself over fabric and lace.

She's oohing and aahing over dress after dress, saying, "Oh, this one. This is ah-mazing!"

Never once does she ask me what I want. Of course, she knows me. Knows I probably don't have a clue, which is probably a good thing because, after seeing all the dresses in the magazines, how does anyone ever pick one? You could try on dresses for years.

I sit down next to Katie. "How did you decide which dress to buy?"

"I think it's kind of like choosing your husband. You keep trying them on until one seems right."

"We might need cocktails for that," I joke.

Katie laughs and then whispers to me, "Lisa dreams of a huge ballgown. You know that's what she's gonna make you try on. I made the mistake of taking Eric's sister shopping with me. She was mad we were getting married before her, and I think she wanted me to look bad. My suggestion is to try on a dress of each silhouette, see what looks good on your figure, and then try on those types of dresses."

"That's a good idea. Kind of narrow it down. How did you do it? Like, plan your wedding? I'm so overwhelmed by choices. How did you know what colors to choose? Did you have a theme?"

The wedding coordinator brings us glasses of champagne and starts asking me all sorts of questions—when my wedding will be, what my colors are, what style dress I want, do I want it casual or formal. I'm pretty sure my eyes glaze over, and I know I just got that deer-in-the-headlights look.

Katie lowers her voice and says to the coordinator, "She just got engaged. It's her first time."

"Yes, it is. Please be gentle with me." I turn back to Katie. "Seriously, how did you do it?"

"Just pick some colors, find your dress, and the rest will all fall into place. I promise."

Although I secretly hated the dresses we wore for her wedding, I'm now sorta applauding the fact that she had the courage to even choose one.

She touches my hand and says quietly, "This probably isn't the best time to tell you, but I don't know if Eric and I are going to make it."

"Make it to the wedding? But I haven't even set a date yet."

"I mean, make it. Our marriage. I'm not ... we're not ... I'm not sure. We fight a lot. I just don't know if it's going to last."

"Oh, Katie!" I hug her. "I'm sorry. Are you okay?"

"Yeah, this stays between us, but Neil and I have gotten close again. He's really been helping me."

"Neil's been helping you? Katie, he's had a crush on you since the eighth grade. He's not the person you should be getting marital advice from."

"I'm not. We're just friends. I mean, there're sparks, but we just go to lunch. Talk. He listens to me."

"They always listen when they want in your pants.' And that's a direct quote from *you*! Do you remember telling me that when I was telling you that Jake wasn't really a jerk because he listened to me?"

She giggles. "I do remember that! God, he was a jerk."

Lisa skips back to where we're sitting and pulls me off the couch. She says in a perky voice, "Okay, we're ready for you to start trying on! I'm so excited you asked us to help you pick out your dress!"

Katie rolls her eyes at me from behind Lisa.

"I'm not sure I'll find a dress today, but everyone tells me I need to start planning."

"Have you set a date?" Katie asks.

"Not yet," I sorta lie. Not really though since we haven't picked an exact date.

KATIE WAS RIGHT. The first dress Lisa has me try on is a huge, poofy hoop-skirted ballgown. This dress looks like something designed by Cinderella, Barbie, and Lady Gaga while they were sitting around, getting high on mushrooms or crack or whatever drug makes you hallucinate. Not that those people would partake in those activities, but if they did, I'm thinking this is the dress that would be born from it. I have never seen so much satin, tulle, lace, glitter, sequins, and fabric roses all in one place.

I look ridiculous.

You know those bobblehead dolls with the big heads and the little bodies? I look like a bobblehead in reverse. A teeny head on top of a big, huge body. I walk out to the middle of the store to give the girls a good laugh.

Katie smiles as Lisa screeches, "OH MY GOD! That's THE most GORGEOUS dress I have EVER seen! Don't you just love it?"

Could she possibly be serious? It looks like a Bedazzler threw up on me.

"Uh, it's quite gorgeous, but I'm not sure this dress is, like, the one," I say.

She disagrees. "I know it's the first one you've tried on, but, oh, JJ, that's got to be your dress. It looks amazing on you. Turn around. I'm dying to see the back of it better."

As I'm trying to turn myself around in this dress, which I'm pretty sure is like trying to maneuver a Hummer into a Mini Cooper–sized parallel parking space, the skirt hits a decorative column with a vase sitting on top of it. The whole thing topples over. If it wasn't for Katie's quick reflexes, the vase would've hit Lisa in the head and probably killed her.

That probably would have put a damper on the occasion.

NEEDLESS TO SAY, three hours and God knows how many Cinderella gowns later, I'm a bridal dress failure.

As in I have no direction, no idea what I want, and no idea when I'm going to figure it out.

I call Phillip and tell him that it's imperative that he meet me at Hooters. I need some hot wings, beer, and *Monday Night Football* to erase the trauma of this afternoon.

Danny texts me.

Danny: Heard you went dress shopping. How'd that go?

Me: Not so well. But it was my first time. First times always suck, don't they?

Danny: Not what I heard.

Me: Yes, I lost my virginity. Again.

Danny: That's pretty funny. You need to get Lori to do a Naughty Dream Week for me.

Me: She's planning a babymoon. Close enough?

Danny: Doubtful. I do have another idea for your wedding though.

Me: Do tell.

Danny: Install multiple stripper poles at the reception to encourage (in)appropriate dancing.

Me: You do know your wife bought our sorority a stripper's aerobic workout DVD and was voted to have the best stripper moves?

Danny: I did NOT know that. WHY did I not know that?

Me: She can show us all her moves at my wedding. On the poles.

Danny: I think I'd rather see those moves in private. On my pole. Gotta go.

Wedding cake and an open bar.

TUESDAY, SEPTEMBER 26TH

I WAKE UP to Phillip kissing my shoulder. My back is spooned tightly into his chest. I'm still half-asleep, but I notice his kisses feel rough. The scruff on his face is tickling my shoulder.

"You need to shave," I whisper.

He runs his scruff up the side of my face and pulls my hips into a serious case of morning wood.

"Dang, Phillip, been having some good dreams?"

"Reliving last week, I think. We should have Naughty Dream Week every week. Starting now."

AFTER AN AMAZING wake-up, Phillip leaves for work, and I text Danny.

Me: *You awake?*

Danny: *Yeah.*

Me: *Video chat?*

Danny: *Cool.*

I open up my laptop and see just part of Danny. One broad, shirtless shoulder, half a muscular pec, an angular jaw, messy blond hair, and one blue eye. Danny sucks at video chatting.

"Danny, the computer is like your center. Line up under the ball."

He grabs the sides of the computer with both hands, and his whole face comes into view.

"You need a haircut," I tell him.

"What are you, my mother now?"

"No. How come you're up so early?"

"Lori was craving blueberry muffins."

"So, you had to go get her some?"

"No, she's baking her mom's recipe. I'm keeping her company."

Lori yells from nearby, "Jade, why aren't you at work?"

She's way too smart for her own good. Who would even think of that?

"Um, I'm going in later. Working from home this morning," I lie.

Danny can usually tell when I'm lying. He says I always look up at the sky. He grins at me. His Devil Danny grin. *Crap.* That means he knows I'm lying.

I try to play it cool by saying, "What?"

"So, I heard the big news." He keeps grinning at me.

What? Phillip promised he wouldn't tell. No. Phillip always keeps his promises. Danny must be talking about different news.

"Um, what big news is that?"

"Naughty Dream Week was a big success."

I inwardly sigh with relief. "Yeah, it was a lotta fun. Phillip seemed to like it."

"He did. I talked to him on his way to work this morning. Heard all about how naughty you were."

"Did he say what he liked best?"

Danny looks at me, confused. "Shouldn't you know that?"

"Oh, yeah, probably. I think it was the baseball. We almost got caught. Like, if Cookie had shown up a minute later, we would've been doing it."

Danny shakes his head at me. "Nope, that wasn't his favorite."

I squish up my nose. "Then, it must've been the tent."

"No. Don't you know your own fiancé? He liked Cancun."

"Really? Cancun wasn't that naughty."

"You attacked him in a beach chair in front of the restaurant where, if it wasn't for your long dress hiding things, people could've seen."

"Oh, yeah, that. That was kinda naughty. Okay, so I have a question for you. Hang on. I'm gonna get some cereal. I'm starved." I quickly pour a bowl of cereal, add some milk, grab a spoon, and then sit back in front of the computer. "Okay, so, how did you set your wedding date? Did it have any significance?"

Lori's face comes rushing into the screen. She has a little bit of flour on her cheek. Danny gently wipes it off as she says, "Jade! Are you setting a date? Did you set one?"

"Not yet, but we're talking about it."

Her face looks bright. "That's so exciting! And, no, we just had a time frame of when we wanted to get married. We picked three resorts and called to see if they were available. They all were, so we chose our favorite."

"It was a really pretty resort. We had a fun weekend. Not that your wedding wasn't great, but Phillip was pissed at me, which sort of made it seem not as pretty."

"You look tanner," Danny says.

"A little. We laid out in the sun a lot. You should see Phillip. He's way darker than I am."

"He always gets tanner than us."

"I know. It's sexy."

Lori sighs. "At least you don't burn like I do. So, what do you think you want? Maybe you should start by picking a season. Which sounds best—winter, spring, summer, or fall?"

I go out on a little limb when I say, "I was thinking a winter wedding might be pretty."

Danny and Lori's eyes both get big.

Lori says, "Like, this winter? That'd be so great! I won't be huge."

"I don't know when. I just thought winter might be cool. It might be next winter."

"Why would you wanna wait that long?" Danny asks. "I couldn't wait to marry Lori. I'm glad we had a short engagement."

"Did people give you crap about that?" I'm a bit concerned about this part.

Lori says, "My parents were sure I was pregnant. That pissed my dad off a bit. I assured them that I wasn't, and they got over it. They love Danny. I mean, who wouldn't?" She plants a sweet kiss on the side of his neck.

Danny says, "My mom thought we might be rushing things."

"She did?" I pause and let out a sigh. "I have been dragging my feet a bit on the wedding planning."

Lori says, "I've noticed that. But why? You love Phillip."

"It's just hard without my parents. Like, my mom would've helped me find the most amazing dress. I went shopping with Katie and Lisa, and I have no idea what I want. Well, I guess I know what I don't want. I don't wanna look like Cinderella."

"Jay—" Danny starts to say, but I keep going.

"And the Macs are great, but Phillip's mom is so, like ... she's ..." I struggle for the right word.

"She's a steamroller," Lori says.

I nod my head at her. "Yes. And I don't wanna get smooshed. Danny, I have a really big favor to ask."

Danny nods his head at me.

"You know your dad's been there for me through, like, everything."

"I know, Jay."

"I wanna know if it's okay with you if I borrow him."

"What do you mean?"

"I wanna ask him to walk me down the aisle."

Danny solemnly stares at me. He knows all the emotions wrapped up in what I'm asking. "Jay, you know he'll be honored."

"I feel bad though. I feel like all I ever do is go out there, eat your mom's cinnamon rolls, whine, beg for advice, or ask them to do something for me."

Danny smiles a soft smile. "My mom said you were out there the other day. She said she always prayed for a daughter, and now, with you and Lori, she has two. They adore you."

Lori's face pops back onto the screen. "Jade, I'm so sorry. I didn't know that's why you've been dragging your feet. I've been pushing you on planning and stuff, and I never even thought about how hard it must be. I'm such a bad friend."

Danny pulls her onto his lap.

"Oh … uh … hang on," she says. She quickly runs off the screen.

"Where's she going?" I ask as I take a bite of my cereal.

Danny grins at me. "To puke."

I drop the spoon back in my bowl. "Nice. I think, on that note, I'll say good-bye."

My phone buzzes with a text.

Phillip: *I love you. We're gonna have an amazing wedding. Have fun looking for ideas today.*

And that motivates me. I pull up a popular wedding planning website. I look at all the pictures of things to choose for your wedding and click on the one choice that I'm sure will be easy.

Cake.

I love cake, especially white wedding cake.

And what's the deal with brides lately? They get all creative on this part. The last two weddings I went to had all these flavors of cake, and not one of them was white! Another wedding we went to had white cake, but they ruined it by adding a gross lemon filling.

Don't brides know that white wedding cake and an open bar are the only two reasons people go to weddings?

I know that's one tradition I'm not going to mess with.

My cake will be white. Plain white cake with chocolate frosting. That's the cake my mom made me every year for my birthday.

I also want fluffy frosting, not the stuff that looks like cardboard.

I start clicking through photos of cakes. There are over two thousand cakes to choose from. They're all quite beautiful, and I save photos of my favorites. I'm not sure if I've found the dream one yet, but I know this …

I want some cake. Badly.

I run to the store, buy a cake mix, bake some cupcakes, and make my mom's chocolate buttercream frosting.

Phillip comes home for lunch while I'm frosting. As he walks in the front door, he says, "Yum. What smells so good?"

I hold up a freshly frosted cupcake. "Cupcakes."

"I thought you were supposed to be planning our wedding?"

"I was looking at cakes."

He laughs. "Let me guess … that made you crave cake?" He grabs a cupcake and puts half of it in his mouth.

"Yes, and I've decided one thing. I'd like to have white cake with chocolate frosting. Sound good?"

He shoves the last half of his cupcake into his mouth. "You can have anything you want. Especially if I can have what I want."

"What do you want?"

He sticks his finger into the bowl of frosting, smears chocolate down the side of my neck, and then licks it off.

"Phillip!" I scream playfully.

While he's licking my neck, I shove my whole hand into the frosting bowl. I attempt to smoosh it onto his face. He's too strong though. He grabs my arm, so I only manage to get a little bit on his cheek.

"Want me to lick it off?" I ask with a laugh.

He grabs more frosting and smears it down my arm.

I still have frosting all over my hand, so I try again to get his face.

He grabs me, spins me around so that my back is to him, and then grabs my hand and rubs it across my face. "Ha! You're putting it on yourself!"

Pretty soon, we're in the midst of a full-fledged frosting war.

I throw a chunk of frosting at him. It hits his shirt.

"Oh, you're in trouble now. You got it on my shirt!"

He pulls his shirt off, grins sexily, takes a step closer to me, and pulls mine off, too. He smears frosting down the front of me and then slowly licks it off. He says, "This is an awfully pretty bra. It'd be a shame to ruin it with chocolate."

"WELL, IT WASN'T your mother's kitchen island, but it wasn't too bad."

He laughs at me.

"What?"

"You should see yourself. You have chocolate, like, everywhere. You need a shower."

"Shut up. You have chocolate all over you, too. You need a shower," I say back.

"Exactly my thought. I'm also thinking I don't really need to go back to work today."

Captain's Log: Day Three of wedding planning.

WEDNESDAY, SEPTEMBER 27TH

Results are as follows:

Number of wedding dresses tried on: 11

Attempted assassinations of bridesmaid with a wedding dress and a large vase: 1

Number of cake photos looked at: 1,279

Number of cupcakes I've consumed: 5

Number of times we've had sex: 7

Number of decisions made about wedding: 0

LORI CALLS ME and asks how the wedding planning is going.

"I feel like I'm drowning in options. I don't think you understand. You just got on the phone, said I want to get married on the beach at sunset, and you did."

"I still had to make choices when we got to the resort. They showed us three cakes, and we picked one."

"I looked at thousands of cakes online. Then, I got hungry for cake, so I made white cupcakes with chocolate frosting."

"Oh, that sounds really good."

"It was good, especially when Phillip came home for lunch. We got in a frosting fight and ended up doing it on the kitchen counter."

Lori screams, "Jade! You and Phillip are naughty. Then, what happened?"

"He told me I was dirty and needed a shower. We did it again in the shower. Then, he decided he didn't really need to go back to work, so we spent the rest of the afternoon in bed. I didn't get much planning done."

"That still sounds fun. You and Phillip seem like you have a lot of fun together. I'm so happy for you. Hey, why aren't you at work?"

"I'm really happy, too. If I tell you something, will you promise me you won't tell a soul? Not even Danny. Like, we're going to tell everyone soonish but just not yet."

"Are you pregnant? Is that possible? It's only been a few weeks, but I guess it's possi—"

"Lori, I'm not pregnant."

"Oh, what is it then?"

I can't hold it in any longer. "Phillip got a promotion. He's going to be running the new Kansas City branch of their business. That means that we're going to *move* to Kansas City! We can see each other all the time!"

"OH MY GOSH! That's the best news ever! I know we talk a lot, but it's not the same. I miss you. I have no one to shop with. When are you going to move? What about your job?"

"I miss you, too. A lot. I quit my job on Monday. I'm going to work for Phillip, if you can believe that. I'm going to help him find temporary offices, design them, and then design and oversee the building of their headquarters."

"Oh, Jade! I'm so excited for you. That's what you want to do."

"I know, and there's more."

"More? Wait. I have to pee. Hang on. I'm taking you in the bathroom with me."

"I really didn't need to know that. Just mute it. I don't wanna hear you pee. So, this is the even bigger news. We're going to get married really soon. Like, sometime this winter. Hopefully December or January."

I hear peeing, and she screams, "JADE! That's the BEST news EVER! I'm so happy for you. But, oh my gosh, you must be freaking out. Trying to plan a wedding so quickly. Wait, you don't seem like you're freaking out. Why are you so calm?"

"I have no idea. Phillip said the same thing when he told me about everything. It just all feels so right, Lori. I can't wait to marry Phillip. I've never been so sure of anything in my life."

"Awww, that's so sweet. Okay, so do you need help? Maybe you should hire a wedding planner."

"Maybe. I don't know. I do feel like I'm drowning in options. So, will you help me a little?"

"I have all day. Let me get some paper." I hear flushing, then water, and then her walking across the hardwood floor in her kitchen. "Can you hear that?" she asks.

I'm pretty sure I just heard way more than I needed to, but I don't know what exactly she's referring to. "Hear what?"

"The workers. They're so noisy. They're sawing tiles outside right now. It's a mess, but the bathroom is starting to look pretty cool, don't you think?"

"It's going to be beautiful, just like you. Did I tell you how gorgeous you look while pregnant? Mrs. Diamond was going on about how you're glowing. They're pretty excited to be grandparents."

"Yeah, they are. It's cool. Okay, so what do you want for your wedding? Do you have any ideas?"

"A few. I want a white cake with chocolate frosting. I'm not sure how I want it to look, but I do want it tall with lots of layers. I found a picture of one that had fluffy chocolate frosting with little white and pink designs. So far, it's my favorite. I was thinking about doing a red velvet cake for the groom's cake since it's Phillip's favorite."

"Those both sound good. So, if the cake has pink on it, does that mean you want pink for your color?"

"I don't think so. I'm not sure on a color yet."

"Okay, what else do you know?"

"My mom and I talked about my wedding reception when I was little. I always thought it would be in a big ballroom with pretty chandeliers and lots of candlelight. I know I'm not the most romantic person, never really been into all that mushy stuff, but, with Phillip, I feel romantic. I want the wedding to feel romantic."

"I think all weddings should be romantic, and you and Phillip have so much history. There will be lots of cool things you can do. Okay, so I have all that. What else?"

"I know it's not all about the party, but we want a great reception. I know Phillip will be picky about the food. He also wants to wear a black tuxedo, and we want it to be formal."

"Jade, I'm so proud of you! You said you didn't know anything you wanted, but you really know a lot. Your theme is romance. You know what kind of cake you want. I think the next thing you need to do is find somewhere to have the reception. That will help you set your date. Then, you need to find a dress. I think you should go shopping by yourself. I wish I were there, but here's what I think you should do. Tell the consultant you want to try on a dress of each silhouette. That's what I did."

"Katie told me to do that, but Lisa made me try on a bunch of ballgowns."

"Just tell them you don't like ballgowns. I figured out pretty quickly what I liked and didn't like. After trying on four or five different styles, I knew I wanted an A-line dress. It looked the best on my figure. Then, we set out to find one that was perfect for a beach wedding."

"Your dress was gorgeous. I loved how simple it was."

"Vera Wang does simple very well. I loved my dress and felt

amazing in it. Think about that, too. You'll be in the dress for hours. Make sure it's comfortable."

"The dress seems like it sorta sets the tone for the wedding."

"Yes, and no. You already know you want a formal wedding, so you're going to want a more formal dress. Your goal for today is to figure out what style you want. That's it. So, go."

"Okay, I'll go. Call you later. And, Lori, thanks."

"You're welcome, Jade, and I promise I won't tell Danny."

I grab a cupcake and slowly lick the frosting off the top while thinking about how sexy the man I'm going to marry is. I click on the internet to pull up a raunchy gift store's website. Maybe I can find a sexy game or some cute coupons for Phillip. Something that will keep Naughty Dream Week going.

OMG!

I come across an item that I have to tell Danny about because I'm dying laughing about this. I believe it's an item that a boy would use to, um, pleasure himself.

Me: *I'm online, looking for some naughty games. Do you think we should have some for the XXX wedding?*

At the wedding store, I look at dresses. I don't know what I want. Like, I've looked at a million dress ads in magazines, but none of them screamed at me from the page, saying they were the one.

I think I want something simple. I don't want lace. I don't want anything flashy.

Something elegant, beautiful, subtle, and refined.

Just like me.

I laugh.

Ha!

Sorry. I even have to laugh at myself sometimes.

Really, I want my wedding dress to be like Danny's old girl-friends.

SSE—simple, smooth, and easy.
Vibrate.

Danny: *What naughty games?*

Me: *Can't talk now. I'm trying on wedding dresses!*

Danny: *That's okay. I'm at a photo op with a few of the guys from the team and some of the cheerleaders. Totally exhausted, but still smiling and signing autographs.*

Me: *Keep smiling and remember :) not :D*

Danny: *Will do.*

I leave the store, feeling a little depressed. I know Lori told me just to narrow in on a style, and I think I did. All the ladies at the bridal store seemed to think I looked best in a strapless mermaid-style gown. I agree on strapless, but I don't know if I picture myself at my wedding, looking like a mermaid.

Get married by a fake Elvis.

THURSDAY, SEPTEMBER 28TH

PHILLIP RUBS MY face before he leaves for work this morning. It might be my favorite thing in the whole world. I fall back asleep and dream of wedding dresses.

I'm in a bowling alley, wearing the huge, poofy, hoop-skirted wedding dress. All my friends are bowling pins with faces.

Somehow, I keep getting pushed down the lane like I'm a bowling ball. I smash into my bowling pin friends with the big skirt and knock them to the ground.

And they are not happy about it.

Pretty soon, all the bowling pins are yelling at me, telling me what a horrible dress I picked, how they hate it, and hate me.

Now, I'm standing above what I think is the pit to hell.

All my bowling pin friends are lying in the pit, all around my feet. They're moaning, writhing in pain, begging to be let out. When I can't bend over to help them because the dress is so big, they try to pull me into hell with them.

I wake up with a jerk, feeling a bit depressed, but immediately get to work.

AFTER FOUR HOURS of online searching, I've decided that planning a wedding seems to vary from being the most joyous of experiences to being the biggest suckfest of all time.

And, right now, it's sucking the life out of me.

Rule number one in all bridal magazines: give yourself a year to plan the perfect wedding.

And here's another wedding statistic for you.

Most brides are engaged for fifteen months!

Fifteen months!

And we want to do this in, like, three months.

Is that even possible?

I called a bunch of hotels this morning. Asked about a Saturday in December or January. I got a whole lot of, "We're booked."

Maybe we should just run off to Vegas and get married by a fake Elvis. I could wear a tacky cheap gown and we could go on the roller coaster later.

No, that's not what I want. I remember my mom telling me she spent way too much on her wedding dress.

"JJ, that is something you should never skimp on."

I know her rhinestones, bling, and love of leopard used to bug me, but it was so her. I feel like I shouldn't be planning my wedding without her. I also know she'd have been pissed to hear me say that. She'd have wanted me to have fun with it.

Then, I think, *My mom's dress! Maybe I could wear it!*

I crawl up to the top shelf in my closet, pull the big box down, and try it on.

And laugh.

And laugh some more.

Oh my. This dress is so eighties; it's almost comical. It has huge, puffy shoulders, full-length mutton sleeves, and is covered with lace and iridescent sequins. I look closer at the fabric and wonder if I could have the dress remade. I really don't love the lace, so probably not. I'm a little surprised at myself though. I kinda like the sparkle. The little sequins. I bet it looked beautiful when she moved. It kind of reminds me of the dress Phillip got me for our engagement party. I've been telling the ladies at the bridal shop that I hate bling, but some of the dresses I've tried on have seemed too plain. Maybe I need a little bling.

I'm pretty sure my mom would have liked that.

I CALL LORI again and ask her to video chat with me. I want her to see that I'm actually miserable and not just faking it.

"Lori, wedding planning sucks. I have no dress. All the places I thought about having the reception are booked, and I can't decide on a color scheme. I think I'm going crazy."

"You just need a different approach. Don't look at this as something you have to do, have to get done. Look at this as, um, a once-in-a-lifetime adventure. You're taking this incredible trip to Bridalville, and you get to shop—no, wait … *search* for the coolest thing from each town to bring back to show your friends. You know, the greatest cake, the most gorgeous dress, the funkiest favors, the yummiest food, the coolest cocktail. Whatever *you* want. How fun is that!"

"Well, that does sound fun," I say cautiously. "A new approach. Maybe that's what I need." I look at her with a shrewd eye. "You're using this stuff on Danny, aren't you? Is Danny going to Babyville?"

"I don't know what you're talking about." She gets a smug look on her face.

"You've gotten really good," I say, complimenting her amazing manipulative skills.

And, well, the conversation works.

I've decided to take a new approach.

Screw the theme.

Screw the colors.

I'm going on a search for what I like best, and that's what I'm going to use.

We'll throw caution to the wind, say, *What the hell*, and just let it all fall into place.

We have a new theme for the wedding, and that theme is me!

Say it with me now!

It's all about me!

Okay, so it's about Phillip, too, but you know what I mean.

THEN, I REALIZE that's what is missing! I need Phillip. I want his input on all of this. I shouldn't decide it myself. We should do it together. Although, lately, it seems like every time we talk about anything wedding-related, we end up in bed or, well, somewhere, you know, having a little fun.

Tonight, I'll take Phillip out for some pizza, and we'll look through wedding ideas.

Shoot.

That won't work. I don't want to drag my laptop and all the crap I've torn out of magazines to dinner.

We'll just order in pizza.

But, if we're at home, I know what'll happen. And what will happen will have nothing to do with the wedding. Well, I take that back. Phillip keeps telling me we're having "rehearsals" for the honeymoon. The honeymoon he is planning but won't tell me about.

So, I text that boy.

Me: *Tonight, I'm just saying no. No sex.*

Phillip: *Did I do something wrong?*

Me: *No, but we have a wedding checklist of a million and seven things to do. I'm ordering pizza. We can have a few beers, eat, and look at lots of ideas. See if we can find some we want to use. There will be no fun until we make some serious progress. Deal?*

Phillip Baby: *Deal. ;)*

I thought he was serious until I saw the little winky face.

Me: *Phiiillliiip!!! No winking either! I know what that means!*

Phillip: *Fine. :(*

Me: *No sad faces either. If you want, we don't have to do any of it. We can just skip the wedding.*

Phillip: *Can't wait!!! Looking forward to it!*

Me: *You're such a liar. I love you.*

Phillip: *Love you, too. We'll find some great ideas tonight, and then we should probably have another honeymoon rehearsal. It's important we get that right.*

When Phillip gets home, he catches me staring into my jewelry box. "What are you looking at?"

"Just my mom and dad's wedding rings. I feel bad they just sit there. It's kinda sad."

I get little tears in my eyes, but I push them back. I'm good at pushing back tears. Well, I used to be. It's gotten harder to do lately.

Phillip wraps me in his arms, and I forget about being sad, especially when he kisses me.

I drag him out to the couch where we chow on pizza and drink beer. I click through picture after picture of wedding ideas. Phillip decides that, if we see something we both like, we should save it. So, we do. We find a cool menu card we both really like. It's black-and-white damask, and it has accents of either teal or purple. Since I like both of those, either could work for a color scheme. We both love a huge white tree centerpiece that is dripping with lights, candles, crystals, and flowers. There's an all-white place setting with a silver snowflake ornament sitting on top.

Since we're getting married in the winter, we both think something like that might be cool. We also save a photo of something I get really excited about. It's the cutest cocktail table that's covered in a black-and-white-damask tablecloth and tied with black ribbon at the base. It has a small purple floral arrangement and votive candles on top of it.

"Let's click back through everything we've saved," Phillip says.

I click back through. "Well, we seem to really like black and white. Should we do that and then accent with either purple or teal?"

"That sounds like a plan," he says.

"I was thinking I'd like to have everything all in one place. I'd like to go from ceremony to cocktail hour to reception to after-party without having to drive."

"Would that mean we wouldn't get married at the church?"

"Yeah," I say sneakily.

That way, I don't have to worry about Pastor John. We'll just find someone random on the internet or something. Or invite a judge. I bet Mr. Diamond knows a judge. He's an attorney; he should.

"Especially since it'll probably be snowy and cold. If we can do it all at the hotel, I think it would be nicer. I mean, if we can find a hotel. I haven't had much luck with that yet."

Phillip closes my laptop, sets it on the coffee table, and kisses me. "You're lucky. We'll find somewhere."

"Speaking of getting lucky," I say with a smirk.

Phillip smacks my butt as he follows me into the bedroom.

It's time to drop the bomb.

SUNDAY, OCTOBER 1ST

PHILLIP AND I didn't talk about when exactly he'd make the big announcement today. It's been so hard for me to keep my mouth shut.

After my meeting with the pastor, I'd really like to give Mrs. Mac a piece of my mind and my middle finger and then say something like, *There's no way Pastor John is marrying us, so there.* I'd even stick out my tongue for good measure.

But then I remember that I'm an adult.

Darn.

Finally, during dessert, Phillip turns to his dad and says, "Dad, I have some good news."

His dad says, "Does that mean you finally asked her?"

Mrs. Mac says, "Asked her what?"

Phillip turns to his mom. "I know Dad told you all about us building in Kansas City."

She nods.

Phillip continues, "The good news is, we offered Jadyn the opportunity to design it, and she's accepted."

Mrs. Mac smiles and starts to say something, but Phillip keeps talking, "And there's more."

"More?" Mr. Mac says with a confused look.

"A lot more. We've decided to start looking for a house in Kansas City. We've also decided to get married right away."

"Why?" Mrs. Mac says. Then, she turns to me with an accusatory look. "Are you pregnant?"

This is the same woman who told me just a few weeks ago that I should get pregnant and make Phillip marry me. Now, she's pissed.

Phillip says, "She's not pregnant." He covers my hand with his. "Although that would be amazing."

I melt. Phillip just makes me melt. Always.

I went from feeling like a cat with her back all hunched up and readying her claws to a little puddle of mush.

"How soon are we talking? You know, most weddings take fifteen months to plan."

"I do know that," I say. *Ha! I've been secretly planning for a week. I know lots of stuff you don't. So there.* "We're still working it all out, but we're shooting for December or January."

"December or January! That's only a few months! I have no idea how we're going to plan a wedding that fast."

She seems really stressed by this thought, which I think is a bit odd, as she managed to help her son plan a surprise engagement party in less than a week. So, I say, "You don't have to worry about it. Phillip and I will do all the planning."

She looks at me, obviously reading my mind and knowing I don't have a clue. "So, have you set a date? That's the first thing you need to do."

"We disagree. We decided to set a time frame. A lot of the places I've called are already booked, so we're not setting a date until we find a place."

Phillip says, "That sounds reasonable, don't you think, Mom?"

His mom huffs, "Are you sure you want to rush this? You just got engaged, and you're wrong. The first place you need to reserve is the church."

I wanna tell her I'm never wrong, but this will be more satisfying.

What the heck?

Call the president. Give him the launch codes.

It's time to drop the bomb.

"We're not getting married at the church," I say.

"You're what? Why not? You *have* to get married in the church."

Here we go. Here's where I'm gonna have to spill it. I haven't told Phillip yet. I've sorta been afraid to.

Phillip comes to my rescue. "We thought that, since it will be winter and there will probably be lots of snow, we would have everything in one place. It makes sense, and it's what we want."

"Phillip, you *have* to get married in the church."

"No, we don't," he tells her. "It's our wedding. We can do whatever we want."

"Well, we still need to call Pastor John and see when he's available."

I grab Phillip's hand and hold it tightly for strength. "I met with Pastor John. I don't want him to marry us. We'll be having someone else do it."

Phillip turns to me. "You said something about that after you met with him. What's going on?"

I look at Phillip and then lower my head and look at the kitchen table. I take a deep breath and say, "Pastor John told me that your mom's concerned about you marrying me, Phillip."

Phillip's eyes get big. He angrily faces his mom. "Is that true? You were so excited about us getting engaged. You've been pushing us to plan the wedding."

She sighs. "I was, yes."

"And, now, you're not?"

"I'm just concerned, Phillip. We heard about Cancun. How

she pushed you away. How she's never had a serious relationship."

"I haven't had a serious relationship either. And you know why that is," Phillip says sternly.

Phillip is pissed. I like it.

He's standing up to his mom for me. It makes me love him more, which I didn't think was possible.

"She went through a lot with her parents' deaths. I don't think she's ever dealt with it. I love you both. I want your marriage to work. That's why I talked to him."

"She is me," I say. "Don't talk like I'm not here. I did deal with my parents' deaths, and if anyone knows that, it's Phillip. He's always been there for me. And, just for the record, I don't feel like my parents abandoned me."

Phillip quickly stands up and glares at his mom and dad. "Did you say that? That her parents abandoned her?"

Phillip's dad says, "We would never say that."

"Pastor John suggested it. Suggested that I have abandonment issues. Maybe your mom is right, Phillip. Maybe I'm screwed up, and you shouldn't marry me, which is fine. Then, I won't have to deal with all this bullshit."

I get up.

I want to run. Run away. Run home. Hide under my blanket.

Phillip pulls me into his arms and looks straight into my eyes. "We're getting married, Princess. Whenever we want, however we want. I don't care what anyone thinks. If my parents don't want to be supportive, then we'll go to Vegas or some beach and get married by ourselves." He turns to his parents. "Do you want to be part of our wedding?"

"Yes," his mom says.

"Then, remember that it's our wedding, our life. We make the decisions. I'm not putting up with this."

His dad says, "Phillip, calm down. We get it."

Phillip sits down, pulls me onto his lap, and wipes a few stray tears from my face. I tried to hold them in, but I lost the fight. A few managed to sneak out.

"You still okay with moving up the wedding?"

I kiss his cheek. "Yes."

I can't wait to be Phillip's wife.

I really can't wait.

His dad says, "So, December or January it is. Your parents got married in January, JJ. That's kinda cool, huh?"

"I kind of forgot that. You're right though. It is cool."

Mr. Mac gets down a picture of my parents' wedding day from the family room shelf and hands it to me. Mr. Mac is the best man. My dad looks so young and handsome. My mom was a beautiful, beaming bride.

WE DON'T STAY long after dinner. Phillip always tries to protect me, even from his own family. I'm sitting on the couch, leaning on his shoulder, and watching *Sunday Night Football*. My mind flits back to the picture of my parents' wedding. I quickly get up, run into the guest bedroom, flip open Mom's hope chest, and dig out their wedding album.

If I'm going to get married near their anniversary, maybe I could find something—I'm not even sure what—some little detail from their wedding that I could incorporate into mine. A way to honor them and a way to inspire me.

I take the album with me and plop down next to Phillip. We flip through the pages together.

The first time I flip through, all I really notice are their faces. How young and happy and in love they look.

Those faces that I miss so much.

I lose the fight to more tears. They trickle gently down my face. I quickly wipe them away, so Phillip doesn't notice.

When I flip through the second time, I start to see details. The way mom's dress fit her perfectly. Her pale pastel flowers.

I turn another page and see the bridesmaids all lined up. Their dresses had fitted black velvet tops with full purple taffeta skirts.

"Phillip, purple was my mom's favorite color."

"It's one of your favorite colors, too," he says.

My mind is racing. I'm picturing the menu card we saved. The black-and-white damask, the black scroll lettering, the deep purple accents.

I get up, run to the huge stack of bridal magazines stacked in the corner of the dining room, and flip through page after page of pictures until I find it.

I run the picture over to Phillip. "Look at this dress. I thought it would be such a cute bridesmaid dress." I point to an adorable strapless dress. The ruche across the bustline meets in the center to form a fabric flower, and then it falls into soft pleats from a baby-doll waistline. "It would be perfect to hide Lori's little bump, and look at the gorgeous, pale ice purple. What do you think?"

"I think the dress is cute. So, are we going with purple?"

"Yes, black, white, and purple. I think Katie was right. Pick a color, pick a few details, and everything will start falling into place."

WHEN I PUT the wedding album away, I see our holiday photo album. It's full of holiday photos from each year, starting when I was a baby.

I look through the photos, and my eyes tear up again. *What has being engaged done to me? Why can't I control my tears anymore?*

I see photos of me as a baby. Of Phillip and me visiting Santa. Me bawling. I never liked to visit Santa. He still kinda scares me.

And then I see it. A photo of Phillip and me when we were seven, in front of a fountain in Kansas City. The Country Club Plaza Lights are shining all around us.

My family, Phillip's family, and sometimes the Diamonds would kick off the holiday season with a trip to shop and see the

Plaza Lights.

Phillip and I never liked to shop much. We would spend most of our weekend running back and forth between the pool and our hotel room. We'd swim, order pizza, and watch pay-per-view movies.

I see another photo of Phillip and me in front of the same big fountain. We're older in this one, about fourteen. I know because that was the last Christmas I was taller than him. He has a big grin on his face and is making bunny ears behind my head. I look irritated. I remember threatening to knock him into the fountain if he didn't stop poking me and putting ears behind my head.

There are more pictures of all the gorgeous Christmas lights. I always loved seeing the lights. Walking from the hotel to dinner was so pretty. When I was little, I used to think the Plaza Lights were practically magical.

Heck, who am I kidding? I still do.

I run back to the couch and shove the photo album onto Phillip's lap. "Phillip, look at all of this! Remember this? All those yearly trips?"

"Yeah," he says. "We didn't go much in college. We should go this year."

A crazy idea has been forming in my head. Actually, it's not crazy; it's perfect. "Phillip, what would you think about getting married in Kansas City, maybe in early January, while the lights are still up?"

I can tell by Phillip's face that he likes the idea, but his brain is trying to work out the logistics of it all.

He finally says, "Princess, I think it would be perfect. Just like you."

I forget exactly what he did then. Ran his hand through my hair and started rubbing my back, I think. But next thing I know, I'm in bed with very little on my body and only one thing on my mind.

Wedding guests and ice sculptures.

TUESDAY, OCTOBER 3RD

WE CAME TO Kansas City yesterday to look at commercial real estate, fill Lori and Danny in on all the good news, and enlist Lori's help in finding a venue.

The first thing Lori asks me this morning is if I have a budget.

"Hmm, I haven't thought of that. I was just trying to come up with ideas."

"You need to figure that out first. I would think a big, formal wedding like what you want will be pretty pricey."

"I have money in my trust."

"I thought you wouldn't get control of your trust until you were twenty-five?"

"I won't. I got a good portion of it right away, but I put most of it back in the trust. I only kept enough to pay for college and stuff. I'll talk to Mr. D about it. We want a big wedding. My parents loved a good party. They'd want me to do it up right."

"So, money's no object?"

"Yes, it's an object, silly. I'll have a budget, but I'm sure that budget will include the ballroom wedding that I'm envisioning. I'm so excited, Lori, and I'm so glad you're helping me!"

We start by scouring the internet for possible places to hold the ceremony and reception.

BY THE TIME Danny takes Phillip to practice with him this afternoon, we have a long list of places to call and get busy on the phones.

I call the places on my list.

One by one, I cross them off the list.

Booked.

Booked.

Booked, booked, and more booked.

Lots of the places I call don't even answer, so I leave them all the same message.

Hi! This is Jadyn Reynolds. I'm calling, hoping you might have your ballroom/art museum/rooftop ballroom/loft/castle/party room/hovel/dive/shack/hole in the wall available for a weekend in January. Please call me back at blah, blah, blah, blah, blah blah, blah.

I've called twenty-seven places and either left messages, been told no, or gotten laughed at.

Seriously. A couple of places literally laughed at me.

"We've been booked up for a year," one woman said haughtily.

I think it might be hopeless.

Lori comes back in from the kitchen. I can tell by the look on her face that her calls haven't gone any better.

"Everywhere I've called has been booked. I even started tossing around the Danny Diamond name, but it hasn't done any good."

"Maybe we'll have the wedding at your house."

"In January? Uh, I don't think so."

"We might have to have it in a tent on the empty lot next to the Diamonds' house. Can you imagine that in January? Our guests would be frozen solid."

Lori giggles. "They could be both wedding guests and ice sculptures."

We laugh about it, although I kinda feel like crying. I finally felt like I had it right.

It would be perfect.

I really could picture it in my mind.

A big ballroom overlooking the Plaza Lights. The ceremony would be mostly white with touches of ice purple. The cocktail hour would have great appetizers and a cool signature drink. There would be a fancy dinner in a chandelier-lit room. The tables would have an icy feel with those white tree centerpieces we saw. There would be cool purple uplighting and lots of candlelight. After dinner, there would be dancing and a lounge area. The colors would get bolder. Black, white, and a rich, deep purple.

Even though I still don't have a dress, I sorta thought I had it all figured out.

Maybe we'll end up in Vegas. After the fake Elvis married us, we could sneak into one of the big hotel ballrooms and pretend that was where we got married. Or maybe we could forget about romance and embrace the whole XXX wedding theme. Fake Elvis could marry us in a strip club. Strippers could jump out of the wedding cake. I could wear a white thong and dance around a pole for my first dance. I could have strippers as my attendants.

Speaking of attendants, I even showed Lori the picture of the bridesmaid dress. She thought it was adorable and loved the color.

A few weeks ago, I hadn't had a clue what I wanted. Now that I have great ideas, I don't have anywhere to have it.

I'm depressed.

Phillip has a meeting first thing in the morning, so we drive back home late. We are both exhausted and fall asleep as soon as our heads hit the pillow.

It's January. Snow is whipping through the sky. The wind is howling through the trees. It's about ten degrees outside, and we're having our wedding in a tent in the empty lot next to the Diamonds' house. We have a whole bunch of heaters in the tent, as we're trying to keep people from getting frostbite.

Phillip and I are cutting the cake when one of the heaters falls over and catches the tent on fire.

Pretty soon, my wedding guests are on fire.

People's faces are burning off in front of me.

Phillip runs up to me, his face on fire.

His face melts off like wax, but underneath the wax is Phillip's perfect face.

Which is really freaky.

I scream in my dream and wake up.

I wanna wake up Phillip and talk to him, but I know how tired he was.

Instead, I decide to pray.

When I was a little girl, my mom and I always used to say my prayers together before I went to sleep.

Since my parents are now in heaven with God, I'm not really sure who exactly I'm talking to when I pray.

Yes, I pray to God, but I also pray/talk to my parents. I figure they're up there with him. I don't know; it's like I need guidance sometimes, and it helps me to just talk to them.

Or to God.

Or to anyone who would like to help me—that's who I really hope is listening.

So, I pray.

Even fold my hands like when I was little.

I ask God to help me figure out a wedding.

I ask my parents for guidance.

I ask my mom how she planned her wedding without going insane.

No one answers me though, and eventually, I fall back to sleep.

A hostage situation.

WEDNESDAY, OCTOBER 4TH

I CALLED MR. Diamond and told him about the wedding and that I needed to talk to him about how to pay for it. We agreed to meet for drinks.

Mr. D has handled my trust and helped me with all the financial decisions I've had to make since my parents died. He's also treated me like the daughter he never had, and I don't know what I'd do without him.

When I get to his favorite upscale restaurant's bar, he's already there, waiting for me.

He has a glass of scotch sitting in front of him, but, as usual, he hasn't touched it. There's a glass of deep red wine sitting across from him.

"JJ, look at you." He stands up, kisses my cheek, and gives me a fatherly hug. "I don't think I've ever seen you look so happy."

"I don't think I've ever been this happy."

"Well, it's good to see. So, I ordered you a pinot noir this time. It's red, but it's pretty smooth. I think you're ready for it."

Mr. D has been teaching me about wine. Getting me to try new things. Like wine that doesn't come out of a box. We started with whites; now, we're working on reds.

He raises his glass, the way he always does when it's just the two of us, and says, "To your parents."

I take a sip of the wine and find it is very smooth. "Wow, this is pretty good. I like this one."

He smiles at me. He looks a lot like Danny when he smiles. It's not his mouth really, more the way his eyes crinkle up. "I'm glad you like it, and I'm glad you're happy. My job though is to consider your financial future. You and Phillip might be perfect for each other now, but you can't foresee the future. We're going to have Phillip sign a prenuptial agreement."

"No, we're not. He'd be offended by that."

"I don't think he'll be offended, honey. Phillip's a strong man. He'll want to earn his own money. He'll agree to it; don't worry." He gets a big grin. "So, I have a confession. There were some extra funds that we had from a small account, and instead of adding them to the basic safe funds we put everything else in, I invested it in a riskier portfolio. You kids were buying Mac computers; Apple seemed like the wave of the future, and then with the iPhones and iPads—well, let's just say, the little fund has done extremely well. I want you to use that money for your wedding. Your parents loved a good party. They would've wanted you to do it up big, and with this amount, you should be able to do just that."

I look at the printout he set in front of me and am stunned by the amount. "Are you sure I should spend all this on a wedding?"

"I think you should. Of course, it's your money. You don't have to spend it, but I really believe it's what your parents would have wanted. Your dad used to talk about how he would surely cry when you got married. How he couldn't wait to walk you down the aisle someday. Well, providing you wanted to marry a good man. He planned on scaring off anyone he didn't think was good enough." He chuckles. "I think you know how he felt about Phillip. Your dad would have been thrilled."

I smile at him. My eyes fill up with tears. It makes me feel good to hear him say that my dad would have been happy that I'm marrying Phillip. All I've ever wanted is to make my parents proud.

"Honey, I didn't mean to make you sad. I know the Mackenzies are great, but I'm sure you're wishing your parents were here with you for this."

"I really do. Honestly, that's why I was dragging my feet about planning it at first. It just didn't feel right to plan it without them."

He covers my hand with his. "They're with you, JJ. You know they are, and so am I." He takes a big drink and then slowly puts his glass down. "However, there's something important I need to talk to you about."

I tilt my head, look at him, and try to figure out what else there is. Based on the tone of his voice, I think I heard the good news first. "Okay."

He points to the printout. "I'm holding this money hostage."

"What do you mean?"

"Your parents put me in charge of your trust for a reason. They wanted me to help you make good decisions. I take that job very seriously."

"I know you do." I wanna ask him to walk me down the aisle, but I think I need to solve this hostage situation first.

He hands me another piece of paper. "This is the money you currently have control of. It's what you have left after paying for college, buying your car, and the down payment on your condo. You recall, you had more than this but put it back in the trust. So, this is the available cash you have left until you turn twenty-five and gain full control."

"I know, but I thought you had discretion. Like, I thought you could take money out of the trust for me if you thought it was necessary. I assumed that's how we'd pay for the wedding, right?"

"That is right. I have discretion. What you have in your control is a lot of money, but I don't think it will cover your dream wedding. And, if you did use it for that, you'd probably have nothing else left."

"Right. That's why you're letting me use some of the trust money."

"Well, I might be."

"You might be?"

"Remember I said I'm holding the wedding money hostage?"

"Uh, yeah."

"I heard that you don't want Pastor John to marry you. That you've refused to go to church for couples counseling."

"Well, yeah. He wasn't very nice to me. There's no way I'm letting him marry us."

"The Mackenzies are very adamant about having him marry you. They feel your parents would've wanted it."

I tilt my head and look at him. "Can I ask you a question?"

"Sure."

"When my parents died, did you think I needed counseling, or did you think I handled it well?"

He thinks about it for a second and straightens the napkin under his drink. "Maybe both. I think we were all shocked at how well you seemed to handle it. We kept wondering when you were going to break down. We worried that you were holding it all in. Not allowing yourself to grieve."

"I didn't do that. The night of the funeral, after everyone left, I went back to my house and lost it. Cried my eyes out. Phillip was there. He knows."

"What about after that?"

"What do you mean?"

"Danny says you never let yourself cry. That's not normal, honey. You're supposed to cry."

I shake my head at him. "Not me. I just suck it up. Although I did cry onstage when we got engaged, so you can't say I never cry."

114

"Okay. Is it true that you've never visited their grave? Not once?"

His comment makes me feel really guilty, especially since he's looking at me in a way that makes me know he thinks I should have. Like I've been a bad daughter for not going.

"Yeah," I say, "but I don't go there because I don't believe they're there. I believe they're in heaven."

Plus …

I can't go back there.

Thinking of their bodies buried in the dirt.

Um, no. Not going there.

Ever.

"What about hospitals? Is it also true that you didn't visit your best friend, Lori, when she had her appendix taken out?"

I start to fidget. I'm feeling a bit uncomfortable about all this. I try to explain myself, "Um, it's true, but I had a test, and Lori was home the next day. I visited her there."

He nods his head at me. I can tell he sees right through me.

And I did kinda lie to everyone about the test.

I hate hospitals.

Nothing good happens there—at least for me—and I didn't wanna, like, jinx her.

He smiles at me. "I'll always worry about you, you know?"

"I know, and I really appreciate it. Appreciate everything you've always done for me."

His smile turns to a grimace. "You might not feel that way after I tell you this. I agree that you should choose who marries you, but I'm going to insist you go to couples counseling. All of us go through it. It's really a good thing. I know you and Phillip get along well, but being a couple is different from being friends. There are a lot of issues to deal with as a married couple. Marriage counseling helps prepare you for that. You're moving very fast, and I'm sure there are things you and Phillip have never discussed before, like money, budgets, life goals, how many kids you want, how to handle conflicts, things like that. So, if you choose to go through couples counseling with Pastor John, you can send me all the bills for the wedding. If you choose not to, then you'll have to pay for it on your own. I'm sorry if he upset you, honey, but I really believe your parents would have agreed with me on this."

"Did the Macs tell you that Pastor John said my parents abandoned me, and that's why I'm mad?"

"I heard that he asked if you ever felt abandoned. There's a big difference between the two."

I can't talk about this. I won't talk about it. There is no way that I'm ever going to talk to Pastor John again, but I adore Mr. D. I won't be disrespectful. He's done too much for me, and I know he's been brainwashed by the Macs into thinking this is in my best interests.

I give him my best puppy-dog eyes. They used to work on my dad when I was little. They probably won't work on him, but they can't hurt. "I'll talk to Phillip about it, but I'm pretty sure I'll be having a very small wedding now. Thanks for the wine."

I WAS FAIRLY calm when I left the restaurant, but by the time I get home, I'm fuming.

I'm trying to figure out if I can sue Mr. Diamond, fight him. I want the big wedding. I think he's right that my parents would have wanted it. It's not his money; it's mine. *Who does he think he is? And why was I so stupid? Why, at eighteen, did I tell him I didn't need that much money? Why did I let him put it back in the trust? What was I thinking?*

That's it. I wasn't thinking.

My parents had just died.

I was under stress.

Or duress.

Or whatever it's called when you don't make the right decisions because you're temporarily not thinking straight. *I'll hire a lawyer. I'll …*

I storm into the house and throw my purse against the wall.

Phillip's sitting on the couch. He looks at me with concern. "What's wrong?"

I plop on the couch next to him. "We're … we can't … I don't … he said …" Then, I start crying.

I tell him how we had our dream wedding planned. How I can't afford it now. How it probably doesn't matter because we have nowhere to have the dream wedding anyway. How I just wanna go to Vegas, have strippers for bridesmaids, and get married by Elvis. How it will just be Phillip and me. How we're not doing couples counseling. How everyone should just mind their own freaking business. How I'm glad we're moving, so we don't have to go to any more stupid Sunday dinners.

Phillip holds me and lightly pats my back. "We'll figure something out, Princess. Don't worry," is all he says.

But it's enough.

Phillip always knows exactly what to say.

I lay my head on his shoulder and stop worrying. Phillip has that effect on me. He calms me down. I know we'll figure out something together.

I can barely breathe.

FRIDAY, OCTOBER 6TH

PHILLIP AND I have decided to elope. We're going to skip Vegas and get married on an amazing beach. We spent all last night looking at exotic locales. We haven't figured out where, but since it's just the two of us going, we're going somewhere really posh. Somewhere decadent. We've narrowed it down to four places, and I'm going to call them this weekend and find out about their wedding packages. It's not what I dreamed of, but it's how it's gonna have to be.

Like Phillip says, "All that matters is that we get married."

And I keep telling myself that he's right.

Even though it doesn't feel that way.

I'M SITTING AT Phillip's desk at work, sketching out some very rough ideas for the front of the new building. They've been floating around in my mind for a few days, and I want to get them on paper.

My cell rings. I don't recognize the number but notice it's the KC area code. "Jadyn Reynolds," I say very professionally, assuming it's one of the realtors we've been working with.

"Miss Reynolds, this is Maggie from the International Hotel in Kansas City. I got your message the other day, and I wanted to let you know that we have had a cancellation for our rooftop ballroom and wondered if you were still interested."

Ohmygosh! Oh. My. Gosh! OMIGOSH! I can barely breathe! The International Hotel is the dream spot! Rooftop ballroom overlooking the Lights! *Can this really be happening? Am I awake?*

"Are you serious?" I ask.

But wait. What happened? Why did it come available? Did some other couple call off their wedding?

Would it be bad Karma to take their place?

Do I really care about Karma?

"May I ask why the event got canceled?"

"It was scheduled for an annual company holiday party, but you know with the way the economy is, a lot of companies are cutting back. They've decided to cut out their party this year."

"Wow, okay." *AHHH!* "What date is available?"

"Saturday, January the thirteenth."

OMG! It's like a bolt of lightning just flashed straight down from heaven into Phillip's office.

January the thirteenth! My parents' anniversary was the twelfth.

"The thirteenth would be perfect," I hear myself say. I'm beyond thinking. I'm just doing. "Wait. Are the Plaza Lights still up then?"

"Yes, it's their last weekend," she says cheerfully.

"I'll take it."

I can't believe my luck, my … blessing—I'm not sure which, but wow. I'm so excited.

It gets even better when she says, "I don't know if you're interested, but the wedding and event planner who normally does this function is free now as well. She's very talented, and she has other vendors you might be interested in hiring. Would you like her number?"

OMG! Yes! A wedding planner and the dream location! Is this really happening?

Thank you, God.

Thank you, Mom and Dad.

Thank you, whoever listened to my prayers and made this happen.

Thank you, thank you, thank you.

"I'd love that," I say.

I do want a wedding planner. I want to go over my ideas with her, my colors, the scrapbook of stuff that I've been collecting in my mind, and have her fret over the tiny details. I want us to enjoy our wedding weekend. I think a wedding planner is exactly what we need.

Then, she says, "The company also had a block of rooms held. Would you be interested in those?"

Uh, yeah!

"Yes, it will be a destination wedding, so we'll definitely need the rooms."

Before I know it, I'm giving her my credit card number to put down a deposit, and she's faxing me over a contract.

This isn't just any venue that became available. This is the dream one. This is the gorgeous hotel with the view of the Plaza Lights. It has a rooftop ballroom, great food, and sparkly chandeliers.

All of a sudden, I can see my wedding again.

I know what I want. I know what colors I want, and I can picture it.

I hang up the phone and scream with joy.

Phillip comes rushing into the doorway.

I look at him and can't help it.

Happy little tears start trickling down my face.

I look up to the sky and say, *Thank you*, again.

I'm pretty sure I just got a wedding gift from my parents.

I excitedly tell Phillip what just happened.

He tilts his head at me. "But that means we're gonna have to do couples counseling. I thought you were vehemently opposed to it?"

SCREEEEECH!

CRASH!

BOOM!

I'm pretty sure the truck carrying all my wedding dreams just crashed into a brick wall, burst into flames, and blew to pieces on impact.

My heart drops.

Oh my gosh. He's right. I can't have this wedding. I'm going to have to call her back and cancel.

I cover my face with my hand. "You're right, Phillip. I forgot. I got so excited that I forgot I couldn't afford it. I'll have to call her back and say no."

Phillip pulls me into his arms. "Princess, you want the big wedding. You never let anything stand in your way of getting what you want. Why are you gonna let a few couples counseling sessions get in our way?"

"You know why, Phillip."

"I talked to Danny about it. He said couples counseling was a breeze. They met with Lori's pastor, like, twice."

"It's who they want me to do the counseling with."

He gently pushes my chin up, so I have to look at his gorgeous brown eyes. "What do you want?"

"I want the big wedding, Phillip. I really do."

"Then, let's do it. We'll go to counseling and make everyone happy, and we'll have the wedding of our dreams."

"What if counseling breaks us up?"

He looks at me seriously. "Really? Nothing will ever break us up. And I'm calling Mr. D right now."

He grabs his cell, calls Mr. D, and says, "Hey, it's Phillip. We're considering going to marriage counseling. I agree a big wedding is what her parents would've wanted, and it's what she wants. But, before we agree to your terms, I want to make one thing clear. We'll go to couples counseling. We'll talk about our future marriage, but we will not be talking about her parents. You cool with that?" Phillip nods his head and smiles at me. "Awesome. Then, you can be the first to hear. We're getting married on January thirteenth at the International Hotel in Kansas City. Yes, sir. I'm excited, too. I'll tell her."

Phillip gets off the phone and gives me a smug grin. "Done."

I wrap my arms around his neck. "I love you, Phillip. You always know the right thing to do. How do you always know the right thing to do?"

"You used to hate that about me, remember?" he teases.

"That's true. Sometimes, it got in the way of my fun. It's more fun when we're on the same team."

"It is. I think you'd better call the wedding planner right away, and then I'm taking you out for lunch. We seriously need to celebrate."

I CALL THE wedding planner. Her name is Amy, and we connect right away. I can't wait to meet her! We talk about my budget, how I want the event to flow, and all of my ideas. I email her a file of all my wedding inspirations.

She tells me, "We have exactly ninety-nine days until your wedding. Normally, the save the dates would go out ninety days in advance, so that's the first thing we need to do. Do you have a guest list you can send me?"

"Uh, well, no," I say. Then, I give her the quick version of our first-date engagement, how we've been engaged for less than a month, why we want to get married quickly, and how adorable Phillip is.

She's like, "Wow. Well, I'm glad you're used to moving fast because we have a lot of decisions to make and a short time to make them. Your wedding will be here before you know it."

I can't even believe it.

I'm going to be Mrs. Phillip Mackenzie in ninety-nine days.

I start to sing in my mind. *Ninety-nine bottles of beer on the wall, ninety-nine bottles of beer, take one down, pass it around, your wedding will soon be here. Hey!*

I agree to get our guest list to her by next Sunday. She'll order the save-the-dates, go through all our ideas, and make a plan.

I IMMEDIATELY CALL Phillip's mom and tell her we have a date and a location.

Normally, my first call would've been to Danny and Lori, but I was afraid, since Mr. Diamond knew, she might get pissed if she heard it from them and not me. Then, I called Lori and Danny and gushed about it some more.

I'M SO EXCITED!

Like, in case no one noticed.

I KNOW I should do what it says in the wedding magazines and take each one of my bridesmaids out for a drink or a special lunch and ask her to be in my wedding in a very personal and loving way.

But they need to know *now*!

Plus, I'm so excited; I feel like I could burst.

So, I call them all. I ask Lori to be my yet-to-be-named honor attendant. For my bridesmaids, I ask my best friends from high school, Lisa and Katie; Phillip's sister, Ashley; and my sorority sisters, Chelsea and Macy. They all excitedly say yes, and since I am on a roll, I also ask a couple of other sorority sisters to help with the wedding. I'm not sure yet what exactly they'll do—probably be in charge of getting the party started, knowing them—but they might have to do the guest book or something first.

PHILLIP TAKES ME to lunch at our favorite Italian restaurant to celebrate.

I'm surprised when he tells the waiter, "We'd like a bottle of champagne, please." Phillip never drinks during lunch.

Over champagne and chicken Alfredo, we decide that Danny will be his best man. His groomsmen will be his brother-in-law, Cooper; Joey, one of our best friends from high school; Nick, the college football kicker who was always hanging out at our townhouse in Lincoln; and his fraternity brothers Blake and Logan.

"What about ushers?" I ask.

"I was thinking Neil and Brandon for sure. What about Katie's husband, Eric?"

"I love Eric, but they aren't getting along great. In fact, Katie and Neil have been having lunch together."

"Lunch? Is that code for sex?"

"No, they really are just having lunch, but I get the impression that she wishes it were more."

"That sucks. It'd suck to get divorced. We're never getting divorced."

"I don't want to go through that either, so that means you're gonna have to be really nice to me. Always."

Phillip chuckles and then runs his hand across my jawline. "I'm always really nice to you."

"I know, Phillip. You're perfect. Everything is perfect right now."

"That might be the champagne talking. And I was thinking, we might need to stop at home before we go back to work. Do a little more celebrating."

His eyes sparkle at me, and I have to agree with him. "That sounds perfect, too."

I'M SITTING IN Phillip's office, waiting for him to finish up a meeting, so we can go out and do some more celebrating. It's a really good thing he works for his dad because, between the restaurant and our little stop at home, we took a three-hour lunch.

I think about what I have to do to get the dream wedding and decide Phillip's right. I'm just gonna do it.

I call Pastor John's office.

A woman answers, "Pastor John's office. Margie speaking."

"Margie, this is Jadyn Reynolds. I'm getting married, and I need to set up couples counseling with Pastor John."

"He's been expecting your call, and you're in luck. I've got his calendar right here in front of me."

Wow! This really is my lucky day. I don't have to talk to him!

Is it un-Christian of me to pray he'll get the stomach flu on the nights of our meetings?

She continues, "How does this Tuesday sound? You'll meet him every two weeks until your wedding."

"We'll be there," I tell her and then hang up as fast as I can.

You do not play fair.

MONDAY, OCTOBER 9TH

OKAY, SO I'VE been a frugal girl. I inherited quite a bit of money when my parents died. My dad sold insurance for a living, so they were extremely well insured. I had access to a lot of money at eighteen.

Did I go crazy?

Did I buy an expensive car?

Did I whisk all my friends away to the Caribbean for a party?

No, I put most all of it back into my trust. Safely invested in things I didn't really understand, but Mr. D said they were safe and are performing well.

And, because of this frugality, I like to buy things like shoes when they go on sale. Because shoes are to me what toilet paper and beer are to Phillip. It's important to him to always have a backup twelve-pack in the fridge, and we can never be without six backup rolls of toilet paper, or we're on—flash the lights—*emergency reserve status.* I feel that way about shoes. A woman needs backups in her closet. I mean, you never know when you might need a pair of leopard-print stilettos with red suede trim.

TODAY AFTER WORK, I ran to a shoe sale at my favorite department store. And did I score! I got three pairs of adorable shoes for what one would've cost at full price.

So, you can imagine my surprise when I walk into my condo, excitedly carrying my sale treasures, and Phillip starts giving me crap about shopping, spending money, and buying another pair of shoes he thinks I'll never wear.

"Phillip, these shoes were a very good deal. I got three pairs for the price of one!"

He's all snotty when he says, "Well, buying no shoes is cheaper than that. You have shoes in your closet that I've never seen you wear. You could shoe a small country. You can't possibly need another pair of shoes."

Who peed in his Cheerios?

"Well, Phillip, since I'm paying for the condo that you're living in and since you aren't contributing to the mortgage payment or the utilities or the satellite dish, you probably shouldn't have any say in what I spend. But, since we're on that subject, let's see what you've spent lately."

I grab his wallet, which I know is full of perfectly folded receipts.

He gets an irritated look on his face, but I go on, "Let's see ... what do we have here?" I shuffle through receipts. "Beer, lunch, Taco Bell, beer, gas. Oh! What's this big one?"

"Nothing," Phillip sasses back.

He tries to grab the receipt from me, but I avoid him and read it. "Wheels for your car? But, Phillip, your car already has wheels. Does she really need another pair?"

He shrugs.

"And wow. Her shoes—I mean, wheels cost fifteen hundred dollars. Fifteen hundred dollars! That's a lot of money. Oh, wait, what's this little note here at the bottom?" I read off the receipt. "*Call when chip comes in.* Who's Chip, Phillip?"

"It's not a who ..."

"I know it's not a who. I know *exactly* what you ordered. You bought the horsepower chip you and Danny had talked about when you thought I wasn't listening." I raise my eyebrows at him. "How much was the chip, Phillip?"

"Four grand."

"Four THOUSAND dollars? You know, I'm having a hard time understanding how you can give me crap for spending one hundred sixty-five dollars on things I don't need when you've just spent over FIVE THOUSAND DOLLARS on things your car doesn't need. Tell me it was at least on sale."

"They don't go on sale."

"Maybe you should've waited until they did."

Phillip's fuming. It's kinda funny.

He says, "This is a worthless conversation. I'm not having it."

"You started it."

He squints his eyes at me. "Yeah, well then, I guess I'll end it, too." He walks out the door to the garage and slams it shut.

I'm still holding his wallet and see his car keys sitting on the counter.

I smile, grab them, walk to the garage door, stick my hand out the door to jingle them at him, and then quickly shut the door.

I know he can't leave without them. I also know his spare set is at his parents' house. I run into the bedroom and strip down to my lacy bra and panties.

Yes, I finally got over hating lingerie. Me and Victoria have made up in a big way, and she and her secret are my new best friends. I've been spending a lot of time at her house. Shoes aren't the only things I've been spending my hard-earned money on, but Phillip never has a bad word to say when I walk in the house with that hot-pink bag.

In fact, he gets pretty excited about it.

He's always like, "Oooh, what's in the bag?"

Not once has he asked me how much I spent.

I wrap his keychain around the side of my skimpy underwear.

I hear him march into the house.

He yells out, "Give me my keys!"

I yell back, "You'll have to come and get them!"

He storms through the bedroom doorway in an angry haze, sees me lying on the bed, and freezes. Well, his body freezes, but his eyes are running down my lace.

"Damn," he states with a shake of his head. "You do not play fair."

"Have I ever?" I ask coyly.

"No," he says madly. He takes two quick strides to the bed, roughly pulls me off it, and takes his keys back.

I thought he was going to take the keys and leave, but he throws them on the dresser, takes off his shirt, and throws me back on the bed.

And there's something really kinda exciting about the way he's sorta manhandling me.

Actually, it's not kinda exciting. What it is, is freaking hot.

Sex is what keeps a marriage good.

TUESDAY, OCTOBER 10TH

I DON'T WANNA be at couples counseling. I think it's stupid. Phillip and I are perfect for each other. We get along amazingly.

Like, last night was amazing.

The way he sorta threw me on the bed.

How he was kissing me hard. The way he madly stripped off my lace.

It makes me hot, just sitting here, thinking about it.

And it's a good distraction because I hate the man sitting at the desk in front of me. If it wasn't for Mr. Diamond holding my wedding money hostage, I'd never be here.

Put me down as a hostile witness.

Phillip held my hand as we walked in the room, and it calmed me down a bit. He told me in the car that, worst-case scenario, we'll learn how to deal with each other even better.

PASTOR JOHN SAYS, "Phillip, JJ, I'm glad you're both here. I understand you weren't very excited about couples counseling."

I don't say anything. I just fold my arms across my chest.

Phillip says, "I think JJ is still upset about you suggesting that her parents abandoned her."

"I didn't say they did. I said some people feel abandoned. JJ

130

might not realize it, but their deaths have affected her. They had to have affected her. I want to make sure that your marriage lasts. I assume that's what you both want as well?"

Phillip says, "Yes, we do."

I don't reply. I just sit there. No one said I had to do anything other than show up. I probably look like a spoiled little brat, but I don't care.

Pastor John nods his head toward me. "Jadyn, is that what you want?"

I roll my eyes. "No, I want an unhappy and miserable marriage, just like every other starry-eyed bride."

Phillip glares at me and says to the pastor, "She's being sarcastic. Of course we want a happy marriage."

"We're all on the same page then. Here's what I'd like you to do first." He hands us each a paper and pen. "I want you to write down three things that you love about each other."

I put the paper on my knee.

Would it be bad if I wrote down three very specific parts of Phillip's body? And, like, how amazing those parts were last night?

Uh, probably.

What do I love about Phillip?

Hmm, I love the way he talks to me. Well, the way he used to talk to me, like every night before I went to sleep. Now, we usually just fall asleep after being exhausted from our pre-sleep activities.

I also secretly love the way Phillip has always rescued me. How he always chooses me over, well, everyone. When I need him, he is there.

I also love the way he makes me feel safe. Like I'm where I belong.

Hmm, those are all really good things. I'm really good at couples counseling. I can't wait to share my answers with Pastor John. I'll show him. They're, like, the perfect answers. Phillip and I will get an A-plus. We'll be done with counseling, and then we can get on with the happily ever after.

I try to hand him my paper.

He says, "Oh, no. They're for you to keep. I wanted you to think about it. Get you in the mood, so to speak. I understand you've set a date."

"Yes, everything has fallen into place. We're very lucky," Phillip says.

Pastor John replies, "Okay, so tell me about your relationship. How long have you been dating?"

"A little over a month," Phillip says proudly.

I roll my eyes. Pastor John has known us our whole lives. He baptized us both, and he was at our engagement party. He totally knows this already, but whatever. If Phillip wants to play along, I'll let him.

"Wow," the pastor says. "That's not a very long time."

"No, it's not," Phillip replies. "But we've known each other our whole lives, so it's not like we don't already know everything about each other."

"Okay, so how are you handling conflicts?"

Uh, what conflicts?

As usual, Phillip reads my mind and answers, "We don't have any conflicts."

I'm quite proud of this.

Phillip and I are the perfect couple.

Pastor John should consider using us as a model for perfect coupledom. Phillip and I never fight. And, on the rare occasion that we do, I pout, and Phillip gives in. It works really well.

"Hmm, that's interesting," Pastor John says. "So, you're telling me, you don't fight? You've never had a fight?"

Phillip admits, "We sorta had a little fight yesterday about her buying shoes, but we, um, resolved that conflict pretty easily."

"Great. How did you resolve it?" Pastor John asks.

Uh, I tricked Phillip into forgetting he was mad at me with a sexy lace bra and a barely there thong.

I give Phillip a worried glance.

Phillip says, "Well, she defused the situation by making me laugh."

Phillip is good. I defused the situation. I sure did.

The pastor drones on, "Laughter is a key ingredient in a good marriage. So, what will you do if you disagree, but you can't laugh about it?"

"Sex probably," I accidentally burst out. I didn't really mean to say that, but Phillip has been totally hogging this conversation. Not that I really wanted to be a part of it, but it's hard for me to keep my mouth shut for extended periods of time.

The pastor raises his eyebrows and gives me a pointed glare. I've seen that glare before.

A few times.

Katie and I used to be candlelighters. We'd go in before the service, light the candles, and have to sit behind a column during the service. We were off to the side, hidden from the congregation but in plain view of Pastor John. One time, Katie had me practically rolling down the pew, laughing. She and Neil dated most of their sophomore and junior years. She was telling me about the first time she touched his boy part. How it felt and how she'd screamed when he made it grow in her hand. She'd thought something was wrong with it! We were clutching our sides, laughing silently, until I accidentally let a laugh escape. It was maybe kinda loud, almost a scream. The pastor stopped in the middle of his sermon, turned, and glared at me. That totally got me in trouble with my parents afterward. I should've hated him then. I mean, he's a professional! He should have better sermon-giving concentration skills.

He says, "I see." Then, he does that thing he always does when he's pissed, but he doesn't want to say it. He runs his hand down the sides of his little beard, stroking it.

At which point—I can't help it!—I glance toward Phillip and start thinking about a part of him I'd like to stroke.

"Well, I guess we can skip the part about saving it for the wedding night," Pastor John says haughtily.

What an ass.

Seriously.

I wanna rip that little beard right off his face. We're all adults here. Surely, we can discuss sex.

Sex is what keeps a marriage good.

I would assume.

"Sex is a good conflict-solver though, right?" I ask because I'm trying to be a good student. Plus, I love asking questions when I know the right answer.

"Actually, no," Pastor John says, "I don't think it is. Why don't you tell me about the fight."

I start because I'm going to prove him wrong, "I went shopping right after work because there was a great shoe sale. The saleslady who always helps me called me and told me that they'd just marked down a bunch of shoes but that the sale didn't officially start until the next day, so I should come in and get, like, first pick. And I did. It was awesome. I found three great pairs of shoes for what I would normally spend on only one. I wear an eight or an eight and a half. Although, sometimes, for a really good shoe, I can squeeze into a seven and a half. I don't think either one of you appreciates what a triumph that is. Like, if I were a size five or a ten, it'd be easy to find shoes on sale, but I'm the most common size, so that makes finding great shoes on sale really hard. And one of the pairs I got was a designer pair, and, oh my gosh, they're these adorable orange suede platform wedges. I mean, I don't actually have anything to wear with them yet, but they're, like, a statement shoe. They'll make a basic outfit look amazing."

Phillip rolls his eyes.

"Phillip, I see you rolling your eyes," Pastor John says to him.

"Why did you get upset about her shoe purchase?"

"I wasn't upset at that point. I just thought it was really stupid to buy more shoes when her closet is already jammed with them."

"Phillip, orange suede platforms are something you don't find that often. You have to buy that kind of shoe when you see it. When you really need a pair of orange platforms, they're impossible to find. Plus, you have no room to talk. Do you know how many pairs of tennis shoes you have? A pair for running, a pair for softball, a special pair for lifting weights, a pair for mowing, a pair of red Adidas just for football games. You also have about five pairs of Sperrys, vintage Air Jordans ..."

"See?" Phillip says to the pastor. "This is why you can't fight with her. You can't get a word in edgewise."

Pastor John says slowly, clearly taking Phillip's side, "Why don't you tell us what did make you mad, Phillip?"

Phillip's pissing me off.

"This is why you can't fight with her."

He should know better than to fight with me.

I always win!

He shouldn't even try.

He should just let me have my way. Our life would go very smoothly, and there'd be no fights.

There. Problem solved. Counseling session over.

I should counsel people.

I laugh to myself. *Ha!*

I'd be a horrible counselor. I'd tell them to suck it up, quit whining like a baby, and shut up about it. Deal with it. Move on. Stop talking about it. All this is doing is pissing people off.

Namely, me.

Plus, Neil and Joey just texted me and said they're at Taco Tuesday at the bar and asked if I would please let Phillip come out and play.

I stealthily hide my phone under my purse and reply.

Me: *Screw you both. I'm coming to play, too.*

Phillip goes on, "Well, then she started going through my wallet and looking at my receipts."

"And that made you mad?" Pastor John asks him.

I butt in and tell the pastor, "I think you need to tell Phillip that what comes around goes around. I'm pretty sure that's in the Bible somewhere. Or maybe it's, like, the Golden Rule. Treat others like you want to be treated yourself. Because, clearly, Phillip did not follow this simple rule. He wanted to talk about my purchases, so he should be prepared to discuss his, too. Don't you think?"

Pastor John squints his eyes at me. "I suppose that would be considered fair, yes."

"Right, and he got mad because—what did I find in your wallet, Phillip? What did you buy?"

Phillip stiffens up his back and sits up straighter in his chair. "I bought wheels for my car."

"Which I thought was *hilarious*! I asked him why he bought new wheels for his car when she already had a perfectly good pair. Get it? Like the shoes. It was awesome."

Pastor John shakes his head at me. "Phillip, how did that make you feel?"

Oh. My. Gosh.

Who cares how it made him feel?

It wasn't like I was being mean. I was just proving my point. And, clearly, I made my point, which was what pissed him off. He wasn't mad about the shoes. He was mad he'd gotten caught being like a double agent.

Or what's that word when you say one thing, but you do something else? Like, when you're in high school and your parents tell you not to smoke pot, but then, one night, you find them getting high in the hot tub? I know; it's hypocritical. Basically, bullshit.

Phillip tells the pastor, "It made me feel mad. I didn't think it was any of her business what I'd spent. Plus, she was mocking me."

"I was mocking him because not only did he buy the wheels, but he also ordered the horsepower chip. The four-thousand-dollar horsepower chip. He's complaining I spent like two hundred dollars on shoes he thought I didn't need when he'd just spent six thousand dollars on things his car didn't need!"

Pastor John folds his hands on the desk. I see him glance at the sky. Probably saying a prayer for Phillip. "So, why did that make you mad, Phillip?"

"I got mad when she started going on and on about how I don't pay rent, but I live with her. How we don't share our money yet. It was all bullshit."

"Phillip! It wasn't bullshit, and you know it. It was true."

"Whatever," Phillip says.

"Okay," Pastor John interrupts, "so you were both mad. You're both mad now, just talking about it. How did you solve the conflict? What happened next?"

"I wasn't mad, Pastor. I thought it was freaking funny. He got all pissed off, stormed out of the house, said he was leaving. I was standing there, holding his wallet, and his keys were sitting on the counter. I knew he couldn't go anywhere, which I thought was even funnier."

Phillip gives me an evil glare. I can tell he's sticking his tongue out at me in his mind.

"So, what did you do?" Pastor John asks again.

"I waved the keys out the door at him, and then I ran in the bedroom."

I glance at Phillip. He's trying hard not to smile, but the corners of his mouth are betraying him.

"That's it? You hid the keys in the bedroom?"

Phillip now has a full-on grin. "No, she stripped down to some sexy lingerie, lay on the bed, and held my keys hostage."

I raise my eyebrows at Phillip. He's not telling the exact truth. "I did not hold the keys hostage. You told me I don't play fair, and then you took them from me."

I sorta forget where we are. I stare at Phillip's adorable face and look deep into his eyes.

He grins at me, grabs my hand, and says, "You don't play fair. You never have."

I wrap a strand of hair around my finger, lick my lips, and think about how he threw me on the bed, how hot it was. "You didn't seem to mind, Phillip."

He slowly runs a finger up the side of my thigh. "Yeah, you're right."

God, he's sexy.

Oh, wait. Speaking of God, we're in church with a pastor staring at us.

Um, awkward much?

Pastor John coughs. "So, you solved the conflict with sex. Here's the problem: you didn't solve the conflict. You just temporarily forgot about it. You solved nothing. Sex solves nothing. Phillip, you got mad again, just discussing it. That's what happens when you don't deal with problems. They sit in your mind and fester. When you do that enough, they eventually grow into an infection. They infect your marriage with doubt, and you stop respecting each other. You have to take each other's concerns seriously, or that infection will ruin your marriage."

I really wanna know where this man did his training. *Is he even qualified to do couples counseling? He's comparing marriage to a disease!*

Who does that?

He really doesn't make marriage sound all that fun. I'm just saying.

Pastor John continues, "It's really not about the shoes, in this instance, or about the money. It's about control. Who wears the proverbial pants in the family. Think about that, and we'll discuss it more next time. Our time is up. See you in a few weeks."

WE GET IN the car, and I say, "Marriage counseling is bullshit. He hasn't taught us anything. Sure, he told us we did it wrong, but he didn't say how to fix it. Talking about it didn't fix it."

"Well, it's something to think about, and there's some validity to what he's saying. There's a gal at work who's going through a divorce, and I heard her talking in the lunchroom about her husband. She was bringing up stuff from the past eight years. I'm thinking she didn't talk to him about their problems, or he didn't listen. Whichever it was, they didn't fix it at the time, and she's held it against him for a long time."

"Phillip, eight years from now, we're going to laugh about the shoe fight. I laugh about the shoe fight now. It was funny."

"Yeah, it was. Plus, you're sexy."

"Really? Like, do you really think I'm sexy, Phillip?"

"Yeah, wanna go home now, and I'll shoe you?"

"Shoe me?"

"I mean, show you. I just said shoe because shoe, the shoes, you know."

"It wasn't that funny," I say, but then I start laughing again. "Okay, it was really funny. I'd like to take you home, but Neil and Joey just texted me. They're at the bar, and they want you to come out and play. They said they'd counsel you."

"That'd be a joke. Do you wanna go?"

"Yeah, for a bit. I'm pretty sure I'm gonna need to go to the bar after every couples counseling session. Plus, it's Taco Tuesday. Margaritas are half-price, and tequila shots are only a buck."

WE WENT TO the bar, had some tacos, and a couple of tequila

shots. For obvious reasons, Phillip is usually the designated driver, so I maybe had one more shot than he did, and when we get home, I am ready for some fun.

I'm stripping my clothes off in the bedroom when Phillip walks in.

He grins at my nakedness and says, "Just so we're clear, I'm the man. I wear the pants in the family." He points down to his pants. "See?"

I tilt my head, grin, and slowly walk my naked ass over toward him. I grab the front of his jeans and unbutton them. "Not if I can take them off you."

The Cheerleader Incident.

THURSDAY, OCTOBER 12TH

APPARENTLY, LORI AND Danny got in a fight about a picture of Danny that's in the newspaper today. In the photo, he has two cheerleaders kissing the sides of his face.

And I guess Danny was like, "It's in my contract that I have to do some publicity things."

And Lori was like, "Danny, I read your contract, and I can say with one hundred percent complete positiveness ..."

At which Danny chuckled and was like, "You've been hanging around Jay too much; that sounds like one of her words."

And Lori continued, "It is not in your contract that you have to pose with cheerleaders kissing you."

Danny got pissed and was like, "I'm not going to sit here and have you attack my moral character. I'm a good and faithful husband. I'll be a great father. What the hell's happened to you? What happened to my confident, never-the-jealous-type wife?"

He stormed out of their house.

Lori sat there, watched the door close, and whispered to herself, "She got pregnant."

SO, WHILE THAT was going on, Phillip and I were watching a movie. Meaning, he was lying on top of me, he had my arms

141

pinned above my head, and he was peppering my neck with ticklish kisses and unbuttoning my shirt.

My phone rings, *Dum, dum, da-dum, dum, dum, da-dum.* Yes, the wedding march is my ringtone. Phillip keeps changing it just to irritate me.

Then, *Dun, dun, dun, duh.* The *Jaws* theme song. Okay, so I might be messing with his ringtones a little myself.

He grabs both of our phones off the coffee table. "Danny," he says, looking at my caller ID and handing me my phone. Then, he looks at his and says, "Lori."

DANNY TELLS ME about the cheerleader incident.

"Danny, she's pregnant. She's got crazy hormones. I mean, what did you have to do besides have a night of fun?"

"Well, actually, it was a day of fun."

"Okay, too much information. Now, she has to deal with all of it. She feels like she's getting fat. Her emotions are everywhere. She's sick half the time. She's cut out caffeine, which would be enough to send me over the edge, and I just think you need to be a little more sensitive. I think your job as the soon-to-be father is to pamper her. To be there for her emotionally."

I hear him groan, so I say, "Danny, do you love her?"

"Yeah."

"You want her to keep loving you?"

"Yeah."

"Then, play nice! She's like your baby's offensive line. She's keeping it safe! Protecting it. Make her feel like you think she's doing something amazing for you because she is! That's your baby in there, Danny. Taking care of her equals taking care of *your* baby."

"Yeah, I know you're right."

"As usual," I tease.

"Shut up."

"So, no simple, smooth, and easy?" I ask.

"Uh, no."

"Do something romantic, Danny. Remind her that she's still your girl. Not just your fat, pregnant, and stuck-with-you wife."

"You can't even tell she's pregnant. How could she be fat? Besides, she looks so hot. I know she's complaining that she feels fat, but I *love* her body right now. It's a little fuller, and her boobs keep getting bigger. It's awesome. She looks sexy, if you ask me."

"Well, you should definitely tell her that because she's gained four whole pounds, and that's devastating to her. She says it'll be fine to gain weight, and she wants a healthy baby, but right now, she thinks she looks fat, not pregnant."

"My offensive line says I should buy her jewelry."

"Jewelry is always nice, but I don't think that's what she needs. She needs a small, sweet gesture. Something to remind her that she's still your girl. You can get her something spectacular when she has the baby."

"Yeah, you're right. We haven't gone out on a date in a while. But it's mostly because she's been either sick or really tired."

"Danny, how do you and Lori solve conflict?"

He laughs like a little boy who just got caught saying a dirty word and then says, "Sex. Always."

"Pastor John says, if you do that, your marriage will fail. That, if you don't deal with the conflict, your marriage will fester and get infected."

"Whatever," Danny says. "I'll let you go. I'm gonna make some dinner reservations, tell her I'm sorry, and make it up to her."

"With sex?"

"Absolutely."

Ha! What does Pastor John know anyway?

I text Lori since she's still on the phone with Phillip.

Me: *Haven't seen the pic yet. Gonna find it on the internet.*

Lori: *What pisses me off the most is he was clearly enjoying himself. He has the biggest freaking smile I have ever seen.*

Me: *Wait … he has a big smile?*

Lori: *Yeah, why?*

Me: *As in this kind of smile :D and not this :)*

Lori: *Uh, yes.*

Me: *I don't even need to look at the picture. If Danny does this :D, it means he's uncomfortable. It's his fake smile. You have nothing to worry about.*

Lori: *You're sure about this?*

Me: *Positive.*

Lori: *Why do I not know this?*

Me: *You do now. Have a good dinner.*

I love checklists.

FRIDAY, OCTOBER 20TH

I'M SITTING IN Phillip's office, waiting for him to finish up a conference call, so we can go to dinner and work on our guest list.

I get on a wedding website where I started a wedding checklist a while ago. So far, all I have crossed off is, *Get Engaged.*

I love checklists. Sometimes, when I make a checklist, I put stuff on it that I've already done, just so I can feel productive and cross it off.

So, here we go!

Wedding Checklist:
Get engaged.
Pick a date.
Book ceremony.
Hire a wedding planner.
Choose wedding party.
Love your groom.

The way things have fallen into place has left me feeling slightly high.

I know there are a lot of details, but now that I have a direction and someone to organize and help plan my wedding, I'm excited about this next phase of planning.

I look through some photos of real couples' weddings. This is so fun! I'm in the best mood!

My life is perfect!

I get a text from Phillip's mom, and I'm actually excited to hear from her! I can handle anything right now!

> **Mrs. Mac:** You REALLY need to do something about your STDs and fast!

I read her message twice and ponder this.

Um …

What is she talking about?

I don't have an STD.

No, wait. She must have mistyped a word, and her phone autocorrected it to STD. I wonder what she meant.

I wait for a minute.

For her to notice the misspell and send me a little * and the word *stand* or *stained* or whatever else has an S, T, and a D in it.

I wait calmly, but nothing comes. I read it again, noticing it says your STDs, like plural. *Is she insinuating that both Phillip and I have STDs?*

My phone vibrates again, and I'm relieved. She must've noticed the typo.

> **Mrs. Mac:** ??? This is important!

Wait. What?

Excuse me?

Does Phillip have an STD?

That he did not tell me about?

Do I have an STD?

Could Phillip have given me an STD?

WTF?

And, if he did, why is his mother telling me about it?
I'm freaking out here! So, I text Lori.

Me: *OMG! I think Phillip might have an STD!*

Lori: *OMG! Really? How?*

Me: *I DON'T KNOW!!! I'm freaking out @!!!!!!!@#^$*&!*

Lori: *Danny says Phillip has always been meticulous in his condom usage. You shouldn't have anything to worry about.*

Me: *True. Okay, that makes me feel better.*

I relax for a second. She's right. I'm being ridiculous.
My phone vibrates again with another message from Lori.

Lori: *Do YOU have an STD?*

Me: *NO! I mean, I don't think so, but Phillip and I haven't been using anything, so if he does, then I probably do, too!*

Lori: *Didn't you go to the GYN this summer for a checkup?*

Me: *Yeah, so?*

Lori: *They usually run tests for that, don't they?*

Me: *I don't know. Do they? I would think they'd only do that if you asked them to. Plus, when he asks if I always use a condom, I always say yes.*

Lori: *Jade! You shouldn't lie to your doctor!*

Me: *I don't want to get yelled at! I KNOW you're supposed to.*

Lori: *Well, I think they check for that sort of thing. So, you're probably clean ... or were then anyway.*

Me: *Yeah ...*

Which means she's implying that I was then, but I might not be now.

And I can't help it.

I'm not a hypochondriac or anything, but all of a sudden, I'm feeling slightly itchy down there.

Like, maybe I have one and didn't know it, but now, the symptoms are manifesting. I'm also feeling a little feverish. I put my hand across the back of my neck. It feels warm.

Maybe I should get online to see what symptoms come from STDs.

> **Lori:** *So, who all have you been with in the last few months?*
>
> **Me:** *Uh, Phillip.*
>
> **Lori:** *and …*
>
> **Me:** *Um, the guitar player.*
>
> **Lori:** *AND …*
>
> **Me:** *I don't know what you're talking about!*

I tell her this even though, well, I'm not very proud of this, but there was this sorta drunkish night before Phillip and I got together. I saw this really cute guy, Jason—who I'd dated junior year in college—at the bar. We started talking and dancing, and, well, drinking, and one thing led to another. And we had done it before when we were dating, so it's not like he was just some random stranger. I mean, we already had. So, when we did it again, it didn't really count. Like, he didn't add to my total or anything. It was kinda like a free throw. It counts for points, but if you miss, it doesn't count against you. When you do it with a guy you've already done it with in the past, it doesn't count against you. It's a freebie.

> **Lori:** *Look, I'm not trying to throw you under the STD bus or anything, but I know that there was a night you maybe got drunkish and probably weren't as safe as you*

should've been.

Me: *Uh ...*

Lori: *As in the night I KNOW you did it with Richie Rich even though you lied and said you didn't!*

Richie Rich's real name is Jason O'Connor. That was the nickname Phillip gave him because his family was wealthy, and he was one of those guys who wanted everyone to know it. He was also quite handsome and adorable most of the time. He was a guy I actually really liked. We'd been dating casually for about three months when I took him to my winter formal. He got drunk and started a big fight. I made Phillip ditch his date to come rescue me. The next day, Jason sent me two-dozen roses as an apology, and Phillip told me I shouldn't take him back. One of the only times I've ever followed his advice on boys.

Me: *Shit, maybe I do have one.*

Lori: *Do you have symptoms? Have you noticed anything rashy on Phillip?*

Me: *Not on Phillip, no. And I would've definitely noticed.*

Lori: *What about you? Do you have symptoms?*

Me: *I didn't, but I'm starting to feel feverish and kinda itchy everywhere.*

Lori: *So, you think you might've gotten one from Phillip? Or someone else?*

Me: *Well, if I got one, common sense tells me it would be from someone besides Phillip. Because, if it was from Jason, I probably wouldn't have noticed it at, like, the time.*

Lori: *I really worry about you sometimes, but I'd have to agree.*

Me: *But what if Phillip has some secret life that I don't* *know about? What if he's addicted to hookers? What if he has another girlfriend somewhere that I don't know about? You see that on TV all the time! And their families never have a clue. Am I clueless?*

Lori: *OMG, Jade. Chill.*

Me: *I'm trying to! So, I could have one, but it has to be Phillip who has one because there's no way Phillip's mom could possibly know I have an STD when I DIDN'T EVEN KNOW MYSELF!*

Lori: *Phillip's mom? Wait. What? WTF are you talking about?*

Me: *She just texted me and told me I needed to do something about our STDs. That's why I'm FREAKING OUT HERE!!!*

Lori: *OMG!!! That seems like an awfully sensitive issue to text someone about! OMG! Maybe Phillip does have something, and he confided in his mom. Maybe she knows it was from you. Maybe it's, like, been dormant. They can do that, can't they?*

Me: *I don't know!*

Lori: *I think you'd better talk to Phillip and quick!*

Me: *I'm scared.*

I was gonna call Phillip, but I'm still a chickenshit sometimes, so I figure, if his mother can be a chicken and text me about it, then it's perfectly reasonable for me to text Phillip about it as well.

Just as I'm about to send Phillip a scathing message, I get another text from his mom. She's very impatient.

Mrs. Mac: *Hello???*

I don't know what to say.
So, I do what anyone would do.

I stall.

Okay, I lie.

Me: *In a meeting. Will get back to you ASAP.*

Now, I'm pissed! I mean, my gosh, she just sprang this on me, and in five minutes, I'm supposed to know what to do? I haven't even talked to Phillip yet. But I'm gonna now!

Me: *It would've been nice to hear about your STD from YOU instead of YOUR MOTHER!!!*

Phillip: *WTF are you talking about?*

Me: *She just texted me and told me we need to do something about them.*

Phillip: *You're joking, right?*

Me: *I wish I were. :(*

Phillip: *I'm in the middle of a conference call. I'm sorry, but I have to say it again. WTF?*

Me: *So, does that mean you're mad at her for telling me because you wanted to tell me yourself? I think you owe me that because, now, I probably have one, too.*

Phillip: *I DO NOT have an STD!*

Me: *I mean, I'm a little freaked out by how you got one and who you got it from, but we can just take medicine or something, right?*

Phillip: *JADYN! Listen to what I'm saying! I DO NOT HAVE AN STD!!!*

Me: *Well, your mother thinks you do.*

Phillip: *I have to go. I'm on a conference call. I'll talk to you about this in a few.*

I don't respond because I can tell he's irritated by all this. It's not my fault his mom told me. *Why is he getting all bent out of shape?* Maybe it's because he wanted to tell me in person, but wait. No. He said he doesn't have one. I mean, if his mom let the proverbial cat out of the bag, wouldn't he fess up if he did?

I'm starting to feel a little less itchy already. So, even though it's still in the back of my mind, I try to get back to work.

I just got an email from the realtor in Kansas City, so I'm scrolling through photos of buildings that are possibilities for temporary offices. I see a few that look promising and am composing a nice email to her to let her know which ones I want to see.

Vibrate.

Phillip: *To my textually challenged and wedding-on-the-brain mom, STD = SAVE THE DATE!*

Me: *OMG!!! Thank you, GOD!!!*

I call Lori. She puts Danny on speaker, so I can break the bad news about our unfortunate STDs to them together.

"So," I say, "STD does not mean sexually transmitted disease."

"It doesn't?" they both say.

"Nope. Not to Phillip's mom. It's wedding speak for *save the date*."

"OMG! That's hilarious!" Lori says with a giggle.

"I know, right? I accused Phillip of having an STD while he was in the middle of a conference call. I was freaking out and feeling itchy and feverish and everything!"

"You're such a freak," Danny says.

Lori says, "A lucky freak, is more like it. Hey, I have to run. Love you!"

Danny stays on. "So ... how come you never told me you slept with Richie Rich this summer?"

"Maybe I didn't think it was any of your business."

"Or you didn't want Phillip to find out?"

"Both. Duh! So, shut up!"

"Bye. Love you," he says.

Don't go telling people about it.

SATURDAY, OCTOBER 21ST

WE'RE DRIVING TO the Macs' house, and Phillip is giving me a hard time about our STD meeting with his parents.

"We're trespassing in dangerous territory," he tells me.

I'm not finding the whole thing all that funny, personally, so I tell him very politely, "Shut up."

He grabs my hand and kisses it. Like that will help.

"Phillip, if I'd texted you and told you I was worried about an STD, you totally would've thought the same thing."

"Well, from you, sure, but my MOTHER?" He starts laughing hysterically.

He's been doing that a lot lately. He calms down a little when I flip him off.

"I'm sorry. I know it caused you some stress, but it's really quite funny."

"Maybe, but I was freaking out. You just don't need to go telling people about it, okay?"

All of a sudden, Phillip looks very interested in the road.

My phone buzzes. I have a text from Logan, one of our groomsmen.

Loggie: *What's the difference between love and herpes? Herpes lasts forever.*

"Phillip, here's a happy sentiment from Logan about our upcoming nuptials."

"That's cool. What'd he say?"

I read Phillip the text. "Did you tell everyone?"

"Uh, hey, we're here," he says as he pulls in the driveway.

NEEDLESS TO SAY, I get all sorts of subtle—and not-so-subtle—shit about the STD because, by now, Phillip has told the whole freaking world about it.

At least with the XXX wedding, I only get funny texts from Danny.

I walk in the door, and Mr. Mac greets me with a slap on the back. "Hey, JJ, do you know how Burger King gave Dairy Queen an STD?" He laughs and then says the punch line, "He forgot to wrap his Whopper. Ha-ha-ha, get it?"

Laugh, laugh, laugh.

Everybody laugh.

Phillip, who I think is going to stick up for me, says seriously, "Dad, you really shouldn't joke about STDs."

See, isn't he sweet?

But then he adds naughtily, "You can't dick around with stuff like that."

And, now, they're both practically rolling on the floor, laughing. Holding-their-sides, trying-to-breathe laughing.

I'm going to kill myself now.

WE ALL SIT down at the kitchen table. Wedding guest lists in hand.

My phone buzzes.

And buzzes.

Our friends are all so witty and clever.

And, right now, I'm flipping them all off in my mind. Mrs. Mac, the very person who started this whole debacle and the very person who should be most embarrassed by this, keeps grabbing my phone and reading the texts out loud. Then, they all hoot with laughter.

> **Katie Bear:** *How does herpes leave the hospital? On crotches! Bahahaha!*
>
> **Joey Loves You:** *I wanted to get on your wedding website, but I heard it was INFECTED!!! Ha-haha-ha!*
>
> **Nickaloser:** *What's the most fatal sexually transmitted disease for a bird? Cherpes because there is no TWEET-MENT!!! Jay, I just have to say that your blondeness is adorable.*
>
> **Blakeness:** *Hey, congrats. We heard they're naming an STD in your honor.*

I say boldly, "If you're through with all your fun, maybe we can actually work on the guest list."

So, Phillip, Mr. Organized, somehow merges all of our lists into one spreadsheet. We have four hundred fifty people on our merged list.

Phillip says, "Obviously, we need to make some cuts."

I say seriously, "We really need to think carefully about this list. I mean, we don't wanna give STDs to just anyone, do we?"

And then I smile.

Mr. Mac says, "Awww, JJ, you made a little STD joke." And then he says, "Let me see this list." He scans through it. "Julie, if we haven't gotten a Christmas card from them in the last five years, you need to take them off the list." He rambles off about twenty-five names of people I've never heard of.

Mrs. Mac is starting to pout.

Phillip says, "Think of it this way, Mom. Don't invite anyone you wouldn't want to spend the weekend with. You'll be shopping on the Plaza, eating dinner with them, looking at lights with them, dancing and drinking with them. Go through your list and mark who you really want there with you."

I look at Phillip's list. A long-ass list of frat and football boys whose idea of a perfect night includes beer pong, beer bongs, keg stands, weed, and probably a few strippers. On a mellow night. Let's just say, these boys like to party.

"You might wanna do the same thing."

"Hmm, you might be right about that," he says.

After we go through that, BOOM, the list is done. I guess we can say, the STD crisis is over.

You are so easily distracted.

MONDAY, OCTOBER 23RD

PHILLIP MUST HAVE told everyone to stop with the STD jokes because I have yet to get one today. But Danny, bless his heart, is still providing comic relief with his XXX wedding ideas.

> ***Danny:*** *Wearing a ball cap low, hoping not to be recognized while doing recon for you at the XXX store. But it's hard to be inconspicuous when you stupidly brought a 6'5", 345 lb. lineman with you.*
>
> ***Me:*** *LOL! I can so picture you two.*
>
> ***Danny:*** *Marcus says he applauds your efforts and hopes he's invited to the wedding.*
>
> ***Me:*** *Tell him the STD is in the mail!*
>
> ***Danny:*** *He says he wants to go to your wedding but not if he's gonna get an STD.*
>
> ***Me:*** *I told you the STD story, Danny. Don't give me any shit.*
>
> ***Danny:*** *I think I'm the ONLY one who hasn't been giving you shit. I totally would've thought the same thing.*
>
> ***Me:*** *That's why I love you.*
>
> ***Danny:*** *Yes, I know.*

Me: *Tell Marcus I wanna come shopping with you guys next time.*

Danny: *Oh my. Will get back to you with some gooood ideas!*

Phillip walks into our office and says, "Hey, I have some free time. Let's talk about the wedding. I just finished my interview with Amy. She asked so many great questions!"

But the texts keep coming.

Marcus: *Why did the blonde wear condoms on her ears? So, she wouldn't get hearing aids.*

I can't help it. I send one back. I know so many blonde jokes.

Me: *What's a blonde's idea of safe sex? Locking the car door.*

Marcus: *What's the mating call of a blonde? I'm so drunk …*

Me: *What do you say to a blonde who won't give in? Have another beer.*

Marcus: *Does that work?*

Me: *It works on Danny.*

Phillip grabs my phone from me and puts it in his desk drawer. "You are so easily distracted."

"Oh, yeah, the wedding. Well, what do you want? What's important to you?"

He pulls me onto his lap. "Obviously, the most important part is that, when it's over, you'll be my wife."

He kisses me for a bit.

Who's distracted now?

I go, "Um …"

He stops kissing me and says, "Wedding, right. I told her I

want good food. Good music. Good cake. A fun after-party. A hot bride."

He starts kissing me again.

Seriously, this is why we never get anything accomplished.

His secretary buzzes him over the intercom at some point and says, "Your appointment is here."

He stops kissing me. "Dang, I have to go."

I get my phone out of his drawer and see another text.

Danny: *I have two words for you: edible underwear.*

Are you listening to this?

TUESDAY, OCTOBER 24TH

As we're walking through the church doors, Phillip grabs my hand and says, "Be nice."

I roll my eyes at him. "If he can't tell us anything that will make us be a better couple, why should I take it seriously?"

He stops and pulls me toward him. "Because it's our marriage, our life. I would hope you'd wanna take that seriously."

"Fine, I'll try to be good."

We sit in the stupid blue-checkered chairs and watch Pastor John rub on his beard for a while.

I'm thinking ahead to another fun Taco Tuesday when he says, "Another big issue in marriage is how much time you spend together."

Well, heck. I've got this one. We don't even need to discuss this.

We've got this aced.

"Phillip and I spend tons of time together. We're together all the time, so we're good."

Phillip gives me a little glare.

The pastor sighs. "It's great you spend time together, but are you spending enough time apart? Everyone needs a little space."

I swear to God—yes, God, you up there? Are you listening to

this?

I can't say *anything* right!

I say we spend lots of time together, and he says it's wrong. If I had said we hated each other and never wanted to be together, he would've been proud.

This is so stupid.

Plus, I can hear the margaritas calling my name.

Well, not really, but I just got a text from Neil that said, *The margaritas are calling your name.* So, like, I know they are.

Phillip says, "We do spend time apart. And I can see how that will become even more important since we've started working together."

I turn and look at him. *Is that really my Phillip? Did he just say he needs time away from me?*

"You want time away from me?" I ask, trying not to sound as crushed as I feel.

"No, I just … like, how you take baths or go shopping. Like, we don't do everything together, even now."

Pastor John says, "Exactly. For a marriage to be strong, you have to maintain your own self-worth and confidence. You should feel comfortable with letting Phillip have hobbies of his own. Occasionally, he should be able to see his friends without you. Just like it's important for you to do the same."

Speaking of friends, ours are at the bar, waiting for us. We should probably get going.

Pastor John continues. "If you're together all the time, it can become suffocating."

I say with just a tad of sarcasm in my voice, "So, first, our marriage is going to fester and get infected, and then we're going to suffocate each other. Gee, marriage sounds like great fun."

He ignores me. He has us do some lame flash-card game where we're given examples of conflicts, and we have to work it out with our words. Phillip and I do awesome on this exercise.

Probably because the things we were supposed to be fighting about were unrealistic. Like, I can't imagine us ever fighting over things like rules for our kids or sex or friendships, but I talk them out with Phillip, like the perfect little bride.

AS WE'RE WALKING to the car, Phillip smiles sweetly at me. "You did a good job at role-playing. It's good to know we can work out conflict. You definitely deserve margaritas tonight."

I don't have the heart to tell him that I was totally faking everything.

One continuous buck-ass-wild party.

THURSDAY, OCTOBER 26TH

LORI'S ON THE phone, whining to me, "Jade, we need to plan your bachelorette party, and I'm thinking maybe you should ask Lisa or Chelsea to do it because I'm pregnant. It kinda sucks that I can't drink, and I'm afraid it won't be fun."

I've been prepared for this conversation because Danny called me the other night while she was taking a bath and gave me a heads-up.

"You know, Lori, I'm kind of over the whole *let's get drunk, eat penis cake, dance, and party* thing. I mean, I'm getting married. I'm supposed to be a grown-up. What I really want my bachelorette party to be about is spending time with my girlfriends. Like, would you be upset if we didn't have a *bar crawl* kind of party?"

"Uh, um …" she mumbles.

She's shocked at me, I think.

"Well, what would you wanna do?"

"I don't know. What about a girls' day? Like maybe we go to the spa, come back to my place, order up food, and have, I don't know, a pajama party sort of. Drink some martinis, talk, and enjoy being with the girls."

"Really? Danny suggested a spa thing, but I know how you

like to party and dance, and I figured that's for sure what you'd wanna do."

"Yeah, I know. I hope it doesn't mean I'm getting old and boring already, but if I'm gonna dance and party, I'd like to do it with Phillip, not some random bar guys."

"I don't think it means you're old and boring, Jade. I think it means you're in love."

"That's probably true."

"This will be so much fun. We'll do it the same weekend the boys go to Vegas."

"The boys are going to Vegas?"

"Oh, I guess I'd better have Danny call you about that."

PRETTY SOON, DANNY calls me. I swear, it's a good thing I have a boss who won't get mad at me for planning my wedding and talking to my friends when I'm at work. One of the benefits of working for Phillip.

"So, I'm planning the bachelor party. Got any suggestions or things I can or can't do?"

"What did my dad say before I went to visit you in Lincoln?"

He laughs and uses a deeper voice. "'She'd better not get drunk, stoned, pregnant, or die.' I will never forget that phone call."

"I'd say something along those lines. I'd like him not to get so drunk that he does something he'll regret. I'd like him to be alive when it's over and preferably nothing involving jail time."

"Cool. I can handle that."

"So, what are you going to do? What's the plan?"

"Well, my plan is to get a few of the bros together for a weekend in Vegas. My bye week is the first week in December, so it should work out great. We could have one continuous buck-ass-wild party."

"Sounds awesome," I say, but truthfully, I don't want Phillip anywhere near a buck-ass-wild party. I want him home with me.

Is that bad?

Am I clingy?

Am I going to smother our marriage before it even starts?

"I thought it'd be awesome, but then I was talking to one of the guys on the team. He said the bachelor party shouldn't be about what I would like but what the groom would like. So, I have an idea. It's maybe a little unconventional, but I know he'd love it. And, based on what Lori wants to do for your bachelorette, it might be perfect."

"Now, you have me interested."

"Phillip, in case you don't already know it, is freaking nuts about you."

"You think?" I giggle.

"Uh, yeah, and when I mentioned taking him away for the weekend, I could tell he wasn't crazy about the idea. So, what if we sorta combine the bachelor and bachelorette parties?"

"I'm not dancing for you, Danny."

"I think we'd all get in trouble for that. So, I haven't worked out all the details yet, but I thought we'd fly in separately on Friday. The girls can go do the spa or whatever. The guys will go golfing, followed by the traditional bachelor party night. The next day, we'll figure out a fun way to surprise Phillip. Then, we'll all go out together Saturday night. Do drinks, have a nice dinner, go dancing. What do you think?"

"Danny, that sounds like so much fun; it really does!" But then I think about everyone having to fly to Vegas, pay for rooms, drinks, and the spa. "I'm just worried about asking my friends to spend their money on a trip to Vegas when they've already bought dresses for the wedding and all that. It feels like too much."

"Jay," Danny says softly.

"What?"

"I've got it covered."

"What do you mean? You've already talked to everyone, and they're okay with it?"

"Not exactly. I mean, I have it covered. I'm gonna pay for it. The flights, hotel rooms, the spa—all of it."

"Danny, you can't do that. It's way too much."

"Jay, listen to me. You guys are my best friends. I'm so excited you're marrying each other, and I wanna do this for you, for both of you. Please just be gracious and say, *Thank you, Danny*, and don't fight me on it."

I want to put up a fight because Danny's going way overboard on this. But it's not very often that Danny asks me not to fight with him. It might be the first time. Um, no, it is the first time. For sure.

Danny likes to fight with me, I think.

"Fine, I won't fight you on it. It sounds amazing and is incredibly sweet and generous of you. But I have one request. Will you dance at my party?"

"Uh, no."

"Ah, come on, Danny. You'd put those Thunder from Down Unders to shame."

"I'm gonna say, no, sorry. So, what do you think about surprising Phillip? Like, not telling him that you're there? Don't you think he'll love that? I was thinking we'd dress you up and have you come to our suite, like you're a dancer or something."

"He will be all hungover and probably won't even notice it's me."

Danny chuckles. "Jay, you know how it'll be. Phillip will be fine, and the rest of us will be hanging."

"True, Phillip never gets all messed up, does he?"

"Nope."

"I kinda like that about him."

"Well, from what I hear, you kinda like *everything* about him. And a few things specifically. Who knew you were so naughty?

And don't you two ever get tired?"

"It's all so amazing with Phillip. And, no, we don't. I really don't know why I didn't take your advice and sleep with him sooner. I could've been having so much fun."

"'Cause you're stupid and stubborn, just like me, and you won't do what anyone tells you is good for you."

I think of something that's been bugging me, so I ask him, "Danny, do you ever think about cheating? I mean, you're like this big, sexy quarterback making the big bucks, and girls are always throwing themselves at you. Do you ever want to? Are you glad you got married?"

"Did Lori ask you to ask me this?"

"Uh, no. Why?"

"Then, why are you asking?"

"Well, couples counseling is sort of freaking me out. The pastor is supposed to be pro-marriage, but it feels like he's trying to talk us out of it. He keeps referring to our marriage as a dead body. It's going to fester. It's gonna get infected. Then, we're gonna smother it to death! I'm just wondering if marriage is a smart idea."

"Do you want someone besides Phillip?"

"No, but what if I change my mind? What if he does?"

"Jay, you can't do this to yourself. He's either the one or he's not. Do you think he's the one?"

"It feels like he's the one."

"So, why are you worrying about it?"

"Danny, did you pay attention to your wedding vows? Till death do you part. Forever and ever and ever. I mean, are there out clauses somewhere? Like, what if Phillip gets a big beer gut or a hairy back? What if we get married and I find out something about him that I don't like?"

"For God's sake, Jay, you've known him your whole life. I don't think you're in for any surprises."

"Maybe."

"And, just for the record, I love Lori. I'm smart enough to know that a roll in the hay with some hot chick isn't worth losing her. Are you smart enough to know that?"

"I don't wanna roll in the hay with anyone but Phillip, but I'm afraid he might want to."

Danny's voice sounds concerned. "What's going on? Why would you think that?"

"I don't know. Well, there's this girl he works with who has a big crush on him. Like, it's so obvious. Phillip takes his team out for drinks sometimes, and when I get there, she's always sitting next to him and flirting with him."

"How does she flirt with him?"

"She's always touching him, and I'm afraid he likes it because he doesn't stop her. If a girl were doing that to you and you wanted to be polite because you had to work with her, would you let her touch you? Is Phillip oblivious to it? Does he like it, or does he want her back? Or worse, could he already be with her?"

"Have you talked to Phillip about this?"

"No, I can't talk to him about it! He'll think I'm being jealous, or if he's doing something, he'll just deny it. I have to find out on my own."

"I see now why they wanted you to go to couples counseling."

"What's that supposed to mean?"

"Jay, talk to him. You have to talk stuff out in your relationship."

"Never mind, Danny. I'll figure it out."

"You looking hot today?"

"Actually, yes. I have on a really cute new dress and adorable high heels. Phillip likes when I wear heels."

"Your legs are, like, a mile long. Every man alive likes you in heels. Veeerry seeexy."

"Thanks, Danny. Your pity flirting is helpful."

"You're hot, Jay. Phillip loves you, and from what I've heard, it's not like he's been ignoring you sexually."

"Oh." I giggle. "Well, uh, no. Definitely not. I know what I'm gonna do. He's taking his team out for drinks tonight, so I'll just go and check it out. I mean, I work here now, so I'm officially part of the team, right?"

"Right," Danny says.

I TOUCH UP my makeup, add a little smoky eye shadow, three more coats of mascara, and some perfume Phillip loves.

When I get there, as expected, the girl is sitting next to Phillip, acting like he's the most amazing and interesting man on Earth. Phillip's even drinking a bottle of Dos Equis.

Ha! That kinda makes me laugh.

I'm pretty good at entertaining myself.

I take out my phone and pretend to do something important. The girl laughs and touches Phillip's arm, but he doesn't seem to be interested. He's kind of leaning away from her.

I bravely glide into the bar with my head held high. And not to sound conceited or anything, but I'm over six foot tall in heels, I'm skinnyish, and I have what Danny terms as *decent boobs* and long blonde hair.

My point being, in a bar, I can usually turn a few heads, and I'm hoping to turn Phillip's.

He notices me as soon as I step into the room. His eyes roll down my legs, and then he gives me an adorable grin. It makes me feel confident, so I walk up behind him and wrap my arms around his neck. I also position my body so that it's slightly between him and the girl.

"How's my sexy fiancé?" I coo.

"Mmm, good now." He swivels in his barstool and plants a big kiss on me.

Ha! Score one for my team! I thought I was gonna have to kiss him. It's way better that he kissed me.

One of the sweet girls from work, who must hide out in her office because I never see her during the day, says, "I need to see this ring everyone has been talking about."

Phillip keeps his arms wrapped around me, and I'm still strategically between him and the girl. I hold my left hand out across the table and show off my gorgeous ring.

"Wow, that's beautiful. Phillip, your dad said you had it designed for her?"

"I had it made," he replies, "but she actually drew the design."

"But you weren't dating at the time, right?"

"No, we were engagement ring shopping with our friend this past spring. We asked her what her dream ring was, and this is what she sketched."

I gush, "And he kept the sketch. That's the amazing part."

"I'm confused," she says. "If you got engaged on your first date after being together for only a week, how did you get a ring custom-designed that fast?"

"Oh," Phillip says with a blush.

Is he embarrassed about this? Is it because of the girl? Is he embarrassed to be engaged to me?

He says, "You know, you're the first person who's asked me about the timeline. But you're right. You can't get a ring custom-designed in a week."

"You can't?" I say. "Wait, then how did you?"

Phillip blinks slowly and looks at me with sparkling eyes. "I've had it since May."

"Like, Cancun May?"

"It was for when we got back," he says, but what he's saying with his eyes is way more powerful than what he's saying with his words.

Oh. My. Gosh.

May.

He'd thought Cancun was a slam dunk.

He says to the table, "I had it for about three months before our first date."

"You two have the most romantic story," she gushes.

The girl hasn't said a word. She's glowering into her drink.

Phillip pulls me onto his lap. "You look surprised."

"I am surprised. May, huh?"

"I told you, I've known for a while. I just had to wait until you were on the same page."

"I think we're on the same page now."

"I don't know. I think we have some, uhhh, syncing up to do. Plus, it's been a long day. I think you need to take me home and put me to bed."

"Are you tired?" I sorta whisper but loud enough for the girl to hear.

"Not at all." He grins, kisses up by my ear, and whispers, "God, you smell good. I can't wait to get you home." He throws some money down on the table and says to everyone, "See ya tomorrow." Then, he takes my hand and leads me out of the bar.

And I just hit the game-winning shot at the buzzer!

My team wins!

AFTER SYNCING UP in bed, I ask him about the girl, "Phillip, what's that girl's deal? She's always like, *Oh, Phillip, you're so funny.* When she touches your arm, I just wanna rip it off."

"She's kind of a flirt, but I'm not the least bit interested."

"Then, you need to make her stop touching you. It's not work appropriate, not professional. If you're gonna be the boss, you can't allow it. And, if you wanna be my husband ..."

"Are you actually jealous?"

"Ummm, well, not really jealous, more like concerned. Phillip, I love you. I don't want some secretary to ruin our relationship, and it concerns me that you let her touch your arm.

It makes me think you like it."

"Actually, it bothers me, but I'm not sure how to handle it."

"Maybe you shouldn't be going out for drinks when she's there."

"That would mean I'd never get to go because she's always there. She's on my team."

"I think you should let her know that it makes you uncomfortable. Maybe say something to her, or move your arm away. If you don't move, you're almost encouraging her."

"Well, next time she does it, that's what I'll do."

"Good, because I really don't wanna have to say, *Phillip, hold my earrings while I beat her ass.* That might not be very professional either."

Phillip laughs at me, and then he smiles that smile that makes me melt.

Every. Single. Time.

I run the backs of my hands down the sides of his handsome face. The way he looks at me makes me know that I was stupid, that I have nothing to worry about.

I kiss him. "So, did you really have the ring for three whole months before we hooked up?"

"Yeah, Danny and Lori were the only people who knew. They sorta thought I was nuts. And, after Cancun blew up, I sorta thought so, too. I was really disappointed."

"I was really disappointed, too. Cancun didn't go at all the way I'd planned."

"You had a plan for Cancun?"

"Yeah."

"Really? What was it?"

"I was gonna get you a little tipsy, dance with you, and then take you back to my room. I never imagined you'd leave me alone with those guys. That was, like, dangerous, you know, leaving me on the beach, drunk and crying."

"I never left you by yourself. I wanted you to think I was gone because I was pissed, but I kept an eye on you. I had to make sure you were okay."

"That was sweet."

"I'm a sucker, is more like it."

"No, you're sweet and adorable, and I'm so lucky you didn't give up on me, on us."

"I couldn't. I just had to believe it would work out, but then you started dating that drummer."

"Guitar player."

"Whatever."

"Hey, don't get smart with me, mister."

"Hey, don't tell me what to do, missy."

"I'm gonna be your wife. I can say whatever I want."

"Oh, say that again."

"I can say whatever I want. I like that part."

"No, the other part."

"What part?"

"The wife part."

"I'm gonna be your wife."

"Yeah, I love that."

"I love you."

"I'm not sure I believe you."

"Huh?"

"I think you're gonna have to show me."

"I think I already did."

He pulls me closer and says, "Maybe you need to show me again."

He was a freebie.

SATURDAY, OCTOBER 28TH

WE'RE BACK IN Kansas City and out at a sports bar with Danny, Lori, some of Danny's teammates, and their wives.

We just ordered dinner, and somehow, the subject has turned to sex.

And not just any sex, but *my* sex life in particular.

Lori—who, now that she's pregnant, seems to think she can say anything and get away with it—decides that this is the perfect time, in front of all these people I barely know, to mention that I might have been worried about having an STD for real because I went home that drunken night with Jason O'Connor.

Keep in mind, I would never in a million years think Jason had an STD. Also keep in mind that Phillip doesn't know I was with Jason this past summer, and Lori knows *damn well* that I didn't want Phillip to know this.

I'm pretty sure Danny's whole team knows the STD story; like I said, everyone thinks it's pretty hilarious.

I can handle a little teasing, but when Lori says, "What made it more humorous is that she had a drunken night with this Richie Rich guy, and she was really worried Phillip's mom somehow knew she had one."

At which, Phillip glares at me.

Shit.

It's not like Phillip went without sex all summer. I mean, I don't think he did. But we're in a group and supposed to be having fun, and I've had a couple of beers. Maybe we can all laugh about it, and Phillip won't care.

So, I say, "Well, so what? He was a freebie anyway."

And the guys are like, "A freebie?"

"Yeah, I'd been with him before, so he was the perfect one-night stand because he didn't count."

Big lineman Marcus says, "Didn't count for what?"

"You know, like, your total."

He smiles at me and nods his head in understanding.

Apparently, the throw-Jadyn-under-the-bus sickness is spreading like a virus because Danny says in his twelve-year-old voice, "So, Jay, how many guys *have* you slept with?"

I have to say, I'm a little embarrassed by this.

One, it is no one's business.

Two, it's no one's business.

And, three, Danny has no room to talk.

"I didn't keep track, but I *know* you did. Has Lori seen your *little*, well, make that *long-ass* list?"

He ignores my comment even though I can see Lori's brain going, *There's a list?*

"Come on, Jay. It's not like we don't know them all anyway. This would be a good way for Phillip and me to test our memory. You know, challenging your cognitive function is very important as we age. This might be more complex than a Sudoku puzzle. Let's start with Matt, freshman year."

I roll my eyes at him.

"Freshman year?" one of the guys named Chase asks. "You started early, huh? Wild child?"

"Uh, no," Danny says, "freshman year of *college*."

"Oh, wow. Did you used to be fat or something?" Marcus

says.

This from a man who is three times my size.

Danny saves me. "Nope, she's always looked pretty much like this."

"Then, what happened?" Chase's wife asks.

Okay, so now, I'm forced to make a statement about the young people of today. Shouldn't they be applauding my ability to wait so long? Do they think I wanted to wait that long for what I hoped was love?

"I thought we were all supposed to wait for love; didn't any of you?" I'm hoping this will steer the conversation toward their experiences and away from mine.

But, apparently, I'm the freak at the table they all want to look at under the microscope because Marcus is like, "Well, sure, but we wanna hear about you."

I roll my eyes, but I don't want to be a bitch and tell them to all mind their own freaking business, so I say, "I was ready to my junior year. I was dating this guy, Jake—"

"DOUCHE," Phillip and Danny both pretend cough.

"Oh, shut up, you two. The only guys you wanted me to date were you, so of course, you never liked my boyfriends. You were both just jealous."

"He was still a douche," Danny says, "and you know it."

"Ignore them," Marcus tells me.

So, I keep going. "Anyway, we'd been going out for, like, a month, and I would think I was ready, and then something would happen—"

"Cheater," both Phillip and Danny fake cough again.

"And we would break up. And they're right; he was a douche, but he was so hot."

This gets the wives' attention.

"What'd he look like?" Chase's wife asks.

"Oh, he had that hot bad-boy thing going on. Longer, dark

hair, his bangs were always in his dark eyes, and you never knew what to expect from him. He didn't give a darn what people thought of him and got into a lot of trouble at school, mostly 'cause he was mouthy. He was kind of a slacker, true, but he was also the quarterback after Danny left, and he had great arm muscles. He could be super sweet, and he was the first boy who told me he loved me."

Like, besides Phillip.

Phillip catches my eye and points to his chest. He's letting me know that he was really the first boy to tell me that. I smile dreamily at him.

"Ah … first love. He sounds adorable even if he was a jerk," Marcus's wife comments. "I mean, what high school boy wasn't a jerk?"

Danny, Lori, and I all look at Phillip at the same time and say, "Phillip."

The whole table laughs, and Phillip blows me a kiss.

Marcus is like, "Go on."

"We would break up and get back together, but usually, when we broke up, it was 'cause he was a jerk. We'd get back together, but I'd make him wait a while. I was trying to see if he was serious, but then he'd be a douche again. That went on most of my senior year. When I was finally ready to do it with just about anyone, I couldn't get anyone to do it with me."

"No way," Chase says.

I nod and tell them the sad truth, "Yeah, way. I was gonna do it with Jake the night he broke up with me. Had on the sexy underwear and everything. It was a fail." I raise my eyebrows at them. "But that was the night Danny kissed me, and I thought maybe I would do it with him instead."

"You did?" Danny says with a shocked look all over his face.

"You really didn't hear Lisa screaming in the cornfield, 'You should do it with Danny'? She always had a huge crush on you."

"So, Danny turned you down?" Marcus asks.

A wave of sadness suddenly washes over me.

Phillip can see it on my face, so he says, "No, he didn't. He got in a fight with Jake, so I took Jadyn home."

Danny looks at me with concern but probably figures the night my parents died is not something I wanna talk about with acquaintances at the bar. He says with a grin, "But then there was prom night."

I smile at him, and he knows I'm thanking him for getting us back into easier territory. "*That* was the night he turned me down, Marcus."

Marcus and this Alex guy say, "You were dumb, dude."

"Jay, you know it wasn't like that."

"Oh, that's right; big stud Danny got scared, drunk, and passed out instead."

All the guys laugh hysterically at that.

"So, you're right; Matt was the first, and after that, it really depends on who you wanna count."

Alex says, "What do you mean, *who you wanna count?*"

"Yeah, we want to know how many," Danny says.

"Well, it doesn't really work like that, does it, Lori?"

She's been awfully quiet through all of this, little bus driver there. She also happens to be the queen of *he didn't really count.*

She smirks at me but keeps her mouth shut.

The other wives agree, "Right."

The guys are looking at the women, all confused.

"I know for you guys, it's all black and white. I slept with her, or I didn't. But I think girls tend to look at that question and see lots of shades of gray."

"Like some guys you did it with don't count," Marcus's wife, Madison, says bluntly.

"Exactly," Lori and I agree.

"Wait," Danny says. "So, who wouldn't count?"

Madison says, "I know one. The guy you met at the bar and thought was hot. But, when you sobered up, you realized he wasn't. Like, not at all. I don't think you'd count him."

Marcus is like, "Why wouldn't you count him?"

To which, I reply, "Because, if you'd been in your right mind, you never would have."

Duh.

Madison tells us, "I had a friend call me one shameful morning and ask me if it counts when you wake up, naked, in a guy's bed, but you don't remember doing anything."

"What'd you tell her?" Chase asks.

"I told her not to worry, that it didn't count. If you don't remember it, you didn't do it, right?"

"That's how Lori kept her numbers down," I tease.

"Okay, I can kinda understand that," Alex says. "So, does that mean, girls don't count *any* one-night stands or drunken sex?"

"I think, if he was hot, you'd count him," Madison says.

"Oh, yes. If he was hot, you'd definitely count him," I say.

Lori finally decides to pipe in on the conversation. "Jade, remember that hot-ass bartender you did? You count him, don't you?"

"What bartender?" Phillip asks.

I'm running boys through my mind, praying that I slept with another bartender somewhere along the way, and that's the one she's remembering.

But no.

She looks at Phillip and Danny like they're idiots. "You *know*, the one from Kegger's who always let Jade drink even though he knew she was underage. He had that adorable, spiky blond hair, those big green eyes, and the longest eyelashes we'd ever seen. What was his name?"

"Bradley?" Phillip says. "You slept with Bradley?"

"Uh ... maybe." I put on my sweetest face.

I hope.

Danny's like, "So, that's why we always got free drinks? And here I thought, it was 'cause I was the hot-shit quarterback. Although, come to think of it, I only got free rounds when I was with you."

"We got free rounds *a lot*," Phillip states adamantly.

"Uh, well, it might have been more than one one-night stand," Lori says. "Did you really not know that, Phillip?"

"No, I did not," Phillip says, his eyes boring into mine.

I give Danny my *I'm panicked here; please do something* look, but he thinks it's funny and is laughing at me.

Fortunately, Alex chips in, "Who else wouldn't you count?"

"If he sucked," his wife says.

There are choruses of, "Yeah," and, "Exactly," and, "For sure," from the girls.

"Oh, and if you cheated on your boyfriend with someone, I don't think you would count him either," Lori says with a grin.

"I could get you in a lot of trouble, you know. I have way more dirt on you," I whisper quietly to her.

"You ladies are scaring me," Marcus says. "So, who *would* you count?"

To that, he gets a bunch of replies.

"Guys you had a relationship with."

"Hot guys."

"Yeah, definitely the hot ones."

"The ones who were good."

"Yeah, even if they weren't that hot."

"Oh, and the memorable ones," I say.

"Memorable how?" Danny asks.

Lori opens her big mouth *again*. "Oh, like the guy who worked at the movie theater?"

"What was memorable about the movie-theater guy?" Chase asks.

"Let's just say, it has to do with popcorn butter and the back of a movie theater and leave it at that," Lori says.

"Oh my God, Lori, you're making me sound like a slut. I dated the movie-theater guy for two months and never had sex with him. It's not like I did him for free popcorn."

Danny gets mouthy. "Two whole months, Jay? That was, like, a record for you."

"Uh, no. Four months was my record, and you have no room to talk, Mr. Revolving Bedroom Door."

"How long will you and Phillip have been dating when you get married?"

"Four months," I shoot back.

Danny pats Phillip on the back and says, "Dude," like in sorrow.

"Danny, maybe we should talk about your sex life. How many girls are on that list? I mean, I lost count sophomore year."

"You were never very good with math, blondie," Danny quips.

"Shut up!" I yell.

Lori says, "Yeah, Danny, how many? We've never really discussed this."

I can tease Danny all I want to, but I love him, and I can see that this conversation is going nowhere good and fast. So, I toss him a life preserver by saying, "Well, how many for you, Lori? Remember that wrestler dude? And who could forget all the things you did with that guy from your Anatomy class in the name of studying?" *Let's put her under the microscope for a little while.*

"Jay, we might need to talk about this later," Danny teases.

"Trust me, Danny; her number is smaller than yours. Even without the mental revisions."

"That's weird," Alex says, "because I think guys count every single girl regardless of the circumstances."

"Even if she was nasty?" I question.

"Uh, yeah, I think so. Guys?"

And all the guys are like, "Yeah."

"What if she was your best friend's girl?" Marcus's wife, Madison, asks.

Marcus says, "Yeah, sure. I mean, I did."

Then, both he and his wife get big grins on their faces, and he continues, "But, then again, I married her."

Living on love.

FRIDAY, NOVEMBER 3RD

I WENT TO look at wedding dresses again yesterday. Still no luck. Lori must have been feeling my frustration all the way down in Kansas City.

While I'm driving to work, my phone rings.

"So, did you find a dress last night?"

"No, I suck," I whine. "I thought the dress would be the easiest part. I might have to go naked."

"That would fit your whole XXX theme."

"Yeah," I say as further depression sets in.

"So, I have a plan. Danny plays the Jets in New York next Sunday, and I think we should tag along and do some serious shopping. I heard there's a store there that has the biggest wedding dress selection in the world. We could leave Friday, shop all day Saturday, and see the game Sunday."

"Sounds like a plan to me, although I'm gonna have to see if my boss will let me off work."

"He will. He's invited, too. We also invited both the Diamonds and the Macs. Are you okay with the moms helping you shop?"

"Just promise me, no STD jokes."

"Deal! Oh, Jade, I'm so excited! I know I'll be able to help you find the perfect dress!"

"I sure hope so, Lori. I sure hope so."

AS SOON AS I get in the office, Phillip shuts his door, pushes me up against it, and kisses me. "You're late," he says. "I'm your boss. I'm probably going to have to write you up or something."

"No, you're just always early."

He grabs my ass. "Maybe you should offer to sleep with the boss, so you can get ahead."

"I'm surprised you'd want me to sleep with your dad, Phillip."

He chuckles and kisses the side of my neck, just under my ear. I swear, it makes me weak in the knees. It's a good thing I'm up against the door.

"I'm pretty sure I'm your boss."

"And I'm pretty sure, if sleeping with you were the way to get ahead, I'd be running the company by now."

He slides his hand into the back of my hair and kisses me again. "I missed you."

"You saw me an hour ago."

"I still missed you. Do you know how sexy you looked this morning? Your hair was a wreck, and your mascara was all smeared. That's how I know it was a good night. The more smeared your mascara, the more fun we had."

"Are you suggesting we had fun last night?"

"Oh, yeah. And guess what. We're going home for lunch today."

"I'm gonna starve, huh?"

"Nah, you're just living on love."

Sweet and sass.

MONDAY, NOVEMBER 6TH

PHILLIP AND I are meeting with Amy, our amazing wedding planner, for some serious wedding planning. Since we hired her, wedding planning has become really fun.

We're basically planning one big, long party, and I love parties!

We've both had numerous phone conversations with Amy about what we want at the wedding. And we know food is high on Phillip's list. We both want the food to be like good, normal food. Sorry, but don't come to my wedding if you're looking for little appetizers with caviar and cream on top.

That is not us.

We meet her at the hotel, view the ballrooms, and sit down to start our food tasting. We taste all the appetizers for the cocktail party. We're having Kobe beef sliders, hot wing bites, twice-baked baby new potatoes, bacon-wrapped scallops, barbecued shrimp, a shot glass of tomato-basil soup served with a mini grilled cheese, fruit kabobs, and crab cakes.

We also want to have a cool signature cocktail. We just need to choose one.

Amy says, "They made three drinks for you to try. I wasn't sure which way you would want to go—a wintery drink or one that matches your wedding decor."

First, we try a chocolate peppermint martini. It's really good, and it reminds me of hot chocolate and Peppermint Schnapps. Then, we taste a gingerbread martini. Phillip is in love with the gingerbread one, but he thinks they both taste too much like dessert. Once they bring out the third drink, I see why. I'm pretty sure this drink was Phillip's idea. It's called the princess martini.

Amy tells me, "It's a combination of Chambord-flavored vodka, citron vodka, and lemonade."

Phillip takes a taste. "This drink is aptly named. It's just like you. The perfect combination of sweet and sass."

"And the glass is rimmed with purple sugar. How cute is that?"

"Like I said, just like you."

I take another drink and then yell out, "Sold!"

Phillip grins at me.

Sorry, I have to say it.

Isn't he just adorable?

I just want to take him home with me.

Like, now.

But we have to do this stuff even though all I can think about is how I'd like to rip his clothes off.

WE TASTE EVERYTHING on our dinner menu. The wedge salad with balsamic vinaigrette, the Kansas City strip steak with a port wine reduction, garlic mashed potatoes, and cheesy corn. It is all really good.

"Jadyn," Amy says to me, "Phillip told me you love desserts. I think it might be fun to do something a little different. While you're doing the toasts, your first dance, and cutting the cake, I thought we should serve a little something sweet to finish off dinner and go with the champagne. And don't worry; people will still eat plenty of cake."

Danny, who is known for his impeccable timing, texts me.

Danny: *XXX desserts = chocolate body paint + whipped cream.*

Gosh, he makes me laugh. I show Phillip the text.

He whispers in my ear, "We'll stop at the store later. That sounds fun."

I bite my lip. I'm practically breathless, imagining Phillip covered in whipped cream and chocolate. Two of my most favorite things.

I'm having a nice, steamy daydream when the chef brings out an array of dessert shooters. Little bites of wonder are what they should be called. They're the perfect size, and we couldn't pick just one. So, we're doing an assortment and letting the guests each try a few. We did narrow the options down to four, Phillip and I each picking our two favorites.

And I have to talk about these desserts because dessert is, like, my very favorite thing in the world. Phillip has always teased me because, if I had my way, I would eat dessert first and see how hungry I was before ordering dinner.

If only our bodies would cooperate with this, diet-wise.

I think God, the architect of our amazing universe, made incredible things—sunsets, rainbows, ripples in the water, our bodies and minds, and everything. He also created sex. Think about that.

But I think the fact that dessert every day would make us fat is a serious design flaw.

Think how happy we'd all be.

Seriously, if everyone in the world could eat dessert first *and* not get fat in the process, I'm convinced there would be so much more happiness and love in the world. It's kinda like the whole '70s thing.

Peace, love, and weed.

Now, sure, weed makes you feel all happy, but, you know, it's illegal and all and frowned upon by many.

However ...

Peace, love, and dessert.

I really think the world could wrap its head around this.

And I plan to fully support this movement at my wedding.

Dessert for everyone.

So, don't laugh at the fact that we're having four kinds of dessert shooters and two kinds of cake.

Okay, now, let me gush about these shooters.

My favorite is something called chocolate overload, which, if I remember right from school, would be considered an oxymoron because it's not possible in Jadyn's little world. There is no such possible thing as *too much* chocolate; therefore, it's impossible to overload it. It starts out with gooey flourless chocolate cake pieces, and then it's topped with homemade chocolate fudge, chocolate ganache, and chocolate whipped cream.

Seriously.

"You can just take a dozen or so of those up to the honey-moon suite and leave them by the bathtub for me on our wedding night," I half-joke to Amy and Phillip.

Actually, I'm not really joking.

My other favorite is lighter and fluffy, but it is equally won-derful. It is similar to a cake my grandma used to make when I was little. It has pound cake, warm caramel sauce, whipped cream, and toffee pieces.

Phillip chooses a mini tiramisu because that's his mom's favor-ite dessert, and then he goes crazy over pumpkin cake with caramel liquor and cinnamon-spiced whipped cream.

"You can put some of these by the tub for me," he jokes.

"I'm a wedding planner, not the dessert fairy," Amy says. "Although, when we're finished up here, we do get to taste cake.

I'm gonna go tell them we're ready for the after-party food."

"This is, like, the best day ever," Phillip says to me.

I'm still picturing Phillip covered in chocolate, so I whisper to him, "If you buy chocolate and whipped cream on the way home, it might just be your best night ever, too."

He gives me the sexiest grin. "I think that can be arranged."

He gazes at my mouth. I'm pretty sure he's going to kiss me, but he says, "You have some whipped cream on your mouth. Here, let me get it."

He licks the corner of my mouth and then kisses me. I'm pretty sure he was lying, but I don't mind.

AMY WALTZES BACK in with a different chef. "Since both of you have fond memories of late-night breakfasts with your friends, that seemed like the perfect food for your after-party."

We taste the cutest stack of mini pancakes that are held together by a purple skewer and drizzled with warm maple syrup. There are paper cones full of mini hash browns, sausage and cheese biscuit sliders, mini French toast points made with cinnamon bread, warm mini cinnamon rolls with thick white frosting, and a little ramekin filled with a mushroom and pepper jack cheese omelet.

The exact type I used to make for Phillip and Danny.

"What do you think?" she asks.

Phillip and I both have our mouths full of something. He gives her two thumbs-up.

I chew quickly and then say, "I think you just pitched a shut-out."

And she's like, "What?"

"It's like you had the perfect game," Phillip tells her. "You did good."

AFTER A LONG drive home, Phillip makes good on his promise.

He stops at the grocery store by my house and comes out with hot fudge and a can of whipped cream.

Let's just say, Phillip is by far the best dessert of the day.

Focus on our future.

TUESDAY, NOVEMBER 7TH

I'M STARTING TO hate these blue-and-white-checkerboard chairs. They're like mini torture devices. I look down at them and study them a little closer, half-expecting shackles to be hidden under the rolled arms and on the wooden legs.

As if it's not bad enough that I'm sitting here, Phillip told me on the way in that, if I wasn't good, I wouldn't get margaritas after.

Does he think he's my dad?

I don't need his permission to get margaritas!

Maybe, today, we need to talk to him about the whole smothering thing. I'm pretty sure margarita-blocking equals smothering.

Can you actually die from lack of alcohol?

Pastor John says, "So, today, we want to talk about the past."

Phillip butts in, "We're not going to discuss JJ's parents."

I smile at Phillip. *My hero.*

Maybe he's not so bad after all.

The pastor replies, "Well, Phillip, you can pretend all you want that it doesn't affect you, but JJ went through something traumatic. You both did. But that's not all we need to discuss. Everyone comes to a relationship with a past. Past loves, secrets, sometimes children. They've had relationships that were successful and relationships that were failures. We want to make sure you're both on the same page. How much do you know about each other's pasts?"

"We know everything! I've known him my whole life!" I say.

Phillip smirks at me. "Not everything. I learned a few things I hadn't known about your past the other weekend."

Oh, please. He's not going to bring up that I slept with the bartender, is he? He hasn't said one single word to me about it, and he's gonna choose now to talk about it?

Pastor John says, "What did you learn, Phillip?"

I give Phillip my evilest glare, but he doesn't look at me.

He continues, "I just learned that I hadn't known everything about her, like I'd thought I did."

Duh. Like I was gonna tell Phillip about every boy I'd slept with.

Sleeping around was fine for Danny, but I wasn't really allowed. Like, Phillip and Danny would've gotten mad at me. Part of the reason I never brought a guy home with me is, Danny and Phillip would've crucified him.

"I don't know everything about your past either," I tell Phillip. "We were close, but, like the dreams we talked about, we didn't share everything with each other. I'm learning new things about you, too."

"True," he says.

His eyes get sparkly, and I can tell he's moved from thinking about my past to thinking about Naughty Dream Week and probably about last night. Phillip doesn't mind being treated like a dessert. He says I can lick whipped cream off anything I want, anytime I want, which I wanna do again very soon. Like, maybe tonight.

When that's what you have to look forward to in your future, why would you care about the past?

Phillip turns to Pastor John and says, "I don't think we should be dwelling on the past. I think we should be focusing on our future."

And this is why I love that boy.

AND I LOVE him even more when we get to his car. He kisses me quickly and deeply, and then he picks me up and sets me on the hood. He's standing between my legs and leaning his torso tightly into mine. He grabs my legs, wraps them around his waist, and pulls me in closer. A couple of things cross my mind before I unzip his pants. It's really a good thing the parking lot is dark and deserted, and I'm really glad I wore a dress.

The sex is all he remembers.

WEDNESDAY, NOVEMBER 8TH

I CALL LORI while Phillip is in a meeting. "Do you think our past matters? Like, does it freak you out that Danny slept with a lot of different girls?"

"Not really. His past is what makes him who he is. Plus, I figure he got it all out of his system. I don't think your past has to define you. I wasn't exactly a saint either."

"That's for sure, and that's a good way to look at it. You kinda threw me under the bus the other day. Phillip and Danny didn't know about Bradley."

"You hooked up with him off and on for two years! How did they not know that?"

"I never told them. I always said I was staying at the sorority house if I wasn't coming home. They don't know much about the hook-ups side of my past. Like, the guys I was in relationships with, they knew about. The hook-ups, not so much."

"Did he get mad?"

"No, we had stupid couples counseling last night. He sorta brought up how he'd thought he knew everything about me, but he really doesn't. Then, I think he started remembering Monday night, and it distracted him. While we'd had our tastings, I'd told Phillip I wanted to cover him in whipped cream and chocolate and make him my dessert. He'd stopped and bought stuff on the way home, so I did. It was so fun. Phillip is so damn sexy. I can hardly stand it."

"Did you really? Didn't that make a mess?"

"It would have, if we'd been in bed."

"Where were you?"

"The kitchen. Like, mostly the counter—well, and then the floor. We cleaned it all up, but I still keep finding little random chocolate smudges. They make me laugh."

"Jade, I'm a little worried about you. Do you really think couples counseling is stupid?"

"Yeah, didn't you?"

"No, not really. I kinda enjoyed it. It was fun, learning about ways to be a better couple. He made us think about issues that we hadn't thought to discuss, and I was glad we did."

"You were always a better student than me."

"I studied harder; that's for sure. You hardly ever studied, but you got good grades. That used to piss me off," she says.

"I just have a really good short-term memory. I can't remember any of it now."

"Well, I think you should take counseling more seriously. You and Phillip need to be able to work through things, not just have whipped-cream sex."

"Danny told me you solve your conflicts with sex."

"No, we don't. He just thinks we do. If we talk it out first, then I reward him with sex. The sex is all he remembers. I think he has a short-term memory, too."

"You're a tricky girl."

She laughs. "So, this weekend! You ready to find the dress of your dreams?"

"I am. Do you really think we'll find a dress?"

"I know we will!"

TONIGHT, WE'RE BOTH sitting in bed. I'm on my iPad, flipping through wedding cake designs, while Phillip is watching—well, I have no idea what he's watching.

He's on the Discovery channel, and every time I glance up, I see huge crocodiles eating something.

It's really disturbing me, so I try not to glance up, but, yuck, I accidentally do.

So, it's really no wonder that, with all this wedding planning going on in my mind, my subconscious would wreak havoc with my dreams.

I walk out onto a stage as an announcer says, "And, on today's journey through the dark recesses of Bridalville, we find our heroine, Princess Jadyn, on the search for the perfect wedding dessert."

I sit at a big golden banquet table, eating dessert after sinful dessert. An audience claps for me when I choose to have purple edible flowers flown in from Guam for my special day.

"She's so creative," the announcer says.

Then, it's my wedding day. Phillip pulls out my chair at our sweetheart table. We sit down, and I feel so lucky. Phillip is beaming at me. Our friends and families are at all the surrounding tables, waiting to be served dinner.

Our amazing Kansas City strip steaks are being delivered. For some reason, we decided it would be very cool to have the steaks carved like an ice sculpture. The steaks are somehow standing on end, and they've been carved to look like a crocodile. Now, you would think this might look a little scary, but at the time we picked it out, Phillip and I thought it was adorable because it looked like the crocodile was smiling at us and wishing us a happy life. He was a cute crocodile, like the one from Peter Pan.

But, just as our guests are oohing and aahing over our creativity and how real they look, the crocs come to life, jump up off the wedding plates, and start to eat up all our guests. One by one, I watch my guests get swallowed up by their crocodile steaks.

I start to scream.

Phillip wakes me up.

I tell him about my horrible dream. "What do you think it means?"

"Maybe you're afraid no one will come to the wedding. That we won't have any guests."

"No, that can't be it. These people were already at the reception, and who comes to the wedding and skips the reception? I mean, the reception is the best part."

"People who don't wanna get eaten by a crocodile perhaps?"

"Smart-ass. Well, all I know is, I'm not getting the steak."

"I guess I might have to agree with that. Maybe we should call Amy in the morning and go with the filet medallions instead."

I look at Phillip. He has bedhead, and the side of his cheek has red lines across it from where he was sleeping on his hand.

I grin at him and move my hands under the sheets. "You know, I think I'm so scared; I might not be able to go back to sleep. You might have to distract me."

He pulls me closer to him as I run my hands down his abs. "How am I supposed to do that?"

I press my lips against his yummy-smelling neck, graze my tongue down the side of it, and rub my hand between his legs. "I bet you can think of something."

I want to look timeless.

SATURDAY, NOVEMBER 11TH

WE'RE IN NEW York, and Lori is quite prepared with a list of stores for us to check out and a car to take us.

She says, "Jade, if you can't find a dress here, you're doomed."

"Nothing like a little bit of pressure to start my day," I mutter back.

"You didn't get coffee yet, did you? You're always cranky without coffee. Did you eat breakfast?"

"Um, no."

She sighs at me.

"Don't give me that sigh. I'm going to try on wedding dresses! I need to look perfect, so I spent a lot of time getting ready." I lean over and whisper in her ear, so the moms can't hear, "Plus, Phillip would not let me out of bed. He's insatiable."

Lori giggles with me and then asks the driver to stop at the next coffee shop. She comes back with a latte and a chocolate chip scone for me. I'm happily sipping coffee and thinking about how Phillip looked when I left this morning. All those sexy muscles lying there, naked, twisted-up sheets down by his feet. The way his eyes sparkled when he spoke. How I can't even remember what he said because I kept thinking about how I just wanted to take my clothes off and pounce back on top of him. I think about what I would've done. How I would've run my hands across his broad shoulders. How I love the way his abs feel in my hands. How muscular his butt feels when he's—

His mom interrupts my thoughts by shoving a file folder in front of me. Mrs. Diamond tells me they clipped out some photos of dresses they thought I should try on.

I thank them and flip through the photos, not really looking at them. My mind is back to sexy places.

WE GO TO a few bridal boutiques. I try on some dresses, but nothing wows us.

Around noon, I'm introduced to a bridal consultant named Hillary. She's short, blonde, and extremely peppy. I like her enthusiasm right away.

Hillary says, "I'm going to steal the bride away for a little while. Enjoy some champagne, and she'll be back out, looking like a bride."

Hillary leads me back to a dressing room where we sit down. "So, tell me about the groom."

"His name is Phillip Mackenzie, and I've known him my whole life. He was my best friend, growing up, and my college roommate. We got engaged a couple of months ago on our first date."

"Wow, really? I've never met anyone who got engaged on their first date. So, how about your budget?"

I tell her my dress budget.

She nods and says, "Have you tried on any dresses?"

"I've tried on about thirty."

"And have you liked any of them? Do you have pictures of dresses you like?"

"I have a stack that people think I should try on. I don't want to waste our time though. I know that none of them are the one."

"Okay, why don't you tell me what you liked or didn't like

about the dresses you've tried on?"

"I hate hoop skirts. I don't want anything heavy. I wanna be able to move."

"Got it. Now, describe to me how you want to look on your wedding day."

"No one has asked me that question before."

"Well, I'm going to help you find the perfect dress. It's my job to ask the right questions."

I think about how I want to look. "I wanna look timeless. I want my daughter to look back at my dress twenty years from now and not know when I got married. I kinda want to look like Grace Kelly. Not her wedding gown; that was too lacy. More like the fifties classic strapless dresses. But, no, that's not really right either because I don't want to look dated. I definitely want strapless. I want the dress to be soft and light, so I can move around in it. I thought I wanted something very tailored and plain, but when I try on dresses like that, they don't seem dressy enough, so I think I need a little bling. I know most brides probably come in and know exactly what they want—like, they want to look a certain way— but all I want is for Phillip to think I look amazing. I did try on a dress of each silhouette. Everyone thinks I look best in a strapless mermaid style. I sort of feel like a bridal failure."

"You're not a failure. You just haven't found the right dress yet. You've told me a lot about what you want and don't want. I'm going to pull a few dresses. Be right back," she says in a very chipper voice.

I say a silent prayer that Hillary can figure me out.

That, today, I will find my dress.

While I'm waiting, my phone buzzes. I pull it out of my purse.

Danny: XXX-themed wedding requires a XXX bridal dress. Hint...

Following is a photo of a woman that you'd assume is a bride since she's wearing a veil and dressed in all white. I'd say she's probably a very naughty bride. She has on a white lace corset, sheer lace thong, fishnet thigh highs, and patent leather platform heels.

Only the classiest shoes for this bride.

Over all of this is a sheer robe. The robe is sporting a feather collar, or maybe it's a white boa; I'm not sure. She also has extremely big hair, bright red lipstick, and a cherry halfway in her mouth. Maybe that's a new wedding dessert I should consider.

Ha!

Me: *OMG! Very classy!*

Danny: *If you decide you wanna try on dresses like this, one that will fit your theme, ditch the women and let the best man help you pick it out. I'm told it's one of my duties to see my groom is well taken care of.*

Me: *You're a goofball. Are you with Phillip and the dads?*

Danny: *Yeshhh :) and Mac likeyyyyyy.*

Me: *Are you drinking?*

Danny: *I have a game tomorrow, so not really, but everyone else is. Lori says brides sometimes wear a second dress to the reception, and it should fit your theme. So, we ordered this for you. You can thank me later.*

Me: *More like, Phillip will be thanking you. Tell him it definitely fits our honeymoon theme.*

Danny: *You have a honeymoon theme?*

Me: *Maybe ...*

Danny: *Phillip says you do but won't tell me. He also said to tell you this outfit reminds him of whipped cream. What does that mean?*

Me: *Well, we can't use XXX for the wedding, so ... and ask*

*him about the whipped cream. OMG, Danny, it was so
HOT! Just don't let the dads hear!*

Danny: *I'm jealous.*

Hillary walks back in the room with four dresses. There must
be something about having a complete stranger see you practically
naked that makes you feel like you can talk to her about anything.
While she's getting me all done up, I find myself telling her that
it's kinda hard for me to be picking out a dress without my mom.
I tell her how my mom loved bling and how I used to fight against
it, but the older I get, the more I don't mind just a little bit of
sparkle. For some reason, it makes me feel more like her.

The first dress she puts me in is actually quite pretty. I know
for sure it's not the dress, but it's probably the first one that I
don't dislike. It's a strapless mermaid-style dress. It has just a bit of
bling across the waistline, but the rest of it is pretty plain. Like the
simplicity of the design is what makes it gorgeous.

I show Lori and the moms.

"This isn't the one," I say, "but it's very pretty, don't you
think?"

Lori loves me in strapless, and the moms love the mermaid
style. Maybe we're getting somewhere. Maybe, today, I will find a
dress.

EIGHT GOWNS LATER.

Hillary knows more about me than my best friends. Not only
have I told her about my parents, but I've also told her how Phillip
and I were going to have a long engagement but moved it up.
How the wedding is going to be romantic. How the date magically
fell into place. How it's the day after my parents' anniversary.
How I feel like they gave me a wedding gift.

I tell her about the ballroom, the candlelight, and the food.

When she goes to grab more dresses, I'm embarrassed to

realize that I've been totally spilling my guts to her.

We've tried on beautiful dresses, but none of them are right. I'm starting to feel like a failure again. And I'm not the only one who's feeling that way. Hillary doesn't seem as chipper. Lori and the moms are starting to look bored and frustrated with me. They've loved quite a few of the dresses, and I'm pretty sure they think I'm nuts.

Naked is starting to sound better and better. Maybe I could just buy a veil and have one of those artists come paint my body white.

Ha! If Kansas City makes the playoffs, I could leave the paint on, add some red and yellow, and go to the game! I'd probably get on TV. Like, if I didn't get arrested first.

HILLARY IS A very patient trooper though, and she comes back in with four more dresses. She's just about to put me in another dress that I already know I'm going to reject when my cell rings. I left my phone sitting on the chair, so I can see that it's Phillip calling me.

"It's Phillip, the groom!" I say excitedly. "Do you mind if I quickly answer it?"

"Sure," she says.

I answer and say, "Hey."

Phillip's soft, dreamy voice fills the room. "Hey, Princess. How's the dress shopping going?"

I apologize to Hillary, "Sorry, I must have hit the speaker button." I turn off the speaker and say to Phillip, "I'm still looking, but I think we're getting closer."

It's a total lie.

Both Hillary and I know this.

I tell him I need to go, and he tells me he knows I'll find the perfect dress today.

As I'm ending the call, I notice Hillary looking at me kinda funny. "He calls you Princess? Is that his nickname for you?"

I nod my head and launch into the story about how, when we were ten, Mary Beth Parker told everyone not to play with me. How Phillip still did. How I told him he acted like a prince. How, since that day, he's called me Princess. How he's always called me Princess in private, but he lets it slip out now in front of our friends. I even get a little misty when I tell her about how we used to play games as kids. How I would be a princess, and he would rescue me from dragons. How, as we got older, he rescued me for real. When my parents died. From bad dates. Flat tires. You name it. How, when I was little, my parents told me I should marry Phillip. How I laughed and told them I was marrying a prince.

I pretty much gush on and on about how amazing Phillip is.

Hillary's eyes light up. She gets a big grin on her face and says, "I have an idea."

She dashes out of the room while I think about Phillip. About how much I love that boy. I need to keep reminding myself that's what this wedding is all about. I'm going to marry the boy I love and have always loved. I think that's why I've been having such a hard time. I'm trying to find a dress worthy of that love.

Maybe I'm approaching this the wrong way. Maybe I should think about what kind of dress Phillip would like.

I think about the dress he bought me for our engagement, freaking covered in sequins but still tailored and simple.

Hillary is grinning as she bounds in with another dress. She looks peppy again. "This dress is not a mermaid style. We've been getting sidetracked by what everyone thinks you look good in. You told me you want classic and romantic. Timeless. Mermaids are fashionable, but they aren't timeless. I want you to try this dress on with your eyes closed. I want you to see it in front of the big mirrors for the first time."

She seems super excited and sincere, so I say, "Okay."

I mean, it's the least I can do for the woman who's probably going to need some kind of deep post-traumatic-stress counseling after dealing with me.

I close my eyes as she slides a dress on me.

Then, she holds my hand and leads me on the now-familiar walk out front.

"Keep your eyes closed," Hillary whispers to me. "I'm going to grab a veil."

I want to open my eyes. I can hear the moms and Lori whispering.

Hillary pulls back half of my hair, slides a comb and veil into it, and then lays a headband across the top of my head. "Okay, sweetie, now, you can open your eyes."

I look in front of me.

Staring back at me isn't me in another dress.

Staring back at me is a bride.

And this bride is wearing the most beautiful dress I have ever seen.

The top of her dress is strapless and satin. It fits the bride perfectly and accentuates her thin waist. Crossing her waist is a band of beautiful crystals. The skirt of her dress is layer upon layer of frothy silk organza. Her hair is half pulled up, her blonde curls are cascading down her shoulders, and there's a long veil with a crystal headband that perfectly finishes the bride's dress.

It takes a second for me to realize the bride I'm looking at is me.

I get little tears in my eyes. I've been looking for so long, and I'm so happy that I didn't buy another dress because this is exactly how I want to look for Phillip. This dress is a combination of my tailored style and, well, a princess. A princess who isn't going to the ball in a big hoop skirt. This princess is more like a fairy princess, and she's going dancing in a frothy, swishy, twirly skirt that feels like she's wearing a cloud.

It's perfect.

I'm dabbing the little tears from my eyes when Hillary says, "Finally, the tears. So, what does everyone think?"

I pry my eyes away from the gorgeous bride in the mirror—I mean, me—and look back to see their reactions. They're all in tears, too.

Danny's mom gets up and hugs me. "Honey, you look so beautiful. Look at those gorgeous crystals." She backs up, looks at the dress again, and sadly shakes her head. "Your mom would have loved this dress. I really wish she were here with us today."

I cover my mouth with my hand. I can't hold back the tears anymore. Just hearing that my mom would have loved my dress makes them flow down my face.

Hillary hands out tissues because we're all bawling.

"So, does the fact that we're all blithering idiots over this dress mean it's the one?" Lori asks.

"Yes," I say. "This is definitely the one."

Mrs. Mac says, "You look a little like a princess," as she dabs her eyes.

Like Phillip's princess, I think.

"I'll take it," I say.

Then, I stare at the bride in the mirror some more.

I can't wait for Phillip to see me in this dress.

Dreams of Their own.

MONDAY, NOVEMBER 13TH

THIS PAST WEEKEND, Lori gave me a book that was written by a mom and daughter about planning the daughter's wedding. She thought it would give me some insight as to what my mom would have been thinking and feeling if she were here with me now.

But I get more out of the book than I expected.

I've realized that I've been kinda selfish. This wedding is not just about me and Phillip. It's really the merging together of families, and those families have dreams of their own.

So, if you're planning a wedding someday, here's my advice to you.

And notice that I'm giving this advice before I put my plan into action, so, that way, if this all ends up with me in a bathroom, screaming, *What was I thinking?*, you will do it regardless of my outcome.

I think back to when we were doing the guest list. Mrs. Mac asked me a question about our plans, and I sort of shut her down and told her that we'd tell her when we figured it out. Like she was just a guest. I realize that Phillip's mom has probably been both dreaming about and dreading the day her precious son got married. She's inviting her friends, and I'm sure she has something pictured in her mind about how it should be.

So, now that Phillip and I have a lot of the basics planned out, I've decided to ask the other important people in my life what they'd like to see happen at the wedding, ask them about their dreams for it.

Who knows? They might have some amazing ideas.

THIS MORNING, I meet Phillip's mom at the Diamonds' for Mrs. D's wonderful cinnamon coffee cake.

I take my idea board and inspiration folder. I tell them about all the food Phillip and I picked out, about the rooftop ballroom, and how I want it to be romantic. I also tell them that Phillip has had about all the wedding planning he can take. He wanted a say in the things that were important to him, like food and alcohol, but the rest is just fluff to him.

I invite them to come to Kansas City with me on Thursday to meet the wedding planner and help me with the rest of the decor details. I still have to pick the flowers, the cake design, and finalize the reception decor. They are especially thrilled when I set a stack of bridal magazines in front of them and tell them to go crazy.

AFTER THAT, I go in the study to talk to Mr. D.

I ask for his opinion. Ask if there's anything he'd like to see happen at the wedding.

He thinks about it for a minute. "I know alcohol is one of the most expensive parts of a wedding, but it would be nice if there was a secret stash of good scotch for us old guys to enjoy. I'd also love to smoke a cigar in your dad's honor."

Phillip mentioned that a scotch and cigar bar would be so cool. Plus, I'm getting him an engraved humidor as his wedding gift, so it would be perfect.

And then it hits me. I never asked Mr. Diamond to walk me down the aisle. I was gonna ask him the night he told me he was holding my wedding money hostage. I've been a little mad at him since, honestly.

But I look at him. The man who's helped me through every major crisis—from financial to what to major in. Who has gently guided me down the path to adulthood. Who has done way more than I'm sure my parents ever imagined he would when they named him executor of my trust. He treats me like his daughter. And he wants to toast my dad at my wedding.

He sees that my eyes are filling up with tears and says, "Honey, I'm sorry. I didn't want to upset you. I know it's very hard on you, not having him here. Maybe it's a bad idea."

"You didn't upset me. I think it's a wonderful idea. I got tears in my eyes because I have a big favor to ask you, and it seems like all I ever do is ask you for favors."

"Don't be silly," he says. "I loved your parents, and you know you're like a daughter to me. I'll always do anything in my power to help you in whatever way you need."

I smile at him through tears. "So, does that mean you'd consider walking me down the aisle? Standing in for my dad?"

He sits there for a minute, which I have to say I appreciate. He understands the gravity of this to me.

He's even a little choked up when he replies, "I'd be extremely honored."

The coolest wedding thing.

TUESDAY, NOVEMBER 14TH

PHILLIP WALKS IN the door with beer under his arm and a magazine in his hand. "Look, I found a wedding magazine we haven't looked at yet! This one looks cool, too. It has spreads on real weddings."

We sit at the kitchen table, drink a beer, and flip through the pages. We're halfway through when Phillip stumbles upon an idea that hits his hot button.

"Look at this! They had custom Nikes made as gifts for the groomsmen! They put their names and the wedding date on the shoes, too. That is *the coolest* wedding thing I have ever seen! I'm doing them. We'll do black shoes with a dark purple swoosh!"

Phillip is really excited, and I don't want to, like, burst his bubble or anything, but tennis shoes at a formal wedding? With tuxedos?

Um, no.

No freaking way.

"Uh, Phillip, our wedding is formal. I don't think you can wear Nikes."

He raises his eyebrows and gives me a little smirk. "It's my wedding. I can do whatever I want. Plus, you got purple shoes. You showed me them."

"Phillip, I got purple satin Badgley Mischka heels with crystal detailing. They aren't black leather Nike tennis shoes. I don't know about this, Phillip. I need some convincing."

He looks at me for a beat and then strips off his shirt.

That totally makes me laugh. "That's not the kind of convincing I meant, Phillip. Look at these pictures. Their wedding was outside, and they're wearing khakis. It was very informal."

"I don't care. By the time I'm done with you, you'll be begging me to wear these shoes."

I'll admit, Phillip with no shirt is already pretty convincing, but I say, "I see you shirtless every day. I don't think that's gonna do it."

He picks me up and moves me to the couch. Takes off my sweater. Kisses my entire upper half.

Every. Single. Inch.

My collarbone, down my arms, my neck, my chest, my stomach. When he gets to my stomach, I'm about to tell him he can have whatever he wants, to please just take off my skirt.

He takes off my shoes instead. He gently massages my feet, kisses up my legs, and then finally pulls off my skirt.

And he's right.

I'm pretty sure I'll be letting him wear whatever shoes he wants.

It's bad luck!!

THURSDAY, NOVEMBER 16TH

WHEN I WATCHED that wedding planning show, the thing that struck me most about the episodes was not how beautifully the weddings turned out. What struck me was how you watched each bride grow up in front of your eyes. The process seemed to give them all a kind of bridal confidence, and I feel like I've sorta gotten my own bridal confidence. At first, I was just plain freaked out by the whole thing. When I first started planning, I wanted total and complete control. Then, I realized I couldn't do it by myself, but I still held tight, only allowing Phillip, Lori, and Amy into my wedding planning world.

Now that I've given up control, I realize that you can't do it yourself, and you shouldn't try.

Mrs. D said something on the drive down about how happy she is to be helping because she didn't get to help plan any of Danny's wedding. So, needless to say, both she and Mrs. Mac are brimming with excitement. When I watch them hug Amy, their new best friend, I think I just grew up a little more. I don't have my parents here, but I do have some very special people in my life.

And I'm gonna start celebrating that.

THE MOMS HAD some great ideas that we incorporated into the

wedding plans. We planned out the weekend's events, starting with a welcome basket in each room and ending with a farewell brunch on Sunday. Mrs. Mac had great ideas about what to put in the baskets. My only real contribution was that I wanted some chocolate included.

Big surprise.

And Mrs. D hit it out of the park. She recommended having chilled buckets of beer waiting for the guests upon check-in.

I'm pretty sure our friends are gonna go crazy over that type of welcome.

We got to play around with place settings and decided on deep purple glass chargers, deep purple water goblets, clear champagne glasses with silver trim, white dinner plates, and an adorable multicolored salad plate. Along with all that is an ice-purple napkin. When Amy handed me a princess crown napkin ring that was Phillip's idea, I almost cried.

EVERYTHING HAS BEEN going well until they completely disagree with me about the one thing I'm most looking forward to. Phillip and I have decided to meet in private before the wedding. When he sees me in my dress for the first time, it will be just the two of us and a photographer.

Mrs. Mac says, "JJ! He can't see you before the wedding. It's bad luck!"

Mrs. D agrees. "Plus, you're getting married on the thir-teenth."

"Phillip and I want to have some private moments on our wedding day. If he sees my dress as I'm walking down the aisle, I won't get to talk to him. I want to hear what he thinks. Then, we're gonna go take photos in front of our fountain."

They're both shaking their heads at me when Amy says, "You know, if we do most of the photos before the ceremony, that means we all get to enjoy the cocktail hour. Otherwise, the guests will enjoy it while you take photos."

Neither one of them wants to miss a second of the cocktail hour, so Mrs. Mac finally says, "Well, if you make it special, it'll probably be okay."

"I'm so excited about Phillip seeing my dress in private. Instead of worrying about walking down the aisle and not tripping, I'll be able to focus on him, to remember what he looks like the moment he sees me. I wanna take his breath away."

Mrs. D gushes, "Oh, JJ, the way you talk about it makes it sound so much more romantic. I wish I could've done that when I got married."

"While we're on this subject of walking down the aisle," Mrs. Mac says, "I want to ask if you'd mind if Phillip escorted Doug and me. Traditionally, an usher would escort me down the aisle. Doug would follow behind, and then we would be seated. Phillip and his best man would be standing at the altar already. I was at a wedding recently where the groom seated his parents. I thought it was really special, but I don't want to upset you."

"Why would that upset me?"

Mrs. Mac looks at me with real concern. "Because your parents aren't here to walk with you, and from what Phillip said, you're walking down the aisle by yourself."

"I thought about walking by myself, like as a way to honor my parents, but I changed my mind. I asked a special man in my life to give me away."

Mrs. D's eyes flood with tears. She turns to Mrs. Mac and says, "She asked Chuck."

I DROP THE moms off and then head home. When I walk into my condo, the lights are dimmed, my mom's crystal candlesticks are holding dark purple tapers, the table is set, and I can smell Italian food.

Phillip takes my coat, kisses me, leads me over to the table, and pulls out a chair for me.

"What's all this for?" I ask.

"This is a big thank-you for including my mom. She called me before you guys headed back home and said it was one of the best days she'd ever had. She's very excited for our wedding and very happy that you included her." He pours us champagne and then makes a toast. "Exactly two months from today, we'll be on our honeymoon."

"That's a good reason to celebrate, and I'm glad I invited them. She and Mrs. D had some great ideas for everything from the welcome gifts to the reception. They adored Amy and loved tasting the cake, and we had a lot of fun."

Phillip takes my flute and sets it on the table. "You know, I think maybe dinner can wait." He takes my hand and leads me into the bedroom where there are even more candles lit.

He strips off my clothes and massages my entire body with an amazing-smelling lavender body oil. I couldn't care less about dinner. All I want is him.

"I'm gonna be nicer to your mom more often, I'm just saying."

A miracle sent down by God himself.

SATURDAY, NOVEMBER 18TH

PHILLIP AND I stop by his parents' before heading to Neil's to watch the Nebraska game. I'm updating Mrs. Mac on a few wedding details when she lets out a big sigh.

"I still haven't found a dress. Ashley and I have gone shopping a lot, but I just can't seem to find anything. The wedding is going to be so pretty and romantic. Is it bad that I don't want to look like the mother of the groom?"

"What do you mean?"

She frowns. "I know I'm the mother of the groom, but I don't want to look old. In all the dresses Ash likes, I've felt like my mother."

"Ashley doesn't have a whole lot of patience either. I'm sure she gets mad at you when she likes something and you don't."

"Exactly. I let her pick out the dress I wore to her wedding, and I hated that thing. I looked like a banana."

We laugh. Ashley's wedding was very yellow.

"Let's go shopping today," I suggest.

"But the game is on soon, and I thought you had a party to go to."

"Even better," I sort of shock myself by saying. "That means the stores won't be crowded. And we see Neil all the time. It won't

217

kill us to miss it."

Somehow—possibly it's a miracle sent down from God himself—I'm able to convince Phillip and Mr. Mac that they need to skip watching the game and come with us.

That it's important.

Mrs. Mac sweetens the deal when she promises to record the game and make her gorgonzola-stuffed burgers with mushroom wine sauce for dinner. Who can refuse that?

MRS. MAC AND Ashley have been shopping in bridal stores, looking at typical mother-of-the-groom dresses. I suggest we look at holiday dresses instead. Phillip whines and says he can't shop on an empty stomach, so we head to an upscale mall and have lunch first. We even have wine. I joke and tell Phillip that, since he was whining, he needed wine.

As we walk out of the restaurant and head toward the dress shop, Phillip says, "Hey, do you mind if Dad and I go to the jewelry store while you try on dresses?"

I am ready to lay into Phillip because the whole point of this shopping trip is to find his mom a dress and not sneak off to the jewelry store where they're probably hoping to find a TV.

Phillip's mom looks at me, sees I'm about to blow, and says happily, "That sounds like a plan. We'll text you when we find something."

She makes a beeline to the dress shop, so I follow along.

When we get out of earshot of the guys, she grabs my arm. "JJ, you never, *ever* tell your man *not* to go in a jewelry store. Seriously."

And I realize she probably has a point.

We go to a great little boutique that's fully stocked with holiday dresses, so we have a lot of nice dresses to choose from.

"Do you have a preference as to what color I wear?" she asks.

"What do you think would look good?"

"Well, I showed my friends a picture of the bridesmaid dresses and told them your colors. They thought either silver, light purple, dark purple, or black."

"Hmm, I love black dresses, but I'm afraid you'd blend in with the boys. Your son is getting married. I think you should stand out."

With that remark, I make her cry.

"I'm so lucky to be getting you for a daughter-in-law," she tells me while wiping the corners of her eyes.

With our criteria in mind, we enlist the salesperson's help and find six dresses for her to try on. And, kinda like with my dress, one just stands out.

The dress is a gorgeous deep purple color. It's strapless with an empire waist, and the skirt flows perfectly over her curves. The bodice sparkles with matching purple beading, and the color looks beautiful with her complexion. Honestly, Phillip's mom is looking hot in this dress.

She loves it. She's grinning, holding the skirt, and twirling around. "Do you think I'm too old to wear a dress like this? Everything Ashley and I tried on at the bridal store looked much more matronly. I'm the mother. Can I wear a dress that looks like I belong singing in a nightclub?" But then she's like, "But look at the way it twirls when I dance, and it's surprisingly lightweight, even with the beading. What do you think?"

"You haven't tried them all on yet, but this is my favorite. You look gorgeous, and I don't think you should look matronly. You certainly don't look old enough to have a son who's getting married."

"You just sold me." She giggles. "But this is fun. I think I'll try on the rest."

"Let me take a pic of you and send it to Mrs. D, so we can get her opinion."

I take a pic of her and send it off. She's in a silver sequined gown that's so heavy, she can hardly walk when Mrs. D texts back, *LOVE IT!*

She tries on the other dresses and then puts the purple one back on. I text Phillip to come look at it.

Phillip says, "Damn, Mom, are you sure that dress isn't too sexy?"

Mrs. Mac blushes, and I swear, I see Mr. Mac slide him a twenty.

AFTER SHE BUYS the dress, Phillip says, "Hey, we haven't registered yet, and the jewelry store has great dishes. Wanna go register? We need to look at wedding bands, too."

I've been dreading registering because Lori told me I needed to picture what kind of dishes I would want to serve my children holiday dinners on. What dishes I want to feed Phillip a lovingly made dinner from every night. What color my kitchen would be, so my mixer would match.

Registering felt like a huge task, but it isn't.

We walk in, look at the fine china patterns, look at each other, and say, "That one."

Then, we pick out flatware, and Phillip's dad picks out a stemware pattern that I love. It's gorgeous, heavy crystal, but the glass is cut in a modern way.

Phillip's mom shows us the items that she loves to use when entertaining and those things that are too much of a hassle to deal with. Like real silver. Yes, it's shiny and gorgeous in the store, but who has time to deal with it?

And, instead of registering being a chore, it's a breeze. I think Phillip and I were just confused by all of the possibilities, but here, with his parents' help, all our picks make sense. Phillip's mom even suggests we register for a few holiday pieces. She says people will love knowing we'll use them every year.

When we are done, Phillip takes me over to look at wedding bands. I'm a bit overwhelmed by all the sparkle in the case, and I don't see one that is slightly curved, like my ring.

"I don't think any of these will fit my ring. I don't really need a wedding band, Phillip. My engagement ring is enough."

"No way, Princess. You're not getting out of wearing a wedding band that easily. I want everyone to know you're married." He touches my ring finger. "I also heard you talking to Lori about what kind of band you thought would look pretty, so I had one made. We snuck over here earlier to see if it was finished. Wanna see it?"

I have to control myself not to jump up and down in the middle of the store and scream, *Of course I wanna see it!*

A salesperson brings out a box and sets it in front of me. I slowly open the lid.

"Holy shit!" I say loudly.

Everyone in the store turns to stare at me.

I lower my head and say breathlessly, "Phillip, it's gorgeous."

My engagement ring has an X on each side that's filled with baguette diamonds. The wedding band has three rows of the same baguettes. I take my engagement ring off, so I can try it on.

Phillip slides the band on my finger. "Just think, the next time I put this ring on your finger, we'll be saying our vows. What do you think about writing our own vows?"

I'm pretty sure I'd agree to just about anything right now. Vows, murder, cheating, armed robbery. Yeah, whatever, I'm in.

I hold the ring up, watch it sparkle in the lights, and then put my engagement ring on top of it. "Sure, Phillip. Vows ... yeah, we can do that." I look at my hand some more. "Wow, this is pretty amazing."

"I think you're just easy to impress with a little bling."

He gives me a sweet kiss on the cheek while I think, *This is a heck of a lot more than a little bling.*

I decide to take a lesson from Mrs. Mac and not say a word.

Because, if he wants to think this is a little bling, I can't imagine the day he tries to impress me with some big bling.

What is it about boys and boobs?

THURSDAY, NOVEMBER 23RD

WE'RE WORN OUT from our annual Thanksgiving football game and stuffed from Thanksgiving dinner, but we head to the bar to meet up with our friends. It's become a tradition, too.

Danny and Lori are in town, so they join us.

I ask Lori, "Have you thought of any baby names yet?"

"A few. I kind of like Sloan or Carly for a girl. And we've been thinking about some meaningful names. Like, Hayden Fry was a great football coach, so Danny thought Hayden might be cool for a boy. I don't know that much about football, so I suggested Madden."

"I love that name!"

"I do, too, but he thought it was hilarious that the only name I knew was from an Xbox game. Of course, he idolizes Tom Osborne, the great college coach, but I don't care for either Tom or Osborne as a first name. Danny thought Osborne Diamond sounded super awesome. I didn't mind that until he told me he'd call the kid Ozzy. Um, no. I don't think so."

Phillip, who has been drinking all day and is a little tipsy, says goofily, "I know! You could name your daughter Carat. Get it? Carat Diamond."

Katie and Lisa say at the same time, "Hope! What about Hope

Diamond?"

I haven't been partaking in the drinking today.

I know; shocker, right?

I didn't drink earlier because I'm so competitive when it comes to the annual football game. Then, after the game, when I was stuffing myself with turkey and all sorts of other goodies, I kept drinking water. I'm hoping the water will absorb some of the hundred million calories I've consumed and will quickly flush them out of my body. I want to make sure my wedding dress fits!

Phillip's doing shots with the boys, so I'm being responsible and just sipping on a martini. I wanted a raspberry martini, but Lori made me get a cosmopolitan just so she could smell it. After a few minutes of her sniffing my drink, I begged the bartender for a nonalcoholic version. Now, she's torn between loving the feel of the martini glass in her hand and being horrified that people will think she's drinking alcohol.

She rolls her eyes at Phillip's suggestion of Carat Diamond and continues our conversation, "I think Damon is my favorite for a boy."

"Damon Diamond. I like that."

"Another Big D," Joey says, slapping Danny on the back.

"Really, it should be Double D," I stupidly say.

It causes all the guys to hoot and holler.

What is it about boys and boobs?

Neil yells, "Double D! Ah, yeah, baby. Gotta love those. You should definitely pick a D name for your daughter. Lori's got big cans, so maybe your daughter will, too."

All the guys laugh and start coming up with D names. They throw out Darcy, Daisy, Daniella, and Dani.

Danny says, "We can't give a girl the same name as me. That would be dumb. I do think Destiny would be kinda cute though."

Joey giggles. "Destiny Diamond. That totally sounds like a stripper name. That'd be so hot."

"You know, I've kinda been freaking out over being a father, but then I read in a men's magazine somewhere that, as long as you can keep your son off the pipe and your daughter off the pole, then you've done a good job."

Lori is sitting next to me. She hasn't moved an inch, but I swear, I just felt the earth shift. Like she's a volcano waiting to erupt.

She gives Danny the evilest stare I've ever seen. Way worse than the death stare she gave me at her candle passing. And that almost killed me.

Danny is kinda drunk, and he's having fun, goofing around. I don't think he realizes that this is in no way funny to Lori.

She grabs his hand across the table to get his attention and says madly, "I've been puking daily, listening to classical music that I hate, and drinking only organic juices. I haven't had a cup of coffee, a Diet Coke, or a beer in months. I've painted the nursery with non-toxic paint, so the baby won't get cancer, and bought baby Einstein toys. And you mean to tell me that your only goal for our child is to not be a stripper or a drug addict?"

"We're just messing around, having fun. Relax, Lori," Danny says.

She pulls her hand away from him. "You're right. That's exactly what I need to do." She says, "Excuse me," to the table and slides out of her chair.

She and her baby bump make their way up to the bar. A few minutes later, she comes back with two shots of tequila and a pack of cigarettes.

She's about to make a point, I think.

Danny and the boys are still enjoying the baby-name game. Danny's laughing hysterically about another stripper name.

Neil says, "How about Dakota Diamond? She could wear a cowboy hat, boots, and a rhinestone thong."

The guys all laugh hysterically. Phillip is wiping tears from his eyes. The only time Phillip laughs so much he cries is when he's drunk.

I watch Lori open the pack of cigarettes. She takes one out, puts it in her mouth, and lights it.

She takes a pretend drag, slides a shot glass in front of me, and says loudly, "To my future child."

I hold my shot glass in the air while I kick Danny under the table.

He looks at Lori in horror and grabs the shot glass away from her. "What are you doing?"

Her voice is surprisingly calm as she says, "Why should I make all these sacrifices for our child when your expectations are so low?"

"We're just teasing. I have goals for our child. Big goals. And I'm so proud of all you've done. I'm sorry, baby."

What a suck-up.

Lori seems to be appeased though. She smashes out the cigarette, moves the ashtray as far away as she can, and then announces that she has to pee.

When she's safely in the restroom, Danny turns to me, clinks the shot glass against mine, and downs the shot. Then, he takes mine and downs it, too.

Somehow, I don't think it will be his last of the pregnancy.

"This isn't going to be easy, is it?" he asks.

I just smile at him because I really don't have an answer.

phillip is picking up bad habits!

MONDAY, NOVEMBER 27TH

I FEEL LIKE I'm out in the wilderness, hunting for my dinner without a gun.

And it's hopeless that I'll ever find myself a meal because Phillip won't let me have a gun. He says women shouldn't carry guns. And, when I ask if I could have a knife or a sword or a grenade or even a bow and arrow, he just keeps saying no, no, no.

And *no* is not a word I like to hear.

I adore Phillip, but he really needs to set foot in this century.

Why do I feel this way?

Because we're looking at houses, and we can't seem to agree on what to spend. Phillip is conservative and has a strict budget in mind, and nothing I say can change that stubborn mind.

I've offered to get money out of my trust, so we can afford something a little nicer. Preferably something in Danny and Lori's neighborhood. Phillip says no. He doesn't want me to spend any of my money on the house. I've even tried to be creative. I've offered a lot of money. I've offered little amounts of money. I've offered monthly money.

But still, no.

He has his mind made up that we can afford X amount, and there is no discussion about it.

Which, I'm sorry, is bullshit. We're going to be married. *Shouldn't we be able to discuss this?*

Does Phillip really believe that he wears the pants in the family? I thought we were gonna have a pants-free relationship!

This is why couples counseling is bullshit.

Phillip is picking up bad habits there!

Where's the calm, reasonable Phillip that I know and love?

Where's the guy who can't stand to see me pout?

Not in the car with me today apparently because I just tried to bring up the budget subject again, and he shut me down. I even gave him my adorable, irresistible pout, and he ignored it!

I'M LAZILY RUBBING Phillip's back. He loves when I rub his back after sex. He's also usually in a pretty damn good mood. Lori says she could ask Danny for anything she wanted after sex, and he'd probably agree to it. She also says that she lets Danny think he wears the pants in the family.

I'm wondering if she might be on to something. My usual tactics aren't working at all, so maybe I do need a subtler approach.

"Phillip, I was thinking that maybe part of the reason we're having a hard time finding a house is because we haven't given the realtor much to go on. All you've given her is a price range. Maybe we should talk about what we really want."

He considers the question, probably trying to gauge its threat level. He must decide we're still at DEFCON 1 because he says, "You might be right. We haven't been very helpful. What do I want? I wanna be able to afford it."

"Yes, that one we already know." I sigh. Maybe this isn't going to work.

But he goes on, "I'd also like a modern kitchen with granite countertops. I'd like a room where we can entertain, maybe play pool, watch TV."

Wow. We might be making progress. I want those things, too!

"I agree with you, Phillip. What else?"

"Having a three-car garage would be nice—you know, in case we decide to get another car."

"You don't want to spend any money on a house, and now, you want another car?"

"Not now, but eventually, yes."

I decide not to start a fight.

I'm so amiable tonight. I don't know what's gotten into me.

"Okay, what else?"

"A big backyard and a hot tub for sure. I miss how we used to sit in the hot tub and talk for hours."

I smile at him, remembering all those talks in college. How we would dream about our futures. "I miss the hot tub, too, and you know how I like the water. I'd love it if we had a big bathtub." Things are going well, so I decide to push it just a bit. "I'd also love to have some kind of view."

"We cannot afford to live by Danny. I'm not a professional quarterback, okay?"

"That's not what I meant, Phillip. I just don't want a backyard where my view is nothing but a tall wooden fence. That would drive me nuts! I get that you don't want to spend any money and have any fun."

"Do you have any idea what they spent on their house? Even with the raise I'm getting, I can't afford that."

"Yeah, I do. And the remodel, too. I don't know why you're being so stubborn about this. Let's take what you're comfortable spending and pay the rest from my trust."

"I can't do that. That's your money, and if something happened to us ..."

"Phillip? What are you saying? Are you saying you don't think we're gonna work out?"

"Well, if you don't stop bugging me about this, we might not work out. I have a good job. I don't need your handouts to buy my wife a house."

My mouth flops open. I quickly clamp it shut because I think we just got to the root of the problem.

I need to think more about the best way to approach this. I'm pretty sure some sex and a back rub aren't gonna work in this situation. Besides, I've been looking at the listings every day, and there's nothing for sale worth fighting over.

Might as well let him wear the pants for a little while longer.

Speaking of pants …

He's not wearing any, so I slide my hand between his legs, kiss his neck, say, "We'll work out just fine," and let him take control.

He needs to learn to compromise.

TUESDAY, NOVEMBER 28TH

IF IT WASN'T for the promise of margaritas afterward, I don't think I could get through couples counseling.

Did I mention how much I hate these stupid, blue-checkered chairs?

I'm fantasizing about how I'm going to sneak into Pastor John's office, steal them, and burn them. That way, no other couple will ever have to sit in them again. I'm going to steal his records and invite all the other couples who've been tortured here. We'll stand around the chairs, have a big bonfire, and roast weenies that look like Pastor John.

Pastor John brings up the subject of money, which catches my attention. I realize that Lori might be right. Maybe we *do* need counseling! Phillip definitely needs counseling in this area anyway. He needs to learn the art of compromise!

The pastor hands us each a financial questionnaire.

After we write down our answers, he takes them from us.

Shit!

I didn't know he was gonna take them! Last time, he didn't take them!

Double shit!

I cringe as Pastor John reads them back to us. "The first question asks what your spending habits are and if you agree on them. JJ, you wrote, *I buy shoes. He buys beer and shit for his car, and we try to pretend it doesn't bother us. So, yes, we agree. Oh shoot, I probably shouldn't say shit on a religious paper. Cross that out.*"

Phillip raises an eyebrow at me. I'm slightly mortified. I really wish I could read his mind because then I'd know if I'm in trouble for cussing or for what I said.

I whisper to him, "I didn't know he was gonna read them! Last time, he didn't read them!"

Pastor John continues, "Phillip wrote, *This is probably an area we need to discuss. Especially since we need to buy a house soon. JJ is pretty conservative with her money, so it will work out well.*"

Awww. Phillip is so sweet, but he's so completely clueless. I've been conservative with my trust money, but the money I make at my job, not so much.

Like, not at all.

That's why I have so many shoes. An assassin would have no trouble profiling me. He'd look at my credit card statements and quickly find my weakness for shoes and drinks. I'd die, holding a cocktail and a bag of shoes.

Not a bad way to go now that I think about it. Actually, scratch that.

I'd die never having worn the shoes.

That'd suck.

Phillip reaches over and holds my hand. I grin lovingly back at him.

Danny's not the only one who can suck up.

The pastor keeps going, "The next question asks if you have set any mutual long-term financial goals. JJ, you wrote, *Uh, no*, and Phillip wrote, *I have quite a few long-term goals for myself, but this is something we need to discuss.* I'd say that's a good idea, Phillip."

Oh, sure. Phillip's the star student. If I had known he was gonna read them, I would've tried harder.

"I think we can probably guess whether or not JJ has made a budget yet, but here's what your bride wrote, Phillip. *If there's money in my account, I spend it. Does that count?*"

Phillip chuckles. I guess at least I can make him laugh.

"Okay," I say, "I think we've heard enough. We haven't talked at all about money. In fact, we've been arguing about how much to spend on a house. Phillip won't negotiate. Couples counseling has corrupted him. Now, he thinks he wears the pants in the family."

Phillip narrows his eyes at me. "I'm not negotiating because we can't afford what you want." He turns toward Pastor John and says, "We'll figure it out. Thanks for making us aware that this could be an issue."

The pastor says, "It's definitely an issue. Money problems are one of the top reasons marriages fail. I think I'll let you go early today. Why don't you go home and discuss how to overcome this challenge?"

He's letting us out early? Taco Tuesday, here we come!

I sneak my phone out of my coat pocket, hide it under my leg, and text Joey.

Me: The warden is letting us out early due to bad behavior! We'll be there soon!

"I agree," I say quickly. "We should go home and work on it right away."

AS WE'RE WALKING out to the car, Phillip says, "So, we're going home to talk about our budget, huh?"

Ha!

"No! We're going to the bar and getting you a few drinks. Then, we'll go home and discuss it in bed."

"I thought we'd learned that sex doesn't resolve conflict."

I think about how my mom used to handle my stubborn dad and say sweetly, "Phillip, we don't have a conflict. I'll do whatever you think is best."

His head snaps toward me, and he looks at me with wide brown eyes. I think I just shocked him.

"Really?" he says. "You don't wanna argue about it?"

"Nope, I trust you. You set the budget, and we'll find a great house."

He looks confused. "Are you trying to trick me?"

"I don't think so," I say.

Even though I totally am. If he picks the wrong house, he'll feel guilty about it. He won't wanna feel guilty; plus, he'll want to please me, so I'm hoping this is like reverse psychology.

Make him feel in control, even when he's not.

Is nothing sacred with these women?

FRIDAY, DECEMBER 1ST

WE'RE IN VEGAS for my bachelorette party!

We got into town early this morning, checked in, and immediately headed to the spa. We all had massages, facials, and body scrubs. We soaked in the whirlpool, ate lunch, drank lots of water and a little wine, and then headed back to our suite. We're going to have a drink while we figure out our dinner and clubbing plans.

I plop down on the couch between Chelsea and Katie. "Are you guys tired?"

Chelsea says, "I'm so relaxed; I don't feel like moving."

"Who knew a spa day could wear you out so much?" Katie agrees.

"So, what do you guys wanna do? Should we get ready to go out?" Lori asks everyone.

Katie and I groan at the thought of getting ready.

Lori happily continues, "Well, if we don't feel like going anywhere, let's get comfy, order room service, and just stay here and chill."

I know Lisa is dying to hit the clubs, but Lori looks tired. I quickly agree with her. "I think that sounds like a great idea!" I'm hoping everyone is either too tired or too polite to disagree with what the bachelorette wants.

The smile Lori gives me sorta melts my heart. She wants me to have fun but wants so much to be a part of everything. I bet it's kinda hard, being the only one who can't drink. If we stay here, she'll be happy, and I want her to be happy.

Lori grabs Katie off the big sectional couch, drags her into the bedroom, and comes back lugging gift-wrapped packages.

"What's all this?" I ask.

"Open them and see!" she says.

I watch the girls open their presents. I love watching people open presents. The girls pull matching purple velour Juicy Couture sweatsuits out from purple glitter tissue paper.

Lori tells everyone, "I got these for us to wear while we're getting ready the day of the wedding, but we can all put them on now!" She notices I haven't opened mine yet. "Jade, open yours! Yours is the best."

I slowly unwrap the present. Savoring it, like I always do. I also have matching sweats.

Lori pulls the jacket out of the box and holds it up. "Look, everyone!"

The backs of all the jackets have *Juicy* written across them. Mine has been customized with black and silver rhinestones that spell out *Bride*.

I am a JUICY Bride.

(Insert your own joke here. I'm really too relaxed to feel witty.)

WE HAVE A great time, just lounging, eating, and drinking. But, as the wine bottles are emptied, what's supposed to be a sweet, relaxing night turns into a wine-fueled roast of the bride.

As in me.

I swear, they're telling every humiliating dating story about me!

Is nothing sacred with these women?

I'm feeling pretty mellow though, and I have to admit, some of the things that have happened with me and boys are pretty amusing.

I should write a book about it.

Not a how-to book. No. This would be a revolutionary book.

It would start a whole new category of books. Screw the self-help books.

Instead of a book telling you what to do, this book would tell you what *not* to do.

A how-not-to book.

Things you should be wary of. Things you should never do. Lines you should never fall for. Basically, how to survive college.

This book would probably be the size of *War and Peace*, especially if I, like, went on the internet and compiled other girls' how-not-tos as well.

Chelsea, my adorable sorority baby sister, starts the whole thing by saying, "Remember when that guy called Jadyn by the wrong name, and she believed his lame-ass excuse?"

They all laugh hysterically.

> **DO NOT #1:** *If a guy calls you another name, you should run away! DO NOT believe him when he says he was just reading a novel for his Advanced Literature class and related to the character and his feelings for his love, who, "Oh, baby, reminds me so much of you that I accidentally said her name."*

Yeah, don't fall for that. He's lying. I'm pretty sure there were no girls named Kelsey in any Advanced Literature books.

Katie laughs. "She always used to fall for the line, *Let's go to my room, so we can talk in private.*"

Lori, who hasn't even had any wine, giggles at me. "Everyone knows that one, Jade. How do you even fall for that?"

I'm pretty sure that's one of those rhetorical questions, so I don't even bother to reply.

DO NOT #2: DO NOT believe him when he says he wants to go someplace quiet to talk, especially if you're tipsy. Talking is the very last thing on his mind.

The girls keep giggling.

Lori half-laughs and half-screams, "What about when everyone thought she was the threesome video girl?"

I decide to defend myself on this one. "It's not my fault I'm nice. He asked me out in such a cute way."

Lori laughs. "He handed you a dandelion! How was that cute? That's, like, the lamest thing ever!"

"No, it wasn't. Phillip used to pick me dandelions when we were kids. It was adorable."

DO NOT #3: If you are best friends with two hot guys and you decide to date a slightly smaller, somewhat insecure guy who's adorable in the I rescued this lost kitten *sort of way, DO NOT bring your hot, buff roommates to the bar to meet him. He will immediately think that all you do when you go home is lie around naked, have sex, and make sex videos.*

Yes, that's what his feeble little mind came up with, and because he was insecure, he also chose to spread that sweet, adorable thought all around campus. For three seemingly unending weeks, I got numerous texts from guys who wanted to *get to know me better* with their cameras. And others who wanted me to send them *just one* naked picture.

It's like they wanted proof to show their friends that they had in fact kissed (or whatever) the threesome video girl.

Chelsea giggles. "Oh my gosh! Do you remember the night she hurled burritos and tequila all over the frat house?"

DO NOT #4: DO NOT get drunk off tequila shots and

*then attempt to navigate through a fraternity party to find
your friend and usual rescuer because, sometimes, you can't
find him in your drunken state, and you're forced to send up
a flare or smoke signals or something.*

In this particular case, the signal was me hurling tequila, beer,
and a burrito dinner all over the dance floor and half the crowd
there.

I will mention though that this is a very effective way to clear
the place out and force your friend to get off the girl he was doing
God knows what with and come help you. It does not, however,
earn you points with the guy who gave you all the tequila shots in
the first place.

Lori grabs my arm. "Jade, wasn't that the same guy who said,
if you squeezed your left hand into a fist, then you wouldn't have a
gag reflex?"

I roll my eyes. "Yes, he's the one. Thanks for remembering."

Lisa and Katie roll around on the couch, holding their sides
and laughing.

Lisa screeches, "Who would ever believe that? Even I'm not
that dumb!"

Chelsea almost spits out her wine; she's laughing so hard.

*DO NOT #5: DO NOT believe a boy who tells you that, if
you squeeze your left hand into a fist, then you will not have
a gag reflex, and therefore, putting something of his in your
mouth will be fine even though you told him you were already feeling a little spinny and nauseous.*

Obviously, the squeezed fist is a myth, and he should've been
thankful that I didn't throw up all over his room.

I cringe. "Can we please talk about something else?"

Lori and Chelsea look at each other, grab hands, and scream,
"SKITTLES VODKA!"

DO NOT #6: *DO NOT listen when football players tell you adding Skittles to vodka makes it less strong and more like candy. It will still mess you up.*

Chelsea screams, "No, wait! I have one. Remember the night we made her wear the Do Not Buy Me Shots button to the bar? Ohmigawd, that night was classic!"

DO NOT #7: *DO NOT ever let your friends make you wear a button to the bar that says DO NOT BUY ME SHOTS. This button is like having a beacon on your body that says DO Buy Me Shots because there are boys out there with that Christopher Columbus attitude. They want to go to new frontiers and explore new worlds. And those types of boys will want to discover exactly what happens when you do. And, without going into detail here, trust me; it's not pretty.*

Lori laughs some more. "What about the slutty hot-tub video?"

"We don't need to talk about that," I say, laughing and covering my face in fake shame. That night was really fun.

DO NOT #8: *DO NOT let a bunch of your best friend's fraternity brothers talk you into seeing how many guys you can fit in the hot tub with. Just say no and go to bed. And, if you can't say that, try to say no when they get out the cooking oil and rub everyone down with it, thinking that will allow more people to fit. I'm telling you, if there is enough Jägermeister involved, anything is possible. And, if you do all this anyway, then at least DO NOT let someone record the process and post it on YouTube. No matter what, it's gonna look slutty. And, on a side note, it might be a good idea to untag yourself from said video, so your future employers don't see it when they Google your name.*

Katie grabs her laptop, finds the video, and plays it for everyone. They think it's hilarious.

I think I'll just have a little more wine.

It's at this point that I really wanna call Phillip, but I know I shouldn't. He's probably at a strip club with some gorgeous, fake-boobed babe gyrating on his lap. But, as Katie and Lisa start telling the *keg in the cornfield* story, specifically how Jake announced my virginity to the world, well, I cave.

I send him a text.

I figure I won't get one back at all, but I guess it makes me feel better, knowing that, if he sees it, maybe he'll think about me for just a minute between stuffing dollar bills down some chick's thong.

> **Me:** Just wanted to say I love you and miss you. This is the first night I've spent away from you in almost three months.

I'm surprised by his immediate response.

> **Phillip:** I miss you and love you more.
>
> **Me:** Are you having a lot of fun?
>
> **Phillip:** I'd be having more fun if I were with you.
>
> **Me:** Me, too!
>
> **Phillip:** Danny will take my phone away if he sees me texting you, but I love you. And don't worry about tonight. There's no one for me but you. <3

And I feel happy for the rest of the night.

Define pretty wild.

SATURDAY, DECEMBER 2ND

THE NEXT MORNING, I'm buzzed awake by my phone, and I hear Phillip's sexy voice say, "Hey, Princess, you awake?"

"Kinda. Why are you up? Are you just getting in? Are you sick?"

"Nah, I got in around four, and why would I be sick?"

"Last night was your bachelor party. Aren't you supposed to be puking this morning? Or did you last night?"

"You know I don't like to get that drunk. There was a lot of shot-drinking though, and it was pretty wild. But you know Danny and, well, the rest of the crew, too."

"Define *pretty wild.*"

Phillip chuckles. "The groom had lots of fun drinking and being stupid. He even greatly enjoyed the strip club, mostly because he was laughing so hard at Dillon and Cooper. But, mostly, he was thinking about how much he missed his Princess. Did you and the girls have fun? Are you hanging?"

"Maybe a little."

"I figured. I miss you."

"I miss you more."

Danny texts me around ten thirty.

Danny: Our suite, 11 a.m. An appropriate outfit is being delivered to your room. There will be other girls dressed similarly, so don't freak.

There's a knock at my door. I open it, and a concierge hands me a little gift bag. I set it on my bed and pull the outfit out. What there is of it.

Me: OMG!!! Seriously? I can't wear that!

Danny: Oh, come on. He's gonna love it.

Me: Are you still drunk?

Danny: Maybe. We haven't stopped drinking. In fact, right now, I'm a doctor.

Me: Let me guess … all you prescribe is cranberry and vodka?

Danny: Yes'm! I'm drinking one right now! YUMMY!

Me: I'm gonna need some liquid courage to even put this thing on!

Danny: Go do two shots. Then, I have a confession.

Me: Did Phillip sleep with a stripper???

Danny: No!!!

Me: Did you?

Danny: No. Shots and then answers.

Me: Fine.

I go to the bar in our suite, pour myself a shot, say a prayer that Danny's brilliant idea doesn't backfire, and then toss the shot back. I do another one and then decide to make myself a screwdriver. Those always taste good in the morning even if you have a slight wine hangover.

Me: Shots fired, Captain. Time for answers.

Danny: *You know how you keep telling me I'm a professional quarterback, so I need to get rid of the old Tahoe?*

Me: *Yeah.*

Danny: *After quite a few shots, things got a little crazy, and I kinda did.*

Me: *Danny! OMG! Did you go to the Ferrari dealership downstairs?*

Danny: *Maybe.*

Me: *Lori is gonna freak!!! I'm so excited for you! Which one did you get?*

Danny: *Red F430 Spider. :)*

Me: *OMG! That's awesome, Danny. I can't wait to see it! Ride in it! Drive it!*

Danny: *That means you'll help me tell her?*

Me: *Yeshhh.*

Danny: *Put on the outfit and send me a pic.*

I put on the outfit. A minuscule black leather bustier, an even smaller thong, black fishnet thigh highs, and a matching leather mask to cover my eyes. I add a pair of black stripper heels I brought to wear to the club tonight.

Me: *I'm NOT sending a picture! You're all about to see WAY more of me than you should! I can't believe you talked me into this! You do realize, this could backfire horribly!*

Danny: *How could it backfire?*

Me: *What if I see Phillip doing something with one of the stripper girls? What if he's not attracted to me? It could break us up. I don't think the bride belongs at the bachelor party.*

Danny: *This isn't the bachelor party. This is just a little fun. If Phillip wanted someone else, he had plenty of opportunities last night. Girls like him. I was a little jealous.*

Me: *What did he do? No, wait, I don't wanna know.*

Danny: *He did the same thing I did. Enjoyed girls flirting with him and looked but didn't touch. I can't say that for the rest of the crew though.*

Me: *Really? OMG, that makes me so happy.*

Danny: *Do another shot. I'm having one. Do one with me. Like, right now.*

Me: *Okay.*

Danny: *Here's to happy endings. Hopefully, Phillip's.*

Me: *You're so bad. Cheers.*

Danny: *Get your skinny ass down here. The other girls are waiting in the hallway for you.*

I put on a coat and walk to their suite. As Danny said, there are three other girls dressed similarly to me. The problem is, they look *way* better than me. They have big boobs, great, curvy hips, and sexy, lush red lips. I remembered to put on some tinted lip gloss, but then I drank most of the screwdriver. My lips are probably orange and pulpy.

I wipe the corners of them just in case.

When the four of us girls walk in, it's going to be like that game they used to have on TV when I was little. There was some song … like, *Which one of these things doesn't belong?*

That would be me.

"So, you're the bride, huh? It's pretty cool you're doing this," one of the dancers says.

"You think so? I was just thinking it could backfire. Like, if he likes me but doesn't know it's me, he's in trouble. If he doesn't think I'm sexy like you guys are, he's in trouble. If he likes one of you, he's in trouble. I don't think this is a good idea."

"Come on, he'll love it. When the time's right, just tell him. Or take off your mask. He'll be shocked, but he'll love it."

"What am I even supposed to do? I'm not that good of a dancer."

"Just go straight to him, shimmy in front of him a little, and then do a lap dance."

I mentally thank Lori for buying the stripper's workout. If it wasn't for that, I wouldn't have a clue.

We go into the suite. The boys are trying to act cool.

Well, except for Joey and Dillon, who are chanting, "Take it off."

I move in front of Phillip. He's so adorable, and, well, I'm in a mask. I might as well have some fun with him. I sit on his lap, straddling him. Run my hands through his hair the way I always do. He has a grin on his face, but he's not touching me. He sorta has his hands limply down by his sides. I grind into his lap, then get up, and decide to dance in front of him.

I do what is probably the stupidest circle-twirl thing ever seen. *Why didn't my mom make me take dance lessons? Why did she let me play soccer? Didn't she know every girl needed to know how to dance at some point in her life?*

When I turn back around to face Phillip, his eyes roll down my body.

I hear Nick from behind me yell, "Come on, Mac, show her what ya got!"

Phillip squints his eyes at me, flashes a big grin, gives Nick a thumbs-up, and then pulls me onto his lap. Then, he puts his hands firmly across my ass and pulls me in even closer!

I swear, I'm going to kill him.

The boys think it's awesome.

Neil hoots, "Way to go, Mac!"

Joey goes, "Ah, yeah, baby!"

I'm super conflicted. Part of me wants to rip this mask off and scream at Phillip and all his stupid friends, *You assholes!* The other part of me wants to stay in character just to see how far he'll take this. I choose the latter.

I wrap my arms around his neck and nuzzle my boobs into his face.

I figure that'll be a good test. Surely, he'll pull his face away!

But he doesn't! He tightens his grip on my ass and starts kissing and licking my cleavage!

Nick screams out, "*That's* what I'm talking about!"

Oh my God! That's it!

I'm going to kill him, and then I'm gonna break up with him.

He licks up the side of my neck with his tongue.

The guys are going crazy, cheering him on. When his tongue touches my ear, I'm about to blow.

He whispers, "That's a pretty sexy tattoo you have there, miss."

He's referring to the little angel wings I have tattooed on my hip. He and Danny have matching ones on their ankles.

I forgot about that. It's clearly visible.

He continues, "You know, this is my bachelor party."

I try to answer in a different voice, "I heard."

"I'm supposed to have, like, random sex with hot girls at my bachelor party. So, I was thinking …"

"I don't think it's your brain that's thinking."

"Wanna go to my room?"

I smile at him. I love this boy, and I'm more than willing to play along. "Lead the way, baby." I start to get up, but then I stop. "Um, you do know that I charge five hundred dollars for that?"

Phillip holds out his hands. "I don't have any cash."

I get off his lap and lean my boobs down into his face. "Oh, that's really too bad. There are these shoes I want, but my boyfriend gets mad at me when I buy shoes, so this is how I earn my shoe money."

He studies my masked face and then slowly runs his eyes down my body. "Don't move."

He strides over to Danny and says a few words to him.

Danny gets his wallet out. I hear Danny mutter, "That's a bargain compared to last night."

Phillip comes back with a handful of ones and five crisp hundred-dollar bills. I reach out to grab the money, but he pulls it back fast.

"Oh, not so fast. You have to earn it first."

As the boys cheer, I take his hand, follow him into his room, and earn myself a new pair of shoes.

DANNY AND I are the first ones down at the bar. He's struggling with buyer's remorse.

"Jay, should I feel guilty?"

"Not at all," I tell him. "Hey, can we go see it?"

"Yeah, if you'll tell me why I shouldn't feel guilty on the way."

As we walk down the brightly decorated hall, I say, "Danny, it's okay to buy yourself just one thing as a reward for all your hard work. Now, if you start buying a whole fleet of *whips*, I'm gonna have to whip you with my XXX wedding favors."

Danny laughs heartily.

I wrap my arm around his shoulders, which causes me to get jealous looks from all the women walking by. "Danny, you've worked your ass off for years to get to this point. You really should enjoy it a little. Speaking of enjoying it ..." I reach into my purse, grab the five hundred dollars Phillip paid me, and hand it to him. "Here's your money back."

He laughs at me. "You probably don't have a fallback career as a stripper. I'm just saying."

"Shut up!"

"I guess you're right though. The only thing I've spent money on is the house. Speaking of that, did Lori tell you the house next door to us is getting ready to go on the market?"

"No, she didn't."

"I think you and Phillip should buy it."

"It'd be fun to be neighbors again."

WE GET TO the Ferrari dealership. The place is like Disneyland for boys with cash. Danny walks in and is greeted like the superstar he is. He and the sales guy lead me to an incredibly sleek and gorgeous bright red car.

"Wow, Danny. I wouldn't need to get tipsy to buy this car. Can I have one, too?"

Danny laughs as he opens the door and lets me slide behind the wheel. "You look good in it. You should buy one for yourself."

"I can't talk Phillip into spending money on a house. He'd have a cow if I brought home a freaking Ferrari! Plus, *I'm not a professional quarterback.*"

"Jay, when it comes down to it, it's your money. You can spend it however you want."

Sitting behind the wheel of this car, I feel like I could have anything I want.

"Phillip said to me, 'I have a good job. I don't need a handout from my wife to buy a house.' And I'm not sure what to do. He won't listen to me about it. It's like a closed subject. Every time I bring it up, he gets pissy with me, and Phillip is never pissy with me. That's your job." I give him a smirk. "Plus, ultimately, I have to get your dad to agree. Why did you tell me to put the money back in my trust? I wouldn't have had to go through stupid couples counseling."

"Because my dad was afraid we'd blow it on a car like this." He studies me and the car. "You look hot in this car. You should do what you want."

"I'm not buying a car like this, but anytime you want me to

drive this for you, you let me know." I stick my hand out and do my best rap-star imitation. "*I'm in my whip. I'm in my ride.*" I laugh. "You know, I totally should've been a rap star."

Danny laughs, crosses his arms in front of his chest, and does a rap-star pose. "Dude, me, too."

"We're gonna need to buy you some gold chains or something first. You're a little too clean-cut-looking."

"I think you're trying to distract me. Back to the subject at hand. Do you know how cool it would be for our kids to be neighbors and for us to be able to hang out like our parents always did? In fact, speaking of that, you need to hurry up and get pregnant."

"No way."

"We want you pregnant soon."

"You sound like Phillip's mom. I wanna be able to drink on my honeymoon."

Danny takes my hand and helps me out of the car. "Go off the pill now, and maybe you can kill two birds with one stone. You can go on your babymoon and your honeymoon at the same time. That would save Phillip money, so he can buy the house next door. You'll love it, Jay! They just finished remodeling it, and the kitchen is so cool. The basement looks like a sports bar. It's awesome."

Danny throws his arm across my shoulders and leads me over to a matching fly yellow Ferrari. "We wouldn't have to match exactly."

The sales guy, who's been following us around, says to me, "This car looks like you."

I'm not sure if looking like a fast, expensive car is a compliment or not, so I ignore him. "A babymoon is the silliest thing I've ever heard. What are you celebrating? That your baby isn't there yet? The soon-to-be death of your romantic and sex lives? I want some time to enjoy it being just Phillip and me. Like you and Lori did. You had romance."

"We still have romance."

"Danny, I've dated Phillip for three months. That's it. I wanna date him for a while. I want it to be just the two of us."

"Having a baby is romantic."

"It doesn't seem like it. Seems stressful, and once the baby is born, it's a lot of hard work."

"So, how long does Phillip wanna wait?"

"I don't know. We really haven't talked about it, but I'm sure he wants to wait, too."

"Come on. Just think, our kids could grow up together, play football together." He gives me a big smirk. "Your daughter could beg my son to teach her how to kiss."

"I did not beg you. I wanted a simple two-minute demonstration. I didn't expect you were going to teach me for hours."

I hear the sales guy chuckle.

"You know me. I just wanted you to be perfect."

"And, besides, you're a year older than me, so I have some time."

"You need to start trying now."

"My luck, I'd get pregnant and be puking through my wedding."

"Fine. After the honeymoon. You have a goal now. Visualize yourself being fertile, fruitful."

"Danny, jeez. Yuck."

Danny looks at the sales guy and says, "This car is really tight. She'll take it." Then, he grins at me. "Just think, Jay, when you're trying to get pregnant, you have to do a lot of trying."

"Danny, okay, enough. If it's supposed to happen, it will." I look at the sales guy. "I will *not* be taking it. We need to get back to the bar."

"Fine." Danny pouts.

"You know, you kinda pout when you don't get your way."

"I do with you."

"Why?"

"'Cause it usually works. Shall I give you my grin, too?"

I smack his shoulder, which doesn't affect him in the least. Danny gives the sales guy a high five on the way out.

"We need to get Phillip over this nonsense and make him buy the house."

"I don't think it'll work. He thinks he wears the pants."

"Tell him you insist. You know, it's funny that the girl who's been giving me a hard time about not rewarding myself can't take her own advice."

"Danny, this is different. I didn't earn this money. I didn't work for it. I got it because my parents died. I'm afraid, if I spend it, it's like I'm glad they're dead."

"You're so dumb, and your parents would have been so disappointed. They wanted to take care of you if something happened. That's why they were well insured. They wanted to be able to give you something if they weren't here to give it to you themselves. So, why was it okay to spend it on college, but it's not okay to spend it on a house?"

"I'm okay with spending some of it on a house! Phillip is the one who isn't. And I've only spent it on things they would've spent it on. Like, they insisted I go to college, so I was okay with it. They would've paid for my wedding, so I'm okay with that. But I'm pretty sure they never would have bought me a Ferrari, Danny."

"True. But don't you think your parents would have loved the idea of you living by us, of our kids growing up together, just like we did?"

"Yeah, they probably would have, but it's not me you have to convince; it's Phillip."

"So, once again, tell him you insist. Tell him it's what your parents would have wanted, and just buy it!"

"I don't think he'll let me. He's stubborn."

"Then, you have two options. Use your feminine wiles on him or make him feel guilty. Tell him you strongly believe it's what your parents would have wanted, and you feel like, if you don't, you'll be letting them down."

"You're devious, Danny."

"Yeah, well, that's why we get along so good."

AFTER A GREAT dinner, we're all sitting around the curved hotel bar, laughing, joking, and reminiscing. As we learned last night, one thing about being friends with people practically your whole lives is that they never seem to forget anything.

So, of course, the topic turns to Phillip and me.

Blake goes to Phillip, "So, now that you're engaged, you can finally tell us the truth. All those nights the two of you went home to watch movies or just chill, you were hitting it, right? I mean, we all knew it even though you were always like, 'We're just friends.'"

Nick joins in. "Yeah, why the big secret? It was so obvious to all of us. Every time you looked at Phillip, it seemed intimate."

My mind flashes back to coming home from hanging out with Nick, Chelsea, and some other friends. Phillip hadn't gone because he had a big test to study for. Phillip is a perfectionist. He likes to do his best at everything he does.

That night, I came home and found his big body sprawled across my bed. I asked why he was in my room. He told me it smelled good and that it helped him relax. I quizzed him for a bit. Then, he laid his head on the pillow next to me and buried his face in my chest. I could tell he was stressed, so I ran my hands through his hair. Sometimes, I rubbed it hard, like they do at the salon when they shampoo you. Other times, I was soft and gentle.

I moved down to his neck, which was a mass of knotted-up muscles. I figured his back was tense, too, so I offered to rub it. I'd rubbed his back and shoulders many times before, but he always had his shirt on. He sorta shocked me when he sat up and pulled it off. I will admit, I didn't really mind rubbing his naked skin. I rubbed his back the same way I had rubbed his hair. Sometimes hard and massaging. Sometimes soft little caresses. Other times, I barely touched his skin with my fingertips. It was slightly hypnotic.

I woke up later, wrapped in his arms, books still lying all around us. I didn't bother to wake him up. I told myself that I wanted him to sleep well before his test, but truthfully, I liked being in his arms.

Nick is right. We *were* intimate. We just didn't have sex.

Nick continues, "You have this connection. I don't understand why you acted like it wasn't happening."

"Because it wasn't!" I exclaim.

Lori says, "Guys, it's true. Sad but true."

"Damn, Phillip," Logan says. "You must've been really in love with her to spend all that time with her and *do nothing*!"

Everyone laughs.

"So, basically, you all lived together for three years, and *nobody* was getting any?" Blake asks.

"Not from each other anyway," I stupidly say.

"That's so disappointing." Logan sighs. "Jay baby, you should've come to Loggie. Oh, wait, you did." He flashes me a cheesy grin.

"Shut up, Logan. I didn't do anything with you either."

"I wouldn't call it anything."

"Fine. I made out with some of Phillip's fraternity brothers, but seriously, that's all I ever did."

"Uh, Matt Fuller," Logan reminds me.

"Well, yeah, I dated him for four months. After he dumped me and pissed me off, I revenge-dated his best friend because it drove him nuts. Those were the only two boys from your frat I slept with. I just … I don't know. I couldn't sleep with Phillip's friends."

"You didn't have any problem sleeping with my friends," Danny teases.

Nick jokes, "You just have a thing for hot football players, like me."

I turn my head and ask Danny, "Is a kicker considered a real player?" Then, I give Nick a smirk.

"Actually, kickers are definitely real players. Think of how many times a kick wins a game."

"True," everyone says, agreeing with Danny.

"Lori, how many football players did I sleep with?"

She holds up her hand, which is forming a big, fat zero.

Danny looks at me in surprise. "Really? Is that true?"

"Yeah, sadly."

Nick says, "Why does that surprise you, Danny? You're the one who told every guy on the team that we could look but not touch."

"YOU TOLD THEM THAT? Danny! That was so not fair!"

Danny and Phillip laugh.

"I never really thought it would work," Danny says. "Glad to know it did."

"Well, it certainly explains a lot. It didn't matter though. Mostly, I did just fine, finding boys without the two of you. And I preferred it that way."

"Yeah, you were sneaky," Danny says.

"I had to be! Here everyone thought it was all hot, wild sex going on, but the truth is, it was like I lived with two FATHERS!"

Danny says, "Please. We used to get into trouble together. I never acted like your father."

"You did if I was *getting into trouble* with anyone but you."

Nick says to Danny, "Like when you guys used to make out at the bar?"

Phillip and Lori both look at us.

Crap. I'm pretty sure neither one of them knew about that.

Danny ignores Nick. "I've always watched out for Jay. Phillip and me both."

"And she's always needed it," Phillip says adorably.

He pulls me into a sweet kiss.

Phillip's kisses are so amazing. I think that's why it was never a big deal to kiss Danny. It didn't really mean anything. It was more like an adventure. I'm pretty sure, somewhere in the dark and scary recesses of my mind, I knew, if I kissed Phillip, it would've meant something more. Something important.

Dillon laughs and goes, "Remember that baseball game when JJ supposedly by accident mixed up the Gatorade bottles with Danny's special Gatorade-vodka mixes?"

Joey is like, "That was messed up, girl."

Phillip laughs. "Joey, you were the one who was messed up." He tells everyone else, "He got drunk during the game and was goofy and stumbling around."

"Everyone thought he had heat exhaustion and was delirious," Danny says.

"Hey, it was an honest mistake. I didn't see the special mark on the top. But I have to say, it was worth it. I don't think I've ever had so much fun at a baseball game."

"I don't even remember it," Joey says.

Neil clutches Danny's arm like he just remembered something super important. "Danny, dude, remember that chick from Park City who was all into you? She'd sit up in the bleachers in that little miniskirt with nothing on underneath? I got hit in the face with a pop fly one time when she uncrossed her legs."

Katie asks, "She was the one who had a boyfriend, right?"

Phillip laughs and says, "We all know how Danny felt about that."

All the guys say in unison, "'Just because there's a goalie doesn't mean you can't score.'"

We all laugh and giggle.

Joey is like, "Oh, guys, have you been out to Westown lately? They got a new convenience store. It's called the Kum and Go. I was seriously pumping my gas and laughing my ass off. Because *pumping?*"

"I know!" Neil says. "I get gas there every time I see my parents. I always feel bad though when I pump and don't go inside to buy anything. Like, I did her, but I didn't stay to snuggle."

Lisa giggles. "I wondered why all the men were lined up outside. Coming and going is like their dream."

Lori quips, "Why? They can do that by themselves at home."

"A man totally named that store," I say. "Can't you see a bunch of high-ass frat boys lying around, making up names for their future convenience stores and laughing their asses off?"

"We need to go there, Logan," Blake says. "We should try and plank on top of their sign."

Logan high-fives Blake and says, "That'd be so awesome."

I look at Phillip and think it's time we go dancing. I can't wait to grind all over him and actually have the ability to back it up. I wanna drive him crazy. The kind of crazy that will make him want to take me back to my suite and drive me crazy.

"You guys ready to go dance the night away?" I ask.

plant a seed and hope it grows.

MONDAY, DECEMBER 4TH

I'VE BEEN THINKING about what Danny said, and I might have stumbled upon a way to do it.

I'm going to plant a seed and hope it grows.

That's how my mom always said she dealt with my dad, and my dad was more stubborn than I am. Somehow though, my mom was always able to get her way while, at the same time, making my dad think it was his idea.

I need to pull out the big guns—or maybe the small, subtle guns—to get Phillip to buy the house next door to Danny and Lori.

What do those ladies say in the movie *My Big Fat Greek Wedding*? Something about the man is the head, but the woman is the neck. How the neck controls which way the head looks.

I need to be the neck.

I need Phillip to look at the house and make the decision to buy it.

I can't be the one to suggest it.

I need to find out how much they want for the house. I need to get Mr. Diamond to agree to let me spend it. Mr. D will be the one to tell Phillip it's what my parents would've wanted.

No, wait! I have an even better idea!

We'll make the money a *gift* from my parents.

Then, it will be *our* money.

We'll go look at the house, and Phillip will say, *Now, we can afford it. We'll take it.*

Or something like that.

Phillip will think it's all his idea while I will act appropriately shocked and thrilled. Phillip will be my hero, and we'll live happily ever after.

Gosh, I hope this works.

I act surprised.

THURSDAY, DECEMBER 7TH

MR. DIAMOND CALLED Phillip earlier today and asked if we could meet with him after work.

We sit in the big wingback chairs in his study, and Mr. D says to Phillip, "So, you know that my job is to protect JJ's financial interests. And, as much as I believe you two will be together forever, I have to think realistically about that. Every time I make a decision about JJ's finances, I always ask myself, *What would Paul have done? What would her dad have wanted, and how would Ronny have felt about it?* When I'm not sure what to do, I've consulted with your dad, Phillip, since he and JJ's dad were so close.

"I want to talk to you about JJ's finances tonight. I want you to understand everything. First off, you know they would've wanted her to have a special wedding and that Jadyn has that budget?"

"Yes, sir," Phillip answers.

"Second of all, I know her parents would have wanted to give you a special wedding gift, so in this envelope is a check made out to both of you."

Phillip grimaces.

Mr. D hands Phillip the envelope. "Phillip, you're going to be getting lots of wedding gifts in the coming month. Those gifts are your friends' and family's way of helping you get started in your new life together. You're planning on accepting these gifts graciously, am I right?"

Phillip thinks about it. "Yeah, I guess."

"That's what this is," Mr. D says. "A gift. Phillip, I know what you're thinking. You're a man. You're starting a new family with JJ, and you want to love and support her.

"When Mary and I got married, her parents wanted to give us money for a down payment on our house. I fought her tooth and nail because I didn't want to feel like I owed them anything. I wanted to make it on my own. In some ways, it felt like a slam to me, like they were saying they didn't believe I could support and provide for their daughter. But her father sat down with me and told me that it was a no-strings-attached gift and asked me to accept it as such.

"So, Phillip, please accept this gift from her parents. It's what they would have wanted. Hopefully, you can use it to find a home that's perfect for you."

He asks Phillip to open the envelope. Phillip's eyes get big when he does. I know the exact amount of the check, but when he shows me, I act surprised.

Phillip says, "Wow."

Mr. Diamond keeps going, "But this is your money as a couple, and it's completely up to you how to spend it. You might do what I think her parents would have wanted and use it to buy your first home. Or you might decide you want to blow it all on a trip around the world. Maybe you'll decide to reinvest it, to start your own business, or buy matching Ferraris. My point is, Phillip, this is your money together, and you should decide together how to use it."

Phillip is listening very closely to Mr. D, and I have to give it to him. He's nailed it.

And, in case Phillip hasn't had enough of a mind fuck yet, Mr. D drops this on his plate.

"Thirdly, like I said, it's my job to protect JJ's finances, so I'm going to ask you to sign a prenuptial agreement that will protect the rest of her trust in case either one of you decides to end your marriage."

In other words, in case Phillip decides to dump me or trade me in for a younger model someday.

Phillip has no problem with this. He reads over the document and signs away.

I'm hoping, now that he doesn't have access to my money, he will feel okay about using the gift money on our house.

I'm so bad. I haven't even seen the place yet, and I'm already calling it our house.

Okay, seeds have been planted.

Now, I'm just gonna stand back and watch them grow or germinate or take root or whatever newbie seeds do.

AS WE'RE DRIVING home, Phillip says, "So, what do you think we should do with this gift?"

I say a little bit pathetically, "Well, I guess just put it in the bank until we can decide what we wanna do with it. I mean, I know you won't wanna spend it on a house, so I guess we'll just reinvest it."

When I decide if I'm going to keep him.

SUNDAY, DECEMBER 10TH

I HATE TO admit it, but I think I might be coming down with a cold. But, even though I'm not feeling great, I still help Phillip's mom clean up after dinner. I'm ready to sit on the couch and watch football, but when I walk in the room, the guys all hold their empty beer bottles up at me.

A not-so-subtle hint to bring them more.

I purposely sniffle loudly, so Phillip will feel sorry for me, but he doesn't seem to notice.

When I walk back into the kitchen, there's an intense conversation going on between Ash and her mom. I really don't wanna get involved.

I just wanna go sit down, but I get dragged into the conversation when Mrs. Mac says, "So, JJ, when are you and Phillip going to have children?"

And maybe it's the fact that I don't feel good.

Or maybe it's the fact that I'm not married yet.

Or maybe it's the fact that Phillip and I haven't even discussed it.

Or maybe it's the fact that the idea of me being pregnant is just plain laughable.

I can't even help it.

I laugh out loud.

Sorry, but I do.

Ha!

I even let out a little snort.

She doesn't look very pleased. She says, "I'm serious."

I rub my hand across my temple. *Think, Jadyn. Say something noncommittal, but something that will appease her. Or better yet, make her forget about you and babies.*

"Um … gosh, I'd say we'll figure that out after the wedding." She gets a sad look on her face, which makes me feel bad, so I add, "But it'll probably be fairly soon."

She smiles at me. It's a touching, heartfelt smile that makes me feel worse. I'm probably going to hell for lying to my future mother-in-law about her dream grandbabies.

But, technically, it's not exactly a lie. I just think her idea of fairly soon and mine are quite a few years apart.

I tilt my head at her. "Isn't that a question more appropriate for your already-married daughter?"

Let's put some pressure on Ashley for a change. Put her in the hot seat.

Mrs. Mac waves her hand. "I don't think they're even trying. Maybe not even having sex."

"Mom! We'll have children when we're ready! And we have sex. I mean, some sex," Ash says.

She looks kinda sad. Like maybe *some* is code for *not so much.*

"So, when will you be ready?" I ask.

"When I decide if I'm going to keep him."

"What?" I exclaim.

"Oh, I'm just teasing," Ash says.

But, the way she's looking at Cooper, who's now sprawled across the couch, shoving chips in his mouth, I wonder if maybe she's not.

I wonder if she's glad she got married. I mean, Lori and Danny are happy, but Katie and Eric are having a rough time. And, now, I wonder if maybe Ashley is having a hard time, too. Although Katie says the best thing about fighting is the make-up sex. She also says, sometimes, she picks a fight just so they can make up. Sounds a little twisted to me, but it's not my marriage, so I just laugh along.

I look at Cooper. I like Coop. He's a cool, relaxed guy. And Ashley can be pretty overbearing. You'd have to be pretty chill to deal with her. But I hardly ever see them all gooey anymore, like they were when they were dating. Maybe Mrs. Mac is right, and they really aren't doing it.

That's a scary thought.

What if Phillip gets tired of me?

What if, someday, he doesn't want me anymore?

Phillip's mom keeps discussing babies, and she's going on and on about how lucky the Diamonds are that Danny and Lori are expecting.

I think she's got grandma envy.

"Just chill, Mom," Ashley says in a snotty voice.

That is a mistake because I can tell Mrs. Mac is about to tell her a thing or two about chilling.

I quickly hold up the beers I just got out of the fridge and offer a wry smile, so they'll understand it's imperative that I get back to the family room and deliver them to the menfolk while they're still cold.

I go in the family room and hand them to the guys.

I sniffle again as Phillip pulls me onto his lap.

"You're sniffling. You need to see the doctor."

"It's just a cold. I'm fine."

He whispers in my ear, "Did I mention that I'm gonna be the doctor?"

My face instantly feels flushed. I whisper back, "In that case, I might need a very thorough examination. We'd better get home."

press my body firmly against his.

TUESDAY, DECEMBER 12TH

COUPLES COUNSELING AGAIN tonight. I tried to get out of it earlier. I sniffled and told Phillip I might be too sick to go. He said the same thing my parents used to when I wanted to stay home from school on a Friday.

"If you're too sick to go, that means you're too sick to go out tonight."

I really want to go out, so here I am.

As we're walking down the hall to the pastor's office, I tell Phillip, "I talked to Amy earlier. Can you believe that, exactly a month from today, we'll be at our wedding rehearsal?"

Phillip snakes his arms around my waist, gently pushes me against the wall outside the pastor's office, and kisses me. "It can't come soon enough."

I put my hands inside his coat, squeeze his sides, and press my body firmly against his.

He can make me want him with just one kiss.

His hands slide under the back of my shirt. I swear, his hands feel like fire on my skin.

I'm about to say, *You're needed in the restroom, Doctor. Stat!*

"Ahem!"

I tear my lips away from Phillip and see Pastor John standing inside his office door. I didn't hear the door open. I think my sense of touch is so overwhelmed when Phillip kisses me that the rest of my senses don't function properly.

"Sup," I say to him with a nod.

Oh. My. Gosh.

I'm so incredibly lame.

Who says sup to a pastor? I think the blood that normally flows to my brain is now congregating in other areas of my body. My dad once told me that boys think with their dicks. He said it's because the blood flows there and away from their brains. I was thoroughly mortified by that comment, but now, I'm thinking it doesn't just happen to boys.

My insides are pounding with desire. And, now that the pastor has seen us, I can't pull Phillip into the restroom for a pre-counseling quickie, like I was considering.

Damn it!

PHILLIP AND I sit in the stupid checkerboard chairs. Phillip looks at me with those eyes. I remember when Danny and Lori used to look at each other with those eyes. Like they had a secret no one knew but them. I remember wondering if I could ever look at Phillip that way. I can't see my eyes, but his definitely have that look. I have a feeling we'll be skipping Taco Tuesday tonight.

Pastor John loudly taps a pen on his desk. I was gazing into Phillip's eyes and not really paying attention.

The pastor says, "So, tonight, we're going to talk about sex."

Oh, great. Like my mind isn't already consumed with thoughts of sex. I've been mentally calculating how many more minutes it'll be before I can attack Phillip. How many more minutes until I can strip him naked. How many more minutes until I can make him—

Pastor John's grating voice interrupts what was just about to be a very hot daydream. "I'm sure it's hard to believe at this stage in your relationship, but many couples fight about sex."

Before I can stop it from coming out of my mouth, I stupidly say, "They do?"

I don't wanna talk about this.

I just wanna go home now and do it.

Phillip slips off his coat. He has on a long-sleeved cream thermal Abercrombie shirt that seems to be losing the fight to contain his muscles.

I imagine ripping the shirt off him, letting those muscles be free to roam wildly across my body.

Pastor John drones on, "Yes, JJ, they do. Many couples go through a honeymoon stage. When it seems like sex is all that matters. There's a lot of desire, but eventually, things simmer down."

I seriously can't imagine things simmering down with Phillip. But then I remember what his sister said the other day. They've been married only a few years, and I think they've simmered down.

"When does that usually happen? I think Phillip's sister might be going through that right now."

Phillip groans. "I don't wanna hear about my sister's sex life."

It's better than talking about our sex life, I would think.

Pastor John says, "It varies with each couple. What matters is that you're able to discuss sex."

"Wouldn't it be better to just do it?" I ask. I mean, wouldn't it?

"Well, of course, but as your marriage grows, you will have additional stresses. Time, money, self-esteem, children, and your relationship will all have an effect on your sex life."

"But, if you love someone, wouldn't you always want them?" I ask because this has been bugging me. I seriously would die if Phillip ever turned me down.

I'd probably divorce him.

I mean, if your own husband doesn't want you, why bother staying married?

"It's not that simple, JJ. Imagine, if you can, Phillip comes home one night and is tired from work. You've been home with the kids all day, and you are exhausted, too. He still has to go out and mow the grass, and you still have to bathe the kids and put them to bed. By the time you eat dinner, do your chores, and get the kids to sleep, do you think you will want sex? Or will you just want to go to sleep?"

Aside from the fact that his example is riddled with stereotypical and chauvinistic things, I get what he's saying. I look at Phillip because I assume he's going to answer the question, but he shrugs his shoulders at me. He doesn't seem to know the answer.

How can he not know the answer? The answer is quite obvious!

"We'd have sex, and then we'd sleep."

Duh!

Pastor John nods his head. And his nod is not in agreement with me.

I FORGET WHAT else he says. He drones on about who will initiate it, keeping the spark, talking, talking, talking. I swear, his position on sex is that talk equals foreplay.

Ha!

Get it? His position on sex? I crack myself up.

I'd have to disagree with that. The last thing I wanna do is talk. I look at Phillip's lips and picture them kissing me, not talking. I can almost feel them on my neck. My eyes glaze over as I think about all the naughty things I'm gonna do to him tonight.

Maybe I'll make him go to Taco Tuesday. I'll flirt with him. Bat my eyelashes at him. Run my hand up his thigh under the table.

Or maybe I'll sit across from him. Slip my shoe off. Rub my foot between his legs. Drive him crazy.

He'll be begging to go home.

But we won't make it home.

We'll barely make it to the car because he wants me so badly. He'll throw me across the backseat, undo his pants, and—

"So, I guess that's it for today," the pastor says loudly with a clap of his hands.

The clap wakes me up. I still feel like I'm in the backseat with Phillip. It's slightly disorienting.

We get in the car, and Phillip says, "So, Taco Tuesday. Yay or nay?"

"Definitely yay," I reply.

Nothing wrong with trying to make a few of my dreams come true.

Let them grow.

SATURDAY, DECEMBER 16TH

WE'RE DRIVING TO Kansas City to pick out office furniture. This is the lie Phillip told me.

Yes, Phillip told me a complete lie.

I know this because Danny told me that he talked Phillip into *just looking* at the house today.

So, I'm not at all sure what that means!

And it's killing me!

I wanna talk about it!

I want him to tell me what he thinks. If he's considering it.

I'm going craaazy with wondering.

And he's sitting there, driving, all calm and cool, while bobbing his head to Aerosmith.

I wanna pin his head to the back of the seat and threaten him with torture if he doesn't tell me what he's thinking.

Why would he want to look at a house he thinks he can't afford?

No. Be calm. Be cool.

Maintain the *I know you don't want to buy it* routine.

You planted the seeds; now, let them grow.

And I'm trying to, but, hey, plants need a little water, right?

Maybe they're not growing because I need to water them.

So, I say, "I'm surprised the commercial office furniture place is open on a Saturday."

Phillip grins. "I lied. We're not really doing that. Danny told you about the house next door that's going on the market, right?"

"Yeah."

"We're gonna take a look at it today. See if it's really as nice as Danny has been going on about."

"But why would we do that?"

Phillip turns his head and gives me a confused look. "I wanted to surprise you with this. I thought you'd be really excited."

I sigh, a defeated, slightly pretend sigh. "It's hard to get excited about seeing something you can't have. Lori says it's gorgeous. All it's gonna do is depress me more when we go look at houses in our price range. It's like dangling Jimmy Choos in front of me and then making me buy my shoes at Target."

Phillip squints his eyes at me. This is the part where he should say, *Oh, Princess, but now, we can afford that house. It would be so cool to live by Danny and Lori, and it would be amazing, and we'll live happily ever after.*

Or something like that.

Instead, he smiles and says, "Well, if nothing else, maybe we can get some ideas from it. Kinda like when my mom tours those dream homes."

"Yeah, I suppose," I say pathetically again. I'm really trying hard not to pout.

But, all of a sudden, I totally am.

And I'm not faking it.

For real.

Because getting ideas was not the seed that I planted.

WE LOOK AT the house. Danny has been whispering in Phillip's ear about what he and Lori spent on their house, what the remodel is costing, and how this is a much better deal. Lori has mentioned how great it would be not to have the mess of a remodel.

And, well, I gush to myself since I can't gush to anyone.

This house is IT!

Like Phillip is the ONE.

Like my dress is the ONE.

This house is the ONE!

Even the house knows he's the one for me. The house is pleading with me like a hopeful lover, *You know I'm the one for you, baby. Let's live together.*

The house has everything on Phillip's wish list. A gorgeous kitchen with granite countertops and sparkling new appliances, a big island with six barstools, an open floor plan, and an incredible basement game room. If he isn't already sold on the kitchen, the expansive master bedroom overlooking the lake with its huge closets and a bathroom where I'd happily spend the rest of my life, the sweeping staircase, and the huge deck, he has to be sold the second he sees the walk-out basement. It's like a boy's wet dream down here. Pool table, foosball, bar, poker table, three flat screens, sound system, huge sectional couch, and a hot tub out on the patio.

I'm so sold.

I wanna run outside, cheer, do cartwheels, and stab a big SOLD sign in the front yard. The sign would say, SOLD TO ME, and it'd have a picture of me hugging the front door.

Phillip and Danny are grinning like maniacs in the basement, which you'd think might be a good sign, but Phillip has said nothing to me to indicate this is any more than a dream tour.

Shit.

Speaking of shit, maybe I forgot to fertilize the seeds, and that's why they're not growing! I try to think of all the bullshit things I could say to make Phillip fall in love with this house.

But I can't.

Truth is, I want him to love it for all the reasons I do. And, yes, I planted seeds, and that sounds sort of manipulative, but I don't want him to get talked into doing something he doesn't want to do. I don't want him to be unhappy.

Even if that means passing up this amazing house.

You know, love kinda sucks sometimes.

It makes you do stupid stuff, like care more about the person you love than you do about yourself.

I watch him grin at Danny. I notice how sexily his forearm flexes when he runs his hand down the bar.

I'm pretty sure I could live in a shack with him and be happy. As long as he was there, it would feel like home.

I'm just so in love with that boy.

AFTER OUR TOUR, we meet with the couple who owns the home. Phillip tells them the house is beautiful, what a great job they did on the remodel, and how they must be sad to leave it.

They agree as they grab us beers from the outdoor kitchen's fridge.

An outdoor beer fridge?

Seriously? Is there anything this house doesn't have?

Phillip discusses pricing with them. What they are going to list it for. What they'd take for it now. When they'd like to close.

I can see the corner of Phillip's jaw twitching slightly. Usually, he does that when he's trying to play it cool. When he doesn't want to smile. It's like his poker face.

But what does that mean? Does it mean he's considering it?

No.

Not going to get my hopes up.

Because I don't think so. I think he loves it, but he's convinced we can't afford it. I still don't even understand why he agreed to look at it.

Nothing like setting yourself up for disappointment.

Or, well, setting me up for disappointment.

Phillip says to everyone, "Do you guys mind if Jadyn and I

take a quick walk and talk about it?"

And I'm thinking, *Talk about what?*

Talk about how the house is great, but we can't afford it?

Talk about which great ideas we should file away in our brains for someday?

Phillip nods for me to get up.

AS WE WALK down toward the lake, he grabs my hand. "So, what'd you think? You didn't say much in there. I thought you'd be oohing and aahing over everything. Didn't you like it?"

"Well, Phillip, I think it's a gorgeous, perfect, amazing house. It has everything I could possibly want. The kitchen is a dream, and the master bath is to die for, but I'd love it for the basement alone."

His eyes light up. "The basement is totally tricked out. Can you imagine the parties we could throw down there?"

"Well, yeah." I look really pathetic, I'm sure. I'm totally pouting—and not because I'm trying to get my way, but because I feel sad about this. I knew looking at something I couldn't have was a bad idea. It's depressing. "Maybe, someday, we can have a house like that." I nod my head and put on my best fake smile.

Phillip pulls me into his arms. He softly runs his hand across my cheek and into my hair. I look deeply into his adorable brown eyes and feel bolstered with confidence.

It'll be okay.

There will be other houses, but there's not another Phillip.

I mentally stomp on the stupid seeds.

I want Phillip, and nothing else matters.

Phillip nuzzles his face into mine and says, "I was thinking maybe today should be someday."

My eyes get big. I back away from him and barely whisper, "What do you mean?"

"I think we should start someday *today* and buy it. I thought you'd be more excited about this."

Ohmigawd. I might start hyperventilating.

"Really? Are you serious? I didn't think you were interested. I didn't wanna get excited because I knew you were against spending that kind of money."

"Well, that was before I had that kind of money sitting in the bank."

I smile. *Big.*

"So, Princess, is that a yes?"

I fling myself on Phillip, jump into his arms, and wrap my legs around his waist. He twirls me around while I kiss him.

"That's a yes," I finally say. "In case you couldn't tell."

"I figured. I didn't get this much excitement from the ring. Should we go tell them we'll take it?"

"Not just yet," I say. I wrap my arms around his neck and kiss him some more.

A cosmic shift has occurred.

MONDAY, DECEMBER 18TH

PHILLIP WAS LOOKING much like Cooper tonight after work. He was lying across the couch with the remote control glued to his hand.

I lay across him and started doing some things he liked, usually a surefire way to get him into bed with me. All of a sudden, this annoyed him.

"I'm trying to watch this," he told me and sort of pushed me aside.

Now, I'm sorry, but you could have a two-hour romp in bed and come back, and the golf game would be going pretty much the same. And excuse me, but isn't this why they created highlights and DVRs?

I probably should have jumped up and down, naked. I probably should have screamed, *I need some attention here!*

Instead, I asked if he wanted to grab a drink with some friends.

He said, "Nah, you go. I'm tired."

So, now, I'm headed to the bar. Talk about looking for attention in all the wrong places. I'm also wondering if Pastor John is prophetic.

Is Phillip getting sick of me already? Is he going to stop wanting me?

I'M SORT OF embarrassed to admit it, but this bar is like my second home. Not quite the home Kegger's was down in Lincoln, but it's where we all hang out here, in Omaha. It's rare that I don't see lots of people I know.

But tonight is different. There are a lot of guys here that I don't recognize.

It's like they dropped off a busload from the hot guys' home.

I mean, seriously, Phillip is hot.

We know that.

And most guys don't even come close in my opinion. A guy has to, like, have it all for me to even give him a second glance. I'm not into skinny guys, and if they wear skinny jeans or have a skater kind of look, they're not for me. The only time I've ever really strayed from that is with the guitar player I dated this summer. He did have great guitar-playing arm muscles though, and at the time, I kinda felt like I needed to try something different. Evidently, I did not learn my lesson with the sex-video guy.

Normally, my typical guy is like a real man. He could be a mechanic or a cowboy or a linebacker, whatever, but he has to have good muscles and an adorable smile.

Oh, and good teeth.

Danny always used to tease me about how I love teeth. Like I was shopping for a horse or something.

But I do like a perfect smile.

And, tonight, it's like someone is holding a casting call for Jadyn's Perfect Type. 'Cause, as I'm scanning the crowd while walking back to our usual table, there are, like, four guys who literally turn my head.

LATER, WHEN I walk back to use the restroom, four guys hit on me. Even after I said I was engaged, they keep trying.

I swear, I didn't even flirt back. I was too shocked to flirt.

When I get back from the restroom and sit down next to Joey, Katie, Lisa, and Neil, I realize a cosmic shift has occurred.

Is it because it's the first time I've been here alone since we got engaged?

Does an engagement ring make a girl more attractive?

Do all the boys realize I'm serious about settling down, and so, now, I'm a more attractive mate?

Or am I more attractive to them because I'm committed, and it could just be a no-strings-attached fling?

Or has the shift changed me and how I look at guys? Like you want what you can't have.

Do I really wanna be stuck with the same guy for the rest of my life?

Phillip is so structured, and there is security in that. But what if I want something different?

Like, I love desserts. My very favorite is chocolate cheesecake, but if I had to eat it every night, wouldn't I get sick of it?

What's so wrong with wanting to have, like, a piece of apple pie one night and maybe a nice pound cake with strawberries the next?

I think Barbie might have been on to something.

A really hot guy sits down next to me. He is one of the guys I turned down on the way to the restroom.

And he's hot.

Not the Phillip sweet, dreamy kind of hot, but more the Danny Diamond, all blond and an attitude kind of hot.

Like, he's really hot. Did I say that already?

But the more he talks, well, the more bored I get.

I guess I do like a little brain behind the brawn. If a guy can't get my very witty and amazingly intelligent sarcasm, then he's a dud.

I want this guy to leave, so I flash the engagement ring his way again, but I think he might be too dense to know what it means.

Normally, Joey and Neil would be all over it. Like, they'd just tell the guy to leave. That I'm taken. But Neil is busy fawning over Katie, and Joey is trying to pick up some chick. Lisa is drooling over the guy, but she's trying to act disinterested.

I touch her arm and say, "I'm going to the bar." I said it in a way that let her know the guy was all hers, and I would take my time coming back.

I grab the two empty pitchers off our table, say something vague about being back, and head to the bar for refills.

THE BAR IS super busy, so I squeeze between two guys sitting there, swing the pitchers onto the counter, stick my boobs out, and flash a big grin in the bartender's direction.

The guy sitting to my right spins his barstool around, and I find myself standing between Jason O'Connor's legs.

Jason purrs, "Jadyn James, look at you, all gorgeous and shiny."

Jason has always called me Jadyn James because his name is Jason James O'Connor. He thought it was cool that we, like, matched. And shiny, from anyone else, would make me think my makeup got greasy-looking, and my face needed to be powdered. But shiny is a Jason word. And shiny equals perfect to Jason. He loves shiny new toys of all kinds.

"I hear you got engaged."

"How did you hear that?"

"My parents told me. They also told me I should've never let you get away. They always ask me about you, how you're doing and stuff. They thought you were smart, funny, and down to earth."

"Aw, that's so nice. I liked your parents, too."

"What about me?"

"What do you mean, what about me?"

"Did you like me?" He gives me an adorable little curve of his textbook lips and a flash of expensive and perfect teeth. "Did you love me?"

I think about how to answer that.

"At the time, I thought I was in love with you."

"I was in love with you," he says sweetly. "I think I'm still in love with you."

I ignore the *still in love with you* part and say, "It felt like we were in love, but you never told me."

"Remember your winter formal?"

"How could I forget that? You ruined it!"

"No, before that, before I got drunk. How did you feel about the night, about me?"

"I felt great. Had a hot date, loved my dress, loved my hair. Honestly, before you got drunk, the night felt kinda special. I mean, it seemed like it was gonna be special, you know, until it wasn't."

"Here's a little secret for you, Jadyn James. I was going to tell you I loved you that night. You would've been the first girl I ever said it to that I felt like I really meant it. Like, when I wasn't just saying it for sex. I was also going to give you my fraternity pin. Make it official."

"You wanted to pin me? I would've passed my candle, gotten serenaded, and everything?"

"Yeah, you would have."

"So, why didn't you ask?"

"I was kinda nervous. I wasn't sure how you felt. It bothered me how tight you and Phillip were. Danny, too. I'd heard rumors about you and Danny. Even asked you about them."

"And I told you, Danny and I were never together."

"I know, but you lived with them both. You never once invited me to stay with you. You always stayed at the frat house, and I don't know. I was nervous, then I got drunk, and then things got all messed up. You know the rest."

"The rest. As in I left."

"I felt so bad the next day that I called my mom. She told me to send you the prettiest roses I could find and to send lots of them. I said I was really sorry on the card. I even signed it, *Love, Jason*, but it didn't work."

"The problem was, it seemed like it wasn't just that one time. Like, you were always looking for a fight. I was used to being around guys who avoided fights. They didn't need to prove their worth by fighting. I realized that wasn't the kind of guy I wanted to be with."

"I'm not like that anymore. I've grown up, graduated, gotten a good job, and I know what I want. I think it's fate that I ran into you tonight."

"I'm glad you've gotten your life together, Jason. I'm happy for you. So, what is it you want?"

"You."

"Me? I'm engaged!"

"Yeah, but you're *only* engaged. You aren't married yet. Officially, you're still single."

"But I wanna marry Phillip."

"I think you should marry me."

"Marry you?"

"You have to admit, we had fun together. And, this summer, when we hooked up, it was good. We have amazing chemistry."

"We were both drunk, and you never called. I wouldn't call that amazing chemistry."

"I got the feeling you didn't want me to call. Like you were maybe, sorta dating someone."

"Oh, so my maybe, sorta dating someone scared you away, but my being freaking engaged doesn't?"

"Let me see the ring."

I proudly show him all two gorgeous carats of it. Even in the dark bar, you can see how it catches the light. I love my ring.

Jason holds my hand and studies it. "I could do way better than that."

I know that's his way of slamming Phillip. Like the ring isn't big enough or something. What he doesn't realize is that it's the ring of my dreams, so he totally just slammed my taste, too.

He gets off the barstool and wraps his arm around my waist. "Marry me instead." I open my mouth to say something, but he's like, "I'm not done. Don't settle for marrying your friend. That's what people do when they can't find anyone else. Like, if we're not married by the time we're thirty, we marry each other."

"It's not like that with Phillip."

"I think it is. I think, if you and Phillip were that amazing together, you would've gotten together in college. I'm serious. Marry me. We'll call Phillip afterward and break it to him gently. Tell him the wedding's off, that we got married. We'll fly to Vegas tonight, get a suite at the Four Seasons, and buy you a new ring. A ring that will put this one to shame. I'm talking massive. Five or six carats, all for you. Then, we'll find you a sexy white dress and get married."

"Your parents would kill you."

"Not once I told them who I had run away with. You'd have anything your heart desires. Always. That's what I can give you, Jadyn James."

With Phillip's coldness tonight and my total insaneness—even if it's happy insaneness—with the wedding planning right now, running away to Vegas does sound sorta freeing.

I look at Jason.

Jason is adorable and sexy, and I'm kinda flattered by this.

I mean, now, I have two guys who wanna marry me. I feel sort of unstoppable. This must be how Danny feels when he scores a game-winning touchdown.

"Jadyn James, I do love you. Marry me, and I promise you a great life. What do you say?"

"I say you should've told me you loved me and pinned me back then instead of getting drunk. I'm also saying that, after we hooked up this summer, you should've called. But you didn't."

He looks embarrassed. "I tried to tell you after."

"What do you mean?"

"I went to your house after I sent the flowers, but you weren't there. Phillip answered the door, told me it'd probably be best if I left you alone. Danny and two massive football players walked up behind him, all nodding, letting me know, if I didn't leave you alone, I'd have to answer to them. Plus, you ignored my calls. I'm sorry. I should've tried harder. I promise, I'll make you happy."

Well, shoot. Now, I feel sorry for Jason. I feel bad I didn't thank him for the flowers and that I didn't hear what he had to say. I got mad and hurt, and I walked away. Someday, I'm gonna grow up and realize that people screw up, and you need to at least listen to what they have to say. Let them explain before you convict them of whatever you think they did. I didn't give Jason a chance to explain, and it could've maybe made a difference. *If I had listened back then, would I be with him now? Or would I have still ended up with Phillip?*

I remember, after Phillip picked me up from the dance, I ate ice cream and whined on his shoulder. I really liked Jason, but Phillip told me I shouldn't be with a boy who didn't treat me with respect. He told me I deserved better. He sounded just like my dad had when he used to talk about Jake, and for the first time ever, I took Phillip's advice concerning a boy.

"Jason, I'm sorry I didn't thank you for the flowers."

"It's okay," he says.

And, seeing a flicker of hope, he wraps me in a hug. I don't mind the hug because it feels like one of those closing-a-chapter-of-your-life hugs.

Well, it does until Jason starts hugging my ass.

"I'm serious, Jadyn. Vegas tonight? Happily ever after?"

Happily ever after.

I can't help it. Whenever those words cross my mind, I see Phillip's face. I know he's my happily ever after even if he did ignore me tonight. I sure hope I'm right about Phillip.

"I can't. I love Phillip. I wouldn't want to hurt him."

Jason gets his haughty look. "He'd get over it."

"Maybe I'm not that easy to get over, *Jason*," I say in a smart-ass tone. The thought of Phillip getting over me easily makes me mad.

Jason snarls back, "Fine, but when you divorce your friend in six months because you were wrong, don't come looking for me. This is a one-time offer."

"Then, you don't really love me, and I've definitely made the right decision. Good to see you, Jason."

He's like, "Whatever."

I grab the full pitchers off the bar, yell at the bartender to put it on my tab, and hurry back to the safety of my friends.

Even though I know I did the right thing, my encounter with Jason has my mind spinning. I sip on my beer as if it were poison and finally go home.

Phillip waited up for me. "So, did ya have fun? Who all was there?"

"Katie, Lisa, Joey, Neil, and, um, Jason O'Connor."

"I hate that guy."

"So I heard. He told me how he came to the house to apologize and what you said to him."

"Oh." Phillip tilts his head and looks at me. "It was for your own good, you know."

"Wanna know what else he told me?"

"Not really."

"The night of formal, he was going to tell me he loved me and ask me to wear his fraternity pin. That's what he came to tell me that day."

"I didn't know that."

"Yeah, I know. I liked him a lot. He came to apologize, and you had no right to interfere."

"Danny and I were watching out for you. That guy was an ass."

"That ass asked me to go to Vegas with him tonight and marry him."

"He what? Did he not see the rock? Did he not know that we're engaged?"

"Yeah, he knew. Saw the ring. Told me I deserved better—at least five or six carats."

Phillip slowly sits back down. He kinda looks like I just punched him in the gut. "It sounds like you actually considered it."

"I'll be honest; there was a part of me that considered it. Before I left tonight, I tried to kiss you, and I did stuff you normally love. You practically pushed me off you. Do you even like me anymore? I don't wanna marry someone who's already sick of me."

Phillip runs his hand through his hair and sighs. "Princess, I just needed a few minutes to relax and unwind. I had a busy day. I just wanted to sit, watch golf, and not think for a few minutes."

"Well, I'm just saying, that's not the send-off your girl-friend—"

Phillip interrupts me. "Fiancée."

"Should get when she's headed off to a bar full of hot temptations."

Phillip looks irritated at me for saying that, but I usually say what's on my mind. And my mind is a little pissed off at Phillip.

"I'm serious, Phillip. You chose TV golf over a romp on the couch with me. And then sent me to the bar."

He considers that. "Probably not a smart move on my part,

huh?"

"I'm thinking, not so much."

Phillip grabs my ass and kisses the spot just below my ear that gets me every time. He puts his lips on my ear and whispers, "So, does that mean you're still horny?"

I have to give him a little shit. "Actually, I already got that taken care of tonight."

I'm probably not very convincing though since I'm running my hand under the waistband of his shorts. Phillip is just so hot. I can't help myself.

"You're a very naughty girl for even thinking about marrying someone else. Young lady, go to your room," he says in a deep, *you just got caught by the principal, filling the school pool with goldfish* kind of way.

And, for a second, I think I might be in trouble, but then he flashes that sexy grin and herds me into the bedroom. And, um, well, you can probably figure out the rest.

Shiny, gorgeous hair.

WEDNESDAY, DECEMBER 20TH

I FINISHED SOME last-minute Christmas shopping this morning. Now, I'm sorting through my condo. I can't believe we get to move into our house right after the honeymoon. I'm so excited, and I'm really trying to get organized. I have piles to donate, piles of stuff to return to friends, piles of shower gifts, and trash piles. I swing open the patio door because I'm sweating from all this organization, grab a stack of magazines I need to go through, and sit on the couch.

All of a sudden, I see something move out of the corner of my eye.

AAAHHH!

OMG!

Like, no, you don't understand.

This is like, *OH MY GOD!*

I'm seeing *the* biggest freaking spider I have ever seen in my life!

The spider is standing just inside the patio door, staring at me. Not even moving. And he is big enough to really creep me out!

Think, Jadyn.

Raid!

I need Raid! Or bug spray of some kind.

JILLIAN DODD

I run into the bathroom and realize I have no Raid, but I do find some mosquito repellent. I run back out to the living room, stand on the coffee table, and fire it down on him. The spider moves toward me, but he doesn't die. It doesn't really even seem to faze him.

Damn!

Now, he knows I'm after him!

I jump from the coffee table to the couch, and then I run back into the bathroom and look for something else.

I slowly come back out, looking for him.

The spider hasn't really moved much, but his little hairy legs are twitching like he's trying to figure out his next move.

I'm armed with more things to try to kill him. First, I spray him with a great hair product that adds shine to my hair. The spider doesn't die, but now, the living room smells like grapes. I throw the shining spray onto the couch and spray him with some Big Sexy Hair Spray.

The spider just looks into my eyes and sends me spider telepathy. He says, *I'm going to have shiny, gorgeous hair when I kill you.*

Ahh!

What else do I have?

I spy my tennis shoe by the front door.

Oh. No way.

Gross.

I jump off the coffee table, leap toward the hall closet, and grab one of Phillip's big running shoes.

I toss it at the spider.

The spider, I swear to God, dodges the shoe, laughs, and throws it back at me.

I decide it's time to call in reinforcements.

I grab my cell and call Phillip.

"Phillip, there's a huge spider in the house. You've *got* to come and KILL IT NOW!"

288

"Princess," he says in a patronizing tone, "surely, you can kill a little spider."

"Didn't you hear me? I said, it's a *huge-ass* spider!"

"Well, kill it with some bug spray or a shoe. I'm kinda busy here."

"I tried that, Phillip. I tried mosquito spray because I didn't have any Raid. When that didn't work, I tried hair shiner and hair spray. And the spider just told me, *Thanks. I hate mosquitos, and now, my hair looks shiny and gorgeous*, and I swear to God, it threw your shoe back at me! That's how big this spider is. You *have* to come NOW!"

"Calm down. Suck it up in the vacuum cleaner then."

"And give him a new home in my vacuum? No way! He's not a genie, Phillip. He won't come back out and offer me three wishes. He'll come back out and be pissed at being all dirty, and he will AMBUSH us in our sleep!" I scream, "AHHH!" and jump back onto the coffee table.

"What now?"

"He's chasing me, Phillip! Don't you understand? I'm under attack here! Stop talking to me, hang up, run to your car, and get your ASS over here! NOW!"

"Oh, who's bossy now?"

"Phillip, when I said I was under attack, I wasn't joking. I'm pretty sure I saw him send out a battle cry to all his spider friends. And he's strategically blocking my way to the patio door because that's where his troops are gonna come in! And, when you finally get home, there will be nothing left of me but a carcass covered in spider webs with a million huge spiders eating at me. Do you know what a horrible death that will be?"

"You're being silly. Just kill the damn spider."

"Fine. I'm done marrying you. I'm gonna go find a real man to marry. One who's willing to take care of me when I'm in a crisis and neeeed him!"

"All right, jeez. I'm coming."

I hang up and see my neighbor Wayne out in his yard.

"WAAAYNE!" I scream my loudest, most horrifying scream toward my patio door.

Wayne turns to look in my direction, but I don't think he can see me because the sun's in his eyes, so I yell, "HEEELP! SOS! SOS! CODE RED! Foxtrot, Unicorn, Charlie, KILO!!!"

Wayne is a retired military man, so I screamed all the military terms I could think of.

Wayne was, like, Special Forces and all that. *That* is exactly what I need! Not some dumb boy who's going to argue on the phone with me as to whether or not I need help.

I must've gotten Wayne's attention because he comes running over to my patio door.

He's just about to cross my threshold into enemy territory when I scream, "Stop! Don't come any closer!"

Wayne is rapidly assessing the area with his eyes. I think he thinks I was attacked, and there's a rapist running loose, and I'm standing on my coffee table, trying to avoid him.

"Jadyn, what's wrong? Why are you on the coffee table?"

I put my finger up to my lips to tell him to shush, and then I slowly, secretly point down at the spider on the floor. The spider has been sitting halfway between the patio door and me. It's been staring at me, sizing me up, trying to figure out just how many webs it will take to catch me and make me a year's worth of meals. But, when it heard Wayne's voice, it moved ninety degrees to face him. I'm feeling a little scared for Wayne, but he's ex-military, right?

He can deal, I would think.

Wayne looks down at the massive spider. And what does this ex-Special Forces guy do?

He shudders and shakes his head at me. "HOLY SHIT! That's a big freaking spider. Spiders give me the willies."

"Me, too. The spider has been staring at me, planning my demise."

"I can see that."

But Wayne's brave, so he says, "You got any big gloves?"

ABOUT TWENTY MINUTES later, Phillip strolls leisurely through the front door.

"Phillip, it's been *twenty* minutes. The office is only six minutes away *during* morning traffic! You didn't even hurry!"

"I needed to get gas. So, where is this huge spider?" He looks at me in that way. That way people do when they think you're a stupid idiot, and they're just humoring you.

Which makes me really mad.

"Phillip, you should've been so worried about me that you drove over here on fumes, and when the car ran out of gas, you should've ditched it and run as fast as you could to save me."

He rolls his eyes at me. "I think maybe you're being a tad overdramatic."

"No! I AM NOT! And you missed out. Wayne was outside in his yard, and so I screamed like a maniac from the coffee table. He came over and saved me, and the spider was so big; it gave even him the willies. And he's an ex-RANGER! And I'm just little old me!"

Phillip starts to protest, so I continue. "Yes, Phillip, the ex-Ranger, Special Forces, top military guy told me he wished he'd brought his gun; it was so big. And, yes, he did kill it. Well, eventually."

"Eventually?"

"Yes, well, first, he put on oven mitts because I didn't have any kind of protective gloves. He also used a spatula, which is now in the trash. Then, he took a paper bag and, like, herded the spider into the bag with the spatula. He has the spider in the bag on his deck if you'd like to go now and see its carcass."

I watch Phillip go over to Wayne's deck. Wayne walks in his condo, comes back out with beers for the two of them, and shows him the bag.

I go on a massive spider hunt. Checking everywhere I can think of, making sure he had no friends in my house.

Phillip comes back over with a beer in his hand. "Wow. I'm sorry. That *was* a big freaking spider."

"I know. I'm very traumatized." I pout.

He sets his beer down, pulls me in close, and starts kissing down my neck. "Let's see if I can help you forget about the spider."

"Phillip, you didn't save me. You don't get to have thank-you sex. I should be having sex with Wayne."

"Hmm, but I'm here now, and he's calling all his friends to come over and see the dead spider."

He lets go of me, and for a second, I'm worried he doesn't want me after all. But he gives me a grin, locks the patio door, and then picks me up and throws me over his shoulder like I'm a sack of something.

I scream and giggle as Phillip carries me through the maze of boxes and into our bedroom. He tosses me on the spider-free bed.

"I think maybe I need to earn my own, uh, Special Forces badge."

And, wow ...

Oh my ...

I really should find big spiders and have a neighbor kill them for me more often.

Seriously.

I don't know about Special Forces, but I'm pretty sure Phillip could medal in sexual Olympics.

You're making me cry.

THURSDAY, DECEMBER 21ST

PHILLIP AND I are in the car, heading to Kansas City. He's signed a lease on a temporary office space, and we're actually ordering the office furniture today. Once we're done, we're meeting Lori and Danny for dinner. Tomorrow, we have more meetings, and then we're hanging out with them this weekend. Lori wants to help me shop for our new house, and I wanna find a couple of new bikinis for our honeymoon.

Phillip excitedly says, "I got an email yesterday. The custom Nikes just shipped!"

I'm about to reply when my phone buzzes. I look down and see a text from Danny.

Danny: *I NEED YOU NOW! WHERE ARE YOU?*

I'm about to type a smart-ass remark about him needing me, but then I notice how the words are all in capitals, and there are no winky faces. A feeling of dread washes over me. Something's wrong.

Me: *Danny, what's wrong? Call me. We're still about two hours away.*

Danny: *Can't talk. Lori. Bleeding. Hospital. Miscarriage?*

Danny: Pray.

Me: Do you want us to come? I'll cancel our appointments.

Danny: Please. I'm freaking out. I'm afraid we're gonna lose the baby.

Me: You won't. Like, you can't. We'll be there as fast as we can. What happened?

Danny: Doctor is here. Gotta go.

I tell him we'll be there as fast as we can, but I can't say anything to Phillip.

Not yet.

I can barely breathe.

I'm in the middle of a flashback.

Phillip was talking on the phone with his dad.
We rushed to the hospital.
Phillip's dad met us at the door.
He took my hands and told me my mom didn't make it.
I rushed up to see my dad.

It's been four years, but it feels like yesterday.

I close my eyes.

I saw my dad.
I heard him say, "Angel."
I laid my head on his chest.
He stopped breathing.

Phillip says, "Princess, what's wrong? Why do you look like you just saw a ghost?"

I close my eyes tight and take a deep breath. "Danny just sent me a text. They're at the hospital. Lori's bleeding. He thinks she might be having a miscarriage, and he wants us to pray. He also wanted to know how close we were. He wants us to go there, says he's freaking out."

Phillip tightly grabs my hand, looks worried, and drives faster. "We'd better hurry then."

While Phillip drives, I say a very long prayer.

I pray that they're okay. I plead with God not to take them away from me, too.

I'm surprised I still pray. I prayed hard for my dad, but it didn't work. I hope it works today. I've texted Danny a couple of times, but he hasn't replied, which can't be good.

After what seems like an eternity but is really only a couple of hours later, we pull up to the hospital. We get out of the car, and Phillip grabs my hand, quickly pulling me toward the hospital entrance.

The closer we get, the more I sweat. I don't know if I can do this.

I hate hospitals. I really do. Only bad things happen in hospitals. I haven't been in a hospital since that night, except for when I had strep throat really bad.

I've never visited anyone in the hospital because people die in hospitals.

But then I think about Danny's message, how desperate he sounded, and I know I have to go. He needs us.

Just like I needed Phillip that night.

We get their room number from the information desk and ride up the elevator.

As we walk down the fourth-floor corridor, I'm bracing myself for the worst. For Danny to tell me that Lori and the baby are dead.

I get super hot.

And then I feel light-headed, like maybe I'm going to pass out.

I stop, lean up against the wall, close my eyes, and take a deep breath.

Phillip realizes I'm not walking next to him anymore and turns around to look for me.

He walks back toward me. "What are you doing? We need to hurry."

"I have to get out of here, Phillip. I can't do this. I think I'm gonna throw up and then maybe pass out."

He wraps me in a one-armed hug and pulls me close, exactly the way he did when he walked off the elevator that night.

My mind flashes back again.

How he was mad at me.
How we'd fought.
How I was so afraid he'd hate me forever.
How I couldn't believe my mom was dead.
How Dad stopped breathing.
How the alarms went off.
How they rushed me out of the room and didn't tell me anything.

My own breathing is ragged. I need to get out of here.

Now.

Phillip touches my face and says, "Princess, it's gonna be okay. I promise."

"You can't promise that, Phillip. You don't know." I start to cry.

I cannot do this.

"Danny said he needed you. If it's bad, he's going to need you even more."

He's right. If it's bad, he's going to need me, and I love Danny. I won't let him go through whatever this is alone even if I feel like I'm gonna be sick.

Phillip holds my hand and leads me down the hall in the same way he led me through most of my parents' funeral.

Tears are rolling down my face.

I've been able to hold my tears back since my parents died, but I can't seem to push them back right now.

WE GET TO room 416. Lori's room.

I'm scared. I don't know what to do. *Should we just stand out here?*

Phillip knocks gently on the door.

Danny opens it. There's a wide grin on his face, and he immediately pulls Phillip into a hug.

"Look at this, Mac!" he says as he excitedly shoves an ultrasound photo in front of Phillip's face.

When I see Lori alive and lying in the hospital bed, I let out a cry of relief. She looks scared, but there's a smile on her face.

I rush to her side. "Are you okay? Is the baby okay? What happened?"

"I'm fine. The baby's fine. I was bleeding this morning, and it was enough that the doctor sent us straight here. I was sure I was having a miscarriage. I think I panicked everyone for nothing. Everything is okay now, and the bleeding has stopped."

I let out a huge, cleansing breath of air, bend down, and tightly hug her. "I was so worried."

She says, "Stop crying. You're making me cry." She wipes her tears and then shakes her head at me. "I really didn't think you'd come. Here. To the hospital. I thought you'd make up some excuse."

"I don't have the best of luck with hospitals, Lori, so I try to avoid them."

"Babies are born in hospitals. They're good things."

"That's true, I guess. I was really worried." I give her another big hug. "I love you."

Danny interrupts my hug by shoving the ultrasound photo in front of my face.

I see a very teeny baby. I'm amazed at how small it is but how much it looks like a baby. Like, I guess I thought it would still sorta look like a squid or something. I look closer because I'm dying to know if it's a boy or a girl.

"Danny, they covered up its boy or girl parts!"

"I know! We don't wanna find out. The little monkey is gonna be loved either way, and we're gonna have lots more kids."

"Lots more kids?" Lori says. "Um, let's see if I can do one right. Then, we can talk about more."

Danny snatches the pic away from me and shoves it back in Phillip's face. "So, look at this, Mac. What's it look like the baby's doing?"

Phillip closely studies the photo. "Sleeping?"

"No, look at this. Look at its arm. Doesn't it look like he's throwing a pass?"

Phillip grins. "Yeah, sorta. Must be a boy then, huh?"

"Hey, girls can throw passes!" I say.

"Whatever," Danny says. "My guess is that it's a boy."

"That's my guess, too," Lori says.

I look at the ultrasound closer. It looks to me like the baby is either sleeping with its arm up in the air or throwing its arm up in a cheer, but I decide not to mention that. "So, everything's okay then? Like, why were you bleeding? I thought all bleeding was bad."

"Not always," Lori says. Then, she glances at Danny, who has a very satisfied look on his face.

"What?" I say.

Lori rolls her eyes and hands me a book on things to expect when you're pregnant. I read the passage that she highlighted.

During pregnancy, it's not unusual to bleed after sex. Your cervix is tender and sensitive. If this happens to you, you shouldn't have intercourse again until you've seen your doctor. Having normal intercourse won't cause you to have a miscarriage.

I read it once and then read it again. "I don't get it. What's that got to do with—ohhh, so you had sex, and *it* caused the bleeding?"

Lori laughs self-consciously and nods her head.

Danny puffs his chest out and flexes a big bicep at us. "What it doesn't mention in that book is that I'm huge. Like, extremely well-endowed."

I laugh and look back down at the book. "You're right. It doesn't mention that. Oh, wait. It does. It's scribbled here in the margin. A little disclaimer. *Danny Diamond is so huge that this does not apply. Danny Diamond should proceed with caution.*"

Phillip raises his eyebrows at me. "So, what does it say about me?"

"Huh?"

"Well, I am bigger than Danny."

"What? How would you even know that, Phillip?"

He grins at me. "Well, aside from years of locker rooms, we measured."

"You measured? As in you got naked together, got them hard, and compared? How did I miss out on all the good stuff?"

Danny chimes in, "Jay, we're not gay. We measured separately and told each other our numbers, but I think Phillip's fibbing."

"Phillip never lies."

"Whatever. So, the bleeding happened because I'm amazing, and pregnant women are super horny."

Phillip and I look at each other with wide eyes.

Danny shrugs his broad shoulders and grins. "It's not my fault she kept saying, 'Harder.'"

Lori blushes down to her toes. "Danny!"

Danny just laughs. He's quite proud of himself. "We're among friends here."

Lori says, "Well, you and your friend can go get me some fried chicken. I'm starving. I want extra crispy with mashed potatoes and biscuits. And make sure you get those honey packets."

"I swear, I'm gonna start a pregnancy delivery service. You know how many times I've had to run out and get whatever she's hungry for?"

THE BOYS LEAVE to go get chicken. I'm still sitting here with an amused smile on my face.

"Wipe that smirk off your face," she tells me.

"So, pregnancy makes you horny?"

She looks at the door and makes sure the boys are gone. "Ohmigawd, Jade, yes. Here, read this."

I read a passage about increased blood flow to certain lady parts and think that's something I really did not need to know.

Pregnancy would freak me the heck out. I'm just saying.

When I set the book back down, she continues, "Seriously, sex with Danny has always been amazing. But, yeah, this morning was like ecstasy." Then, she changes the subject. "So, Danny told me something about you seeing Richie Rich at the bar. Did he really ask you to marry him?"

"Lori, you need to be thinking about you and the baby and taking it easy, relaxing."

"All I've been doing is thinking about the baby. I wanna talk about your life. Tell me a story. Some gossip. Something. Distract me."

I lie on the bed next to her. "He did. I don't think he was serious though. Did Danny tell you, the night of formal, he was going to ask me to wear his fraternity pin?"

"Oh, Jade. You would've gotten to pass your candle!"

"I know. I'm kinda bummed by that. He also said something that's been bugging me. Do you think I'm settling by marrying Phillip?"

"Are you nuts? Phillip is fine. He's hot, he's sweet, and he adores you. Why would you ever say that?"

"Jason said it. I just ... I don't know. Couples counseling is not going well, Lori. I'm pretty sure we're failing."

"You're not failing. No one fails."

I grab her hand and try to change the subject by saying, "I hope not. I'm so happy the baby is okay."

"Me, too. So, I know you. You have to have some gossip or some funny story. You always do."

"I have some kind of baddish news."

"Do I want to hear baddish news right now?"

"It's more baddish gossip. You know how Katie and Eric haven't, like, been doing that great, like, in their marriage, right?"

"Yeah, I did hear that."

"Well, did you hear that she's been talking to and going to lunch with Neil?"

"I didn't hear that! What's that all about?"

"I don't know. I don't think they know for sure, but it sounds like she's considering getting a divorce and dating Neil."

"Scandalous." She giggles. "Seriously though, it's really sad. It would suck to go through a divorce."

"You're lucky. You and Danny have a good relationship."

"He cried today, about the baby. I've never seen Danny cry. And I've been giving him a hard time. I just feel so—I can't even explain it—like I'm not even in control of my own body. Like I have this alien thing growing in me, changing my body, and kicking me. It's kinda freaky, but at the same time, it's so incredible. I've been sick and crabby and probably not very nice to him."

"He's worried about being a good dad, but he really loves you, and he really loves the baby."

"Yeah, I know. I'm incredibly lucky. We've decided that we really can't understand what each other is going through and to just focus on the baby."

"Good. You know Danny's going to be an amazing father."

"That's one of the reasons I wanted to marry him so bad. He's so much fun, so full of life and love. And speaking of that, when are you two gonna have kids?"

"Not for a very long time."

"You're going to be amazing parents, too. And Danny's right; having our kids grow up together would be so cool. You know, you're more like my sister than my real sister."

"Really? You have no idea what that means to me. You know, because it's just me." Tears start leaking out of my eyes again. *What is wrong with me? Why can't I push the tears back anymore?*

Lori grabs my hand and puts my palm across her belly. "Feel that?"

"Oh my God! The baby kicks hard! Lori, that's so freaking weird! Does it feel like that all the time?"

"It is kicking a lot now. I was telling Nick about it, and he keeps teasing Danny. Telling him the baby is gonna be a kicker and not a quarterback. That's why Danny's all, 'Look, the baby looks like it's throwing a pass.' Wouldn't it have been hilarious if the baby had looked like it was kicking?"

"Nick's a loser. He was so funny in Vegas. He was giving me crap about being kinda drunk, but he was dancing with me."

"He only dances when he's drunk!"

Then, I tell her about the spider, Wayne's reaction and rescue, and Phillip strolling in for sex. And I maybe confide a little about how freaking amazing sex with Phillip is.

"I remember the first time you introduced me to Phillip. I think it's funny that we didn't get to be good friends until junior year."

"Well, that's 'cause you never seemed like you wanted to have any fun."

"And it seemed like all you wanted to do was have fun. Do you remember when I asked you to introduce me to Phillip? We all thought he was so cute, but I'd never met him before."

"I don't remember that."

"We were dressed as slutty secretaries, and the guys were all in suits. Phillip looked good."

"Phillip always looks handsome in a suit."

"You were like, 'Come on, I'll introduce you. He's my best friend and my roommate.' I'll never forget it. He and Blake were literally surrounded by girls. You sauntered over and walked through the girls. He wrapped his arms around you and kissed you on the cheek. The girls all gave you the dirtiest looks." She laughs. "Then, you told him his tie was all messed up."

"Oh, I do remember that. Phillip could never tie a tie. I always did it for him. And they were probably surrounding Blake. You know that's how he got his nickname, right? His Royal Hotness? Blakeness?"

She laughs. "I didn't know that. That's funny. Blake is a cutie. So, anyway, you undid Phillip's tie and retied it. Then, you stood back and looked at him. I swear, I knew then that you loved him."

"You were always too smart for your own good."

"You introduced us and then totally checked him out. Like, stood back and looked him up and down. You told him he looked too uptight, stole his tie, and put it on. He grabbed the end of the tie and pulled you in close to him. I really thought he was going to kiss you. Instead, he whispered in your ear. I've always wondered what he said."

I laugh. "He told me I could tie him up later at home and that my skirt was so short that it was almost a crime."

"He always flirt with you like that?"

"I always kinda thought he was just playing around, but yeah, he did."

"Then, we got drunk together."

"I didn't get drunk. You did though. I think I created a monster."

"You did teach me how to party."

"I think you always knew how to party. You were just afraid to let loose."

"That's true. We had a lot of fun. You wanna know what surprised me the most about you?"

"Sure."

"You kinda had a reputation as a party girl. And you knew so many guys. I thought you were slutty. I was surprised, once I got to know you, how good you were. Like, you made out with a lot of guys, so I just assumed you did more."

"I'm not a good girl, Lori."

"Jade, you didn't have sex until college."

I roll my eyes at her. "I knew lots of guys 'cause of Phillip and Danny, and I just wanted to wait until I was in love. That didn't really work out so well."

"Like I said, closet good girl. Well, until Bradley."

"Yes, Bradley the bartender. He was supposed to be my first one-night stand. But then it was so much fun, and it turned into a bunch of one-night stands."

"What about Danny?"

"What do you mean?"

"In Vegas, they were talking about you and Danny making out. It sounded like it was often. Was it? I always thought prom night was the last time you kissed."

"No, we kissed in college some. It wasn't a big deal."

"You never told me that."

"Because it didn't matter. Danny and I were friends. Sometimes, we'd get drunk together and kiss. Usually after a loss. I think it was, like, comforting to him or something."

"So, was it just kissing?"

"Pretty much."

"Just tell me, please."

"Why? It doesn't matter anymore. If I wanted Danny for myself, I would've never set the two of you up. When we kissed, he had yet to find love, and I'd found it, but I didn't know what to do with it. It didn't mean anything. It was just for fun. Like most things are with me and Danny. We've just always had fun together."

"Danny says you always got into trouble together. I think you did more than kiss."

"Fine. We did more than kiss. There was even a time when he attacked me on the couch. It was, like, spur of the moment. I thought we were finally going to."

"What stopped you?"

"Phillip came home. It was pretty funny. Danny and I looked at each other, jumped up, and ran into our rooms. We never kissed after that."

"When was that?"

"Fall of my junior year. And I'm glad we didn't. Danny means a lot to me. I think sleeping with him would've been like crossing *Sleep with Danny Diamond* off my bucket list. Like, every girl I knew wanted to sleep with him. My competitiveness sort of made me want to, too."

"I didn't want to sleep with him."

"You were lying to yourself."

She giggles.

"Speaking of that," I say, "I think I might be lying to myself about Phillip."

She looks concerned. "Why would you say that?"

"I told you, we're failing couples counseling."

"I thought you didn't care about couples counseling."

"On the surface, I'm not taking it seriously. But I'm there. I'm listening, and I'm trying hard not to because I'm hearing stuff I don't wanna hear. What I'm hearing is that our marriage is going to be a failure."

"Oh, Jade, don't be silly."

I was gonna argue with her, but I remember something else

I've been wanting to tell her. "Oh, I almost forgot! I had another weird dream the other night."

"Tell me about it." Her face brightens.

She loves reveling in my misery, I think.

"I'm still worried that, with all these dreams, someone is trying to tell me something, or maybe I'm trying to tell myself something. I'm not sure."

"Stop being so dramatic, Jade, and tell me about it."

"I'm not dramatic! That's, like, twice in the last few days someone has accused me of it. And I don't like it!"

"Fine. You're not being dramatic. Tell me!"

"Okay, so it's my wedding ceremony. It's gorgeous. There are candles lit on top of every pew, on every surface. I walk down the aisle in a beautiful Balenciaga gown. I have a gorgeous, long, flowing veil."

Lori interrupts me, "How do you know who Balenciaga is? Do they make wedding dresses?"

"I'm not sure. *Sex and the City* maybe?"

"I know. I was telling you about that Balenciaga motorcycle bag that Mark Conway's wife got, like the only one in Kansas City and how it cost, like, two thousand dollars."

She likes to think our conversations are so significant that they're affecting my dreams.

"What's that got to do with the dress?"

"Nothing really. Go on."

"So, I go up to the altar. Phillip and I say our vows, and when the minister says, 'You may kiss the bride,' Phillip lifts the veil off my face. That's when I FREAK! I can't do it! I can't go through with it! So, I run down the aisle with my veil flying behind me. Of course, with all the candles, it catches fire, but I don't know that it's blazing behind me until people start screaming in horror."

"Oh, how awful," she says, but then she laughs.

"You're laughing at my dream?"

"Just a little. Go on. You are entertaining, I will admit."

"So, it's awful. I'm on fire—well, my veil is anyway. But, luckily, when I get toward the back of the church, I see the back rows are filled with firemen."

"Firemen? What are firemen doing at your wedding?"

"I'm not sure. Did I tell you about Mrs. Mac's Facebook status about the hot fireman working on the fire hydrant on their street? And how she, Mrs. D, and two other neighbors were pretending to sit outside and talk, just so they could drool over him?"

"No, you didn't! They both friend requested me, but I ignored them."

"You did? Ohmigawd, you should totally add them. They're hilarious, and they share waaay too much information. I laugh every day. It's cheap entertainment.

"So, anyway, I left work and went out to join them, and it turns out, the hot fireman was Ryan, this guy I dated freshman year. He was a senior and the first boy I ever French-kissed. Well, technically, I guess that was Danny, but that was more of a tutorial thing."

"Danny taught you how to French kiss? Why have I never heard about this before?"

"It was dumb. I was super nervous about kissing Ryan because this other guy, like, shoved his tongue down my throat once, and it was awful. I didn't wanna be awful, so I begged Danny to tell me how to do it right. It's just one of those things you kinda have to do, so he took pity on me and showed me.

"Anyway, so I go over there and get out of my car, and he calls out my name. I told him about the ladies watching and asked him to pretend to get hot and take off his shirt. So, he did even though it was, like, fifty degrees out."

"Oh, that's hilarious."

"What's even better is, when he was shirtless, they took pictures with him. They posted the pics on their Facebook!"

"No way! Show me your phone."

I pull up the photos and show her. She laughs a hard, full-belly laugh. It's good to see her happy. I was so worried earlier.

"So, back to my dream. I either invited the firemen to the wedding or I had to invite them because of all the candles. Like, maybe some fire code. Kinda like when they supervise fireworks shows."

"Oh, that sounds reasonable. Okay, so then what?"

"This totally hot, buff fireman runs up to me."

"Is he in his fireman's outfit?"

"They all are, but they aren't wearing shirts. Just, like, their jackets, pants, and those hard red hats with the yellow tape on them. And their jackets are open, so you can see their sexy abs."

"Nice. So, was it that Ryan guy?"

"Let me finish. So, this sexy-ass fireman runs up to me, tackles me, and rolls me."

"Rolls you? Why doesn't he just take the veil off?"

"Stop, drop, and roll. Don't you know anything? And stop interrupting. This is serious."

"Okay, sorry."

"So, he puts out my veil fire. And, after rolling me, he ends up lying on top of me. He grins this gorgeous smile at me and starts kissing me. At my wedding! And this fireman is so freaking hot! I want him, like, right there. And, for a minute, I think we're gonna have sex right there, in the aisle at my wedding, with everyone watching! But, all of a sudden, he pulls me up off the ground, and we run, hand in hand, outside the church. We grab the bars on the back of the fire truck as it pulls away."

"So, you left your wedding with a fireman? I see two problems with this. One, you'd already said your vows, so you were legally married to Phillip, and—"

"Let me finish."

"Okay, but—"

"The fireman was Phillip."

"What? So you left Phillip the groom at the altar to run away with Phillip the fireman?"

"Yep."

"But that makes no sense."

"No shit."

"Okay, let's analyze this. Do you have some secret fantasy about firemen? Maybe you should have Phillip dress up as one and come and *save* you."

I roll my eyes.

She snaps her fingers. "It could mean you want more adventure with Phillip."

"Maybe."

"You know what it really means? I think your mind is telling you what you already know. That, no matter where you go, Phillip is the guy of your dreams and is perfect for you. It just means that you're destined to be together."

"I think it means that I can run away, but he'll always find me. It means, I'm trapped. I'm stuck with him."

"I wish I had dreams like yours. They're always so good. I never remember mine."

"I thought pregnant women had lots of crazy dreams?"

"Not me. Not so far anyway. But I swear, I could put a bomb-sniffing dog out of work. I can smell *everything*! Speaking of which, I'm pretty sure I smell Phillip and Danny coming back with the fried chicken."

And she is right.

About thirty seconds later, I smell fried chicken coming down the hall.

PHILLIP AND DANNY burst in the hospital room.

Danny says, "Mark Conway is announcing his retirement

today. He's supposed to be holding a press conference in, like, fifteen minutes. I just got a text about it."

We turn on the TV, eat chicken, and watch him announce his retirement. Although we're very excited about what this means for Danny's future, it still makes us all a little sad because we know, someday, Danny will announce his retirement.

"Not for a long-ass time though," Danny says. He actually looks a little teary-eyed.

Lori says, "I've never seen you cry, and now, you're getting misty-eyed twice in one day."

"I'm excited about what this means for me, but I know, someday, that'll be me up there."

Lori grabs his hand and says, "Not for a long time, baby. Not for a long time."

I really hope and pray she's right about that.

One time in middle school, when Danny was a lot smaller, he got a concussion. Ever since then, I say a prayer before every game. And, so far, Danny's been blessed. He's never really gotten hurt. He broke his non-throwing arm once in high school and slightly sprained his ankle in college. Well, he did sprain his ankle, and it did slow him down, but it didn't stop him. And, of course, there were lots of games where his body was pretty bruised up and sore but never anything to keep him from playing. I pray it continues that way.

PHILLIP AND I left the hospital to let Lori rest. They're letting her go home soon. We did a little shopping and had dinner at our hotel. We're staying with them this weekend, but we have an early appointment here, at the hotel, tomorrow morning and decided a hotel would be easier. Phillip and I had a bottle of wine at dinner, and I tried to get him drunk enough to tell me where we were going on our honeymoon. I tried to reason with him about how I needed to know what to pack. I tried to pout. Nothing worked.

Then, I tried sex.

I'm lying on his shoulder, thinking about how amazing he is. There's something about the time right after sex. I feel so close to him and so in love. I think that's how it's supposed to feel. All those nights I was with other guys, I would lie there, thinking it was great but just wanting to get home. Well, or do it again—you know, so I wouldn't have to talk to him.

Why is it that Phillip and I never brought people home with us?

Danny? Oh my gosh, I once threatened to replace his bedroom door with a revolving one.

"Phillip, how come you never let a girl spend the night at our house?"

"I don't know. Probably the same reason you never had a guy spend the night."

"That's weird, don't ya think?"

"I don't know if it was a conscious thought, but it was, like, our place. I think I would've felt like I was cheating on you. We were pathetic, huh?"

"Yeah, I think that's kinda why I didn't either. Sorta out of some weird respect. I also think you would've been terribly jealous," I tease.

"I would've been," he says very seriously. "I never liked any of your dates or your boyfriends. I never really understood why. I told myself that I was just protecting you, but, really, I was jealous. I was jealous of every boy who had ever kissed you. I wanted to kill every boy who'd ever hurt you. I wanted you. All to myself."

"Hmm, do you want me now?"

"Again?" He chuckles. "Well, let's see." He puts my hand down south. "What do you think?"

I grin because, well, you know. "I would say, someone wants me."

"Yeah, me," he says as he pulls me on top of him.

Can't sleep.

SATURDAY, DECEMBER 23RD

IT'S THREE A.M. I'm not sure what woke me up, but I can't seem to fall back asleep.

Things have been crazy. I've been planning the wedding, going to showers, getting ready to move, designing a building, and getting ready for Christmas.

I have a lot on my plate, but I know it's the wedding that's keeping me awake.

I have my dream wedding pretty well planned out. I'm lying here, looking at my dream guy. I know Phillip's the one. I can feel it in my heart, my soul, and my bones.

I don't doubt it for a second.

But, at the same time, I'm a little nervous.

I'm clearly not going back to sleep, so I pop on Facebook and see Danny has just posted *Can't sleep* as his status.

I gently slide out of bed, so I don't wake Phillip. I go in the living room and give Danny a call. "Hey, I can't sleep either. Why can't you sleep?"

Danny gives me a huge sigh. Like the weight of the world is sitting on his shoulders.

"Do you think I'm gonna be a good father? After last week at the hospital, the baby seems so real. Before, it didn't seem so real."

"Danny, you're gonna be an awesome dad, but I get what you're feeling. I think I'm having the exact same thoughts, only concerning my wedding. It's a bit surreal. I'm afraid I'm gonna suck as a wife, and Phillip will wonder why he married me."

"I think Lori wonders sometimes why she married me. And who could blame her? I wasn't that supportive of her when she was feeling bad. I got kinda tired of it."

"Sometimes, I feel like I'm ticking and ticking. I don't know when I'll explode, but when I do, I'm afraid I'll ruin my relationship with Phillip. It's a lot of pressure."

"I feel that way, too. Like I'm trying to make an offensive game plan when I have no idea what the defense is gonna do. They're an unknown. There's no film, no scouting reports. I'm gonna have to adjust on the field, on the fly. And that's not easy to do. I have no control."

"That's why, sometimes, I'm afraid to marry Phillip. I feel out of control."

"Love makes you feel out of control. I think that's how you know it's right."

"I can't imagine how that will be magnified when you have a baby, Danny. I can see why you can't sleep."

"You're a big help," he says sarcastically.

"Danny, knowing what you know now, having been married, if you had a do-over, would you make the same play again? Would you marry her again?"

"Definitely, yes. Honestly, I can't imagine my life without her. But it's still hard."

"Uh, speaking of hard. Is it bad that Phillip's gone from being my BFF and wanting to sit around and talk to me all the time to wanting nothing but sex from me?"

Danny chuckles. "Now, that's the one thing that *is* normal."

"So, seriously, should I marry him?"

"Yeah, I think you should. You have to know he's crazy about you."

"Maybe, but these counseling sessions are freaking me out, Danny. Phillip and I are failing! We don't handle conflict right. We don't talk about money, and we spend way too much time together. I think we're doing great. But, when we go there, I feel like a big, fat failure!"

"You and Phillip aren't going to fail. You're good together. He's always been good for you."

"I know that, but am I good for him?"

"That's exactly what I wanna know! Am I going to be a good dad? Am I going to be good for them? No bullshit, Jay. Do you think I'll be a good dad?"

"You'll be the best dad, Danny. Seriously. Think about it. You stand on the field, calmly waiting for a receiver to get open while three-hundred-pound men come rushing after you. I think you can handle a little eight-pound baby."

"Well, when you put it that way, true."

"I just realized something. You're confident about everything you do. I don't know anyone with more confidence than you. In fact, you being scared makes me feel more normal. Maybe being scared is normal."

"I think you're right. Get to sleep."

"Okay. You, too."

I sneak back into bed. I'm so glad I got to talk to Danny. I feel so much better.

Everything will be fine.

Is my mind messing with me?

THURSDAY, DECEMBER 28TH

PHILLIP IS LYING in bed, watching TV, while I take a hot bubble bath. I'm not feeling great. Phillip made me go to the doctor today because the cold I've been fighting for a couple of weeks has turned into a stupid sinus infection. He gave me some strong antibiotics, so I should be feeling better quickly.

The holidays were a blur. We had an amazing first Christmas together, and we're on the countdown to the big day. I can't believe, in a couple of weeks, we'll be married! I think I was just nervous before. I know Phillip is the one for me.

I'm sure of it.

How can I not be sure of it when he's so sweet to me? He got my prescription filled, brought me home chicken noodle soup, and watched a movie with me. I slept through most of the movie because I was lying with my head on his lap, and he was running his fingers through my hair. He woke me up after the movie and told me I should take a hot bath and then come to bed.

I get out of the tub, lie down next to him, and immediately fall asleep.

I'm on the phone with a friend, telling her that I'm marrying Phillip.

I'm not sure who exactly I'm talking to, but I'm telling her how excited I am.

How Phillip and I will be the perfect married couple.

How we were made for each other.

I gush on and on about how amazing Phillip is. How I'm sure he's the man for me.

But, as I'm gushing on about him, all of a sudden, I watch myself burst into flames.

I'm on the phone, speaking, but yet I'm burning. I'm like the burning bush.

Apparently, God believes I've just spoken blasphemy, that I'm not right for Phillip.

I wake up to Phillip shaking me.

"Princess, wake up. You're screaming."

I guess you tend to do that when you spontaneously burst into flames.

I'm shaken by the dream.

Was the dream a sign from God that I shouldn't marry Phillip? Or is my mind messing with me?

Phillip kisses my forehead. "Are you okay?"

"Yeah, just a bad dream."

He rolls me into his arms. I rest my head on his chest and listen to his heartbeat. I think fleetingly, before I fall back asleep, that God must be wrong.

Because I belong in this exact spot.

Forever.

Are you scared about getting married?

SATURDAY, DECEMBER 30TH

"THAT WAS AMAZING," Phillip says. "I did damn good."

Phillip's usually pretty impressed with himself after sex. It'd make me laugh if he wasn't completely right. Everything he does is, like, perfect. I've always joked that he knows what's best for me, but I was talking about in life, not in bed. In bed, he definitely knows exactly what to do to me, like, at exactly the right time. And I'm not sure how he does it because I still haven't figured everything out about him.

I've been thinking about telling Phillip how I've been kinda nervous about the whole *till death do you part* thing. About the whole *being together forever* thing. I've always been able to talk to Phillip about how I feel, but now that the boy we're talking about is him, it's not as easy.

And, as much as I keep trying to push it away or smother it, I can't help it; the burning bush dream is still on my mind. I can't figure out if it was a sign that I shouldn't marry Phillip or just plain old cold feet. I read on a wedding website that getting cold feet was completely normal, so I'm trying to be calm about it.

"Phillip, do you ever get cold feet?"

"Are you scared about getting married?"

"Me? Oh, no," I lie. "I just wondered if you do. I read on

317

some wedding website that it was completely normal. I mean, I don't wanna be left, standing at the altar, 'cause you changed your mind."

"Princess, no way am I changing my mind."

"And you don't think we're settling, right?"

"What do you mean?"

"Like, we couldn't get anyone else, so we're best friends getting married."

Phillip backs away like I slapped him. "Is that what you think?"

"No, not at all. Someone just said that, and I want to make sure you don't feel that way."

"Let me guess … Richie Rich?"

"Um, maybe. So, you don't think we are?"

Phillip doesn't answer. Instead, he kisses my neck. "Do you like that?"

"Uh, yeah, but we're supposed to be talking."

He runs his hands down my sides and says, "How about that?"

"Phillip, what does that have to do with cold feet or settling?"

Phillip moves super fast. Before I know it, he's sitting on top of me, and he has my hands pinned above my head. He leans down close to my face and runs his scruffy jaw across mine.

"Settling for marrying your friend means there's love but no physical attraction."

I just put on a T-shirt. He strips it off with one strong hand and pins my arms down against the bed again.

God, I love how strong he is.

"What are you doing?" I say breathlessly.

"I think I need to prove to you that you're not settling."

"How are you gonna do that? Aren't we supposed to be talking about this?"

He kisses down my neck and murmurs into my ear, "Talking

is overrated in this situation. I'm gonna do stuff to you. If it makes you want me, then you're not settling, and we get married. If it doesn't, we won't."

"So, if I can resist you, we can call off the wedding?"

He nods his head and then kisses the top of my outstretched arms, across my wrists, down my tender and slightly ticklish forearm. He's not even to my elbow, and I already know I'd never be able to resist him with any conviction. Especially now that he's kissing my chest and my stomach. I'm trying to pretend to be disinterested, but the truth is, I wanted him the second he rubbed his cheek against mine.

He kisses down my stomach, and I think he's going to really make me crazy by going down a bit further. Instead, he moves back up to my mouth and kisses me deeply.

"You're being a tease," I tell him.

"Oh, I haven't even begun to tease you, Princess. How much more can you take?"

I try to steady my breathing.

My friends used to tell me that all I ever looked for in a guy were muscles and a pretty face. That I should look at his personality, his mind. I joked back that there was nothing wrong with wanting my happily ever after wrapped in a really hot package. And, if Phillip is my happily ever after, then I've gotten my wish.

I'm so not settling.

My eyes can't help but take in every curve of every muscle. The rock-solid hardness of his biceps. His lean stomach. The abs. Oh, how I love Phillip's abs. Even though my arms are still pinned above my head, my fingers move slightly, like they do when I trace my fingertips down his stomach.

Phillip slides his boxers off and gives me a whole different kind of hardness to look at.

But I can resist him.

I resisted him my whole life; surely, I can resist him this once, just to make a point.

"I can resist you. I resisted you for years," I tell him.

Of course, he was always clothed when I resisted him.

He pushes all his hardness against me.

"That's not really fair," I murmur. "It's not fair that you're naked."

He kisses me again.

"Wow. You can resist. Guess I'll just go watch some TV, and we'll call off the wedding." He moves his body a fraction of an inch, like he's getting ready to get off me.

I can't let him go, so I say, "No, you're not."

AFTER A VERY thorough convincing, I know for certain that we're not settling.

But there's more.

"Phillip, you know that we're solving our conflicts with sex, right? You know our relationship is probably already infected."

Phillip brushes a stray strand of hair off my face. "Princess, I think we solved the conflict, and then we had sex."

"I don't really even remember what the conflict was."

We both start laughing.

Phillip says, "Then, we don't have to worry about it festering and growing. We're all good."

"So, what about the feet? Aren't you a little scared about getting married? About making a lifelong, *till death do you part* commitment?"

His brown eyes softly look at me. His mouth turns up into a grin, like he just thought of something happy. "Feel my feet," he says.

I move my cold feet against his always-warm ones. I don't know how he's always so warm, but it's one of the many things I adore about him.

"Do my feet feel cold?"

I laugh. "No, they're never cold."

"And yours always are. That's why we're perfect for each other. Mine are always hot. Yours are always cold. You cool mine down. I warm yours up. Together, they make the perfect temperature."

"So, I actually do something that helps you?"

"You make me a better man, Princess. That's why I wanna marry you."

"Really?"

He pulls me in close and kisses me. "Really."

A few shots.

TUESDAY, JANUARY 2ND

I'M AT WORK, and I'm feeling uninspired in the New Year.

We had a really fun Jersey Shore–themed New Year's Eve couple shower. Everyone took it as an excuse to dress slutty, drink too much, and fist pump. I'm praying the horrible orange spray-on tans everyone got will wear off by the wedding!

In Joey's brilliance, he decided that, rather than make everyone buy us a "stupid" shower gift, they should bring us something practical.

And what's more practical than alcohol?

Now, we have a fully stocked bar from numerous people who had invited themselves to come "break in" our new house. Phillip acted just like a bride usually does at her showers. He was oohing and aahing over every bottle of alcohol. He almost got tears in his eyes when Blake and Logan presented him with an "amazing" and expensive bottle of tequila.

I didn't really drink much at the party. I don't know what's been wrong with me lately. I used to be able to party and have fun.

I think it might have something to do with my quickly approaching wedding. I also think it might have something to do with the fact that one thought keeps going through my mind. Over and over.

No matter how right things feel with Phillip, God is never wrong.

I can't seem to shake the feeling of bursting into flames. Every time I close my eyes, I can feel the fire engulfing my body. I know God was burning me for saying Phillip and I were perfect for each other.

Why would he do that?

And, even worse, Phillip and I have another counseling session tonight. Our schedule got mixed up because of the holidays, and we haven't been there for three weeks. Part of me wishes I could talk about it, but I don't dare. Pastor John would probably have me committed, and Phillip would probably think I'm nuts and decide not to marry me.

I look down at the crap I've been drawing, wad the paper into a ball, and toss it into the trash.

Maybe I just need to get out of here. Maybe I need to be in a different environment to feel inspired.

I TELL PHILLIP I'm gonna go to the Sheldon Museum of Art in Lincoln. He knows that's a place I often go to when I need inspiration. I'm able to forget about my project and immerse myself in other people's creations. Usually, when I do that—stop thinking so hard—the answers seem to come.

But, as I'm driving, I'm thinking I'm maybe looking for inspiration that's more divine.

I think about which of my friends is the most religious.

No, that's not right.

Which of my friends is the most open-minded, religiously? And, more importantly, who will not laugh in my face when I say God might have set me on fire?

That'd have to be Nick. So, I text him.

Me: *What's up?*

Nickaloser: *Just finished unpacking from the bowl game.*

Thinking about getting drunk.

Me: What happened to the whole "my body is a temple" and all that?

Nickaloser: Kickers aren't really football players, remember? And, now that the season is over, I can have some fun. And I fully intend to.

Me: You know I was just teasing about that.

Nickaloser: Yeah, I know. So, what's up?

Me: I'm on my way to Lincoln. Wanna hang?

Nickaloser: Heck yeah! Is Mac with you?

Me: He's not. I'm going to the museum. Come with me?

Nickaloser: That doesn't sound fun!

Me: Please! I need to talk about some stuff, and you're my most open-minded friend.

Nickaloser: I find I'm at my most open-minded after a few shots. Meet me at the bar.

Me: Fine. Kegger's? Are you going alone?

Nickaloser: No. I'm not a loser.

Me: You're in my phone as Nickaloser. :)

Nickaloser: True. But I'm not a loner. Moose and Chaz are meeting me.

Me: Are they religious?

Nickaloser: Are you possessed? Do you need an exorcism?

Me: I don't think so.

Nickaloser: Then, they will be fine. You freaking about Phillip?

Me: Uh …

Nickaloser: Fine. Museum first. Bar second.

Me: Thank you! Twenty minutes?

Nickaloser: *Sure.*

I walk up to the museum and see Nick standing outside, waiting for me. I adore Nick, and even though I love to tease him, he's no loser. He's adorable. Actually, don't laugh, but when he kicks off the football, I don't know, but the way he sorta skips and then, like, boom, kicks the ball is extremely sexy.

He and I had a very short-lived romance—well, maybe more of a booze-filled romance. It lasted all of about two weeks. I never slept with him; really, we didn't do much more than kiss. The one night I thought things might go further, he threw up on my shoes as we were staggering back to his apartment. I spent the night with him, cleaning up his puke and constantly cursing myself for goading him into those last two shots.

He never asked me out again, but we became good friends.

I guess when you clean up someone's puke, it sort of bonds you, but it also makes me wonder.

I greet Nick with a hug and blurt out, "Why didn't we work out, romantically? Is it because I got you drunk?"

He laughs. "No, that woulda been a good reason to keep you." He moves his head back and forth, like he's thinking of how to say what he's about to say. "There were a couple of reasons, I guess."

"And they were?"

"I wasn't going to listen to Danny's warnings 'cause you were fun, but then Danny told me I didn't stand a chance because you liked Phillip."

"Danny was dumb. I was into you," I say as I pay our admission into the museum.

We stroll through the gallery and look at the paintings.

"When it was just us, sure, but when Phillip was around, seriously, it was obvious who you were into."

"No way."

"You're still delusional. And, no offense, but I just don't see how a bunch of colors swirled around equals art."

"Give me an example of how I was into Phillip when we were all sitting at the bar and I was running my hand up your leg. And it's abstract. It's supposed to evoke a feeling, not look like something."

"Yeah, that turned me on. Like, you were this bad girl who wanted me and your boyfriend was sitting right there, clueless." He laughs. "And the art is making me feel like I need a drink."

"My boyfriend? That's dumb. Phillip and I were *just* friends!"

"Jay, you freaking light up like a Christmas tree when you're around Phillip. The way you two look at each other. The connection you have with your eyes? Seriously, I felt like a Peeping Tom, watching someone having sex. It's intimate. Why do you think everyone thought you were having sex? Because you acted like you were. He'd lower his voice when he talked to you, and you hung on every word he said. At first, I thought he just crushed on you, but the more we all hung out, it was pretty obvious who had your heart. Danny was right. I couldn't win. Plus, I was messing around with this hot girl from my sports medicine class, so I was cool with it."

I stop and look at him. "You were two-timing me? I'm appalled!"

He laughs at me and shrugs his shoulders, like it's no big deal. "Jay, we didn't do anything. How could I have been two-timing you?" We stop to look at a bright, modern painting, and he changes the subject. "So, what are you freaking out about? And why the museum?"

"I always come to the museum for inspiration, and I do think contemporary art is the way to go in the new building. But, honestly, I probably shoulda gone to a church."

"You need religious inspiration?"

"Nick, has a higher power ever spoken to you?"

He looks at me kinda funny, so I give him my pathetic look.

"Um, uh, no. Well, I don't know. Maybe once, but I didn't know if it was him or, like, my own brain."

"That's exactly what I've been wondering! Tell me!"

"In high school, besides kicking, I played wide receiver. I got tackled when I was up in the air. Helmet to helmet, knocked me silly. I fell hard to the ground and had a concussion, and for a few scary minutes, I couldn't feel my body. I thought I was paralyzed. They wrapped me up on one of those backboards and carted me off the field. My mind flashed, *I can't move. I'm paralyzed.* Then, quickly, another voice that wasn't my own flashed in my head. It said, *You're going to be fine.* And then I, like, knew I was. At the time, I thought it was God's voice, but who knows? So, did God talk to you?"

"I think he did in a dream. When I told my friend that Phillip was the one for me, he set me on fire and turned me into a burning bush. And, in my mind, it was like he felt that was blasphemy. And I've been having a lot of dreams that are, like, tragic. At first, I thought, you know, I'm freaking, but I don't freak over guys. I really never have."

"You never used to, but Phillip is different. You're different with him. Probably because, for the first time in your life, you have skin in the game. You care about him. You're in love with him. You want it to work. Plus, you're planning a wedding, and you're moving. Your stress is just coming out in your dreams."

"I can see that with the other dreams I've had but not this one. I really don't know if I should marry Phillip now. I'm almost positive God was trying to tell me not to, or he was threatening me or something."

Nick bursts out laughing hysterically and extremely inappropriately for a museum. "You're funny. You know that, right?"

"Stop laughing. I'm telling you this because you're my most open-minded friend, and I thought you wouldn't laugh at me."

He regains temporary control, wipes tears from his stupid

eyes, looks at me, and then starts laughing again.

I walk away, pretending to be intrigued by a Pollock painting.

"I'm sorry," he chokes out while trying to control his giggling.

"Are you high? What's with the giggling?"

He straightens out his face and says seriously, "Kegger's it is. I can't have this conversation here."

We leave the museum with very little architectural inspiration and zero divine intervention.

Maybe the bar is a good option.

WE WALK IN Kegger's, and there, behind the bar, is my favorite hot and former fairly regular hook-up, Bradley. He's drying a glass with a white rag, and he has a phone cradled on his shoulder.

He looks irritated when Nick and I walk up to order drinks. But, when he sees me, his green eyes sparkle.

"Jadyn, baby, you looking for drinks or a little fun?"

Nick holds out my engagement ring and says with a tone that's *way* too serious for a bar, "*Definitely* just drinks."

Buzzkill.

Bradley says, "Phillip?"

And I am like, "How'd you know?"

"Well, it doesn't take a rocket scientist to know who you've always had the hots for," he says as he pours three tequila shots.

"Bradley, in this bar, I always had the hots for you," I flirt.

Sorry, I can't help it.

"You wanted to hook up with me, yes. But you've always had the hots for Phillip."

"Of all the boys I've kissed in this bar over the years, you tell me I had the hots for the one boy I *never* kissed?"

Bradley ignores my question and raises his shot glass. Nick and I follow suit.

He says, "Here's to hook-ups."

"Hear, hear," I say.

He pours us each another shot. "And here's to finding true love. Congrats, Jadyn."

"Hear, hear," Nick says.

Bradley leans across the bar toward me and lowers his voice. "Although I'm still *extremely* available if you came here for a hook-up."

Nick gets a disgusted look on his face. "We're going to our booth. Bring us a pitcher, okay?" Then, he drags me away. "God, you're a flirt, and what's all the Jadyn baby bullshit?"

"I don't know. He just always called me baby. It was cute, but I wasn't flirting with him. I said one sentence, and it was about Phillip."

"You said, 'Hear, hear,' to hook-ups. I'd call that flirting, considering you've hooked up with the guy on numerous occasions."

"What, all of a sudden, you're anti-hook-up? I'll be sure to let all the girls who talk to you tonight know that."

"That's not a bad idea actually. They'll think I'm a good guy and that I'm not looking for a hook-up. So then, when we do hook up, they'll think it's 'cause they wanted to. It's like reverse psychology. You just might be brilliant. So, do you wanna go back and flirt with him? If you hooked up with him, I probably wouldn't tell Phillip."

"You're such a liar. You would so tell Phillip, but it doesn't matter. I don't wanna flirt with or hook up with him! I'm engaged to be married! *And* I have enough to worry about. Plus, I could never cheat on Phillip."

"You cheat on other guys?"

"Um, not on purpose."

"I'll take that as a yes. Accidental cheating. Ha! This is why I love you. You make me laugh."

Just as I say, "So, can we *please* get back to the burning bush?" Moose slides in the booth and says, "Ooohhh, I heard you had an

STD, but I thought it was just a rumor. Does it really burn?"

Oh. My. Gosh.

Nick starts laughing hysterically again.

Seriously, can no one have a serious conversation anymore?

I should have known before I even opened my mouth that I couldn't have a serious conversation with a guy named Moose, but I keep trying anyway. I mean, I drove all this way.

"Uh, no, I don't. We're talking about the *religious* burning bush."

But he's a boy. And, apparently, his mind is not on the religious side of the bush right now.

Bradley brings us a pitcher and three glasses just as Moose says, "I love hot bushes."

That causes Bradley to sit down.

Why, oh why, isn't the bar busy?

"My favorite subject," Bradley says. "Are we talking about Jadyn's? 'Cause I can speak from experience on that one."

"Do tell," Moose says.

And I'm not going to say what he said. If I told this story, our ears would probably bleed. Mine might be bleeding right now because I can't seem to totally tune out Bradley's discussion of my, uh, well … oh, never mind.

My ears just perk up though because he's now telling Moose, Nick, and Chaz, who just slid into the booth, what it was like to have wild, alcohol-fueled sex with me. He's telling them about the time I fell *up* his stairs. They all laugh about that.

People fall down stairs. They don't fall up them.

But I'm getting nervous because I know what's coming next in this story.

I try to get him off track by saying, "Chaz fell down the dorm stairs one time. It was really funny."

They ignore me.

Bradley says, "She was kinda drunk when we got to my

apartment. I was dragging her up the stairs with me, but she was giggling and kept kissing and grabbing me. I just wanted to get her to my room before she woke up my roommates. We were about halfway to the top when she fell up the stairs. She giggled and then pulled me down on top of her. It was hot."

I tune out the rest. I know the rest. I possibly coaxed him into, um, *doing it,* uh, right there, on the stairs.

This is all allegedly, I might add.

He might be making it up.

Because, clearly, I was drunk.

At least, that's what I'm gonna tell the boys.

I say, "I don't remember that. Obviously, I was drunk, or maybe you're thinking of another girl."

Bradley seems hurt by this and slinks back over to the bar.

A few minutes later, I feel guilty and decide to go for a pretend pee.

As I walk by the bar on the way back from the restroom, I stop and ask Bradley for a round of shots.

While he's pouring them, I confess, "Sorry about that. I do very vividly remember the stairs, and I wasn't drunk. I just really wanted you, but you telling that story was pretty embarrassing. You know, talking about it in such graphic detail."

"So, you do remember, huh?" He gives me a smoldering look.

"It was one of the hottest experiences of my life," I say truthfully.

And it was.

Oh my gosh, was it.

His face lights up with a grin. "Me, too. You sure you're not up for a replay of that, like, tonight?"

"Bradley, I'd never try a replay of that."

"Why?"

"It was perfect as it was."

"Mmm. True. I was so afraid my roommates were gonna wake

up."

"I don't think I cared."

"Yeah, that was the best part. We had fun, huh?"

"Yeah."

"And, now, you're getting married. Where is Mr. Wonderful anyway?"

"At work."

"And why are you at the bar with a bunch of boys?"

I look back at the boys loudly discussing their sex lives and sigh. "Well, I went to the museum. Really, I've been trying to talk to Nick about the burning bush, but it's not working because they keep turning it all sexual."

"So, are we talking the religious burning bush? Like Moses saw?"

"Yeah."

"You know my undergrad major was in philosophy, right? Next semester, I'll finish up my doctorate."

"Really? And here I thought, you were just the hot bartender." Who knew he had brains, too? I sorta never got past the hot physical parts.

"So, talk."

And I do.

It just all comes out. How cliché. Spilling my guts to the bartender.

"So, how do you know if God is speaking to you versus your own subconscious telling you something versus a premonition versus a warning versus a hunch versus an omen or versus your mind just freaking out?"

"Do you want my professional opinion?"

"Please."

"Right off the bat, I'd say it sounds like you've been doing way too much thinking."

"Yeah, probably." I let out a big sigh.

"Tell me what happened."

So, I tell him about the dream.

"Jadyn?"

"Yeah."

"You driving home tonight?"

"I don't know. Yeah, maybe. Well, probably. I mean, I haven't really thought about it yet."

"I know you pretty well and can see where this is heading. So, you're not now. You can crash with me if you need to."

I raise an eyebrow at him.

He says, "Okay, hang on."

He walks over to the loser table, says a few words to Nick, and comes back.

"You're staying with Nick. He swears he won't do what I would do to you if *I* took you home."

And, sorry, but my mind can't help but think about the things that he'd do to me.

Oh, boy.

He grabs three bottles and simultaneously pours them into a shot glass. Then, he dramatically flips the bottles and hands me the shot.

"That was cool," I say.

"Drink and then listen."

So, I drink. "Mmm. That's good."

"Thanks. It's my own creation. I still need to figure out a catchy name for it."

"Okay, so back to my problem."

"Baby, you're freaking out about getting married. About having to love the same guy, sleep with the same guy, for the rest of your life. God is not speaking to you. God is not going to set you on fire. From what I can tell, you're lucky enough to have found your true soul mate. You should be celebrating this, not second-guessing yourself. Plus, you've found true love with your best friend. That's even cooler. Have you ever heard of Seneca, the Roman philosopher?"

"I don't think so."

"He said that love is friendship gone mad. You just had a bad dream. Don't try to see something divine in it."

My phone buzzes. I look down at it.

Phillip: *How's the inspiration?*

Me: *Very inspirational.*

Phillip: *Nick told me you're at Kegger's, doing shots with Bradley. That you've had quite a few shots already.*

Me: *Tattletale. Did he also tell you Bradley is getting his doctorate in philosophy?*

Phillip: *Uh, no.*

Me: *Like I said, it's inspirational. Or maybe philosophical-ish.*

Phillip: *I don't think that's a word. So, you're getting drunk?*

Me: *Uh, not yet, no. I don't think so.*

Phillip: *Nick says Bradley says you're staying with either him or Nick tonight.*

Me: *He thinks I'm thinking about getting drunk. The inner workings of my mind are tricky, so it's hard to predict.*

Phillip: *Do you want to go home with Bradley?*

Me: *No. I'm pretty sure.*

Phillip: *Pretty sure? Or FOR sure?*

Me: *I really haven't thought about it yet. Um, let me think …*

Phillip: *Okay …*

I don't get to respond to Phillip because I was messing around

334

with the philosopher's hand, trying to steal a bowl of pretzels, and my phone sorta went flying out of my hand and into the bartender's sink full of soapy water.

Bradley quickly fishes it out of the sink.

He takes the battery out, lays it on a bar towel, dries it off, runs in the back, and comes back with a Ziploc baggie. He tells me to run across the street to the Chinese restaurant and have them put rice in it for me.

I do and proudly come back with a bag of fried rice. I'm expertly eating it with chopsticks.

Kinda.

Bradley looks jealous, so I try to feed him some rice.

He shakes his head at me. "You're so blonde. My waitress called in sick, and her replacement can't be here for a few hours, so come stand behind the bar and look pretty. If someone comes in, just pour them a beer." He goes in back, grabs another baggie, and runs across the street.

I eat my rice, and since no one comes in, I pour myself a beer and am drinking it when two cute boys come sit up at the bar.

"Beer?" I ask like the professional that I now am.

"Pitcher," Cutie One says. "Are you new?"

"No, I'm old. I've been a regular at this bar for years."

"Oh, we meant, are you the new bartender?"

"No, I'm just eating rice and drinking."

I pour them a pitcher and have Cutie One come get it from behind the bar along with some glasses 'cause I'm kinda still eating. I finish my rice and am just doing a shot with the cuties when Bradley jogs back in.

"Oh, more rice for me?"

"Did you just do another shot? You need to stop drinking."

I shake my head. "Just trying to do my job."

Cutie Two says, "She's really good at her job." Then, he grins lasciviously at me.

Cutie One says, "Yeah, but she really should have on something sexier."

Bradley is messing with my phone and the bag of rice. We all stop and watch. He puts my phone in the baggy full of uncooked rice and zips it up.

Cutie One says, "Dude, that doesn't work."

But Cutie Two disagrees, "Yeah, it does. Well, it worked for me. What happened to your phone?"

Bradley replies, "It's her phone, and I'm pretty sure it could tell the way the night was headed and tried to commit suicide." He takes the rice baggie over to the booth, drops it in my purse, and walks back behind the bar.

"Hey, maybe I should work tonight. Help you out."

Bradley looks at me. "I'm not sure that's a good idea."

"Oh, come on. I've always wanted to wear one of the server outfits. They're so cute! It'll be just like Halloween."

"You remember last time you spent Halloween here?"

"Uh, mostly."

"Hmm. I clearly remember your naughty little nurse outfit and how good it looked on my bedroom floor."

Oh my.

The cuties are rapt with attention.

I change the subject. "So, is that a yes? Can I go change?"

He laughs. "Sure. Why not? Ought to provide us with some entertainment."

I GO IN back and change into the server outfit. Little black spandex shorts and a black-and-white referee shirt that's cut quite low in the front and doesn't even attempt to cover my stomach. I add the tall white socks. Luckily, I wore black pumps with my dress today. I walk out, and all three of them whistle. I take a tray off the bar and go wait on my friends.

"Another pitcher, boys?" I ask.

I'm even expertly holding the empty tray on one hand above my head.

They grin at my outfit.

"You should work here part-time. We'd get free beer," Moose tells me.

"I gotta get this on camera," Nick says. "Say *sexy*."

They send the picture to Phillip. I'm sure he'll get a kick out of it. And my new career path.

Was I supposed to be texting him back about something?

Shoot, I forget. Oh well.

I take their empty pitchers and put them on top of my tray, lift it above my head on one hand, and saunter back over to the bar. I refill the pitchers from the tap and put them back on the tray.

I'm a little shocked that I've had a few shots and I am still functioning at peak-performance levels.

I did have a big lunch though, and fried rice must really be good at soaking up alcohol.

As I walk by Cutie One, heading over to deliver the beer, he decides it would be fun to smack my ass.

And, well, I might not have been prepared for it because it causes me to become slightly unbalanced, and I'm afraid the full pitchers become slightly unbalanced, too. And said pitchers might currently be crashing down, cascading beer on two cuties, who probably don't deserve it but who are being soaked in beer as we speak.

"Oh my gosh, I'm so sorry," I tell the drenched cuties as the tray falls out of my hand and clatters to the floor.

Bradley rushes around with towels and tries to dry off the cuties. He snarls at me about my lack of coordination.

"He slapped my ass!" I say, defending myself.

Bradley gets his serious half-bouncer, half-bartender look. "That true?"

"Uh," the boy says sheepishly.

"You deserved it then," he says as he throws the towels at them. He fills up a couple of new pitchers and carries them over to my friends.

As he walks past me, he goes, "I can't blame the boy for smacking your ass. You look extremely hot." He stares into my eyes for a beat. "Tell you what; you take the orders, and I'll carry the drinks."

"I like working here," I tell him when he's back behind the bar.

Whew. I'm starting to feel a little spinnyish.

Bradley hands me a tall drink over ice.

"What's this?"

"Vodka and water."

I taste it. "It tastes like straight water."

"That's because it's made in Iceland. Very high quality. Very expensive, top-shelf stuff."

"Oh." I take another drink. "It's good."

A group comes in and sits at the high-tops in front of the pool tables. They're already racking up a couple of games when I go take their order.

But, by the time I get back to the bar, I can't remember it, so I say, "Two pitchers."

Bradley takes them over.

He comes back and says, "They didn't want pitchers."

"Just tell them it's happy hour, they're cheap, and I was ordering in their best interests. I want more Chinese. Bradley, do you want some?"

Cutie One says, "I want some."

"Dude," the other one says, "I want some from you, too."

"But I don't have any more."

Bradley says, "I think they want, um, *some* of you."

"Oh, really? Why?"

"'Cause you're hot and probably drunk enough to say yes."

"I'm not drunk. And I'm engaged! Hey, this vodka is really good. I'm gonna go see if the pool guys want shots. I'm good at upselling, and I've changed my mind, Bradley. Order us some pizza from Val's."

"You're not supposed to bring food in here."

"I had hot, drunken sex with you on the stairs, and you just told my friends *all* about it. I think I can do whatever I want."

"True." He grins, and the cuties are like, "Uh ... dude, details."

WHILE HE TELLS the boys details, I suggest Jäger shots to my new pool-playing friends. I might have said they were on the house; I forget. Bradley gives me a tray of them, and since no one touches my butt, they arrive in one piece. I work my way back over to Nick, Moose, and Chaz.

"I ordered us pizza," I tell them.

"They don't serve food here," Moose informs me.

"Oh, well, that's just details," I say back.

Nick gets serious. "Okay, let's talk about the burning bush."

But they have each had pretty much a pitcher apiece, plus shots, and they can't be serious.

So, the talk turns to Moose's recent sexual experience.

"Nicky!" I squeal. "Stop talking about boy parts."

"You only call me Nicky when you're trying to convince me to do something you know I don't wanna do. The rest of the time, I'm Nickaloser."

"Ah, you know I don't really think you're a loser. But, if it bothers you, I'll make up a new nickname for you right now. Tonight. You're so lucky! Okay, let's see. Nicky, pricky, picky, slicky, dickey, mickey, hickey, kicky. Wow! A lot of good words rhyme with Nicky. Oh, I've got it! Licky, licky, make a hickey, have a quickie with Nicky's dic—"

"Jadyn!"

"What?"

"Seriously, you can't say that."

"I can't say dickey? A dickey is just a little fake shirt you wear under another shirt. Don't be so sensitive."

"Fine. It's a great nickname, but it's probably too long."

"It's long, huh?"

"Jay!"

"What? You're the one who said it was *long*."

"I meant, the name, not my, uh, part."

I consider that for a moment. "Yeah, you might be right. I don't think that would fit in my phone anyway."

"You're drunk. You get silly when you're drunk, and then you'll wanna start danc—"

"OMG! Nicky! I love this song!"

I start dancing a bit. I can't help it.

I love this song!

Oh, maybe I said that already. Sorry.

"Nicky, come dance with me."

"See? I told ya. And I don't wanna dance."

I do a little shimmy in front of him. "I guess I could go ask Bradley."

"I'm such a pushover." He sighs, acts like he's doing me a big favor, gets out of the booth, and dances with me.

I twirl around, fist pump, do a little harmless grinding on Nicky.

"You're so lucky that I'm a good guy," Nick says.

"Why's that?"

"You're drunk."

"Not any drunker than you are. You're a good dancer when you're drunk."

Nick grabs me and pulls me in closer. "And you're very naughty when you're drunk. Bradley is totally watching you."

"Really?" I kinda gush.

I turn around and look at Bradley, and he's definitely watching me, but I'm not sure why.

"Jay?"

"Yeah?"

"The song is over."

And I realize it is. New song. Not so good to dance to.

"Thanks for dancing with me, Nicky. Oh, hey, I gotta go. Bradley is waving at me." I dance my way behind the bar. "So, Bradley, is there anything I can get you?"

Yes, I'm kinda flirting with him.

But I think it's harmless.

Just-for-fun flirting.

"Yeah," he says. "You can get naked."

Uh, well, maybe not completely harmless.

THANKFULLY, A GROUP of girls walks in. I leave Bradley to go wait on them, yummy vodka in hand. I suggest vodka to them, but they say they just want the bartender. Apparently, they've been trying to hook up with him but to no avail. And here I thought, Bradley hooked up with everyone.

I go back to the bar. "Oh, Bradley, sweetie, they only want *you* to wait on them." Then, I whisper, "I thought you hooked up with everyone."

"No, baby, just you. I don't have a problem with hooking up. I just don't with girls I meet on the job."

"So, I was special?" I can't help but grin.

He looks at me struggling with the tray and my high heels. "Yeah, special ed."

The cuties laugh.

He works for tips though, so he goes and flirts with the girls and gives them false hope. But the false hope will keep them here until closing time. That's a drill I know well. Although, in my case, I guess he gave in and took me home with him. I feel so lucky. Like I won the bartender lottery or something.

He comes back, and I say, "You're pretty sexy when you get your flirt all on."

"Come here. I need to show you something." He drags me in the back room and pins me against the wall. "I'll be glad to show you sexy if that's what you want."

He pushes his body up against mine. It feels familiar and sexy.

It also feels all wrong.

Has Phillip ruined me?

Am I never going to be able to flirt with or get turned on by another guy again? What if he dumps me?

I'll have to become a nun!

"Bradley, can you become a nun if you've already had lots of sex?"

"Are we back to religion again? How 'bout I get off early, you come back to my place, and I'll make you say, *Oh God*, over and over again?"

His long eyelashes bat at me, and he's very hard to resist for two reasons. One, I can feel that he is in fact hard. And two ... um, I forget what two was for.

Just as he leans in—I think to kiss me, a kiss I will somehow have to avoid—we hear, "Pizza's here!" from the cuties.

Bradley stays pinned against me for a long second. Then, he shakes his head at me, throws an apron around the front of him, and walks out front.

I stay pinned against the wall.

And think.

Well, I try to think.

I love Phillip, but is loving him enough? Can I make him happy forever?

Will he get sick of me? Will our relationship fester? Will I smother him?

I don't know any answers, so I go eat pizza.

Chow it.

Oh my gosh, it tastes so good. I even take a piece back behind the bar and let the girls drool while I feed pizza to Bradley. I let the cheese get all stringy and put it on his tongue.

After the pizza, I tell Bradley I'm thirsty for another shot. Bradley tells me I should do one of the special vodka shots, so I do.

LATER, I'M OVER at the pool tables. One of the boys is trying to put a tip into my cleavage when Phillip walks in.

It's like I'm a deer caught in headlights. I freeze.

I feel like a kid caught with her hand in the cookie jar. Except, in this case, I'm the slutty jar who's letting everyone put their hands on her.

He gives me that look. That *I am probably in trouble* look, that *my dad caught me seriously making out with my boyfriend on the couch after curfew* kind of look. I feel like I'm in trouble.

But I haven't done anything wrong.

Have I?

No, I haven't. I'm just helping out a friend, delivering a few drinks.

Phillip doesn't come talk to me or come beat the boy's face in. He calmly sits next to Nick and eats a piece of pizza. I grab the tip out of the boy's hand and go back behind the bar.

"Bradley! What am I supposed to do? Phillip just walked in, and that guy practically had his hand down my shirt."

"Yeah, I saw that," Bradley says.

"Who's Phillip?" Cutie One asks.

"Her fiancé," Bradley drawls.

"Oh, this is gonna be good," Cutie Two says.

"You're waiting tables. Helping me out. Tell him you were gonna slap the jerk, but you were afraid you'd get me in trouble."

"Philosophers are good liars, huh?"

"We just see all angles of the truth."

"We really should've done more talking."

He laughs—well, he and the cuties laugh.

And they say, "Tell us another story."

I walk away and think, with the way they're all huddled together, he does.

I go to Phillip.

I figure I'll stay in character, break the ice.

It's all just fun and games.

Plus, you can't get into trouble when it's just fun.

In theory.

"Hey, can I get you a drink?"

"Only if I get to tip you like that guy." He gets up, grabs me, and pulls me in close to his face. I think he is gonna kiss me, but he says quietly in his deep, mad voice, "You're very lucky I didn't go over and rip his hand off." Then, he smiles and looks up and down my uniform. "You look damn sexy though. I suppose he couldn't help himself."

"You think I look sexy?"

"I do. So, you stopped texting me."

"Oh, I knew there was something I was forgetting! But I couldn't 'cause my phone got in an accident."

"Oh, really? An *accident*?"

"Nicky, show him my phone!"

Nick holds up the baggie full of rice and my phone.

"See? It's in rehab. Drying out." I laugh. *Ha-ha-ha. I'm veeerry funny! I crack myself up!* "Get it? Rehab? Drying out?"

"How many shots have you had?"

I run my hand through my hair, thinking. "Uh, I'm not sure. Three, fourish, five maybe?"

"What are you drinking?"

I give him a taste.

"It's water," he says.

"Oh, no, it's water mixed with this special vodka. High-quality, top-shelf stuff. That's why it's so smooth. You want one?"

"Nah, I think I'll go talk to Bradley. Looks like your pool boys need more drinks."

And then I come up with a brilliant name.

"Kicky Nicky! Get it? 'Cause you're a kicker? And kicky can also mean, like, fun. And you're always very fun, especially when you take me to the bar. Aren't we having fun?"

"How 'bout we see if you remember it tomorrow?" Nicky says.

"Oh, okay." I go wait on the pool-table group while Phillip walks up to the bar.

I realize that Phillip didn't kiss me. That's really not like him. And, now, he's sitting at the bar, chatting with Bradley, who was just discussing my past sex life with the cuties.

Um …

I think this calls for an intervention. No, wait, I mean, an interruption. I don't know. Whatever. I need them to stop their talking!

I walk up to Phillip and wrap my arm around his shoulders. "This is my fiancé."

"We already know that," the cuties reply in unison and give me shit-eating grins.

Shit is right.

Uh, what to say? What to say? Uh …

"Hey, Bradley, let Phillip try that special vodka and maybe one of those special shots, too. You know, the one you haven't named yet."

"I just decided on a name actually," Bradley says. "It's called Sex on the Stairs."

Phillip says, "That's a good name. I will definitely have one of those and a couple more pitchers."

The cuties are snorting with laughter.

I shut my eyes.

I'm freaking dying inside.

Bradley winks at me. "The special vodka is just for you."

"You'll have to text me the name of it, so I can get some. I like drinking vodka that's sooo smoothy-woothy."

"Why don't you take these to the pool-table group while I make you another one."

I go, come back, and tell Bradley, "They want another pitcher and two more glasses. Oh, and more Jäger shots. I'm good at up-selling."

Phillip says to the cuties, "Why are you all wet? Was it raining earlier?"

They tell him about my dropping the pitchers. About it raining beer all down their heads. They make it sound like I was just a clumsy, klutzy klutz.

I stand up for myself. "I only dropped them 'cause I was startled when he smacked my ass!"

Phillip narrows his eyes at the cuties and stands up.

All six foot three inches of prime Nebraska beefcake.

My God, that boy is hot.

I'm feeling a little warm myself. Shots make me kinda horny if I'm completely honest.

He says, "Don't do it again."

The cuties cower slightly. "No problem."

Phillip takes his Sex on the Stairs shot and the pitchers over to the booth.

"Seriously, Bradley? *Sex on the Stairs?*"

"Yeah, I just decided it was the perfect name. It'll catch on, and, baby, you'll be famous … or infamous—something like that."

"I don't wanna be famous." I pout. "I think I'll just go get drunk with my friends."

"I'm pretty sure you're already there."

"Already where? No, I'm not there yet. I was just saying, I'm going to go get drunk with my friends."

"Never mind, but you can't. You're not off work yet. My waitress isn't here."

"I'm just pretending to work. I think you know that."

"Well then, you need to go in back and change, and I'd better help you. Make sure you get it all off."

"Uh, maybe I'll just keep working."

"Thought so."

I GO EAT another piece of pizza and pretend wait on Phillip's table.

Phillip gets back up, grabs me, and kisses me deeply. "You're drunk," he says.

"Not really. Like, maybe, sorta."

"And what in the world was Bradley talking about? Your burning bush? Do I even want to know?"

Ack! Why did Bradley have to tell him that? I cover my face with my hand. "Uh, not my, um, uh, I had a dream. I became a burning bush. Literally burst into flames. God was punishing me."

Phillip peeks through my fingers and moves my hand off my face. "For what?"

I make a sad face. Well, I try to. "Um, you."

"Me? What did I do?"

And, okay, so I might be a little drunkish 'cause I usually don't gush over a boy like this unless I'm drunk. "Made me fall hopelessly and irreversibly in love with you," I tell him sweetly.

"So, why were you burning?"

"'Cause God thought my being in love with you was against his wishes, I think, and so he burned me. I was being blasphemousious. Is that a word? No, wait. I was blasphemic. No, that's not it either. Nicky, what is that word?"

347

"Blasphemous."

I snap my fingers and point at him. "Yeah, that's it. That's what I was. Good job, Nicky."

Nick says, "Yeah, she turned into a"—*BAHAHAHA*—"burning bush."

They all start laughing again.

Well, all of them but Phillip. I'm thinking God burning me because I'm in love with him is probably not very reassuring in regard to and concerning our future.

Really, I'm sorta having a hard time thinking exactly, but whatever.

Phillip turns around and grabs his shot. "I think I'm gonna need this." To the guys, he says, "Hey, did Bradley give you guys one of these shots? He says it's something new he came up with. I mean, I've heard of Sex on the Beach before but never Sex on the Stairs."

Now, the boys have the deer-in-the-headlights look. They freeze and watch Phillip throw back the shot.

He says, "Damn, that was good."

"So we've heard," Nick says slyly and arches an eyebrow at me.

Thankfully, Phillip changes the subject. "Okay, so back to God. I think you're having bad dreams because you're nervous about marrying me. Are you nervous about marrying me?"

"Uh, I don't think so. I'm doing great on the planning, and I've been having fun with it. We're planning the *best party*! Right?"

"Yeah, but it's more than a party, right?"

"Yes, and so that's why I came to the bar after the museum. To talk to Nicky. To see if I'm having, like, a premonition or something. I mean, you don't want me to burst into flames at our wedding. It would sorta ruin the event."

He chuckles. "Well yeah, it probably would put a damper on things."

"I'd watch out for lightning if I were you, Phillip. Oh, hey, I've gotta go work. The cuties are yelling for me."

"The cuties?"

"Oh, yeah, Cutie One and Cutie Two. I don't know their names."

"Bradley seems to be awfully cool about this. Is he hitting on you?"

"I don't think so."

"JJ," he warns.

"Uh, no, well, I don't know. Nicky, has Bradley been hitting on me?"

"Definitely flirting. No, that's not right. He said, if you wanted to hook up, he'd have no problem with that," Nick tells us.

"So, you know, not really," I say.

"I see."

"Why are you here anyway? It's a long drive just for beers."

The cuties wave their empty mugs and yell at me.

"Wait, hold that thought. I think they want me to do a shot with them."

"How many shots have you had again?"

"Uh, Nicky? We had two when we got here, right? I had a special one, and, uh, maybe a couple more mixed in there somewhere, but I mean, I've been here for, like, hours, and I had rice in a baggie and some pizza. It's not like I'm drunk."

He looks at me. Gives me that glare. That *tell me the truth* glare. You know the one, the one that makes me spill my guts to him. Always.

"Fine, I might be tipsy. Maybe a little drunkish. I can feel it, but you know, I'm fine. Pretty much fine."

"I don't think you should do any more shots."

"Oh my gosh, Phillip, I'm earning tips here."

"If that guy puts another tip down your shirt, I'm pounding him. Just saying."

I go up to the cuties. "Jeez, what? You have no patience."

"We're empty. Bradley said you have to wait on us. We think Bradley might be jealous."

"Bradley?"

"Hey, you wanted a job. Just making sure you do it. What did Phillip think of the shot?"

"He said it was really good."

Bradley winks at me. "Yeah, baby, it was."

"You should totally do it with the bartender again. He wants you," Cutie One says.

"You're just taking his side, so you can get free drinks. Can I get you a drink?"

"A couple of shots for us and one for you, too."

I turn and tell Bradley, "Three shots, please."

"You can't have any more shots."

I love how boys think they can tell me what I can and can't do.

"Why not?"

"You're working. I can't have you any drunker than you already are."

"What did you say to Phillip? Or what did he say to you?"

"Just guy talk."

"Guys don't talk; they threaten."

"No, he didn't really. He's cool. Unfortunately, I like the guy. I was just telling him about your special vodka."

"Oh, good. He can buy me some for home."

"I think he already has some at home."

The cuties giggle.

"What?" I ask the cuties.

"Nothing," they reply.

Bradley says, "So, what did you decide? You coming home with me tonight?"

I start to feel sad. I feel like my fun single life is ending. It's like the end of an era. And I want the era to end. I want to marry Phillip, but I don't know if he should want to marry me. If he was smart, he wouldn't.

I get little prickly tears in my eyes. "Phillip wants to marry me. I don't know why he does. Look at me."

Bradley takes the opportunity to do just that. His eyes slowly survey every inch of my body. I want to tell him that I meant, look at me, like, I'm a mess. I wasn't telling him to actually look at me.

When he works his way back up to my eyes, he says, "You're fun. Maybe you should ditch him and start a relationship with me."

"Relationships are like a disease, Bradley. You should think twice before you go getting into one. Did you know, if you're not careful, they will fester on you, infect you, and smother you? Then, I'm pretty sure you die."

"If you feel that way, maybe God was trying to tell you something. In fact, if you listen really hard, he will probably say, *Go home with Bradley tonight.*"

To which the cuties raise their voices high and whisper, "*Go home with Bradley tonight. Go home with Bradley tonight.*"

"See? God just spoke to you." Bradley smirks.

"I'm not that drunk," I tell the cuties.

Bradley pulls me toward the other side of the bar, away from the cuties. "What's all this about festering and infections?"

The tears start to fall now, and I can't even stop them because the idea of my and Phillip's relationship dying makes me really sad. It's the whole reason I'm here. Plus, I might be drunk. "Pastor John told us that would happen to our relationship because we solve our conflicts with sex."

"Don't cry, baby. Sex sounds like a fun way to solve a conflict."

I cry a little harder. "I know, but it's wrong, and so we're failing couples counseling. I've never failed anything, Bradley. But

I am. And our wedding is going to be a disaster. Our guests will catch fire, be eaten by crocodiles, I'll be pulled into the pits of hell because they don't like my dress, my veil is going to burn, and I'll run away with a fireman who looks just like Phillip, straight down to his abs."

Bradley says, "I think you should go change now."

I sniffle. "Okay."

I go in the back, change, and try to compose myself.

When I come back out, Bradley has a special vodka shot for me. He toasts, "Here's to good memories and a happy future. Your wedding is going to be amazing. None of those things are going to happen, I promise. Now, go sit with your fiancé."

So, I do.

PHILLIP TAKES ME home. We don't have sex on the stairs because my condo does not have stairs. But I'm drunk enough to be feeling quite naughty, and Phillip doesn't seem to mind that at all.

The smoothest stuff I've ever tasted.

WEDNESDAY, JANUARY 3RD

I HAVE THE kind of massive headache that comes from mixing alcohol.

And sixty-eight dollars' worth of tips in my coat pocket.

I really should know better than to mix alcohol like that.

Phillip is a sweetie. He took the day off with me. He's been watching movies while I sleep with my head on his lap.

I think maybe I was just scared.

There's no way God could not be Team Phillip.

It's just too right.

I think.

I'm still worried about what my head thinks though.

Then, I remember that we were supposed to meet with the pastor last night. "Phillip, we skipped couples counseling!"

"It's okay. I called and rescheduled for tomorrow night. Told him you got called out of town."

"Oh, thank you!"

"Although I think we need to talk about what last night was all about."

"What do you mean?"

He shakes his head at me. "Princess, I know you. Last night was one of your spiraling-out-of-control nights. Well, it could've

353

been had I not been there and had Bradley not been surprisingly cool."

"Oh, I need to check my phone. He was supposed to text me the name of that vodka. It was the smoothest stuff I've ever tasted!"

Phillip was taking a drink of beer as I uttered these words, and he spit-sprayed beer out of his mouth, all over the coffee table and my head. Now, he's laughing.

"What about vodka is so funny?"

He tries to control his laughter as he blurts out, "It was so smooth ... because, because ... ha-haha-haha-haha-haha. Oh, I'm sorry, but it's just quite funny." He laughs some more.

"Never mind, Phillip."

I'm sorry, but he's being a bit of a jerk about it.

I get up and look for my phone. At some point last night, Phillip took it out of the rice bag. Thanks to Bradley's quick trick, my phone was rehabilitated. Thing powered right up.

There's a text from Bradley.

Hot-Ass Bartender: *You ever need a job, I will totally hire you, and then I'll be the one to take you home.*

Phillip is still snickering and pissing me off, so I'm like whatever and text him back.

Me: *I might be looking for both soon. Last night was fun. Thanks for letting me play waitress, reviving my phone, and introducing me to that vodka. What is the name of it?*

Hot-Ass Bartender: *It wasn't vodka, baby. It was just plain water. You were drinking too much, and I was afraid, if you got too drunk, you might do something with me you would've regretted. And call me callous, but I would not have resisted.*

I look over at Phillip, who's still trying not to laugh every time he looks at me.

Me: *Let me guess … you told Phillip about the vodka?*

Hot-Ass Bartender: *Yeah.*

Me: *He thinks it's hilarious.*

Hot-Ass Bartender: *He's laughing at you?*

Me: *Yes. :(*

Hot-Ass Bartender: *Do you recall that he drank a shot named Sex on the Stairs last night?*

Me: *Yeah …*

Hot-Ass Bartender: *You win.*

Me: *You're the best bartender ever! And thanks for saving my phone!*

Hot-Ass Bartender: *You're welcome, baby. Don't be a stranger, okay? And Phillip's the right guy for you. Stop freaking out.*

Me: *Thanks, Bradley.*

Hot-Ass Bartender: *Anytime, and I mean ANYtime. ;)*

I stop texting and say to Phillip, "So, I get it. He made me think the water was some kind of amazing special vodka. Laugh all you want, but I think it was sweet of him." I decide I really don't feel like talking to Phillip right now. "I'm gonna go take a shower. Get ready for dinner."

"Oh, good. I need a shower, too. I'm very dirty." He raises his eyebrows at me.

For the first time in our relationship, I can honestly say that I have no desire to have sex with Phillip.

"Uh, I think I'd rather take a shower alone." I don't give him a chance to reply. I just walk in the bathroom and lock the door.

And, in the shower, I'm thinking.

I'm thinking that I might have to lie. I'm gonna have to pretend to my friends that everything is fine with Phillip. That I can't wait to marry him and that we'll have a happy and love-filled life.

Truth is, I'm thinking maybe God really was trying to tell me something in my dream. I'm not sure I should marry Phillip.

What if I'm just overwhelmed right now by the surprising fact that sex with Phillip is amazing? And that's overshadowing the fact that life with Phillip is not going to be as easy as I think.

Pretty soon, I find myself crying in the shower. I don't know why I'm crying. I just feel sad. Helpless. Confused. Scared.

Alone.

Very alone.

I calm myself down, wash my hair, get out of the shower, and get ready.

PHILLIP'S POUTING ABOUT the no sex in the shower. He keeps looking at me kinda funny. I can't decide if he's sad or pissed.

Finally, he says in a very flat tone, "Amy called while you were in the shower."

"Oh, I'll call her back."

"You don't need to. She called me since you didn't answer."

"What'd she want?"

"She said we should have a little celebration today." Phillip's words are saying that we should have a celebration, but his face doesn't look like he's in the mood for any kind of celebrating. In fact, he's looking like he wishes he had told her the wedding was off.

"Why's that?"

"She got our ceremony programs, menu, and reception cards back from the printer. Only ten more days."

"Uh, yeah. I'm gonna go grab some shoes, and then we'd better get going. We don't want to be late."

While I'm grabbing an adorable pair of leopard heels with red trim that I'm hoping will put me in a better mood, I'm trying not to freak.

Ten more days!

Ten more days?

I feel sick.

It's okay. Everyone says don't freak.

I'm trying. Really, I am.

Deep breath.

No, that won't work. I can't breathe right now. I might be having a heart attack.

Things are not good.

THURSDAY, JANUARY 4TH

PHILLIP AND I have barely talked today.

Last night, we met Katie and Neil for dinner. Katie had just filed for divorce. I'd really felt like canceling dinner and hiding in the shower all night. I didn't want to face Phillip, but I told myself that she needed me. Needed my support while she went through this horrible ordeal even though she seems really happy about it. She said, now that she's done it, she feels like this huge weight has been lifted off her shoulders. That she was just afraid to admit defeat. Afraid to tell her parents it wasn't working.

I wondered if that's how I'd feel if I called off our wedding.

She and Eric are supposed to have an amicable divorce. And, of course, Neil is super excited. He totally loves her.

When we got home, I stayed in the bathroom until I was sure Phillip had fallen asleep.

Today, at work, we've both pretended to be very busy.

I'm afraid to say anything to him. I'm afraid he's going to ask me questions.

And I don't know the answers to any of them.

On the drive to counseling, he doesn't really say anything to me. He seems to have given up.

I'm still mad that he laughed at me about the vodka. I'm still

358

mad that he didn't seem to care that he'd hurt my feelings, but what's worse is that it feels like more.

It feels like our relationship is breaking down.

Have you ever had your car run out of gas? You know that sputtering it does right before it dies?

That's what this feels like.

WE SIT DOWN in the stupid chairs. If the pastor were any kind of decent counselor at all, he'd be able to tell just from our body language that things were not good. Phillip is leaning away from me. My arms are crossed tightly in front of me. I don't even really want to look at Phillip.

What I'd like to do is puke in the trash can, but I'm trying to hold it in.

Pastor John starts our session with, "Today, we want to discuss intimacy."

"You mean, sex?" I say. Even though I hate him, I have to admit, some of his topics have been timely.

"Not just sex. We talked about that last time. I'm talking about being close, giving him a massage, whispering in her ear, showing your love in other ways, staying close, talking. As we discussed last week, you'll go through a honeymoon period, and then things will level out. It's important that couples agree on timing and frequency. If one person in the couple wants physical intimacy and they don't get it, it can cause hurt feelings, feelings of inadequacy. You might think they don't love you as much as they used to."

"We had our first argument about sex yesterday," Phillip says.

"No, we didn't," I say. "That's bullshit. We didn't argue about sex. I told you no and shut the door. We haven't argued at all. We really haven't talked."

Phillip turns to me, crosses his arms in front of his chest, and glares at me for disagreeing with him. "Well, you didn't want to do, um, that thing with me that you usually like to do."

This pisses me off. *Why can't Phillip keep his big mouth shut?* We're not supposed to be discussing specifics, only sex in general terms, so we can use the information down the road someday.

But, if he wants to talk about it now, so be it.

"You're right, Phillip. I didn't want to have sex with you in the shower after you sprayed beer on my head, laughing at me. It really wasn't a turn-on." I maybe say it a bit bitterly.

Phillip's eyes get huge.

He glances at the pastor, who takes it all in stride.

"Why were you laughing at her, Phillip?"

Phillip visibly cringes. "I think we can figure this out at home."

"No, I think we should talk about it now. You brought it up."

Phillip narrows his eyes at me. "Well, if we're gonna do that, I guess we'll have to start with what went on at Kegger's."

I narrow my eyes at him. "Nothing went on at Kegger's, Phillip. I went out with some friends. We talked in counseling about doing things on our own. About not spending all our time together. I needed to get away, Phillip. Wedding planning, building planning, a new house. Those are all very stressful things."

He replies in a pissy voice, "Like I'm not stressed, too?"

"I'm sure you are, Phillip, but Kegger's had nothing to do with you not getting sex in the shower. You didn't get sex because you'd made me feel stupid. You'd laughed at me. That's not very effective foreplay."

"You don't even get it," Phillip says with a big sigh. He shakes his head and looks at Pastor John. Then, he says with a wave of his hand, "Why don't you just tell us whatever else you have? I don't think this situation requires any further discussion."

Pastor John nods at him.

I roll my eyes at Phillip. Right now, I kinda hate him. I wonder if now would be a good time to bring up the burning bush.

I decide not to. Worst case, I burst into flames on my wedding day. And, if I do, I'll probably be dead, so I won't have to die of embarrassment.

Win-win situation.

Pastor John goes on about intimacy, caring about each other, doing little things to make each other happy. I'm not sure really; I've kinda tuned him out.

My body might not be literally burning, but my mind is still on fire with questions.

As we're ready to leave, Pastor John hands us each a questionnaire to fill out and bring back next time. He looks at the two of us, both pissed and not even wanting to look at each other. "Well, if there is a next time. Maybe you need to rethink this whole wedding thing."

He might be right, but he had no right to say it out loud.

Do voodoo dolls work?

Does anyone know? And do you know where I can get one?

Actually, maybe I'll take two. One for Pastor John and one for Phillip.

Right now, I hate them both.

I'M STILL PISSED when we get back home. I take a couple of Advil for the headache that has been pounding, plop down on the couch, and cover myself with a blanket.

Phillip sits down next to me. Phillip has a voice that reminds me of my dad. Especially when he's mad. It's that same authoritative tone. "We're going to talk about this."

"There's nothing to talk about, Phillip," I sass back.

"I disagree. We're pissed off at each other. We have to be able to talk about this stuff if we're going to make it."

If we're going to make it? If? Does Phillip think we might not make it? He's the one who's always so sure about us making it!

JILLIAN DODD

How am I possibly going to get through this if Phillip doubts it?

He continues, "So, you were mad I laughed at you, and that's why you didn't wanna shower with me?"

I nod. "Yes."

"Do you think I should be mad at you about Kegger's?"

"After Kegger's, you said we had the best sex of your life. Why should you be mad?"

He moves closer to me and gets in my face. "I'm talking about what went on at the bar. Not what happened after we came home."

"Well, if you had a problem with me, we should've talked about it then. You shouldn't have attacked me. Sex doesn't solve conflicts, remember?"

"I attacked you?" He laughs. "You stripped your clothes off the minute we walked through the door."

"What? You can't resist me?"

He doesn't answer my question, probably because it's obvious that he can't. Instead, he says, "I was texting you. Asked if you wanted to go home with Bradley. You said you didn't think so but that you'd think about it. You never replied. Again. Why do you think I drove all the way down there?"

"I thought you came to party with us."

"No, I didn't want you to go home with him. I was afraid you would."

"So, you don't trust me? How are we supposed to get married if you don't trust me?"

Sputter, sputter. The car dies.

I try to start it again. Nothing. I'm pretty sure it's out of gas, and I'm stranded on a dark road in the middle of nowhere.

"Did you have fun at Kegger's?" he asks me.

"Kinda. I think I just needed to blow off a little steam."

"So, this isn't about the burning bush?"

I sigh madly. "Stop reading my mind." I turn my head away

362

from him.

He grabs the back of my head, specifically the base of my ponytail, and forces me to look at him.

Phillip's being just a little rough, and it's extremely panty-melting. That boy just turns me on. Even when I hate him.

I can't even help it.

Plus, it's been nearly forty-eight hours since we last had sex.

I must be in withdrawal.

He's still talking, "I swear, you will not burst into flames at our wedding. Think of how everything fell into place. We're meant to be together. You know we are. I love you, Princess."

He's so freaking sweet. I gaze deep into his brown eyes for a second and then press my lips hard to his. He responds by letting go of my ponytail and pulling me into his hips. I don't bother with his shirt but go straight for his belt.

He responds with equal intensity. He roughly kisses me, pushes up my dress, and pulls me on top of him.

Let's bring out the highlight film.

FRIDAY, JANUARY 5TH

I WAKE UP, happy and in a good mood. I'm ready to walk out the door when Danny calls me.

I answer, "Hey, what's up?"

"What's going on with you?"

"Not much. I'm on my way to get a massage. Phillip wants me to relax."

"No, I mean, the other night. What went on at the bar?"

"Did Phillip tell you about that?"

"No, Nick did."

Oh, boy. If Nick told him, he knows everything.

"Uh, just went down to the museum. Met up with Nick. Had a few drinks. The usual. Why?"

"Jay, I swear, I don't know how Phillip puts up with you."

"I didn't do anything, Danny. I really didn't."

"Oh, really? Let's bring out the highlight film. You said, 'Hear, hear,' to hook-ups. You flirted with Bradley. You stopped texting Phillip after he asked if you wanted to sleep with the bartender. You drank way too many shots. You were grinding on Nick. You dressed up as a waitress—"

I interrupt him, "I was working. A girl called in sick; I was helping out."

Danny ignores me. "You were flirting with the customers. You let some guy put a tip down your shirt. You went in the back room with Bradley for over four minutes. You let Phillip drink a Sex on the Stairs shot. You were feeding Bradley pizza. Am I forgetting anything?"

"Well, jeez, when you say it like that, it sounds bad."

"It is bad, Jay."

"I didn't do anything wrong, Danny."

Danny gives me a huffy sigh.

"Okay, fine. Maybe I drank too much, but I wasn't that drunk. Like, I didn't get sick or anything."

"Oh, yeah, I heard about the special vodka, too."

"Bradley's a good guy."

"Jay, you just got with Phillip. Don't screw it up already. If Lori did something like that, I would've dragged her ass out of the bar."

"You wouldn't have dragged her ass anywhere. She would've stomped her little foot down, put her hand on her hip, and told you to chill out or go home by yourself. She did that once, remember?"

"Shut up. Yes, I remember, but it was a completely different situation."

"Do you remember when you were in a similar situation? That night after you scored four touchdowns? When she got to the bar, and you were surrounded by girls? You were dancing and doing shots. She whispered in your ear that, if you ever wanted to see her again, you'd leave now. You ran out of the bar with your tail between your legs. You were whipped."

"No, I was in love."

"What would I have done if Phillip had told me to leave?"

"Jay, you're supposed to be whipped. That's my point. Why do you seem so determined to screw it up?"

"You didn't have to plan a wedding, Danny. You just showed

up. You dated her for over a year. I'm just a little stressed. I just needed to have a little fun. Phillip's not mad at me, so stop worrying about it. It's none of your business. And here I was, just thinking how nice it'd been lately. Since we aren't living together anymore, we hardly ever fight. Just stop trying to tell me what to do. I hate it!"

"All I'm saying is, you keep doing stuff like that, you're not gonna have to wait for the BOOM. You're gonna trigger it yourself."

He hangs up on me.

I hate Danny sometimes, and I especially hate him when I know he's right.

A little case of cold feet.

SUNDAY, JANUARY 7TH

WE HAD OUR typical Sunday night dinner at the Macs'. Phillip's parents talked excitedly about the wedding.

Mrs. Mac kept saying, "Only SIX more days!"

When she said it, I kept picturing myself walking the plank instead of down the aisle.

It's all fine though. It's normal. I just have a little case of cold feet.

I look at Phillip sleeping.

And I know for sure, he's the one I want forever.

I put my head on his shoulder and fall asleep.

I'm in my wedding dress, standing outside the ceremony, waiting to walk down the aisle. My dad walks up to me. He's wearing a black tuxedo. He looks so handsome, and I'm so happy he's here. He tells me I look beautiful, that I'll always be his Angel, and then he holds his elbow out.

I hear the wedding march start to play. My mom is standing by the door.

She nods at us. It's time.

My dad turns and looks at me. His eyes are suddenly panicked. He pulls me off to the side, through a small door. When the door shuts, the room disappears, and we're in the clouds.

"Are we in heaven?" I ask.

He doesn't answer me, but I know it's heaven because Dad looks younger than the last time I saw him.

"Angel," he says, "are you sure you want to do this? You know, you don't have to go through with it."

"Are you saying, I shouldn't go through with it?"

"I think you're rushing things. You're going way too fast."

Next thing I know, I'm in the tree in our backyard, and Phillip is sitting on the same limb with me. I'm still wearing my wedding dress, but I'm only eight years old.

We're hiding from my dad because he's really mad at me. He just found out that I'd lied when I told him I didn't break the neighbor's window with a baseball.

I know I'm in big trouble for lying, and I'm scared he's going to spank me.

Phillip is holding my hand and telling me it will be okay. That we can stay out here all night. That he's not scared of the dark even though he knows I am.

Dad comes marching over to the tree. There's nowhere for us to hide, so I try not to move a muscle. Dad pulls me out of the tree, and I'm forced to let go of Phillip's hand.

Dad says madly, "If you can't make good decisions, then you're not playing with Phillip anymore."

I start bawling.

Phillip wakes me up. "Are you okay? It sounded like you were crying."

"I was. Do you remember when we were little, and I lied to my dad about us breaking the neighbor's window? Remember hiding in the tree?"

"I do remember. He was pissed."

"He told me I couldn't play with you anymore."

"We never listened, did we?"

"No, we didn't."

Phillip falls back to sleep.

I lie there, thinking. *Did my dad just try to tell me not to marry Phillip?*

First, God, and now, my dad?

I'm seriously ready to walk the plank just to make these horrible dreams stop.

perfectly adorable and well-matched

MONDAY, JANUARY 8TH

PHILLIP'S ALREADY GONE to work. I'm being snoopy and trying to find any clue I can as to where we're going on our honeymoon. He won't tell me anything other than to bring bikinis. He's been teasing me, telling me that we're going to the North Pole. That it's a new honeymoon hot spot. I search through his underwear drawer. That's where he used to hide stuff when he was little.

I find a folded-up piece of paper and think, *Ohhh, maybe this is something!*

I unfold it and find Phillip's counseling questionnaire. His neat handwriting is under each typed-out question.

I go grab my questionnaire to compare our answers. I'm pretty sure this is like our final exam.

The final exam that we have to pass.

I set his paper next to mine and read his answers. *Please let them be exactly like mine.*

What do you want out of your married life?

Me: To live happily ever after.

Phillip: A great, long relationship with the love of my life. To be happy and healthy, have a family.

Aww. Isn't that cute? We're perfectly adorable and well matched. I'm so glad I decided to peek. What's next?

How are you different?

Me: We're very different in pretty much every way. Phillip is controlled. I am wild. Phillip is methodical. I'm schizophrenic. Phillip is neat. I'm kinda messy. Phillip is an early bird. I'm not.

Phillip: We have different ways of thinking. I'm an introverted thinker. She speaks before she thinks.

Uh, I mean, yes, I know I do that, but the way he wrote it kinda sounds like a slam. I don't think I like that answer. I fight the temptation to cross it out.

Where will you live? How did you decide to live there?

Me: We just bought an amazing house in Kansas City, and we decided to live there because Phillip needed to move there for his job.

Phillip: We decided together that we would move to Kansas City, and we bought an amazing house. She's really excited about it.

Yes, I am. But shouldn't Phillip be saying that we're very excited about it? Isn't he excited about it?

Have you discussed how many children you want and when?

Me: Not really. I do want kids, but I don't want them for at least 3–5 years. And we'll have, like, 1, maybe 2 kids.

Phillip: We want them right away. And, like, 3, 4, maybe 5 kids.

WTF? Five kids! RIGHT AWAY! Is he nuts? We NEVER discussed that!

What do you do when you spend quality time together?

Me: We have sex. Oh, no, I can't write that. Cross that out. We jog together, watch football, hang out, stuff like that. I really do like hanging out with Phillip. We have fun together.

Phillip: We do everything together. We work out together, and we love sports, going out, and hanging out with friends. She has always been my best friend.

What will you do if you have a disagreement?

Me: Honestly, I will probably pout until I get my way. And, if that doesn't work, I will be mad and ignore him until he caves. It's worked well in the past.

Phillip: We'll openly discuss it. We really don't have many disagreements though. She does get mad at me sometimes, but I can usually talk her out of it.

He can talk me out of being mad? He's never talked me out of being mad! Who does he think he's marrying?

Do you ever hide from your true feelings? Do you ever use the silent treatment, lie, blame each other, or stop talking to each other?

Me: Yes, to pretty much all of the above.

Phillip: No, I'm very open with my feelings. At least, Jadyn always knows what I'm feeling. And she tells me everything.

Oh, boy. We're in big trouble.

What went wrong with your longest relationship?

Me: He decided to marry someone else.

Phillip: She was jealous of my relationship with Jadyn.

Describe your courtship.

Me: We spent a week hanging out, got engaged on our first real date, and have been living together and dating, I guess, since. Actually, we've only had a few real dates. So, maybe we didn't have a courtship? Or we had the longest courtship known to man.

Phillip: Basically, we've been best friends forever and been in love with each other for a very long time. We just were afraid to make the jump from friends to a relationship. When we finally did, there seemed like no reason to wait. Our courtship has been amazing.

I swear, he's delirious. We didn't really have a courtship. No late-night make-out sessions in front of my house; no, *Should I let him come in?*; no wondering if he was going to call again; no, *How far should I let him go without him thinking I'm a slut?*

How did I miss out on our amazing courtship?

How will you make major decisions together?

Me: Talk about it, I would imagine. Kinda like we did about moving to KC.

Phillip: Talk about it together. Over wine.

In other words, get Jadyn tipsy, and she'll agree to just about any crazy idea.

Is it easy for you to talk about your feelings?

Me: I used to tell Phillip everything. Now, I can't. I'm afraid he wouldn't like me anymore if he knew what I was thinking.

Phillip: We talk about everything.

Uh, wrong.

I can't read anymore. I wad the questionnaires into a ball and throw them in my bag.

It's clear. We're failing couples counseling.

I GO TO work and am surprisingly productive. I just finished up the rest of my preliminary drawings and am feeling really good about them. Going to the museum and letting off a little steam must've been just what I needed.

I check my emails and see one from Amy. She wants to know what our first dance song will be.

But Phillip and I don't have a song!

Apparently, when you don't have a courtship, you also don't have a song.

Sure, there are lots of songs that remind me of him. The song we all danced to like maniacs at his house whenever it came on the radio. The song that was playing in the car the night of my parents' accident. The song we danced to when he was my mercy date for winter formal. Songs from summers by Danny's pool. But they're not songs you'd want to play as your first dance. I don't think anyone wants to see us dropping what our mamas gave us or having us get low, low, low. Pretty much all the songs we love are more like dance and party type songs.

Then, I remember that movie, *The Wedding Planner*, and how the wedding planner could tell by the song a couple picked how long their marriage was going to last. How crucial the first dance song was to the success of a marriage.

I picture the dream. My dad telling me that we were moving too fast. I think he might be right. Phillip and I are moving very fast.

We're talking warp speed.

If we were on a Starfleet spacecraft, we'd have gone into hyperspace by now.

We got engaged on our first date.

We bought a house.

We've only been dating for four months.

And we don't have a song.

I don't need a wedding planner or a pastor to tell me …

We're doomed.

And I don't wanna be doomed with Phillip.

I need Phillip, like I seriously need him, but maybe we need to slow down.

Maybe we should postpone the wedding.

No, calm down. It's just cold feet. Every bride feels this way. It said so on the bridal websites. It's normal to feel this way.

You love him.

It doesn't matter that your wedding guests almost got eaten by crocodiles. It doesn't matter that God turned you into a burning bush. It doesn't matter that you answered all the pastor's questions wrong. It doesn't matter that you solve conflicts with sex. It doesn't matter that you don't have a song.

You love Phillip. That's all that matters.

Everything will be fine.

It's a freaking song. It's not a barometer of your relationship.

I'll text Phillip, and we'll figure out a song. No big deal.

Me: *Just realized we don't have a song. Like, a first-wedding-dance-appropriate song.*

I'm just getting on the phone when Phillip sneaks up behind me and kisses my neck.

"Phillip, you're distracting me. I'm working hard here."

He chuckles. "You just sent me a text about wedding songs. I have a feeling your mind isn't completely on your work."

"Actually, it is. I'm ready to show you my designs. They're still rough, but they're all in very different directions. I need to set up a meeting with your dad, but I thought maybe you could look at them, tell me what you think. Like, if you think he'll like them or if you have suggestions or whatever."

"Sure, I'd love to see them."

I move off my chair and spread my big sketchbook out in front of him. Phillip flips through the pages. He goes back and flips through them again. He has an odd look on his face. I'm pretty sure he doesn't like any of them.

He finally says in an extremely shocked voice, "Princess, these are, like … really good."

I know he said good. He might have even said really good, but what I keep seeing is that shocked look on his face.

Why is Phillip shocked? He hired me, wanted me to do this, and now, he's shocked?

WTF?

He shouldn't be shocked. If he hired me because he thought I could do it, he would expect them to be good.

And then it hits me. Why he really hired me.

"OH MY GOSH, PHILLIP! I was a pity hire? You didn't think I was talented; you just hired me, so I would move to Kansas City with you?"

I can't tell you how pissed I am.

No, scratch that. I'm not pissed.

I'm really hurt.

I feel like I just got the wind knocked out of me.

"What? No, I just—"

"Why are you acting shocked that they're good then? If you'd hired me for real, you'd have *expected* them to be good."

"I did expect them to be good, but …"

No way. I saw the look on his face. I saw his shocked expression. I know exactly what he was thinking.

"Never mind, Phillip. I don't wanna hear it. Here, take these." I shove the plans into his hands while I fight back tears. "If you want, you can use them when you hire someone else."

"Hire someone else? Why would we do that?"

"Because I'll be damned if I'm your pity hire. Some stupid family member you carry along in the business because you don't think they can make it on their own. Well, screw that. I quit."

I grab my purse and march out of the office and to my car.

I PUT THE key in the ignition and realize I should probably call Phillip's dad. Regardless of why they hired me, yelling, "Well, screw that. I quit," is not very professional.

"JJ," he answers. "How's it going?"

"Um, not great. I just wanted to let you know that I appreciate the opportunity, but I'm afraid I have to quit. Well, I just quit."

"You quit? Why?"

"No offense, but I want to work someplace where people believe I'm talented and creative, not because I'm marrying the boss's son."

"Are you in your office? I'd like to talk to you about this in person."

"I'm in my car. I told Phillip I quit, and I was getting ready to leave, but I thought I should tell you first."

"I'm not letting you quit until we talk in person. Come to my office and bring what you've worked on so far."

"I don't want Phillip in the meeting."

"Fine," he says and hangs up.

I take a deep breath.

Okay, so I'll go back in there, take him my drawings, and officially quit.

My phone buzzes.

It's Phillip.

The only reason I answer is because I'm on my way back in there. "Hey," I say coldly.

"Hey," he says back.

"What do you want?"

"What do I want?"

"Yeah, why did you call me?"

"Because you just quit on me!"

"Yes, Phillip, I quit, and I'm on my way back to your office to get my drawings, so I can give them to your dad. Then, you can all move on and hire someone who has talent."

"Jadyn, you have talent."

"I *know* that I do, but *you don't*!" I say.

I walk in the office, grab my papers out of his hands, and leave.

He follows me down the hall. "You need to stop and listen to me."

"No, thanks. I've heard enough." I try not to, but when I look at Phillip, I get tears in my eyes because, honestly, what Phillip did hurts.

I was willing to overlook all the warning signs. I was willing to believe it was just cold feet, that it didn't mean anything, but this I can't overlook. I totally anticipated, foresaw, and predicted the BOOM, but I didn't really expect it to happen so soon.

Or in this way.

I WALK INTO his dad's office and shut the door in Phillip's face.

Of course, he's stubborn. He opens the door and walks in like he owns the freaking place.

"Phillip," his dad says, "I would like to speak with JJ privately."

"Dad," Phillip says with pleading in his voice, kinda like he used to when he was younger and wanted to do something that his dad didn't think was a good idea.

"I'll come talk to you when JJ and I are through," he replies in the tone dads get when you'd better not argue.

Phillip looks at me. He looks at me angrily.

My eyes are kinda full of tears. I swallow, put on my game face, and turn to face Mr. Mac.

Mr. Mac gently says to me, "So, why do you want to quit? Did you and Phillip have a fight?"

"No, sir. I quit because I was hired under false pretenses."

"How so?"

"Well, I believe I was only hired because of Phillip, not because of my skills, my talent."

"And why would you think that?"

"Because I just showed Phillip a few of the ideas, and he was surprised they were good."

"And it upset you that he thought they were good?"

"No, I'm upset that he was *surprised* they were good. If you had hired someone else, you would've looked at their portfolio, known what they were capable of, and been upset if their work *wasn't* good. I don't want a job like this. I know I haven't been working all that long, but at the job I left, at least I felt valued. I can't work like this."

And, quite honestly, I'm pretty sure it's a deal-breaker for the whole relationship.

But I don't say that. A few tears leak out of the corners of my eyes, but I quickly brush them away.

He gets a resigned look on his face and gets up. "Well, I disagree with you. You're right; Phillip is one of the reasons we hired you but not the only reason." He grabs a bunch of rolled-up plans that were standing in the corner next to his credenza, takes them to his conference table, and unrolls them. "Come look at these. I've built this business from the ground floor up. It's been my dream to have a facility that's exactly how I want it."

I quickly flip through them and see that none of these plans look like Mr. Mac. I don't know if that makes sense because how could a building look like a person? But I suppose it's kinda like when you walk into someone's house, how they have it decorated—the colors that they've chosen and stuff—and it looks like them.

Mr. Mac is sort of a style contradiction. He loves rich, classic things. A bottle of good wine. A nice cigar. You could picture him sitting in an old library, surrounded by rich, dark colors and lots of leather-bound books. But, at the same time, he's still young—I mean, for an old guy—and kinda hip. His clothes are expensive, but they always have a flair to them. He drives a luxury-brand car, but the model is a sleek black sports car.

I look at the drawings other people have done and can see why he hasn't built any of these buildings. They just aren't him.

"It looks like you spent a lot of money on plans. Why haven't you used any of these?"

"Why do you think?"

"Because they all suck," I say a little too bluntly.

"Exactly. That's one thing I love about you, JJ. You're just like your dad was. You always cut to the chase and tell us exactly what you're thinking. So, why do you think they all suck?"

"Well, I probably shouldn't have said that. It's not really that they suck; they just … they don't look like you, like something you would like."

"And that's exactly why I haven't. I don't like any of them. It's frustrating to me because I have a vision of how I want it to be, but I can't explain it, evidently because none of these are it."

"I can see that. Like, this one is way too modern for you. And, in this one, they went the complete opposite direction and made it, like, too boring and stuffy."

"So, can I see some of your ideas?"

I want to show him my favorite idea. The building I drew is modern, but it has architectural elements that are classic. It's a building that feels like my wedding dress. Timeless. I want to show him the pictures I sketched of the inside. The cherry wood walls have insets of stainless steel, which give it a sleek, modern edge. The interior colors are dark and rich, like a men's club. The entry lounge has oversized contemporary wingback chairs covered in charcoal pinstripe velvet. The artwork is modern with bright colors. I have no idea if he will like it, but at the time, it felt right.

Just like things with Phillip used to feel right.

I can't stay here any longer. I'm going to cry. I lay my favorites on his table and run out the door. I run into my office. I need to compose myself before I go running out of the building like an idiot.

I lean my back against the closed door. When I open my eyes, I realize I'm not alone. Phillip's sitting at his desk.

"Princess, why did you quit? What's this really about? I saw our questionnaires in your bag. Is that why you're so upset?"

"You went through my bag?" That should piss me off, but I feel like I have no emotions. I feel empty because I know there's nothing else I can do.

"No, they were sitting on top, wadded up. I saw my handwriting."

I sigh, look at my adorable Phillip, and tell him the sad truth, "Phillip, we're not gonna make it. We're failing couples counseling. We handle our conflicts with sex. We don't agree on money. I'm sorry, but I totally tricked you into buying the house. I planted seeds and got Mr. Diamond to gift us the money, and I tricked you. I have a sucky past. There's baggage there that even you don't know about. I pout to get my way. I probably do have abandonment issues. And I read our questionnaires, Phillip. We don't agree on anything. And, really, I probably could've gotten through that all. I could've pretended we were gonna be okay. But you didn't rescue me from the spider, I found out I was a pity hire, and we don't have a song." I take the ring off my finger and gently lay it on his desk. "I hope we can stay friends."

I RUN TO my car, get in, and drive away.

I end up at our old elementary school. I sit in the car and stare at the swings.

I have that same sort of numb feeling I had after my parents died.

Probably because that's what just happened.

Our relationship died.

Can it be revived? Can they shock my heart? Will it ever work again? Or is it fatal?

It must be fatal because I didn't let Phillip try to resuscitate us.

Really, I'm not even sure what all I'm thinking.

Maybe I should drive to Kansas City and talk to Lori. Have her hug me and tell me I'm going to be okay. Break out the chocolate ice cream. And wine. Large amounts of wine. Or margaritas.

Speaking of margaritas, I'm gonna have to return my shower gifts. Most of them I haven't unboxed yet, but I've already used the Margaritaville blender twice.

All of a sudden, the blender seems so important.

If I give it back, it will all be real.

I'm gonna say it now. I hate when people say this because it seems so depressing, but here it is.

FML.

Maybe it was just a matter of time.

Maybe I wasn't supposed to be happy.

It's like someone's played a cruel trick on me.

Give her a taste of real happiness, let her know what it feels like, and then snatch it all away.

Or maybe I'm an idiot, and he wasn't the right guy, wasn't the one. In that case, maybe I should be grateful that this all happened now, before we were married, before we had kids.

But it doesn't feel that way.

I mean, the whole wedding, the venue, the way it fell into place. I really felt like it was a good sign, that I was finally, for once in my life, choosing the right path, the right guy, my prince, my happily ever after.

But I'm thinking fairy tales are bullshit right about now. They should really make fairy tales more realistic.

Here's what I'm gonna do. I'll move to California and start a new life. I'll rewrite fairy tales. I'll make a fairy-tale reality show. A behind-the-castle look at Cinderella and Prince Charming's lives.

I think we'd all take wicked pleasure in seeing Cinderella scream, "Asshole," at Charming, and then, in a fit of rage, she chucked her glass slipper at his head. Hopefully, it's made from, like, bulletproof glass, so it doesn't shatter and rain glass down on Charming's head and, like, disfigure him or anything. Oh, but if it did, we could change it to a *Beauty and the Beast* sort of thing.

Until now, nothing like that has ever happened between Phillip and me, but I did hear recently about a couple I know—cough, Katie and Eric—who was having a bridal shower. She had cleaned her house for three days straight because she wanted everything to be perfect. And, after totally getting all the food, decorations, and games ready, she walked into their sparkling and spotlessly clean bathroom three minutes before the guests were due to arrive to take a quick pee, only to discover her Prince Charming's dirty underwear was lying on the floor. She might or might not have thrown those dirty underwear at his head and yelled a few obscenities. She also said that it was the last straw. That he didn't respect her.

What about the dude who wrote all the fairy tales? Can you imagine being his wife? I'd be willing to bet she chucked a frying pan or two at him when he was sitting there day after day, writing about love and little pigs while he hadn't taken the trash out for three days in a row.

Maybe fairy tales don't exist.

Really, I probably couldn't write the show anyway because I wouldn't know the ending.

What would happen after she chucked the shoe at Charming?

Would he catch it, laugh at her, make her smile, and then lead her into the bedroom?

Would they have hot make-up sex?

Or what would happen if she and Charming failed couples counseling and didn't have a song? What would Charming do after she set the shoe on the desk and ran out of the castle?

What would she do next?

Would she go back and live with the wicked stepsisters, be miserable, and live with mice and cats?

Would she end up marrying the guy who had guarded their castle and always had a crush on her?

Or would she move away from Neverland—no, wait, that was *Peter Pan*. Well, that's it. Maybe she could move to Neverland and make Peter grow up.

And what would Charming do?

Would he go after her?

Would he try to get her back?

Would he have the birds spell out *I Love You* in the sky?

I have no idea.

What I really wanna do is call Phillip. He's the person I always run to when I have a problem or need support or help.

But I can't go to him about this.

I think about calling Danny. I adore Danny, I really do, but Danny is a fixer. It's like he's in a football huddle, and he's trying to get around the defense. He'd make me tell him the problem, and then he'd figure out a way to fix it. He'd make me review the play-by-play. We'd break it down. We'd figure out what went wrong. He'd form a game plan for what to do next. He'd strategize about the best way for me to handle the problem, so I could overcome it and achieve my goal.

If I wanted to fix it, I would go to Danny.

If I wanted support, love, hugs, and sympathy, I would go to

Phillip.

That means, I always went to Phillip first.

IT'S STARTING TO get dark. The school kids are long gone. I realize I've been sitting here for hours. I get out of my car, walk over, and sit on the swings.

I look down at the swing on my charm bracelet.

The bracelet that's the story of our lives.

The story that's over.

At the end of this story, it just says, *THE END.*

There is no, *And they lived happily ever after.*

The bracelet suddenly feels very heavy on my wrist. Like it's trying to strangle me.

I have to get it off.

I slide open the clasp, take it off, hook it to the swing, and then go back to my car.

I'M NOT SURE if I knew where I was going when I left the school, but I find myself at the entrance to the cemetery.

I haven't been here since the funeral, but I know exactly where to go. The spot my parents are buried is burned forever in my mind.

I get out of the car, trudge through the snow, and stand in front of it.

I read the headstone that Phillip and I picked out, but I never came to see.

> *Beloved husband and father, Paul Michael Reynolds.*
> *Beloved wife and mother, Veronica James Reynolds.*

I drop down into the snow and cry. I cry all the tears I've been pushing back inside me since they died.

AFTER CRYING AND crying, I feel kinda refreshed in a weird way.

I start to think with a clearer head. I think Mr. D might have been right. I haven't dealt with it. I thought I had to be strong for my parents to be proud of me. I thought if I didn't let it show, it meant that I was coping. That I'd gotten over it.

I don't think they would be very proud of me now.

They'd probably be embarrassed.

I've made a mockery of everything they taught me. I stood up at their funeral and told everyone about how they lived. About how they appreciated daily life. About how they cherished every day they had.

I haven't done that.

I haven't been smelling the roses. I've been using the roses as an excuse to do whatever I wanted. Sure, I've had fun, but I haven't really appreciated the amazing things right in front of me. I haven't stopped to smell the roses. I've been like a little girl riding by some roses on her bike. I'd take a whiff, and then I'd swat the petals off with my hand. I wasn't appreciating their beauty.

I was destroying them.

I thought, since my parents weren't here, that it was okay for me not to give a shit. That it was okay to pretend like I could do whatever I wanted because the world owed me something.

It doesn't.

I think it's up to me.

I reach out and trace my finger across their engraved names. Above their names is a pair of angel wings. Phillip found the design when we picked out the headstone. I trace over the wings, too.

My hand instinctively goes down to touch my hip.

I hate needles, but I went all by myself a few years ago and got a tattoo. Even though I'd never seen the headstone, I still had the rough drawing they'd made when I ordered it. I took the drawing and had the tattoo artist replicate the wings on my hip.

I didn't tell anyone I had done it because I really wasn't sure why I had done it. Eventually, Phillip and Danny saw it. The next day, they came home with matching angel wing tattoos on their ankles. I was so incredibly touched; I almost cried.

I think of Phillip.

Holding my hand in the hospital.

Holding my hand at the funeral.

Letting me sleep on his shoulder.

Taking me to the swings.

Always, always there for me.

I reach down to touch the cross charm on my wrist.

I panic.

My bracelet. It's gone!

Of course it's gone, you idiot. You left it on the swings.

I have to go get it.

"I have to go!" I say to the grave.

THE SHORT DRIVE to the elementary school feels like it takes hours.

What was I thinking? Why did I leave it there? Some little kid's going to take it in the morning and not appreciate all it means.

All it means.

All it means.

The phrase runs through my head over and over. I squeal my tires, turning into the parking lot. I cannot get there fast enough. I'm gonna get my bracelet, and then I'm gonna find Phillip.

I can't let him go.

I don't care what anyone thinks. I don't care if we're stupid. I don't care that we're failing a stupid class. I don't care if it ends in divorce after six months.

I don't care.

Pastor John was right that first day. I've been running away from Phillip every time things get tough. I always make him come running after me and make him rescue me. I've created drama on occasion just so he'd rescue me because I like it. It's not fair to him.

Is that what my dad was trying to tell me in my dream? That Phillip and I never listened to anyone?

We didn't listen when they told us that girls and boys shouldn't be friends. We didn't listen when people gave us shit about our friendship. We didn't listen when the people we were dating threatened to leave us if we didn't stop spending so much time together.

Our relationship has survived over twenty years because we didn't listen to anyone.

Not even my dad.

I picture Phillip in the tree. How his arm stayed stretched out, his hand empty, long after my dad pulled me away.

Phillip has always fought harder for us than I have. It's no wonder he's tried to move so fast. He's afraid I'm going to run. I don't ever want Phillip to doubt my love. This time and from now on, I'm gonna run to him. I'm gonna fight for him. I'm so in love with him.

But, first, I have to get my bracelet.

I tear out of the car and race to the swings.

My bracelet is gone.

I look around, but I don't see anyone.

What kind of kids would be out swinging after dark?

Shit.

Bad kids.

Katie and I used to sneak out of her house at night and smoke on these very swings.

Maybe it fell off.

I drop to my knees and frantically run my fingers across the dark, snowy dirt. I don't feel it. I need some light. I need my phone. *What did I do with my phone?* I think I turned it off and threw it in the backseat.

I turn around and run straight into Phillip's broad chest.

"You looking for this?" he says, holding up the bracelet.

Without even thinking, I hug him tightly with relief. I take in a big breath and am engulfed by Phillip's scent. The scent that smells like home.

"Phillip, oh my God, you have it! I thought I'd lost it when I was here earlier!"

"Don't act like you lost it. It didn't fall off you. I found it hooked to the swing's chain." He gives me that look. The look you get when you get caught in a lie. "Where have you been? Why did you leave the bracelet here?"

"Because I thought we were over, Phillip. I couldn't stand to look at it because it represented failure. My failure."

"But you came back for it. Why?"

I get tears in my eyes. "Because it's the story of our life."

Phillip looks around. "And this is where it all began."

I smile. "I know."

"Is it gonna end here, too?"

"Phillip, we really need to talk."

"Well, that doesn't sound very promising." He sighs big and sits on a swing.

"Why did you ask me to marry you on our first date?"

He grimaces. "However I say this, it's gonna sound bad."

"Just tell me."

"We were finally together, something I'd wanted for a very long time. I felt like I had to move fast. Get engaged, get married, before you could change your mind. I know I've been pushing you. You kept trying to tell me how you were feeling. I avoided it. If you wanna back out, I understand. I just thought, if we could make it a few more weeks, we'd be married."

"And I'd be stuck with you?"

"Yeah, maybe." He looks at me with pleading eyes. "Do you have any idea what you do to me?"

"I make you horny?" I give him a teeny smile.

"Jadyn."

"I'm joking, but here's the more important question, Phillip. Do you have *any* idea what you do to me? You seem to think it's this one-sided thing. That you love me more than I love you just because you think you figured it out before I did. I know everyone thinks I'm oblivious. That I didn't see it. But I knew. Remember when we were kids, and we'd stare up at the stars and think about how infinitely big the universe was and how small we felt in comparison? How it was, like, awe-inspiring?"

"Yeah."

"That's how I've felt about you all these years. When you asked me to marry you in fourth grade, I prayed that I would. When you told me you loved me after Spin the Bottle, I wanted to say, *I love you, too*. When we were in the chapel at the hospital, you told me you loved me again. I knew you meant it. When you took your shirt off in front of me, I would try so hard not to drool. Every night, when you answered your phone with, 'Hey, Princess,' I would melt. When you fell asleep, studying in my bed, I never woke you up because I loved waking up in your arms.

"I kinda hurt Danny's feelings when I didn't ask him to sit with me at the funeral. I lied and told him it was because I was confused about our relationship, but really, it was because there was no one else I wanted by my side but you.

"And I'm not dumb or oblivious, Phillip. I just felt so small in comparison to how big our love felt. I wasn't ready for it yet. That day we first slept together, I thought I was ready. I thought I'd grown up, but I hadn't. Since my parents died, I haven't really cared about anything that much. Win. Lose. Succeed. Fail. It was all part of the adventure, all part of the game.

"With you, I care. I care so much."

"Do you really feel that way?"

"Yes, I really do. Why did you come here, Phillip? To the playground?"

"What do you think I've been doing for the last five hours besides calling you? I've been looking for you. Have you even checked your phone?"

I look down and shake my head. "I was crying, Phillip. I haven't really let myself cry since the night of the funeral." I look at him and bite my lip. I don't even try to push back the tears. I don't think I could stop them if I tried. "I went to their grave."

His eyes get big. "You did? You said you were never going there."

I clutch my hand to my chest. "I know. I think maybe I haven't dealt with it, Phillip. I think I'm broken. I've been pretending I'm okay, but I'm not. It still hurts, and I cried. I cried a lot."

Phillip chuckles and points to my face. "Um, I can kinda tell you've been crying."

"Do I look like a raccoon?"

"Maybe just a little." He pulls out a hankie and hands it to me. I wipe some of the mascara from my face. "You still look beautiful to me."

"I think I cried all four years' worth of the tears I've been holding inside me. I miss them, Phillip. I don't think I'll ever stop missing them."

He nods his head at me.

"We did a good job on the headstone. It turned out really nice."

Phillip pulls me into his arms, the way he always does when I need him. "I know it did. I've been there a few times. You know, you don't have to be strong with me." I nod my head as he continues, "And I'm sorry. I've been looking for you because I need to tell you something. I knew you were gonna blow. I saw the signs that night in Lincoln. You told me about your cold feet, about settling, and about all your bad dreams. I knew you were getting scared, but I kept pushing you. I'll wait. If you need more time, I'll wait. We can postpone the wedding. I'm done pushing you."

He gives me those eyes, those eyes that make me melt, that are like some sort of stealth ray that sneaks in and wipes out my defenses.

"Remember how I said you always know what I need?"

He nods. "Yeah."

"I needed a push, Phillip. I needed you to push me; otherwise, I wouldn't have freaked. I needed to feel like we were over to know that there's no way I'd ever let us be over. I never want us to be over, Phillip. Never, ever." I give him a little smirk. "Although we're clearly failing couples counseling."

"Couples counseling was shit."

"You told me I needed to take it seriously."

"Maybe I was wrong." He tilts his head. "You're shivering." He stands up, takes his coat off, and wraps it around me. Then, he leans his body into mine. "No wonder you're shivering; you're soaking wet."

"I was maybe lying in the snow when I was crying." I chuckle. I'm such a freaking loser.

He runs his warm hands inside my shirt to warm me up. I want to throw him into the snow and kiss him, but I can't. We have to get through this first.

"So, I wrote down everything you said," he tells me as he pulls out his phone.

I can see he's typed a little list. Only Phillip would write down everything I jumbled out and write a rebuttal. I don't even remember what all I said.

"But, first, I have to know. Did anything happen when you were in the back room with Bradley? Did you kiss?"

"No, Phillip. I couldn't. He sort of leaned up against me, which should've felt familiar, but it felt all wrong. I think you've ruined me. I don't think I could ever be with anyone else. I told Bradley, if you dumped me, I'd have to become a nun."

Phillip laughs. It's good to see him smile. "Okay, good. So, I made a pros and cons list."

I laugh, too. "Like the one you made me in high school when you wanted to talk me out of sleeping with Jake?"

"Yep. And like the one I made when I decided to tell you how I felt about you."

"You made a list for that? Can I see it?"

"Let's stick to this list, okay? So, the pros. First one is that we solve our conflicts with sex."

"Phillip, that's supposed to be a bad thing."

He flashes me that sexy grin. "Yeah, I know, but I respectfully disagree with Pastor John on that one." He touches my cold cheek with his warm hand. "Next on the list is that you know how to manipulate me."

"What? That should be a con, too. I'm not supposed to manipulate you."

"That's where you're wrong. I love that you can. I love that sexy little pout. I love letting you think you got your way. You didn't trick me into buying the house. I wanted it just as much as you did. I was being stubborn about the money part of it, trying to wear the pants. You knew what was best for us."

"I hope the pants are on the cons list."

He looks deep into my eyes. "Princess, there's nothing on the cons list." Then, he smiles at me and says, "Moving on. The next pro is that you have a past."

I squint my eyes at him. "That makes no sense either."

"You're the single biggest part of my past. I love that. And the last pro is that we spend too much time together. I love that we do, so maybe that means we're both a little screwed up.

"And that stupid questionnaire? So we answered the questions differently. So we haven't figured it all out yet. We will. We're different people, and we have different ways of thinking. We aren't the same. We complement each other."

"Two messed up halves that make one perfect whole?"

"Exactly," he says.

"I wanna marry you, Phillip. I don't care what anyone thinks. In fact, tomorrow, we're going to our last couples counseling session, and we're going to tell Pastor John his counseling sucks, we're getting married, and he can kiss our asses."

"We're also going to burn those chairs. Do you not hate those stupid checkerboard chairs?"

I told you he could read my mind.

"I love you, Phillip. So, I'm in, like, if you still are."

Phillip gets an excited look on his face. "Speaking of that, I've found us a song."

"You can't just find us any song. We have to *have* a song."

He puts his finger up to my lips, shushing me, and then puts an earbud in my ear. He loads up a song on his phone. "This is a country song by Keith Urban. I know you don't really like country, but just listen to it."

As I listen to the song, my mind is transported back to Phillip's spring formal.

He walked up to me, grabbed my hand, and led me out onto the dance floor.

He looked so incredibly handsome tonight. His broad shoulders in a black suit, the silver paisley tie he bought to perfectly match the silver dress he helped me pick out. The one he told me I looked so hot in that every guy in the room would be jealous of him.

He wrapped his arms around my waist and pulled me close to him.

The song is slow, and we were barely moving, barely swaying.

My face is nuzzled into the corner of Phillip's neck.

The spot where I feel like I've died and gone to heaven.
The spot that I once kissed, trying to make another guy jealous.
The spot that I'm was dying to kiss right then.

OH MY GOSH!

I rip the earbud out of my ear.

"Phillip! Is this that song? That song we danced to at your formal? When you sang in my ear? Something about being a lover and a friend? Is this that song?"

Phillip grins at me. "Yeah, it is."

The tears come rushing back, but these are different tears. These are happy tears. Our marriage isn't going to fail. We're going to be just fine.

"So, we already had a song?"

"Yeah, Princess, we already had a song."

He puts an earbud in his ear and then one in mine. He restarts the song, pulls me into his arms, and dances with me. I cry happy tears through the song. All the words so sum up our relationship.

WHEN THE SONG is over, I wrap my hands around Phillip's cheeks, look him straight in the eyes, and slowly kiss him.

A long, slow, amazing kiss.

The kind of kiss that feels like the stars.

The kind of kiss you want for infinity. Forget happily ever after. I'm going to be happy with Phillip for infinity.

"You know, I was going to bring you to this exact spot to ask you to marry me. Then, I felt like it wasn't enough. Like it wasn't big enough, like it wouldn't impress you. I went way overboard. I'm gonna fix that. Do this right. The way I should have." He drops down on one knee in front of me, takes my hand, and says, "Will you marry me, Princess?"

I drop to my knees and throw my arms around his neck. "The answer to that question is always going to be yes."

Slow, tender, amazing.

TUESDAY, JANUARY 9TH

LAST NIGHT, PHILLIP held my face in his hands and looked me straight in the eyes. It was a little unnerving at first, but then he would kiss me and run his hands through my hair and tell me over and over how much he loved me.

And I wouldn't say we had sex. I wouldn't say we had make-up sex. I would say, for the first time in my life, I really understand the difference between having sex and making love.

Because I'm pretty sure that's what we did.

Like, pretty much all night.

Slow, tender, amazing.

Phillip walks into the bedroom, coffee cups in hand. He grins at me. "I love what you're wearing."

"Phillip, I'm pretty sure I'm not wearing anything." I can't help but laugh.

'Cause I'm completely naked.

Shame on me.

He gently puts his finger on mine and tips my left hand up, so I can see that he snuck the engagement ring back on my finger while I was sleeping.

I smile what might be the biggest smile of my life. "I like what I'm wearing, too."

He sits on the bed next to me and holds my hand up. "I want you to take a good look at this ring. This ring has nothing to do with the wedding, nothing to do with our commitments, none of that. This ring means one thing. That I love you. Promise me that, no matter what, no matter if we fight, no matter how hopeless things might feel, that you will look at this ring and know that, when you love someone, that's all that really matters. That we'll always figure it out together."

"I promise," I whisper as I pull him back into bed with me.

WE WALK INTO Pastor John's office. I tightly squeeze Phillip's hand. I'm mentally gearing up for a big fight.

We don't sit down in his stupid chairs. We stand in front of his desk and rapidly take turns telling him all the reasons we don't give a shit what he or anyone else thinks.

"We know all our answers are different," Phillip says as he tosses our questionnaires on his desk.

"And we know we solve our conflicts with sex," I say.

"And we know we spend too much time together."

"And we know we're not perfect. We might even be a little messed up."

"But, when you put us together, we're a perfect match," Phillip says.

"And we love each other," I say. "Deeply and passionately. And we don't care what you or anyone else thinks. We're getting married."

Pastor John leans back in his chair and slowly claps his hands three times. "Bravo. Bravo."

I'm instantly pissed. "Bravo?"

"This isn't an act. We're serious," Phillip says. He's pissed, too.

"I know you are," the pastor replies. "And don't move. I want you both to remember this moment forever. How it feels. The two of you. Hand in hand. Fighting against something you think is trying to tear you apart. I was playing devil's advocate a bit. And, honestly, after last week—the way you argued, your body language—I didn't think you'd make it. Thought you'd call off the wedding. What you're going to face in life is going to be a whole lot harder than facing what you did with me. My job is to try to prepare you for that.

"I remember your parents' funeral, JJ. It was the hardest one I'd ever done in my career. I was the same age as your parents and fresh out of school when I married yours, Phillip. I'd become friends with them. Watched you both grow. They were so proud of you both. I didn't think I was going to make it through the service, but I looked out and saw you, JJ, standing there, in the pew. Your eyes were dry. Your chin was up. I saw such strength. I wondered what your parents had done that made you so strong at such a young age. But then I noticed you were tightly holding Phillip's hand, just like you are now, and I knew where all that strength came from. It's from each other. You get strength from each other.

"Whatever you face in life, I hope you face it like you are now. Hand in hand. United. If you do that, you'll make it. You'll have a wonderful marriage."

I turn my head into Phillip's chest and cry with relief.

"It'd also be my extreme honor to marry you." Pastor John grins at us and holds up our save-the-date card. "I mean, you did give me an STD a couple of months ago; you kinda owe me."

I squeeze Phillip's side, and we can't help it. We both start laughing.

You were crashing.

THURSDAY, JANUARY 11TH

I WAKE UP with a start. I look at the clock. It's almost seven, so I wake Phillip up.

"Phillip, I'm not sure we should go on our honeymoon. I'm pretty sure the plane is gonna crash."

"What are you talking about?"

"Well, I just had this dream, and it was horrible."

He doesn't even roll his eyes. "Tell me about it."

"Okay, so we're already married, and all our wedding guests are on an airplane with us. I'm in my wedding dress, and you're in your tux. We're in the cockpit of the plane. You were flying."

"Sweet."

"I take that back. You were not flying. You were crashing."

"Well then, I promise not to fly or crash the plane on our honeymoon."

"What if it's a warning? Like a premonition?"

"I'm gonna be glad when we're finally married, so you can stop with the disaster dreams. And, hopefully, if that's the case, we crash on the way *back* from the honeymoon."

He smirks at me, and I playfully smack his arm.

"Phillip, that's not funny!"

"Okay, fine. If all our wedding guests were on the plane, we

399

couldn't have been going on our honeymoon anyway."

"Oh my gosh, Phillip. I didn't think of that. What could that mean?"

"Did we actually crash and die?"

"What? I don't know. I woke up when we were getting ready to crash, but no, we hadn't hit yet."

"You just didn't see the end of the dream then. I know what happened."

"No, you don't."

"I do. I took control of the plane, pulled up the wheel, and safely landed it. The wedding is going to be brilliant, and our honeymoon is going to be like a fantasy."

"I'm pretty sure it didn't end that way."

"My mom used to tell me, when I had bad dreams, that the ideas were coming from my brain, and if it was scary, I should just use my mind to change the dream. Like all those scary, awful ones I used to have where you would attack me."

He pretend shudders, so I make a sad face.

"What's with all the dreams?"

"I don't know. I've had vivid dreams my entire life. I guess the good news is, they've moved from wedding disasters to honeymoon disasters."

"Our honeymoon is going to be amazing. You in nothing but some skimpy bikinis and some sexy lingerie all week sounds like heaven to me."

"You suck. Why won't you tell me where we're going?"

"Because I wanna surprise you. If I tell you, you'll look at it on the internet and know what to expect. Trust me. It's practically paradise. So, hey, speaking of dreams, you ever have any about me?"

"Maybe a few."

"Tell me." He's holding my hand and slowly twisting his fingers through mine. It's like he can't be near me without touching some part of me.

"Remember that night I was out with Mark and whined to you while sitting on the kitchen island? I had a dream that, when he brought me home, he turned into this werewolf/vampire creature. I don't remember, but it was scary. You saved me. Opened up the car door, stabbed him, and dragged me safely away."

"Sounds a lot like real life. I was always rescuing you for some reason or other."

"Yeah, but unlike real life, after I was safe, I kissed you."

"Now, this is getting better."

"Not really. I think it's like an unwritten princess contract of some kind that, after you're rescued by a prince, you have to kiss him."

"I think you were just hot for me."

"Ask any little girl, and she'll tell you. It's in every fairy-tale movie. You get rescued. You pay him with a kiss."

"Well, that sucks."

"There might have been another one that I had, um, quite often actually."

"Is it a good one?"

"I think so. Remember that flag-bikini day when our feet got accidentally tangled up, and we both fell down?"

"Of course I remember it; however, you tripped me on purpose. Admit it." He tickles me.

"I will say that it was a planned accidental entanglement of our limbs."

"You're such a liar."

"Regardless of how we fell, remember how you rolled me over, sat on top of me, and then leaned down to yell at me?"

"Like this?" Phillip rolls on top of me and leans down close to my face.

"Yeah. Only, in the dream, when you leaned in, you kissed

me."

Phillip leans down and kisses me. A lot. Eventually, he stops. "Then, what?"

"Then, you kissed my entire body and took off my bikini, and we kinda did it right there, in the grass."

"See, I knew you wanted me all along." Phillip pulls off my nightie and kisses down my body.

"Well, no. In the dream, you wanted me. You know, that was the first time I ever did that, like in a dream."

"I was your first sexual dream partner. What an honor," Phillip teases.

"I should tell you that I didn't like the dream."

"Why?"

"I felt very conflicted about it. I liked the dream, but then, you know, you were kinda like a brother to me. It felt a little wrong."

"But you kept having the dream?"

"Yeah. And I kept wanting to have the dream, which was even worse."

"You should've just attacked me."

"Maybe I was waiting for you to attack me. Like you did in my dream."

"You're right; I should have." He kisses down my neck. "I'll try to make it up to you."

your last night as Jadyn Reynolds.

FRIDAY, JANUARY 12TH

LOTS OF PEOPLE have been arriving at the hotel today, and we have fun welcome bags waiting in each room. I love the bags. They are adorable creamy-colored totes with our wedding monogram printed on them. Inside the bag is a map of the Plaza, the weekend itinerary, water bottles, a Kansas City pennant, cookies, nuts, cheese and crackers, and chocolate truffles. Also waiting in each room is a bucket of locally brewed Boulevard beer.

I've already eaten the truffles out of my bag, and Joey and Nick quickly robbed me of my beer.

The rehearsal went well and was followed by a casual barbecue dinner for everyone in town. There were lots of toasts, and we gave our wedding party their gifts. The guys went crazy over their custom Nikes and are beyond excited that they don't have to wear the shoes that came with their tuxedos.

Phillip and I are on one of the trolleys his parents rented to take people on a tour of the Plaza Lights. The Country Club Plaza is pretty at any time of the year, but it is amazing during the holidays. It was one of the first shopping centers in the country and was modeled after Seville, Spain, so the buildings have great architectural details. Like beautiful Spanish domes, towers, arches, and columns. The Plaza Lights are eighty miles of lights that highlight those architectural features.

I snuggle into Phillip's arm. "It's really breathtaking, isn't it?"

Phillip looks straight at me, ignores the lights, and says, "You are."

"Phillip, I mean, the lights, silly. I'm so glad I looked through that holiday album, and we decided to get married here. It feels practically magical."

He nods his head, pulls me closer to him, and kisses the top of my head. "Our whole wedding is going to be magical, Princess."

AFTER THE TROLLEY ride, we head back to the hospitality suite where we're serving warm gingersnaps and adorable snowflake-shaped sugar cookies. There's a coffee and hot chocolate bar to complement the cookies, and Phillip's mom also decided to serve her son's favorite gingerbread martinis as well as the chocolate peppermint martini I loved.

Just when it feels like the party's getting started and I've enjoyed a couple of tasty martinis, Amy says to me, "It's the bride's bedtime."

"Really? It's only, like, ten thirty!"

"You want to look gorgeous on your wedding day, am I right?"

"Yeah, you're right. I guess I can party tomorrow."

"Exactly." She turns to Phillip and says, "That goes for the groom, too."

Phillip says, "No problem. I'll walk her to her room and make sure she's a good girl."

The way Phillip slowly slides his hand down my back, I doubt that his version of me being a good girl and Amy's are the same, but either way, I'm pretty sure I'll be in bed soon.

OUTSIDE MY HOTEL room, Phillip says, "So, tomorrow is the big day."

I smile big. Again. I think my mouth has been in a permanent grin all day.

"Can you believe it's finally here? I can't wait for you to see my dress. I hope you love it as much as I do."

"I'm sure I'll love it. I mean, I love you."

He leans one hand against the door above my shoulder. It reminds me of how he used to lean against my locker when he had a secret to tell me.

I stand on my tiptoes and kiss his cheek. "Good night."

He gives me a long, sweet kiss. I can tell he doesn't want to go, but we're supposed to, right? Like, everyone says we're not supposed to spend the night together before our wedding day.

"Make sure you don't let the guys talk you into partying with them tonight. I want you looking all handsome tomorrow."

"I didn't tell them my room number. They'd be banging on my door all night." He touches my face and looks lovingly into my eyes. "Good night, Princess."

I shut my door, wishing I had invited him in. I mean, I don't really require that much sleep, and I usually only get baggy eyes when I'm hungover, which I obviously won't be.

I'll call him and tell him to come back down.

But, first, I wanna change into some comfy yoga pants and finish up a couple of things.

A FEW MINUTES later, there's a knock on my door. I look out the peephole and see Phillip's adorable face. I open the door and quickly let him in.

"What are you doing?" he asks, pointing to the purple permanent marker I'm still holding in my hand.

I look down at the marker I forgot I was holding. "Oh, I just finished writing on the bottom of my wedding shoes."

"Why are you writing on your shoes?"

"It's kinda like in high school when you'd write math formulas up your arms before a test. You know, so you wouldn't forget. I'm writing on the bottom of my shoes, so I don't forget."

He squints his eyes at me in confusion. "Show me."

I flip up my purple satin pumps and show him where I wrote, *I do!*

He laughs at me. "It's your wedding. Do you think you'll forget that part?"

"I don't know. Maybe," I tease. "So, what are you doing back down here? I thought you were supposed to be getting your beauty sleep."

"Yeah, I know. I just wanted to check on you. Are you nervous? Do you have cold feet?"

"Nope, I put on the socks you gave me." I point down at my fuzzy socks. "I'm all good."

"Have you had any more bad dreams you haven't told me about?"

"No, but I have been thinking a lot about my parents." I tilt my head at him. "Phillip, do you think they'd be proud of me now?"

He pulls me into his arms and sweetly looks at me. "I know they'd be proud of you. You're learning about life, about love, and you're playing the hand that was dealt to you the best that you can."

"It took me a long time to figure things out. I think I'm finally dealing with it. With losing them. I still can't believe I stood up at their funeral and preached about appreciating what you have, and I didn't do it myself."

"Irony, right?"

"Yeah, and it's only taken me four years to figure it out."

"At least you realized it. Speaking of that, do you realize this is your last night as Jadyn Reynolds?"

I pull him down onto the bed with me. "Jadyn Mackenzie. I'm not sure I like the sound of that. I might have to keep my name." I slowly slide my hands down his sides.

He tightly grabs my hands. "No sex."

"What do you mean, no sex?"

"No sex if you keep your name."

I struggle and try to free my hands. Phillip has a smart-ass grin on his face. He loves being stronger than me. He might be stronger, but I'm pretty sure I'm smarter. I lean my face into his shoulder, like I'm going to kiss it, but I bite it instead. It doesn't hurt him, but it startles him enough that I'm able to get one of my hands free.

I run that hand down the front of his jeans. "You drive a hard bargain." I press down a little firmer on his jeans. "Get it? A *hard* bargain."

He laughs. "You're bad. Is it bad that I want to?"

"I don't think it's bad at all. I want to, too. But, before we get to that, can I read you the poem I wrote for the service tomorrow? Like, Lori's gonna read it, but I kinda wanted you to hear it from me first."

Phillip smiles. That smile that makes me melt. "I'd love that."

I grab the poem out of my bag and sit cross-legged on the bed, facing him.

My eyes get teary as I read to him.

Phillip does that to me. He makes me cry.

I remember one night in high school when Katie was crying because she and Neil had broken up, Lisa found some quote. It was something like, *No boy is worth your tears, but once you find the one that is, he won't make you cry.*

I've decided that quote is wrong.

Phillip makes me cry. I cried about him on the beach in Cancun. I cried about him the night I said yes. Phillip has been chipping away at the hard exterior I put around my heart since my parents died. I didn't let myself cry, and I wasn't letting myself feel much either. I locked all my emotions away. Kept them balled up inside of me. I didn't want to feel anything for anyone because I knew how much it would hurt when I lost them.

But Phillip's love got through.

Straight through to my heart.

I feel free now.

Free to feel, free to cry, and free to live my life. And the tears I've been crying aren't sad tears; they've been happy ones. I'm so happy with Phillip; I can hardly believe it.

Phillip gazes into my eyes the whole time I read. I say a silent prayer that, if I'm lucky enough to see those brown eyes every day, I will have lived an amazing life.

What It Means to Marry Your Best Friend

It means he knows you, all of you.

You can't hide your bad parts because he's already seen them.

You can't surprise him with your good side because he already knows it.

He knows what you want before you know you want it yourself.

He knows how to make you laugh, and he knows exactly what to do when you cry.

He knows you see the world differently than he does and embraces your outlook.

He knows, on the rare occasion when you get quiet, that he'd better start talking.

He knows you tend to stretch the truth and knows exactly when to call your bluff.

He knows when to go along with your stories and when to make up a few of his own.

He usually knows when you're teasing him and how to get back at you.

He knows you act tough, but you have a soft heart.

He knows you're fiercely independent, but you secretly love when he rescues you.

He knows when to let you fly and when to reel you in.

And, most importantly, he knows how to love you.

And you know all you need is him.

Phillip pulls me into his chest and hugs me. "That's amazing, Princess, really. I can't believe you wrote it."

"Well, it's kinda amazing what comes out of you when you start to feel again. Somehow, this whole process, from the planning to the stupid counseling, has helped me feel again. I can't thank you enough for putting up with my crap and for helping me get through this. I love you, Phillip. I really do."

"Is there a reason we're not supposed to be together tonight?"

"Well, I think, traditionally, it was to protect the bride's virtue. But, since I don't really have any virtue left, we don't have to worry about that. It's also supposed to be bad luck to see the bride on the wedding day. You're supposed to wait until you see her walking down the aisle in her dress or whatever."

He gives me a sexy grin. "Wasn't it you who said we never listen to anybody?"

"I think that was me." I put my hands on his biceps and give them a little squeeze. "Does that mean I get to wake up in these sexy arms on my wedding day?"

"Most definitely," he says. He gets up, turns off the lights, puts the Do Not Disturb sign on the door, strips down to his boxers, and slides into bed with me. "We'll order room service for breakfast, relax, and I'll sneak out when you go get your hair done. What time is that?"

"My appointment isn't until noon," I say as I happily snuggle up next to him.

I'm seriously blessed.

SATURDAY, JANUARY 13TH

LORI BANGS ON my door at ten thirty. I'm leaning against Phillip's naked chest while he feeds me bites of pancakes.

I get up, peek my head out the door, and whisper to Lori, "Didn't you see the Do Not Disturb sign? That's kinda like hanging a sock on the door. I have a boy in my bed."

She pushes through the door. "Jade, don't joke about something like that," she says like I was hooking up with some random stranger the night before my wedding.

Her eyes get big when she sees Phillip. "Phillip, what are you doing here? You're not supposed to be here!"

"It's not my fault she wanted one last single-girl fling."

I slide back in bed to finish breakfast. "Lori, don't act all shocked. I know you and Danny spent the night before your wedding together."

"No, we didn't."

"You left early. Don't act all innocent."

"Okay, so maybe we spent some time together the night before, but we went to different rooms to sleep. I didn't want him to see me the morning of the wedding. It's bad luck, you know."

"I think it's good luck. I also think it's a stupid tradition and why some brides call off their weddings at the last minute."

"You think sleeping with them the night before will guard against cold feet?"

"Definitely. When you're all alone the night before your wedding, you have nothing to do but think. To question yourself. Contemplate all the lifetime-commitment stuff you're about to say." I give Phillip's thigh a little squeeze. "It's hard to think about cold feet when you've got a hot guy in bed with you."

"Fine, joke all you want."

"I'm not joking at all. I'm dead serious. I'm glad Phillip spent the night with me."

Phillip kisses my cheek, pops the last piece of bacon in his mouth, and gets out of bed. He's only wearing boxers, so he pulls on his jeans, tosses his shirt over a broad shoulder, and picks up his shoes.

"I think I'd better leave you girls to this."

"You're a chicken; you know that, right?" I tell him.

After watching his sexy backside walk out the door, I turn to Lori and say, "You want some food?"

"Are you really doing okay? Like, you seem very calm."

"Does that surprise you? I've always been pretty chill about stuff."

Lori rolls her eyes at me and shakes her head. "You used to be chill about everything until you started dating Phillip. Then, you got a little dramatic. So, is there anything you need? I feel like we should be doing something."

"I'm gonna finish eating and then take a long bath. The hair-stylist doesn't want me to wash my hair, so that's all I have to do."

"You seem too calm. It's kinda scaring me."

"Lori, I wanna marry Phillip more than anything. I'm excited, happy, and incredibly blessed. I've found a man who is so amazing in bed that it makes me cry." I grab a tissue and dab at fake tears.

She slaps me on the arm. "Jade! Do you ever take anything seriously?"

"Yes, actually, I do. In all seriousness, I'm *seriously* blessed. Like, he's amazing. Last night—"

"Okay, I give up. You're calm. Danny sent me down here early because he was worried you'd be freaking out."

"You don't need to babysit me. I'm not going anywhere. I didn't even have any bad dreams last night." I grab a ceremony program off the nightstand and toss it toward her. "Take a look at this."

She watches it float down to the ground, and as she's leaning down to pick it up, she says, "What's this?"

"The ceremony program."

She looks at the front of it. The black-and-white brocade print. The purple trim. Our wedding monogram. She turns it over, flips it open, and then closes it. "It's pretty."

I smile. "No, you need to read it."

"Why? I know everyone."

"Fine, there's something I need to tell you. If you'd read the program, you'd have seen that you're not my matron of honor."

She puts her hand to her chest and cries out, "What did I do wrong?"

"No, silly. I mean, we're not calling you matron of honor."

"Oh, you scared me, and, Jade, I'm so sorry. You didn't have to do that. It was so selfish of me to want to change your wedding."

"Well, I looked up the word *matron* in the thesaurus for a different word to use. The synonyms were even worse. Words like *biddy, dowager, dame.* So then, I decided to buck tradition. I searched the internet and found that other people felt the same way. I found lots of ideas. A nice one was *treasured friend,* but I thought that sounded like we were fifty years old. There was *honor attendant, lady of honor, best woman, chick of honor, goddess of honor, homegirl,* and *the bride's babe.*"

She puts a hand up to her mouth to hide her giggles. "Oh,

that sounds like we're having an affair!"

"Scandalous, right? What about *executive vice president in charge of bridal affairs?*"

"That sounds like you're having affairs, and I'm in charge of them!"

"That'd make you my pimp!" I laugh, but then I get serious. "So, read it."

She opens the program and reads from it. "Lori Diamond, Hot-Ass Best Friend." She chuckles. "Very funny. Did you have this program made just for me?"

"No, that's the actual program. Ask Amy."

She looks down and reads some more. "The bridesmaids are The Hotties? Danny is the Hot-Abs Best Friend? And the groomsmen are The Abbies? Ohmigawd, Jade, only you could write *ass* in your wedding program and get away with it!"

"Nobody reads them anyway. I think it's awesome!"

"I think you're crazy!"

I start to tear up for real. "You're my best friend; you know that, right? Danny and I will always be tight, but you really are like a sister to me."

She gets tears in her eyes, too, and gives me a big hug.

Something borrowed, something blue.

I'M READY. READY to go meet Phillip. Ready for him to see my dress for the first time.

Mrs. Mac and Mrs. Diamond are gushing about how pretty I look.

Mrs. Mac says, "So, you haven't followed any traditions, but we're making you do this one. Do you have something old?"

Lori nods her head. "Yes, the satin at the base of her bouquet is from one of her mom's bridesmaid dresses, and she has lots of new things."

"What about something borrowed?" Mrs. Diamond asks.

I squint my eyes. "Um, I don't have anything borrowed."

Mrs. Mac grins. "I was kinda hoping you'd say that. I have something for you to borrow." She rummages through her bag and pulls out a beautiful four-strand pearl bracelet. "It was my grandmother's. Both my mother and I borrowed it for our weddings."

"I'd be honored," I say and hold out my arm.

She slides it on my wrist. "It looks really pretty with your dress."

I hug her and try not to cry. Even though we went with the waterproof mascara, I don't want to mess up my makeup right before I see Phillip. "Thank you. It's beautiful."

Chelsea says, "What about something blue?" She has a sneaky

little grin on her face.

"Hush," I say.

"What? You don't want Phillip's mom to know you have a sexy *something blue* thong on under there?"

The only moment I really care about.

I'M STANDING OUTSIDE a doorway at the top of a winding staircase. Phillip's waiting for me at the bottom. I can't see him, but I know he's there. I can feel him.

I love the way I look. I love my dress, the way my hair is perfectly curled, the way my veil poofs out, and my soft bridal makeup.

I know brides are supposed to fret and worry about every detail of their wedding.

I'm not.

This is the only moment I really care about. I want to remember the way Phillip looks at me for the rest of my life.

I want this moment to be perfect.

Amy is getting the photographer all set up. After this, we're going to take pictures at our fountain and a few other places around the Plaza, and then we'll come back and do more photos with the wedding party.

Amy says, "Okay, we're ready."

I glide through the door. There is something about this wedding dress. I've never felt so beautiful or so graceful or even anywhere so close to perfect in my life.

I pause at the top of the stairs. Phillip turns around to face me. I've been so focused on how I would look for him that I didn't think about what he'd look like.

Oh. My. Gosh.
He looks perfect.
Seriously.

He looks so incredibly handsome. His freshly shaven face, his perfectly styled hair, his big brown eyes, and that gorgeous smile. His black tuxedo drapes exquisitely across his tall, muscular frame. I love the way his shoulders are broad and how his chest tapers down to his lean waist. Phillip is perfect all the way down to his custom black Nikes with their purple swoosh.

I'm looking at my dream. My prince.

Our eyes meet. He looks at me so adoringly, and I can't believe I ever doubted this. All the worrying I did. All the, *Should I marry him?* All the, *Will we work out?* All the tears.

They all come down to this very moment.

This moment when I know I'm exactly where I belong.

He holds my eyes the whole time I'm slowly descending the staircase. When I'm about to the middle, he starts walking up toward me. Like he can't help it, like he can't wait any longer to touch me.

Three stairs from the bottom, he touches my face and says, "You look like my dream come true."

I get tears in my eyes because that's exactly how I hoped I'd look.

He continues, "You look amazing, gorgeous, beautiful. I don't even have the right words."

"Those sound like pretty good words to me. So, do you like the dress?" I ask as he leads me down the final three stairs.

"I love the dress. My mom cut out all those mermaid dresses. I really thought that's what you were getting. This is so much better." He grins and tilts his head at me. "You kinda look like a princess."

I grab the skirt of my dress and twirl it a bit. "I know. I think that's why I loved this dress so much. But, even if I had gotten the dress all wrong, I know I did one thing right."

"What's that? Your shoes?"

"No, silly. You. I can't believe I'm marrying you today. You're everything I've ever wanted and more. And you're looking pretty damn fine yourself. I even like the tennis shoes."

He holds his pant leg up, so I can see them better. "I love the shoes. Everyone loves the shoes. So, turn around. Let me see this dress."

I do a slow spin.

He looks me up and down and tilts his head. "I think you're missing something."

I look down at myself. "I don't think I'm missing anything."

"Yeah, you are. Let's see ... do you have something old?"

"Yeah, on my bouquet." I show him the fabric.

"How about something new?"

"Pretty much everything is new."

He scrunches up his nose, like he's evaluating me. "Something borrowed?"

I hold out my wrist. "Your mom let me borrow the bracelet both she and her mother wore at their weddings. It was her grandma's."

"I don't see anything blue."

"You don't get to see what's blue until later." I smirk.

He gives me the kind of sexy grin that makes me want to drag him up to my room.

"What about something from the groom?"

"Um, I'm wearing my engagement ring." I hold my right hand up and show him.

"No, that doesn't count." He pulls a little wrapped box from behind his back and holds it in his palm in front of me.

"Phillip, you already bought my wedding band. You didn't need to get me anything else."

"Oh, so you don't want it?" He snatches the box away from

me.

I put my hands on the sides of his waist and pull my body close to his. "Oh, I want it."

"You're bad. Be good and open this."

He puts the box back in front of me. I gently untie the ribbon, pull the small velvet jewelry box out, and open the lid.

Inside is a breathtaking pear-shaped diamond pendant. The larger center stone is surrounded by different-sized smaller diamonds set in platinum. It's funky yet classic.

"Phillip, it's beautiful! And it's pear-shaped, just like my mom's ring."

"It *is* your mom's ring. I took the diamonds out of your parents' wedding rings and had them made into this."

"My parents' rings?"

It feels like all the air just got sucked out of the room. I clutch my arm to my stomach like I just got punched, cover my mouth with my hand, and start to cry. I can't pry my eyes away from it. Their diamonds are together now, and they look so happy.

Phillip looks worried. "Oh, Princess, I'm sorry. I thought— well, you said it was sad that they just sat there in your jewelry box. I wanted you to have them with you. I saved the settings. I didn't ruin them. We can put them back. I can fix it."

I poke my fingers into the corners of my eyes in an attempt to stop the tears from ruining my makeup.

I can't speak. I can't mutter out words. My heart feels like it's in my throat.

"It's beautiful," is all I manage to say.

I lean my head back and fan my face, trying to stop the tears. Phillip leans in and kisses my cheek, which makes me smile.

I reach out and touch his face. "Phillip, I'm so touched. I adore it. I'm trying really hard not to cry here, but ..." I lose the tear battle.

Phillip pulls a hankie out of his pocket and hands it to me. I dab my eyes with it.

Then, I look at it and laugh. "Your hankie has our wedding monogram on it!"

"Amy seriously thinks of everything."

We both laugh.

I clutch my chest. "This necklace, I never would've thought of doing something like this. Thank you. And to get to wear their wedding diamonds, like, today, on my wedding day—it's amazing. You're amazing. I think I'm the luckiest girl in the world."

"I thought it was the universe," he teases.

I laugh and dab away the rest of the tears while he puts the necklace on me.

WE WENT ALL over the Plaza with the photographer and took a bunch of great photos in front of all the fountains and the cool old buildings.

We're in the limo, heading back to the hotel.

"Hey, we just passed the hotel," I say.

"Amy and I have a little surprise," Phillip says. "We thought it might make for some cool photos."

The driver pulls up to a park. Phillip pulls me out of the limo and leads me down a snowy path. We round the corner, and I cover my mouth.

"Oh my gosh, Phillip. Swings!"

And not just any swings. Amy had these swings decorated. The chains have garlands running down them, and there are purple ribbons hanging from the snow-covered trees. It's beautiful.

"Come on!" I grab Phillip's hand like I used to when we were little and drag him across the snow.

I can't wait to see these pictures. I even change out of the purple UGGs I've been wearing out in the snow. The photographer takes photos of Phillip pushing me on the swing, so that you can see the *I do!* I wrote on the bottom of my shoes. I'm pretty sure it will be my favorite picture ever.

Mind if we have some privacy?

IT'S ALMOST TIME!

The girls just left to get lined up for the walk down the aisle. I'm getting my makeup touched up when Danny strolls in.

He always looks so handsome in a suit.

"You look handsome, Danny."

"I had to come tell you how beautiful you look. Really, Jay, you look amazing. Hard to believe the raggedy little girl who punched me in the face could grow up to look like this." He gives me a big hug and gets misty-eyed. "I love you."

I tear up, too. "I love you, too."

The makeup artist says, "Don't cry. We just got your makeup all fixed."

Danny gives the makeup artist his dazzling grin, probably because he knows any girl will let him do anything he wants in hopes of seeing that grin just one more time. Then, he says to her, "Mind if we have some privacy?"

The makeup artist flashes me an irritated look. Like it's my fault. She probably thinks I'm getting ready to have a pre-wedding romp with him. Or, at least, I know that's what she's fantasizing about. Only she'd be the bride.

Danny shuts the door, raises his eyebrows up and down at me, and gives me his Devil Danny grin.

"What? What'd you do?"

"Nothing." He points his thumb toward the door. "You know, she probably thinks we're having sex."

I giggle. "Well, you are the best man."

"Come on, baby, just one last time? He'll never know," he says loudly to the door.

The makeup artist probably has her ear up to it.

He whispers in my ear, "Maybe you should make some appropriate noises. Then, we'll walk back out, and I'll be zipping up my pants."

I laugh and smack his shoulder. "You're so bad."

He laughs with me, but then his face gets serious. "So, I have something to give you." His voice gets that aw-shucks sound to it. The sound that has drawn so many people to adore him. That slight Southern twang he can't seem to get rid of. "I want you to have good luck today. Anyone else would laugh me out of the room if I gave them this, but I know you'll understand."

I nod my head as he reaches in his pocket.

"I'm only letting you borrow this. Like, you *cannot* lose it. But I wanted you to have it for today."

He hands me a black Adidas bicep band.

"Really? Your bicep band? This is practically a state treasure!" In my hand is the sweatband that Danny has worn for every game since he won his first collegiate game.

"Today's your big game, Jay. I thought you should wear it."

"Danny …" I can't even say anything.

You'd think Danny just gave me the Queen of England's heirloom tiara. I know how Danny is with his luck. The year they went undefeated and won the national championship, he wouldn't let anyone wash his game socks.

"I promise to take good care of it." I wrap it around the base of my bouquet. "The black even goes with my wedding colors."

I throw my arms around him and give him another hug.

"I can't believe my two best friends are getting married today.

You really are good, aren't you? You don't seem the slightest bit nervous."

"I'm not. I love him, Danny."

"And it's thanks to me that you're together; you know that, right?"

"No, it's not."

"Jay, we'll be sitting in rocking chairs at the old folks' home, and I'm *still* going to be reminding you of how I told you he was getting serious with that Moaning Monica chick. It was Lori's idea, but I'm the one who pulled it off. I know that's what made you attack him. Admit it."

"You're right. Although I'm pretty sure it's the first time you've been right about anything."

He opens the door, looks up and down the hall, and pretends to see if the coast is clear. He says, "Sup," to the makeup artist and then looks down at his fly. "Shit, that would have been bad," he says and pretends to zip his pants.

I follow him into the hallway.

He smacks my butt, like I'm getting ready to do the tunnel walk. "Go get 'em, Jay."

Every detail. Every thought.

I'M HOLDING MR. Diamond's arm while waiting to walk down the aisle. The ceremony is decorated so perfectly. Guests are sitting in white Chiavari chairs. There are huge glass hurricanes placed down the aisle with pale candles flickering inside them. The aisle runner is black-and-white damask. Even Pastor John, who I wanted to burn in effigy just a few short weeks ago, looks perfect, standing at the end of the aisle.

My bridesmaids look beautiful, wearing their ice-purple dresses and carrying pale pink-and-purple bouquets. The groomsmen look handsome in their black tuxedos. Their deep purple boutonnieres and custom Nikes add pops of color.

One by one, the bridesmaids walk down the aisle.

When it's time for the flower girls, I can't help but tear up. The flower girls are wearing the most adorable blush-colored dresses with tutu skirts. Their hair is done up in curly little buns. They're each carrying a floral-covered magic wand, but it's what's on their backs that make me cry.

Each girl is wearing white feather angel wings. The wings are decorated with halos of pale roses and purple lavender.

Our way to honor my parents.

Phillip tried to find some way to incorporate angels into our ceremony. We looked and looked but couldn't find anything but cheap angel charms. Mr. Mac did some kind of magic Google search and found a photo of an angel flower girl. He printed it out, rolled it up, and put it in my Christmas stocking. I cried then, too, because I knew it was just so perfect.

We've left the front row, opposite the Macs, empty on purpose. During the ceremony, we'll pause in silent remembrance. Phillip and I will walk down to their empty seats and place the two dried roses I saved from the funeral on their chairs. I'm so glad we're recording our wedding. I want to remember every detail. Every thought.

Mr. Diamond interrupts those thoughts. "I want you to look at Phillip and tell me why I should let you walk down this aisle. Because I know, if your dad were here and you had even a shred of doubt about marrying him, he would tell you it's okay to walk away."

"I don't wanna walk away."

"Honey, you broke up with him just this week. Gave him back the ring. If you go up there, you'll be married. You won't be able to just break up next week."

I give him a flippant response. "Sure I can. Isn't that why we had him sign a prenup?"

He says, "Not funny. I'm serious. Are you sure?"

"You know, I kinda hated you for it, but thanks for making me go through counseling. I did need it. I wasn't allowing myself to feel. I think it just hurt too much, but I've realized that's no way to live. I want to walk down that aisle because I love Phillip. With every single bit of my heart."

"I'm proud of you, and I'm glad you're finally dealing with it. I also have to tell you that it means a lot to me to walk you down the aisle, to be able to stand in for your dad."

I give him a hug and say seriously, "There's no one else I would've asked."

Lori takes her place at the altar, and I catch another glimpse of Phillip.

God, he looks so handsome.

Our eyes meet, and those eyes make me melt for the millionth time.

He grins just as the wedding processional starts playing.

My emotions swell inside me. Mr. D has to literally hold me back because all I want to do is pick up my skirt and run as fast as I can down the aisle.

I can't wait to marry that boy.

The boy I've loved my whole life.

The boy who knows what a freak I am and who loves me in spite of it.

I smile and walk slowly down the aisle, like I'm supposed to, and take Phillip's hands.

When this is over, I'll be his wife.

Above our head is a hanging altar made of white branches. It's adorned with purple flowers and dripping with crystals. The branches remind me of the trees we used to climb as kids.

Our wedding is a blur of scriptures, songs, and poems. Before I know it, it's time to say our vows. Phillip and I face each other and hold hands.

"Phillip David Mackenzie, I love you. I love how you've always been there for me. How you think you need to protect me. How you make me coffee every morning. How you always know exactly what I need. How, when I lay my head on your shoulder, I can fall asleep in a heartbeat. I love that you've called me Princess since I was ten, and I love how you can practically read my mind. I love the way you look at me and how your smile lights up a whole room.

"When I was little, I used to tell my parents I was gonna marry a prince. They told me I was silly, and I should marry you. Little did we know, we were both right. For a long time, I didn't think my prince existed, but then I realized he'd been standing next to me my whole life.

"Thank you for believing in us, even when I wasn't so sure. Thank you for loving me, even when I'm stubborn and convinced I'm never wrong. Thank you for making me believe true love, the fairy-tale kind, actually exists. It will be my extreme honor to spend the rest of my life with you. To cherish you, to love you, and to be yours forever."

Danny hands me the ring, and I gently slide it on Phillip's finger.

"With this ring, I promise to not freak out over the trivial stuff, to trust in our love, to not be so stubborn, to always listen to you, to always smell the roses with you, to laugh with you, to adore you, to dream with you, and to love you with my whole heart. For as long as I'm lucky enough to have you."

Phillip's eyes are glistening, and he's grinning at me. Phillip has always grinned at me, but this is different. The depth of happiness we're both feeling, the things we're publicly saying to each other, make this feel different and very special. I can't wait to hear the vows he wrote for me.

"JADYN JAMES REYNOLDS, I love you. I loved growing up with you. I loved fighting you with swords and climbing trees with you. I really loved watching you end relationships with all the dumb boys you dated and how you'd always run to me for comfort. I love how I'm the first person you call when you need someone. I love how, all our lives, no matter where we are or who we're with, whether we're all alone or in a crowd, when you flash that little grin at me, I know exactly what you're thinking. I love the way you look at me, like I'm the only guy in the world, and how, when I hold you, I feel like I could conquer that world.

"I asked you to marry me when we were ten, and I'm here today, making good on that promise. No one has ever compared to you. You've always been my world. You're my best friend, my love, my life. My Princess."

I'm trembling as Danny places my wedding ring in the palm of Phillip's hand.

And not because I'm scared.

I'm overcome with emotion.

So many emotions that I don't think I could even name them all. I just look at Phillip through happy tears and smile.

Phillip slides the band on my left ring finger. The finger every girl dreams of having a prince slide a ring on. The finger that's supposed to connect straight to your heart.

"When we were kids, I used to pretend to be your knight in shining armor, and now, with this ring, I promise to be the man to protect you, to cherish you, to support your wild ideas, to not get mad when you bring home another pair of shoes, to love you, to rescue you, to not be bossy, to adore you, and to continue this adventure of life with you, right by my side, for the rest of our lives."

Pastor John grins at us and says, "I now pronounce you husband and wife. You may kiss your bride."

Phillip pulls me into his arms and kisses me. He was supposed to give me a sweet, sorta chaste kiss, but this is not that kind of kiss. This is a lean-me-back, kiss-me-until-I-can't-breathe kind of kiss.

I'll remember this kiss forever.

"I present to you Mr. and Mrs. Phillip Mackenzie," the pastor says.

Our university fight song starts playing, and everyone claps and cheers as we walk down the aisle as husband and wife.

I'm pretty sure I win.

WE TOOK A few more photos and then enjoyed the last half of our cocktail hour. I didn't get much to eat, but I made sure I got a Princess martini. After the cocktail hour, we all head into the reception.

It looks even better than I dreamed.

The big ballroom overlooking the Plaza Lights, the huge crystal chandeliers, the icy tree centerpieces dripping with crystals, the pale purple uplighting, my four-tiered chocolate cake, the sparkling place settings, and the beautiful silk linens.

Phillip holds my hand and says, "Did you notice I changed the centerpieces?"

I look around some more. I'm a bit overwhelmed because all I can think about is how much my mom would've loved this. Then, I notice that the tables don't each have a tree centerpiece. Some have huge arrangements of the palest pink roses I've ever seen.

"The roses?"

Phillip smiles. "Yeah, each one has four-dozen roses. I'm pretty sure I win for biggest bouquet you've ever gotten."

"You already won that contest when we got engaged."

"I know, but I told Amy that story, and she said that four-dozen roses would be the ultimate profession of love. I love you, like, in case you didn't know that yet."

He kisses the tip of my nose.

I press my lips to his and say, "I think I have a pretty amazing husband."

Some duct tape and a bungee cord.

ABOUT MIDWAY THROUGH dinner, I really have to pee.

Again.

And this is something you never see in a Disney princess movie. They never show the production it takes to pee in a ballgown.

I have a sudden epiphany while a troupe of my bridesmaids is stuffed into the restroom stall with me.

"This is the real reason Cinderella had mice and why Snow White had those pesky dwarfs. She needed them to hold up her dress while she peed!"

"Maybe you should stop drinking so much," Lori tells me.

"It's not my fault Phillip keeps handing me bottles of water. The bottles of water that I don't remember ordering but must have since they have my wedding monogram on them. He keeps telling me to stay hydrated, like it's my big game."

"Well, it kinda is," Lori says.

"That's true, but when he has to pee, it doesn't require a small army of groomsmen to unzip his fly."

And, just when everyone is in place, my dress is held up, and I'm in position to pee, Lisa says, "Uh, hang on a sec." Then, she drops her corner of the dress and runs into the neighboring stall.

Katie says to me, "You need to pick your dwarfs a little more carefully."

We all laugh and try not to get grossed out by the sound of her puking.

I find myself mentally calculating the cost of it. Appetizers, three Princess martinis, a couple of shots, filet dinner.

Damn, that's about a three-hundred-dollar puke there.

It is at that point that I decide to say screw the water and start hitting the alcohol a little harder.

Had Phillip been in charge of holding up my dress while I peed, he probably would've rigged up a way to hold the dress above my head with his belt, some duct tape, and a bungee cord.

Jadalicious.

AFTER DINNER, IT'S time for the toasts, cutting the cake, and the first dance. I can't remember exactly what all Danny and Lori said.

Lori said something like, "We all know weddings are about those three little words. I. Love. You. But, in the case of these two, it's more like, it's. About. Time."

Danny said some sweet stuff that made me cry and some funny stuff that made me laugh, and then he ended the toast with, "To the nights you'll never remember with the people you'll never forget."

The curtains on one side of the dining area are opened up to reveal the swanky nightclub portion of the reception. It has a huge monogrammed dance floor, deep purple lighting, white leather furniture with furry purple pillows, and lots of candlelight. Beyond the dance floor is an outdoor terrace covered in white lights and snow.

Phillip and I cut the cake. Of course, I have to smoosh it in his face a bit. He is smart though and doesn't try to get me back. He's already proving to be a good husband.

Then, we dance our first dance as husband and wife.

I love dancing with Phillip. I know there are lots of guests watching us, but with the lights low, it almost feels like we are alone.

Just like the night we danced at the swings.

AFTER OUR SORORITY and fraternity serenades, I sit on a chair in the middle of the dance floor while Phillip finds his way through the layers of my dress. He's making a big scene of taking my garter off. He runs his hand up the wrong leg and pretends he can't find it. Then, he slowly runs his hand up my other leg, finds the Nebraska garter, and pulls it off with his teeth. The DJ starts playing stripper music.

Guess I'm getting a taste of that Vegas wedding after all!

Just about the time Phillip almost has the garter off my leg, the music scratches, and the DJ yells, "Hold up, wait a minute."

Then, the song "Fergalicious" starts playing—only, somehow, they've changed the words to Jadalicious. Danny and all the groomsmen run onto the dance floor, toss off their jackets, and do a wild choreographed dance. It's hilarious, watching them dance. They do the Stanky Leg, the Dougie, some random breakdancing, and the Moonwalk. You name it; they included it.

I scream, clap, and laugh my ass off. It's classic Danny.

Our love is worth celebrating.

WE'RE DONE WITH all the official stuff. Now, it's time to party!

"Phillip, I wanna give you your wedding present now!"

I drag him to a covered area by the doors that go out onto the rooftop deck. Right now, this area is hidden by curtains.

"So, unwrap your wedding present," I tell him.

He pulls me toward him. "I thought you were my wedding present. How 'bout I unwrap you instead?"

"Phillip, be good and open it! I'm so excited!"

He kisses me and then slides the curtains open. Sitting on a table are five crystal decanters of varying shapes and sizes filled with what is supposed to be the best kinds of scotch. I had to conspire with Mr. D on this surprise. Mr. D tells me I need to acquire a taste for scotch.

I don't know about you, but I have no desire to acquire a taste for something that smells like gasoline.

Next to the decanters is a tray full of cigars, and behind them, there's a gorgeous cigar humidor made of shiny burled wood.

"Scotch and cigars? I think I might keep you."

"The decanters and the humidor are my presents to you. Won't they look cool on the bar in our new house?"

"Very cool. I love them." He kisses the side of my face. "I love you."

"I love you, too. Open the humidor."

He opens it and reads the engraving on the gold plaque inside. *"Phillip and Jadyn. Our love is worth celebrating. January the thirteenth."*

"Your dad always said he was celebrating when he smoked a cigar."

"I know. Now, when you smoke a cigar, you'll be celebrating our love. You won't even have to come up with a lame excuse like my dad always did, and with the date on there, you'll never be able to forget our anniversary."

"No way I'll ever forget this day. I've never been happier. My face hurts from smiling so much." He pulls me in for another kiss. "Thank you. I love it."

"Okay, so now, you can have some scotch and smoke a cigar with the guys while I run upstairs and change into my reception dress."

"Change? What? Why?"

"Well, I love this dress, but it's full, and I wanna dance. I was afraid people would step on it, so kinda last minute, I bought a dress for the reception. It's sparkly and sexy. You'll like it. I'm gonna change really quick. No one will even know I am gone."

I kiss him and start to walk away.

He grabs my waist with one long arm, like he just caught a fish and is reeling it in. "Uh, not so fast there, missy."

"What?"

"I'm coming with you."

"But I was gonna let you smoke a cigar."

"I can smoke a cigar later."

"But I planned it all out."

"Well, you're married now, so you have to think about what your husband wants."

My husband!

"Okay, what does my *husband* want? That sounds so weird. My husband."

"Your husband loves this dress. He thinks you look beautiful in it, but I'll tell you a dirty little secret. All he's been thinking about is how he can't wait to take it off you."

His eyes are dark and smoldering. I know what that means.

"No, Phillip. I seriously need to take this dress off, put the other one on quick, and then get back down here. I'm talking a max of, like, five minutes."

He grins at me and lowers his voice to that sexy volume. "Fine, but I'm gonna help you."

He has a stubborn look on his face.

"You're not going to give in on this, are you?"

"Nope." He grins sexily at me.

"Fine. Come on." I grab his hand and rush him out the side door.

WE GET TO the honeymoon suite, and Phillip says, "Do you have a key?"

Crap. The key.

"Well, yeah, I have a key, but, um ..."

"What?"

"Uh, well, it's not like I have a purse or pockets in this dress."

He pulls the top of my dress outward, stares down my cleavage, and looks for the key. "I don't see it."

The grin on his face makes me laugh. Seriously, it's like he just saw boobs for the first time.

"Just turn around."

"Just where *exactly* is this key?" he asks in a raspy, breathless voice.

"Remember the day I took your car keys when you got mad at me for the shoes?"

"Oh God. This is even better than I could've imagined. But don't worry your pretty little head. Phillip has this all under control."

He gets down on his knees, and I pray no one walks down the hall while his head is under my dress, retrieving the key. Although, honestly, he could probably almost hide under there.

He slowly runs his hand from my ankle to my knee. Then, he kisses his way up my thigh. I let out a big breath because, now, he's running his hand across the edges of my *something blue*. I'm getting a little worried that he's going to forget about the key completely.

"We need to hurry, Phillip."

He ignores me, as usual when there's only one thing on his mind.

Finally, thankfully, a few seconds later, he kisses my hip and says, "Got it!"

I feel the key slide out from the side of my panties.

He gets up fast, unlocks the door, sweeps me off my feet, and carries me across the threshold of our honeymoon suite.

His eyes look even darker.

He shuts the door and gets right down to business. And that business is not taking off my dress as planned.

He kisses my exposed shoulders, my neck, my lips. Then, he looks at the back of my dress like it's a difficult golf putt. Like how they get down and look at it from all different angles.

"There isn't a zipper."

"No, Phillip, you have to unbutton every single button."

He looks some more.

"I can get Lori to come up and do it."

"Oh, no, you're not. I've got this."

He stands behind me, concentrating on the buttons. And the funny part is, he starts with the bottom button and works his way up to the top.

"Phillip, you're, like, doing it backward."

"No, I'm getting the right effect. Just you wait." He undoes all the buttons, except for the very top one. Then, he stands in front of me. He wraps his arms around me, unbuttons the final button, stands back a little, and lets it go.

My dress slowly slides down off of me, and I'm now wearing nothing but a *something blue* thong.

Phillip lets out a heavy breath and says, "God, you take my breath away."

In one quick motion, he puts his hand around my waist, lifts me up out of the frothy fabric pile, and pins me on the bed.

He kisses me deeply and then pulls off his shirt and pants. He never breaks eye contact with me.

I seriously have no idea when he even took off his jacket.

Okay, I have to say this, and then I'm going to tell him, *Uh, no.*

My husband is so freaking sexy!

He's not the only one who can't breathe.

I read somewhere in the millions of wedding articles and websites that you should take time for a few private moments on your wedding day, and I guess this would be considered a private moment.

But still, we planned this.

"Phillip, we can't do this now. It's our wedding night. We discussed this. Remember? Come up after the reception, take a warm bubble bath, drink champagne, relax, and then, *you know.*"

"You changed the plans when you changed the dress."

"Phillip, I don't wanna look back on our wedding night as nothing but a quickie!"

"No problem, Mrs. Mackenzie," he says as he pulls the last scrap of lace off me. "I see no reason why we have to compromise. I see no reason why we can't have both."

And then, well …

It's my wedding night! Well, kinda almost my wedding night. I'm not gonna tell him no.

The. Coolest. Wife. Ever.

WHILE EVERYONE WAS drinking and dancing, the ceremony area was being totally transformed. Phillip knows we're having an after-party and helped pick out the great food, but he thinks it's being held here.

At midnight, the DJ stops playing and announces that the after-party area is now open and to head that way for food and fun.

I grab Phillip's hand to lead the way.

He steps into the room and sees the college-themed sports bar that Amy suggested. We had pool tables, ping-pong tables, dartboard machines, karaoke, and foosball brought in. Drink options are coffee or kegged beer out of red cups. There's white lounge seating with red and black pillows and portable white bleachers. There's even a replica game-day scoreboard that says Bride and Groom instead of Home and Visitor.

Phillip gives me a wide, half-drunken grin. "You're seriously the. Coolest. Wife. Ever."

We laugh and watch our friends' looks of surprise as they come into the after-party. I also notice that Joey, who caught the garter, has his arm tightly wrapped around my sorority little sis and bridesmaid, Chelsea, who is still clutching the bouquet she caught.

Everyone seems pretty excited.

The ping-pong tables are quickly converted to beer-pong tables. The groom is bodily carried off to the keg to do a keg stand. Blake, Nick, and Danny do a hilarious karaoke rendition of "I Kissed a Girl."

I laugh so hard.

By the time we leave the after-party, Nick is passed out on the white couch, and Katie is making out with Neil behind the bleachers. Some things never change.

PHILLIP UNLOCKS THE door to our honeymoon suite and carries me over the threshold again. The room looks amazing. There are candles lit, rose petals sprinkled across the bed, and two of the rose bouquets from the reception are sitting on the nightstands.

Phillip does a silly little dance. "Let's get this wedding night started."

I think he's pretty tipsy.

I wonder if the wedding night is going to go as planned, but Phillip suddenly gets very serious.

We slowly undress each other, and then he leads me into the bathroom. In the bathroom are four more of the rose arrangements and more gently flickering candles. A bath has already been drawn, and sitting next to the tub is a silver tray with our favorite dessert shots and tea light candles. Attached to it is a note that says, *Congrats! Love, the Dessert Fairy.*

You know your wedding was a success.

YOU KNOW YOUR wedding was a success when …

You got married.

All the parents show up at your farewell brunch, wearing the matching black plastic sunglasses from the hangover kits you handed out.

Most of your groomsmen are still wearing their tuxedos and are still tipsy because they have yet to stop partying.

Your sweet sorority sister is doing what appears to be the walk of shame.

Granted, Chelsea isn't still wearing last night's dress and clutching her heels and her underwear, but she and Joey both arrive fashionably late at the exact same time. They're grinning at each other in that naughty, inside-joke kind of way. And, knowing Joey, he was very naughty.

The YouTube video of a certain young quarterback doing the Stanky Leg at your reception already has over 87,000 views.

Our XXX honeymoon.

I KNEW WE were going somewhere warm, but I had no idea Phillip's parents would splurge like this on our honeymoon. Talk about a gift we'll never forget. We're at a gorgeous, luxury resort in the Bahamas where we have an amazing beachfront suite.

I guess he wasn't lying when he said that me in nothing but a bikini all week sounded like his idea of heaven.

We just got back to our room from our quick tour of the resort.

Phillip says, "So, this isn't really a love letter, but it's my lame attempt to tell you all the things I love about you. Remember I told you about the pros and cons list I made? I wrote it the night before I told you I wanted to go out with you for real."

"So, I finally get to read it?"

Phillip nods and hands me the paper. "Yeah, provided you promise not to laugh at me."

I read the list. "Phillip, are you serious? You like all the bad things about me. All my flaws. Like how I always think I'm right, how I'm stubborn, how I blurt out stupid things before I think."

He pulls me into his arms. "Yeah, those are the things I love the most. I love you, Jadyn James Mackenzie."

"Oh, wow. That sounds beautiful when you say it."

Phillip grabs the present Danny and Lori sent with us and sets it on the bed. "We were given strict orders to open this as soon as we got here."

I ignore the box and put my hand down Phillip's pants. I'm not feeling the need to be particularly subtle right now.

Phillip moans, "Our XXX honeymoon."

"Well, if you're a good boy."

"I'm a very good boy."

"Yes, I already know exactly how good you are, but, you know, it's our honeymoon; you're maybe gonna have to step it up a notch."

"I think I can handle that. So, open the box."

I take the lid off, and we both go, "Holy shit!"

Because inside is, um, I don't even know if I want to know all that's inside this box. There are all sorts of XXX-type goodies.

"No wonder the guys in airport security were laughing at us!" I scream.

"I think we're gonna have fun on our honeymoon," Phillip says. He's wearing his own version of a Devil Danny grin.

"I think our honeymoon is gonna be like Naughty Dream Week on steroids."

Phillip paws through the box. "Hey, what's here, at the bottom?"

I look at the sweet sign he's pulled out of the box. "I think that is Lori's contribution. Don't you love how she cutified our XXX honeymoon?"

Phillip tickles my sides. "Cutified? I'm pretty sure that's not a word."

"Well, it should be. It means, she made it all cute."

"I think Lori just gave us the best marriage advice of all. Our marriage should be full of hugs and kisses with a lot of XXX thrown in to make it fun."

I put the hotel's Do Not Disturb sign on the outside of our door because I don't want anyone to take Lori's, and then I put the one she made on the inside. It's definitely coming home with us.

I walk back toward Phillip, shedding my clothes along the way.

"I think we'd better get this honeymoon started, Phillip."

"Mmm, Princess," he says as he grabs me and throws me on the bed.

Our XXX honeymoon favors cascade onto the floor.

But I don't think I care about that right now.

Why I should tell her I love her.

Pros:

She makes me laugh.

She's fun to be around.

We have fun together.

We can party together. She is funny as shit when she's drunk, but she thinks she's not.

We can chill together.

She loves football, is a good pool player, and loves sports.

She thinks she's low maintenance.

Her smile. Her laugh.

The way I feel when she lays her head on my shoulder.

How, even though she's tough around everyone else, she's always soft around me.

Her skin is so soft. Always.

Her hair always smells good.

The way she smells. How, when she borrows my sweatshirts, they smell like her.

Her mile-long legs.

I always want to be around her. No girl has ever compared.

How she curls up with her feet tucked under her when she sits on the couch.

She gives the best back rubs ever.

She's extremely sexy, and she really has no idea that she is.

She has the cutest toes.

She's so smart, but she can be completely clueless.

She calls me every night before she goes to sleep even though we live together.

The way she looks first thing in the morning.

She's freaking adorable.

Her little freak-outs.

How she has me wrapped around her little finger, and I don't even mind.

Her sense of adventure. Her outlook on the world.

How she thinks she can still take me on. And how fun it is when she tries.

Her creativeness.

Her naughty sense of humor.

The way her smile slowly builds from a little smirk to a full-blown smile when she thinks something is funny.

Her stubbornness. How she stands up for what she thinks is right, no matter what anyone else thinks.

How she always thinks she's right.

Her voice.

How she tells me everything.

How I can figure out what she's thinking without her saying a word.

Her eyes.

Killer body. Seriously killer body.

She's my best friend.

She's a good athlete, but she's such a klutz. It's the cutest thing.

She never thinks before she speaks, so you always know what she's thinking.

The way she looks at me. I think she might be in love with me, too—well, I hope.

The way all her boyfriends get jealous of our relationship and break up with her.

I'm pretty much madly in love with that girl.

Cons:

She's gonna freak when I tell her how I feel.

Read the next book in the That Boy series, *That Baby*.

ABOUT THE AUTHOR

Jillian Dodd is a *USA TODAY* bestselling author. She writes fun romances with characters her readers fall in love with—from the boy next door in the *That Boy* trilogy to the daughter of a famous actress in The Keatyn Chronicles to spy who might save the world in the Spy Girl series.

She is married to her college sweetheart, has two adult children, and has two Labs named Cali and Camber, and she lives in a small Florida beach town. When she's not working, she likes to decorate, paint, doodle, shop for shoes, watch football, and go to the beach.

www.jilliandodd.net

Made in United States
North Haven, CT
21 March 2023